ELLA'S LEGACY

BOOK THREE OF THE LOST WARRIORS

CHRISTINE PRIESTLY

Cover design by JV Arts www.justventurearts.com

Magic chart illustration by JV Arts www.justventurearts.com
Map creation by the author and Mr Lee using inkarnate.com

Chapter and scene break graphics by Mr Lee
Sigil design by Mr Lee
First edition 2025
christinepriestly.com

To my lost warriors,

Let us share something worth burning for.

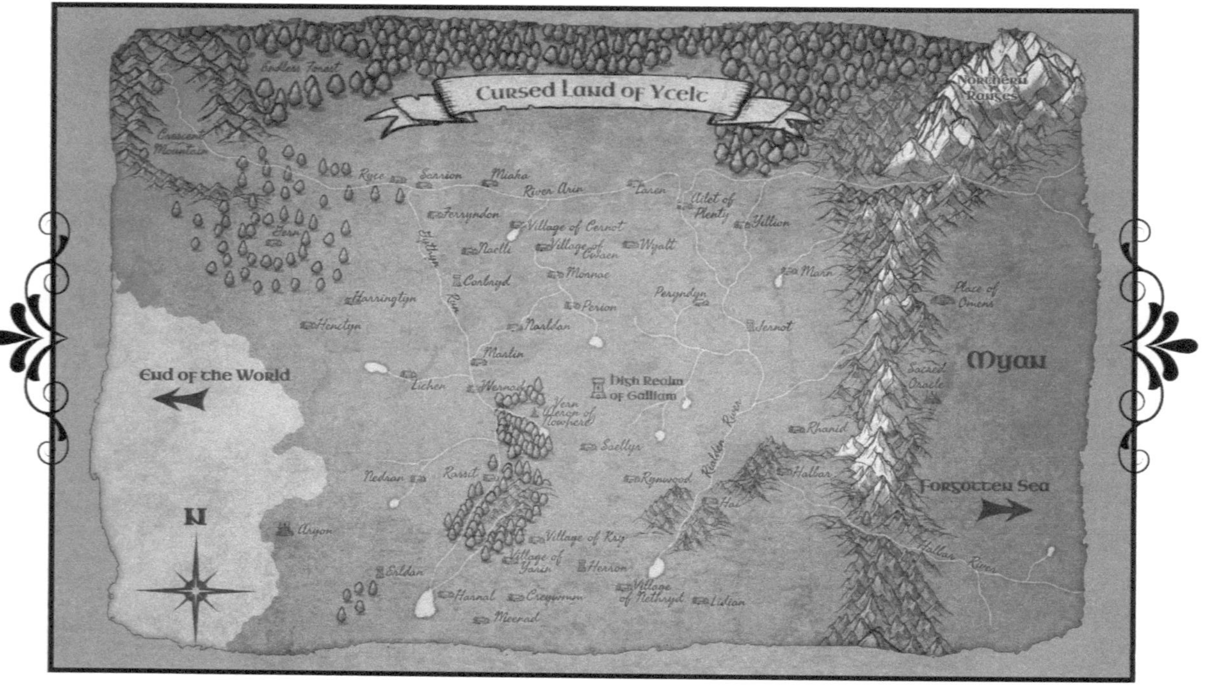

Cursed Land of Ycelc
Endless Forest
Northern Ranges
Crescent Mountain
Ryce
Scarrion
Miaka
River Arin
Taren
Ailet of Plenty
Yillion
Fern
Ferrynden
Village of Cernot
Naelli
Village of Coaen
Wyalt
Mann
Place of Omens
Conbryd
Monroe
Peryndyn
Harringtyn
Perion
Jernot
Henclyn
Norldan
Martin
End of the World
Lichen
Wernoch
High Realm of Galliam
Myau
Yern Heron of Nowhere
Sacred Oracle
Saellyn
Rhanid
Kiahlan River
Nedran
Rossit
Rynwood
Hallar
Hai
Forgotten Sea
Aryon
Village of Ksy
Village of Yarin
Herron
Eildan
Village of Nethryd
Listian
Harnal
Creywrmn
Meerad
N

Author's Note

A note on language:

Ella's Legacy is written in UK English. Readers more used to US English spellings may be unaccustomed to the quirks of UK English, such as the additional 'u' in words like 'colour' and 'honour', but trust this will enrich your reading experience as you become immersed in the author's world.

A note on content:

Content advice is available from: christinepriestly.com/content/
Please reach out with any questions or concerns. Your wellbeing matters.

Glossary

You can find a glossary of world-specific terms and sigils (glyphs) at the back of this book, and on my website: christinepriestly.com/glossary/

Discover

Visit christinepriestly.com to discover a full-colour map of Ycelt, character portraits and more.

ELLA'S LEGACY

BOOK THREE OF THE LOST WARRIORS

And what constitutes a man's legacy?

Is it the lore he writes?

The life he leads, a love he shares,

What he discovers, or creates?

I tell you; a legacy is not determined by what a man does,

Or even who he is,

But by what he leaves behind.

The Lost Warriors by Ynad of the Gern

PART ONE: UPHEAVAL

The Kingdom of Erldan, Ycelt

Winter, 797 A.S.

ONE

C hill struck Gohran's skin, a familiar tingle travelling the length of his spine as he and his men approached the village, pursuing his wretched brother-in-law. The last time he'd ridden this way, it was to hunt down Jarrod's killers, and he had the strangest sense the gods were laughing at him.

Quiet cloaked the night as the villagers hunkered behind barred doors and shuttered windows.

They were right to fear him.

His riders pounded on residences, dragging men, women, and children out beneath the crescent moon, their shouts and whimpers cutting across the dark.

Perched atop his steed, ice and fire settled in his chest, his stomach, his loins. Another breath and he froze.

He opened that special sense that was neither watching nor listening, yet somehow encompassed both, like scrounging for a memory that wouldn't quite form. Ella was close by. He knew it as he knew his own name.

As quickly as the feeling gripped him, it dispersed.

'Your Highness!' The rider ripped Gohran's focus from Ella's echo to the cacophony of their interrogation.

He dismounted and confronted the villagers his troop had rounded up, cowering as he paced before them.

'Your lord isn't here, Your Highness. I swear,' rose the plaintive voice of a man clutching a small lad and a lass. Frightened, tear-smeared faces clung as though their father's trouser legs could shield them.

'No such man has ventured this way in seasons.' A woman inched between them, as if her skirts could protect them any better.

Gohran's gaze pierced. 'No men?'

'Our Lady of the Dark Sun as my witness, not one.'

Others affirmed this, heads shaking and murmuring, 'No men.'

But the odd skip to their words, blankness to their eyes and slackness to their mouths, made Gohran wonder.

Another tingle, like insects crawling along his skin.

Wind tugged at his cloak as he strode before these grovelling peasants. For the briefest glimmer, Ella's presence engulfed him. He sucked in his breath. Blinked. Peered at these wretched souls, searching for any trace of her among them.

He felt nothing. Less than nothing. A void.

She was not here. But had she been?

Terror clutched him. He asked again about visitors, and again the villagers told him no, not the man he sought.

'Any women?'

Heads shook slowly as their focus drifted, and when they spoke, they appeared puzzled and hesitant.

'Not that I recall...'

If these folk had encountered his sister... Ella's existence, what she knew, and what they shared, threatened his very soul.

Dread gave way to simmering rage. His voice a low growl, more beast than man, he turned to his troop and rumbled, 'Burn them. Burn them all.'

Chaos erupted as the kneeling settlers scrambled.

His riders seized bodies and shoved them within their homes, boarding doors and windows, shuttering the inhabitants inside. Panicked screeching followed as his men dragged torches, setting straw and thatch alight.

The roar of catching flames surged through his limbs. Heat and embers rose in concordance with the fire in his heart, as satisfying screams scorched his ears.

All the while, Jonas's smirk and his sister's terror flickered behind his eyes. If the lord was there, they would smoke him out, and if he wasn't, no one would survive to wag their tongues—about anything.

Smoke.

Billowing clouds rose above an orange haze, turning the sky from sable to violet, ochre, and cinnabar. Dread sank like lead in Jonas's stomach as distant wails punctuated the night.

He choked back a sob, slid off his steed, and slumped to his knees. A shivery sweat broke across his temples as his guts wrenched over and again. He'd not even been there, had sought to spare Tymot and every soul in that village, but Gohran took his vengeance just the same.

The spasms abated, and he wiped spittle, tears, and snot from his face, then stuffed his fist into his mouth to stop from howling.

Gohran was a monster. So much for his façade of piety. This savagery was not the will of the goddess, but of a demon incarnate.

A flurry of snow melted across his flaming cheeks as Jonas ducked between spindly, misshapen branches. He'd no shelter, no weapons, not even a warm cloak.

'Keep to the edge of the End of the World until you reach Henctyn,' Amber had told him before she veered towards her haven. 'Then travel north and west. Within the forest you'll find another sanctuary, the Gern.' She'd torn a strip of fabric from the hem of her stinking robe. 'Take this with you to show the lore masters there. They accept male refugees, and if they question you, tell them the High Priestess, Breeyan of Aryon sent you.'

He fingered the stained cloth. Peered west into the barren wilderness and mounted his steed, wishing he had water to rinse the bile burning in his throat.

Amber and the gold-eyed girl had ridden towards a grove he recognised. The exact way he'd travelled following a pitiful woman and her starving children two seasons ago. He remembered the pattern of the trees where apparent smoke had risen—nothing compared to the blaze that raged to the north and east of him now.

He'd wanted to ask if Amber's haven was out there, where those folk had sought refuge. Had Ella been there that day? Would he find her there now? But Amber's withering glance had silenced him. She may not be able to control him or suck his energy, but he didn't care to test the limits of her powers. Not after what he'd witnessed.

Amber thought he hunted Ella from desire. From selfishness. But he wasn't searching for Ella for himself. Not anymore. Her existence was the only way to prove to the priests that Venn's marriage to Raeyn was invalid and to force an annulment. To free Nedran from Gohran's clutches.

Embers sparked the sky over the razed village in the distance. How could they remain entangled with the man capable of *that?*

Amber's focus had drifted, listening to the night's secrets. Eventually, she spoke. 'I don't say this to deter you from following me, but Ella is not where I'm headed.' *Where I expected her to be.* Her unspoken thought had slid into his mind.

She had every reason to lie, yet seemed earnest. 'Then where is she?'

'I don't know.'

Jonas swore.

'Even if I did, I wouldn't tell you.' *And I don't.*

Whimpering like a frightened pup, the gold-eyed girl had roused from her nest in the sorceress's lap atop their shared steed.

Amber's gaze drifted again. 'We need to go.'

Gohran wasn't likely to stop until he'd hunted Jonas down, destroying everyone in his wake. If the robes caught Amber and the girl prisoner, they would re-torture and burn them both alive.

Amber had leaned close, clasped his hand in hers. 'May the gods remember your compassion and smile on you, Lord Jonas of Nedran.'

Terror had gripped him. Gohran and his men were coming. Amber must have slipped the notion into his mind, for he'd known it with a certainty that did not belong to him.

'Go, my lord. Go now!'

He'd shuddered, unsure he would ever get used to the sorceresses' strange faculties. He fought the urge to dally and watch where they rode, then mounted and kicked his steed to a gallop.

Now, as he picked his way past the razed village, distant sounds of horror fading into the night, an inferno seethed through his veins.

He glanced up at the sliver of Xenon's smile peeking between blood-tinged clouds and smoke. Through cupped hands, he called to the heavens: 'I vow to every god and goddess, Gohran will not live to see his firstborn heir take a living breath.'

Thunder boomed and rolled, but instead of reverberating, it petered to a dead, muffled silence. He would kill Gohran, or he would die trying.

Two

Raeyn watched her strange new husband's skin pale, her brother's letter dangling, as if dripping with poison that he dared not let go. What was Gohran playing at? She'd scarcely been gone a week, and he was putting their futures in jeopardy. Whatever Venn's brother had done, it can't have been drastic enough to warrant his arrest. Though if he somehow slighted Gohran... Gods, her brother was as fragile as overblown glass.

Once, she imagined her husband handling vexing matters with equanimity, but at that moment, standing across from her in the drawing room, his cheeks unshaven, with hair curling in unwashed clumps, he appeared wild.

Breathe.

She stood to rest her hand on his arm. 'My lord, let me ride home to speak with the king—'

'*Nedran* is your home now,' Venn snapped and shrugged her off.

The candelabra's flickering shadows haunted his eyes, and she staggered back. 'Yes, my lord.' Her tone low. 'I misspoke. My *former* home—'

He studied her with a curious expression, as if he peered into her soul, needing to determine... What? He started to speak, then halted. Then tried again, his mouth gaping open and shut like a river trout.

She waited while he struggled to compose himself, to consider his next words.

He cleared his throat. 'I don't doubt your intentions. However, I worry your brother may gain...' he stalled, voice catching, '*undue influence* over any single person.'

Did he distrust her loyalty? 'My lord, I spoke my vows before our people and the gods.' She almost said *goddess*, but wanted Venn to know she held no particular love for the Dark Sun Cult Gohran worshipped. 'Our provinces are now allied, our ambitions aligned, and while I remain the Princess Elder of Erldan, I am first and foremost your wife. It is as much in my interest as yours to ease relations with my brother.'

Years of measuring Gohran's moods, and their mother's before him, had schooled her to study Venn's brow, the twist to his mouth, the rise and fall of his breath, to judge when it was safe to proceed. 'Gohran likely regrets his lapse of judgement. Let me speak to him. See if I can persuade him to release the lord without compromising his pride.'

Lynden stirred from where she'd sat quietly on her silk-covered chair, wiping her tears and nose with her handkerchief. 'I agree with Princess Raeyn.' Her eyes were hopeful. 'Gohran's pride...'

Raeyn supposed she didn't wish to expose how intimately she knew the king. She needn't worry. Raeyn hardly cared where her brother stabled his steed—though it would become her concern if he'd sired a foal on her. She hoped they'd had more sense than her sister, Jay.

Venn sought her gaze, and then Lynden's. 'We can't afford to step a single foot wrong.'

'I understand, my lord.'

'No,' he said. 'You don't.' Eyes hard. Mouth tight. She eased off. 'No one approaches the king.'

'My lord?' A nervy page hovered in the doorway.

Venn swung around to address him. 'Tell King Gohran I require the immediate release of Lord Jonas. Whatever spurious nonsense my brother has conjured, I will provide recompense. Offer a blood price if you must. Be sure the king knows if he fails to return Jonas a free man, the next time he sees me, I shall aim my sword at his throat.'

Gasps crossed the room, Raeyn's among them.

'Venn, no!' Lynden leapt to her feet and grabbed Venn's arm, pleading.

Venn shrugged her off just as forcefully, and she recoiled, shielding her face as if she feared he would strike her.

Raeyn could not imagine Venn using violence against anyone. But more and more, she realised how little she knew him. Had she married a man as vile as her brother?

Raeyn positioned herself between them, used to fending off Gohran and their mother before him. She would not allow Venn to conduct their household with aggression and fear.

Something in her expression, in her movement, must have given Venn pause, because his fire abated. Shoulders slumped, face in his hands, he whispered, 'This is my fault. I'm sorry. So, so, sorry…'

Raeyn fought the urge to reach across and comfort him, instead ushering Lynden out of the drawing room and into the women's quarters. To safety.

By every demon, what had he done? The terror in Lynden's eyes when Venn pushed her away sat like a stone on his chest. He was supposed to protect her. And Jonas. Safeguard them all.

A memory fought to surface, of himself as a boy, his fifteenth summer not yet past, thrust into the role of dryhten. His father's men surrounded him: servants, advisors, warriors; while his aunt, Servan, squeezed his arm.

'All boys play at being their fathers until the gods force them to wear their boots.'

He remembered looking down at his oversized shoes, shuffling to hide their scuffed leather. How was he supposed to wear his father's when he'd not yet filled his own?

Then he wondered why he worried about shoes when his father lay cold before him, when solemn eyes awaited his care and command. His sister wept beside Jonas, sullen and silent. With his father's last breath, his people had become Venn's. He would wear his father's boots, wield his sword, and bear his staff.

The wood that settled into his throat refused to be swallowed away as the walls narrowed, squeezing in, the weight of Nedran's souls heavier than his scrawny shoulders could carry.

'It only takes a whisker pulled from the wrong cat to raise hackles,' his father used to say. 'Stroke them as they like, and they will rest on your lap. Ignore their favour at your peril.' Claws out, they would hiss, or they would swipe.

With his aunt's guidance and the help of his steward and advisers, he'd steered his people through the storms that followed and matured into a leader they respected and whose judgement they honoured.

Older than his seasons, those around him used to whisper.

But now he was that lost boy once again, tossed into a maelstrom with no rudder to steer them to shore, no one to confide his reasoning or doubts.

Jonas was the only person who might understand, and he had left his brother to the whim of a monster.

A monster. That's how Raeyn saw him now too, he was sure; her censure painted across her usually staid features as she witnessed Lynden's fear.

He'd tried to hear Raeyn out. She was right. Someone needed to placate Gohran, and it couldn't be him. When he contemplated confronting the king, his entire body trembled, a shivery ice-fire that tore through his limbs, knowing how easily he'd been swayed. Manipulated. Controlled. Could anyone defend against that invisible force? Could Raeyn? He would not take that risk. Not when Jonas's life depended on it.

When he'd sought a match with one of Erldan's daughters, it was with his people's security in mind. He hadn't suspected their queen, and her son, bore the stain of heresy.

Even after the priests Cleansed Queen Prya, he did not take heed. He'd never understood why Elnora's servants were so determined to rid Ycelt of witches and heretics, had not quite believed in their supposed powers. Now, he recognised the threat they posed, taking a rational man and bending his will unawares. Turning him mad.

Faced with that threat, he had no one to turn to for help. He could not defeat Gohran with words or reason, so threatened the sole weapon he knew Gohran feared: his blade.

Three

'You made it.' Breeyan heard the woodenness in her voice when Amber reached the lookout post where she and Shira camped, waiting.

She resembled a spectre, her loose and matted tresses stirring in the wind, while her stained and torn vestment flapped. Beside her limped a strange, wretched waif with pale stringy hair and bright yellow irises, but no magic that Breeyan could sense.

Even at this distance, Amber's power was evident, soothing and quietening the girl, but Breeyan caught snatches of panic breaking through. What had their captors done to them?

Shira grasped Amber's arms, choking back tears. 'Thank Xenon, you're alive!'

Breeyan stiffened. She wanted to caution her apprentice not to get too close. 'Shira, escort Amber's companion to the citadel.' When Shira hesitated, Breeyan eyed their clasped hands. 'Felda should tend to her.'

'Take her, Shira,' Amber said, and Breeyan caught the murmur of their private thoughts.

As Shira ushered the girl and their steed away, Breeyan handed Amber a blanket and placed more wood on the fire. Apart from one drift of snow the previous night, the sky remained clear.

'Is that Ella's babe?' Amber nodded toward the infant girl strapped to her chest.

'Xarion, yes.' The heat soothed her nerves, while restoring Amber's, who thankfully did not question her decision for them to remain out at the grove.

Breeyan needed to gauge to what degree the novice had defied Xenon's laws, and to what extent her captors had violated His decrees.

'I sensed you searching for me,' Amber sipped the fresh water Breeyan offered, 'when their draughts wore off... But I had to keep my mind shuttered.'

Breeyan opened her god-sight to read Amber's aura. Strange roiling currents tugged and pulled, expanding and contracting. She summoned power from their campfire and let her gaze stretch further, then halted. If it was the Curse, did she want to know?

'I thought Nykki would be with you...' *But I am glad she is not.*

When Nykahlia alerted Breeyan to Amber's approach, she'd had to shield against the young priestess's protest at remaining within the citadel, while she and Shira headed to the grove.

Instead of answering, Breeyan passed Amber a bowl of stew and a hunk of grain-filled bread.

'Erldan's head priest knows about Aryon,' Amber said between mouthfuls. 'But by Xenon, it wasn't me who told him. My presence merely confirmed what he already knew.'

Breeyan's jaw tightened. 'Go on.'

'He has uncovered his king's magic.'

A sharp inhale. She'd not shared with Amber that Xenon had blessed Gohran, yet an image flashed behind Amber's eyes of the crosses marked on Breeyan's genealogy map. When had she spied Breeyan's work?

Now, he risked discovery by his head priest. She sucked in another breath. She never should have abandoned her son. Didn't realise her sister would not prepare him, that she didn't know how to.

Gods, the seeds she had sewn, and for what? To claim the passion Prya stole. To satisfy her carnal hunger. Was it worth it?

Brittle determination set Amber's mouth in a hard line, her eyes dull, like grim stones. 'They understand a great deal about our magic and its limitations.' Flickering images revealed Erldan's High Priest testing her. Experimenting. Torturing—

Breeyan held up her hands, blocking the novice's brutal memories. 'They terrorised that girl to evade the Curse?'

Amber nodded.

It wasn't the priests who had distorted Amber's aura, then.

Breeyan sensed Amber's realisation that she was not their first prisoner tortured in this way. A follower of Xenon, but not someone from Aryon, at least, not in Breeyan's time here.

Xarion stirred, seeking. Always needing. Breeyan laid more wood on the fire and coaxed it aflame, drawing power to soothe.

They fell into silence, each guarding their thoughts from the other, but not before Breeyan caught Amber reflecting on the male prisoner who had accompanied them.

'Who was he?' she asked.

'Lord Jonas of Nedran, the dryhten's younger brother.'

She sensed Amber struggling to decide how much to share, and considered using power to impel her to speak, but her mere contemplation sent Amber's knowledge tumbling forth. The lord realised Ella was alive. Foolishly believed he was in love with her. *No doubt Ella's beguilement.* This thought, Breeyan kept buried.

'The lord also knows Ella has magic. And the king.' Her gaze drifted from Xarion to Breeyan and back again.

Breeyan did not respond. Would not acknowledge Ella's dark gift, nor Gohran's crime.

'Also—there is something strange about the lord. He seems immune to certain powers. I couldn't influence him...' *Or draw from him.*

Breeyan eyed her. That last thought escaped unintended. Amber's weakened state impaired her shield.

Amber brushed the tears from her cheeks, her mouth crumpling as she gathered strength and composure, drawing each inhale deep from her chest. 'I defied Xenon to save our lives, but defied Him nonetheless.' A statement, not a plea for mercy.

'I do not wish to bring harm to anyone else. I did not come back for me...' Amber's reasoning slipped into Breeyan's psyche. When she swallowed, she tasted the guilt of the tortured girl's pain. She wanted the yellow-eyed lass healed, and to share what her captors revealed.

'I know I cannot return....' Amber finished.

Neither needed to voice her fate. They must Cleanse her.

Her thoughts were on her beloved. The single boon she dared not request. To see Nykahlia a final time. But she would not risk her beloved's life. Not if she carried the Curse.

Too late, Breeyan thought. Amber crossed that line long before her abduction. It was the god's reckoning she should fear now, not hers. 'Get cleaned up and rest. We'll talk more once Elnora rises again.'

Heaviness weighed. She yearned to send Amber and Nykahlia far from her people and their haven, but there were too many unknowns. Sequestering them bought her time to decide how to proceed, and how best to inform her council.

When Amber arrived safely at Aryon's grove, Breeyan did not hold her. Offered no comfort, merely studied her, that strange child cradled against her chest. Tears had rolled down her mud-smeared cheeks as she'd relinquished the gold-eyed girl's care to Shira. She had remained strong for so long, fending off those monsters and containing her fellow prisoner's pain. Surviving.

Finally, she could breathe.

And as Breeyan settled into her blankets, she'd relayed her tale. The High Priestess kept the glowing flames between them and held the babe to suckle milk through a cloth nipple, fussing and cooing in an astonishing display of affection.

Oddly quiet, the infant emanated power so potent it was frightening. Ella's daughter, she presumed. But where was Ella?

Though Amber feasted and drew from the fire, she could barely soothe herself. She had nothing in reserve to search for her former pupil, nor fortify against Breeyan's probing. She stopped fighting and lowered her shield, letting Breeyan plunder her mind. What use was hiding anything? She would burn either way.

Her belly satisfied, she heated water to scrub herself, dabbing around the dirt-crusted scabs where the priests' ropes had bound her, then polished her teeth with the charcoal surrounding their fire. She soaped and rinsed her matted hair before pulling on a fresh robe. Her stinking vestment, she scrunched into a tight fist, imagining it burning to cinders, but she couldn't risk creating more smoke, so hurled it beyond the grove. It could rot for all she cared.

When Elnora's sinking rays faded the sky to indigo, she lay down, shut her eyes, and tried to sleep. Her body craved rest, should feel at ease, but her nerves had ruptured.

She gazed into the dwindling embers and pictured Jonas. Behind him, the horizon held a peculiar glow, as if he rode alongside a fire, but that was impossible. She turned away and peered through the treetops into the distance, ignoring the eerie orange light. She couldn't think about what that might mean.

Desperate for rest, her mind raced inside her twitching body. She shuffled again, begging sleep to come. But each time her eyes drifted closed, and her muscles relaxed, terror surged through her and she woke gasping. The jolt of being carried, blinded, bindings abrading, flooded her. When last she'd camped out this way...

Tears sprang, and she choked them back. She'd made it this far. She was home. And yet, she had betrayed Xenon to get here.

She stared into the night. Breeyan's muffled snores grated as Ella's strange child slept cradled beside her, sharing the black hair and wide blue eyes of its mother.

And father.

She wondered again how Gohran had come to bed his sister. Had Ella been willing? Surely not. But if she was desperate, afraid, might she have bartered using her body? No doubt the king forced her, but was his mind truly his own? Not when Xenon's beguilement bound everyone to Ella's will.

When she'd first witnessed Gohran's strange, twisted aura, entwined with Ella's, she hadn't understood what it meant. Had Ella's binding of him already begun?

Regardless, Lord Jonas of Nedran was right. Gohran was a monster.

Yet Amber pitied him, navigating his magic alone, abhorring his very essence, with only that vile priest to guide him.

What had happened to them both?

So many unanswered questions. Across from her, Breeyan slept soundly. How much did she know?

Amber's thoughts whirled, worrying at anything other than her immediate fate. She hugged her blanket tighter, and placed more wood upon their fire, shivering despite its blaze. She shuffled and twisted. Couldn't get comfortable. Couldn't relax.

It was too still. Too quiet. She'd felt calmer while fleeing for her life with Jonas and the girl by her side.

What if Davith's priests commandeered their king's army and headed this way, hunting her down? Would Gohran attack Aryon?

Or would their fear of the Curse prevent them?

She wished she'd paid more attention to the Marked Prince while she was living at Erldan. Her focus had been on her pupil and the queen. On staying hidden and remaining alive. On keeping Ella safe.

Something—or someone—pinched her mind. An intense discomfort that tore and squeezed. Needing.

Ella's babe had roused.

Breeyan woke and settled her, drawing power reflexively, sucking the fire to mere embers, until the intrusive pain eased.

Amber marvelled at how easily she balanced feeding the child's need with sustaining sufficient reserves for herself.

With Xarion nestled and quiet against her, Breeyan's curiosity scratched Amber's psyche.

'I can't sleep...' Amber said, trying to disguise the hitch to her breath.

'My foresight shows no immediate threat,' Breeyan assured. Yet the god's omens had not spared her, as they had not spared Ella nor her mother all those years ago.

Amber forced herself to lie still, wondering if she would ever sleep again.

Ice rippled along her spine.

Soon she would rest, undisturbed, for eternity, her consciousness extinguished with her body and her soul.

Four

When Elnora finally crested the horizon, Breeyan bid Amber gather their blankets and follow, heading away, instead of back towards the citadel. On the cusp of winter, the sun still carried a dry heat, milder than the nights when the temperature would dip and freeze their water stores.

Stubby dried grass and leaf litter crunched beneath their feet, brittle rather than sodden. She inhaled their familiar eucalyptus scent. Further west, not even this spindly vegetation would grow.

Breeyan halted before a large boulder, brushing dirt and moss away to reveal a ringed diagonal cross etched into one side: the symbol of Xenon.

'Help me,' Breeyan said, setting Xarion on a pile of dried leaves. She did not ask Amber to hold the child, and Amber did not offer.

Xarion studied them with eyes that comprehended more than any babe ought.

Side-by-side, they pushed and shoved the heavy rock, but it would not budge.

'I recall this being lighter,' Breeyan grunted. 'But that was a long time ago.' She wiped her palms on her robe and massaged her back. 'Step aside,' she commanded, then retrieved Ella's daughter. Eyes half closed, blue light surged, and chill blasted between them. The boulder rolled as if made from down instead of granite, revealing a metal grate covering some kind of cellar.

Xarion giggled, delighted.

Amber hugged her chest. Did that power belong to Ella's babe?

Breeyan stooped and hefted the grate open with a rusty screech, and Amber tasted stale metal.

'I can't shelter you within Aryon,' Breeyan said, 'but you might feel safer down here, out of sight of any pursuers, at least until the council decides your fate.'

'We know my fate already.'

Breeyan didn't respond, simply motioned for Amber to lower herself using the hand and footholds carved into the dugout walls.

Still wobbly, she clung on and climbed down. Dim light filtered through the upper corner of the space. The rest remained in darkness. Clay filled her nostrils and throat, reminding her too much of Erldan's dungeon.

With Xarion strapped to her chest, Breeyan passed Amber the blankets and leftover supplies. She checked that the ground was dry, and set each item down, then grasped the footholds, ready to climb out.

'I'll return with a brazier,' Breeyan said. Another screech and the grate slammed shut above her.

Panic clutched her throat.

A chain jangled, followed by a loud clunk, and then footfalls fading through rustling leaves.

Breeyan had locked her in.

☾

Guilt-tinged relief washed over Breeyan as she secured the lock in place and headed to Aryon. The Curse was like a wound that needed to be cauterised. It must not fester and spread.

Back at the citadel, she retreated to her study and summoned Shira.

When her apprentice arrived, shadows circled her eyes. 'How does the girl fare?'

Shira shook her head. 'Chrysanth is resting in the infirmary. I bandaged her wounds. It looks like someone used her for some type of ritual blood-letting, and the gods know what else. As for her psyche, I've managed little more than Amber—a temporary salve, no more.'

Breeyan plucked her gnawed cuticles from her mouth.

'If a few of us channel together...' Shira shuffled nearer, glancing at the infant sleeping against Breeyan's chest. She appreciated Xarion's potential as a powerful source. 'Failing that, if we can't heal her...'

Severance. Shira did not wish to utter that word, not now. For Amber, it would have been cruel, but for Chrysanth, it would be a mercy.

'How does Amber fare?' she asked, stacking Breeyan's hearth.

Breeyan ignored her question. 'Once you've finished here, head to the archives and locate any lore on the Curse. Find what you can on the effects once evoked.'

Shira paled.

The threat of the Curse had always loomed, but too late, Breeyan realised how little she understood of it.

The novice had defied Xenon's laws. She wasn't sure to what extent, but they were not safe if Amber stayed.

If Breeyan was right about starting one chain of the Curse, Amber had likely created another. In her vision, she saw Xarion rising from the wake of destruction—an end to that chain. Where did Amber's chain begin and end? Did it include Chrysanth? What about Nykahlia? She needed to isolate them until she could be certain.

Amber assumed they would Cleanse her, but Breeyan wanted to know if there was another way.

Only if you let it be... That line of lore must hold some significance. It implied she had a choice. She would not choose Cleansing for the child at her breast. Not if she could prevent it.

'On your way out, send Nykahlia to me,' she said. Amber desired to see her beloved a final time, and she would have her wish.

T ime slowed while Amber waited. Without the rhythm of her captors' movements, transporting her to be tortured, delivering food and water, the hours dragged. She remained sober and alone, with no certainty of when or if Breeyan would return.

Why had she locked her in? Did she believe Amber would flee or attempt to enter the citadel? She had returned of her own volition, had already accepted her fate.

She wanted to howl, but no one would hear. Needed to fight, but there was nothing to pound or kick except the dank clay walls.

The dim outside light didn't reach far, so she cast her eyes aglow and peered through the gloom like a cat. A narrow passage, blocked by rubble and stone, led away from the cavernous space, presumably back to Aryon's citadel.

What was this place? Part of the original fortifications? Somewhere to store supplies in times of war? Or prisoners. She shuddered.

Strange currents swirled at odd moments. Was there an opening she couldn't see? Wind whispered, carrying a faint howl, and another, higher-pitched wail. If she stretched her mind, she sensed agony and loss. People had died here. Slowly. Painfully.

The shiver along her vertebrae settled into a cold ache in her bones. She hoped Breeyan returned with that brazier soon. Prayed she would release her when she did.

She drew her blankets around her, and huddled in a shadowed corner, eyes and mind shut against the haunting wind that carried ghostly echoes of long-lost souls.

She should rest, but her body tensed, panic shooting whenever sleep approached. Breathing hard into the cold, she ripped her limbs clear, reminding herself she was free.

Except she wasn't.

She swiped the tears scattered across her cheeks, stuffed her anguish down, and steeled herself for whatever was to come.

FIVE

Lynden lay against her pillows, hugging her blankets. Her bed seemed empty. *She* was empty—empty without Gohran.

She longed to trace the toughened leathery scars crinkling his back—for it was his back she saw when they slept. Craved those rare sparks when his arms wrapped around her, burying his face in her hair and neck. Never lingering, only as a precursor to slaking his lust.

Why had she forgotten his arousal pressing into her in those moments? Not tender, but demanding.

And yet, he completed her in a way she had never experienced. It was a light that shone warmer than Elnora's rays on her naked back.

But afterwards, when he rolled away, leaving her alone—and he always left her—she felt like she did now: dark, hollow, used.

This time, *she* had left *him*, but she felt bereft just the same.

Even as he thirsted for her sex, he controlled his rigid movements, his veneer detached, as if he searched for something that wasn't there. When he watched her with practised concentration, locked inside himself, she wondered if he would ever find it.

How had she imagined she could be the one to break through? That he would find what he sought and let her in. That he would change for her.

She'd been blind. Having witnessed his ferocity, she gave herself to him. But he was the exact monster everyone else saw. And now he'd turned that anger on her brother. She choked off a sob.

Earlier, the vehemence of Venn's shrug rocked her, and for a moment, she expected to look up and find herself transported back to Gohran's bed, forever awaiting his next eruption.

Raeyn had sat her down in the women's hall, and encouraged her to sip heated hallit spirit between slow, deep breaths, until she calmed enough to retire to her room. But alone, her walls taunted, and her thoughts echoed.

As a girl, panic often clutched her limbs when she woke, screams stuck in her throat, certain someone had stolen her loved ones. She would crawl into her brother's bed, where Jonas would stroke her hair until she fell back asleep, safe knowing he was there. Later, Bess would stay up and play tiles with her, or read to her, until she outgrew her childish fears.

It had been a long time since that familiar dread gripped her. But now her old trepidation seemed close once more. What if Jonas never returned?

The moon's sliver yielded the barest glow, and she peered through the dim light, trying to reassure herself. Gohran couldn't be foolish enough to face Venn with a sword in his hand. He would forgive any slight, and Jonas would saunter into the dining hall when they least expected, eyebrow cocked, teasing them about their sombre faces.

She wished Venn had permitted Raeyn to persuade him—or allowed her to try. She ought to take the carriage and confront him herself. If she leveraged his guilt and shame over striking her, he would have to let Jonas go.

A knock.

'My lady?'

It was Bess.

'What is it?' She threw back her blankets and pulled on a cloak over her nightdress before opening the door. Winter's chill was setting in.

Eyes wide, Bess looked ready to burst if she didn't speak. She inspected the corridor, leaned close, and whispered, 'Follow me, my lady.'

'It's the middle of the night!'

Bess's staid expression cautioned her, so she slipped on her shoes and followed her lead, tiptoeing in silence. The corridors were eerily quiet. Not even punctuated by the jangle of keys or distant footfalls.

Bess cupped her candle, which cast flickering silhouettes along the walls and ceiling. She led them down the servants' stairs, and through the kitchen, then into Nedran's root cellar. Dirt and milled grain and a hint of rot mingled with sour ale and vinegar.

'Bess—?'

A shabby, unshaven man stepped out of the shadows.

'Jonas!' She threw her arms around her brother, stifling her half gasp, half sob. His shirt and hair reeked. But beneath the stench of anxious sweat, smoke, and the gods knew what else, she smelled *him*. She squeezed tighter.

His familiar palm stroked her tresses, and she longed to drown in the comfort of him. Too soon, he pulled away, but rested his hands on her shoulders.

'I thought Gohran arrested you!'

'He did, and he mustn't know I returned home.'

How had he ended up in this mess?

'Lyn, I can't stay. I've been a fool. I only came to warn you. No one is safe from that demon king.'

She had never seen her brother so intense, so earnest. 'Gohran can be ill-tempered, but—'

'Remember old Tymot?'

She nodded. Tymot was one of Jonas's curious acquaintances.

'Gohran's men razed his entire village, searching for me.'

'What? Why would—?'

'Take the carriage to Lichen before the snows set in. You won't be safe here. Not when Gohran comes hunting.'

'Gohran wouldn't hurt...' But she couldn't finish the sentence. Gohran had hurt her already. She swallowed. 'I might have some sway over him.' She would expose him if she needed to. It wasn't her shame, it was his.

Or would her reminding him of his mistreatment push his troubled roots deeper into the soil? That strange, private torment that led him to harm himself over and again, only to spew all his hate and anger outwards.

'Stay away from Gohran, Lyn.' Eyes beseeching. 'Our demon king has a way of influencing people...'

She startled. Venn had said something similar, hadn't he?

If he meant the way Gohran drew her in, how his presence crowded everything else out, all sense, all reason, lost in the here and now. Wasn't that how love was supposed to feel?

And Venn loved him, too. They were like brothers. Or had been.

Jonas frowned, his mouth tight, as though he fought the urge to say more. He pulled her close against his chest, breathed into her hair. 'I must leave, but promise me you won't let him near you again. No matter what he says or does. Keep your distance, and never meet his gaze.'

He released her, and his absence left an aching void. 'No, Jonas—don't go!'

He fought his tears as much as her.

'My lord?' Bess handed him a pack. Lynden hadn't even realised she'd been gone. 'Spare clothes, a blanket, and some food.' Last, she passed over a dagger and a sword, hilt first, followed by a purse. 'There's a fresh steed outside, but you'll need to swap over the saddle. I couldn't lift it on my own.'

'My thanks, Bess.'

Jonas pulled Lynden close one last time. 'Stay calm and focused and do whatever it takes to keep Venn steady and Nedran safe.' He kissed her forehead. 'I'm going to set things right. When you see me next, this will all be over, and we'll be free of him.'

Six

Jonas could have kissed Bess as he pulled on the peasant's shirt, trousers, and cap she packed for him. Nothing bearing Nedran's insignia. Even the fresh steed bore no brand. She had thought of everything.

Mounting, he turned towards the city gates. He needed to be gone before Gohran's men headed this way. For now, they assumed he wouldn't be so brazen—or foolish—to return home, but he didn't dare linger.

He studied the grotty torn cloth Amber gave him. She'd urged him north, but he would need to veer further west to avoid Lichen. Much as Vera's parents might harbour him, knowing they held no love for Erldan's monarch, he would not expose them to Gohran's limitless vengeance.

'His magic is broken.' That's what Amber had said. He had no moment to register it then, but it was this information he risked going home to deliver. Not that he could speak of Gohran's sorcery, only warn Lyn to stay away and protect herself from his influence. He would not leave his family unarmed. The man was a living, walking demon.

The queen, her son, and her daughter—all sorcerers. Surely not Raeyn or Jaydyn. Those poor women were likely victims of their brother as much as Venn. Even Gohran's mother had been his victim. But if Gohran had magic all along, why had he denounced her? Why permit Venn's marriage to Ella, but then hide Ella away, falsify her death? Nothing made sense.

He shook the questions aside. He needed to find Ella. But how? She might be anywhere in Ycelt. Or somewhere beyond it.

The last time he'd sought answers that lay outside the known realm, he called on Alina, with her strange potions and dangerous eyes. Though they looked nothing alike, shared no mannerisms, Alina reminded him of Ella, and now he suspected the reason.

What if he made one more stop before heading out? He halted, pivoted, and rode for the centre of town.

At this chill hour, the streets were almost empty. With his hood pulled up to shadow his face, he ducked and weaved between the occasional stragglers who wandered the alleyways year-round and through the back entrance of Alina's tavern. Now that winter had set in, not even her patrons were up drinking in the hours before dawn.

He handed a coin to the dozing guard and crept inside. The servers had long since retired, but a lone drunkard snored before the cooling coals of the fireplace, with a couple of hounds curled against his legs and back. Two pairs of canine eyes watched, their snouts twitching and ears perked, neither willing to sacrifice warmth to pursue their curiosity.

He rapped on Alina's door, hoping she didn't have overnight company. No answer. He knocked louder.

A groan. 'What have I told you about letting me sleep?'

With the trapdoor half open, Alina squinted through the dim light. Her complexion and features appeared muted without her usual cosmetics. 'Jonas? Is that you?'

She helped him through the manhole and rubbed her eyes. Dark hair fell around her shoulders, and her brown skin peeked through a loose, modest night dress. 'I scarcely recognise you with that growth all over your face. What are you doing here?'

'Please, I need your help, and I have little time.'

'Jonas—'

He placed his finger to her lips. 'Listen. The king's men hunt me, but I must find someone before I flee. The person I seek has magic.' He held up his other hand to silence her. 'I know sorcery exists, and that you can access it.' Her potions, the visions she provided to her patrons, and her strange glass sphere told him that.

He retrieved the sphere from its perch on her shelf and shoved it towards her. 'Help me find her. Please. My life, my family, and every soul in this city, depends on it.' He pictured plumes of smoke and distant screams, hoping his guess was right, and that Alina could read his thoughts as Amber had done.

Alina's focus drifted, and the colour drained from her cheeks. She sucked in her breath, drew her shoulders back, and took the glass in both hands. 'Come, help me light the brazier.' She nodded to the kindling and flint stacked nearby.

He didn't have to ask why. She needed fuel for her magic, and he was useless as a source.

He laid the wood, picked up the flint, but she waved her hand, and the timber caught alight before he could strike it. He staggered back.

'Sit.' She motioned towards her worn chair and knelt on a cushion opposite. He tried not to think about its usual purpose as she settled on her knees before him, the glass sphere balanced between her splayed fingertips. 'Place your hands over mine and picture the person you seek.'

Ella's memory was never far away, her raven hair and her soft, kissable lips...

'Be as specific as you can,' Alina said.

He tried to describe her, but she was so much more than her melodic, teasing laugh, her noontide eyes that deepened whenever she smiled... it was the way he felt *invigorated* in her presence. As if she understood him as no one else could.

'Keep going,' Alina coaxed.

The fire in the brazier flickered, and a cool draught swirled between them.

His mind returned to their evening beneath the stars, studying Ella's shifting expressions of fear to curiosity, to pleasure and surprise. Nothing he could put into words.

'Let your imagination guide you,' Alina said.

But his reverie veered to the night's disastrous conclusion. Her brother and Venn overshadowing them the following morning, witnessing her terror and her shame. The memory seared into his mind.

Curse Gohran.

'Concentrate, Jonas.'

He dragged his attention back to before that night. Before Ella's return to Nedran, already changed by her brother's wrath. He imagined her nimble fingers wrapped around his lumbering ones as he tried to thread a needle to repair his shirt, the thrill of her bare skin on his and the brush of their thighs. Later, he pictured her flushed cheeks as she wrestled him, and the fire behind her gaze as he pinned her to the grass...

'Look into the sphere.'

As though spying through a fogged window, a cloudy image formed. He squinted, trying to see past the haze to where bodies appeared to move, wishing he could wipe the surface clean. Another draught, and the mist cleared.

A miniature scene came into focus, of folk moving through a forest. He tried to enlarge the people, their faces, as if he might draw them nearer with his will alone. More cool air rushed past, and he discerned the woman in the centre of the glass, her slight frame and straw-coloured cropped hair.

'It's not working—' he began, but then she looked up, staring straight back through her unmistakable azure eyes.

The world tilted and his breath stopped, heart thudding until he feared it bursting from his chest. Moisture skimmed his cheeks. It was her.

In the moons since they last spoke, he'd pored over his recollections like a series of abstract dreams. In weaker moments, he imagined them continuing into a future where he apologised, and she forgave him. Where they abandoned their past and respective duties to build a humble life together. A futile fantasy.

Seeing her through the glass now, weathered and hardened, but very much alive, pierced him like an arrow. Her cheeks hollowed, her jawline more defined, and her skin tanned. She had outgrown her naivety. Warmth flooded his loins, tingling his legs and spine.

Those eyes were no longer vulnerable, but powerful. He drew a sharp breath. Powerful and dangerous.

He'd never desired her more.

Beside her perched a dark-skinned man with thinning white hair, and a tall woman with greying honey-coloured tresses, full lips, and hazel-green eyes. The feeling that he should know the woman nagged, but he could not establish from where.

'You don't recognise this place?'

He shook his head. 'Do you?'

She nodded. 'Maybe.'

'Tell me, Alina.'

'I've seen woods like these to the north and east, close to the High King's city. It's already snowing there. Thicker than here.' The vision widened to reveal a blanket of white covering a series of huts and trees alongside an opening carved into an escarpment. 'I cannot say where, exactly. Between Rassit and Wernad, perhaps?'

A picture slipped into his mind's eye of the location Alina referred to. He clung to the image, along with every detail contained within the glass. Imagining reuniting with Ella there—alive—created a resonance like a lodestone for his heart to follow.

The lightening sky peeped through Alina's attic window, signalling the false light of uhtan.

'I must go.'

Travelling through any town between here and Galliarn by daylight was risky. Over the years, Jonas had made a point of befriending everyone he encountered. Even without his family's insignia marking his clothes, people would recognise his grin.

He would veer west and north as Amber suggested, then cut across the Gythyn, circle back to the woodlands behind the High City and pray to every god it was the location Alina's sphere revealed.

His chest thudded again as he recalled Ella's altered face meeting his. He only hoped she would still be there when he arrived.

SEVEN

'Is she dead?' A light-skinned woman peered down at Ella.

'Nay,' said a darker man with peculiar violet eyes. 'But the blue mist left her colder than the snows.'

Don't... I'm Cursed... Ella emitted a wordless, strangled croak.

'Help me carry her.' The strangers wrapped a blanket around her and bundled her into their arms. Why was she naked? Who were these people? Where were they taking her?

She tried again to speak. 'Leave me...' *I'm Cursed.* Her warning slipped away as she fought the cold, flitting in and out of awareness.

Her frame bumped with each step. Everywhere they touched ached, yet the pain seemed to belong to someone else, unconnected to her body.

Somehow, she perceived the stars winking in the night sky, and the layer of snow that their boots sank into, while the icy air bit through her bones.

The man's thought slipped into her mind. *Had the gods not smiled upon you when they showed me the shifting currents of your magic, lass, you would have died from this night's frost.*

Aloud to the other woman, he said, 'It has been an age since I witnessed anyone porting.' His wispy white hair formed a halo around his dark skin, which glimmered in the moonlight. Not tanned or bronze, but indigo.

He grunted, arms shifting beneath her as he tried to get a better hold.

The woman rolled her green-grey eyes. 'Really, Yorg? She's so slight!'

'Maybe so, but my bones grow weary.'

'Ha! I've never known someone to begrudge the years blessed upon them as much as you.' She shook her honey-tinged tresses away from her comely features.

'The gods have been kinder to your folk, Lyn,' Yorg said.

'And it's been an age since anyone called me by that name. Does your memory slip with your body?'

He chuckled. 'Doubtless. Apologies, Vorlyn.'

They carted Ella into what appeared to be a cave. Dim light from a fire cast flickering shadows along the grey stone walls. They set her down before the blaze, still wrapped in a blanket. Heat rushed to fill the void, burning and tingling. It stung her mind and body, and she moaned.

The man clutched his temples and winced in obvious pain, speaking through gritted teeth. 'She has life enough yet!'

Ella observed herself through his eyes, as if looking through a window. The slight rise of her chest, the glow from the blood flowing beneath her pale skin, and the blue currents of her magic pulsing.

The woman's expression softened. 'I'll fetch a draught. She's in no state to permit your power to enter her.'

'Please do. She's a fierce one,' Yorg said, wincing.

'In all my seasons living among the god-touched, I have never envied the way you experience another's pain,' Vorlyn said.

Yorg smiled wryly. 'It's my fault for letting down my shield.'

Warm hands brought a lacquered cup to her lips, and Ella sipped. The liquid drew her consciousness to her flesh, not quite attached, as if it could peel away at any moment.

Yorg's strange violet eyes pinched into a frown. 'She's not fully as one,' he said. 'Look at me, lass.'

She forced her physical gaze to find his, though her mind wavered, and wandered again.

Drifting. Her body below. The sky above and all around. She floated in a sea that traversed space and time. Eddies tugged and pulled, and she allowed the currents to carry her where they willed.

A thought reached her. She didn't know whose. *The soup of the gods.*

She could not gain purchase on her leaden flesh. Her simulacrum passed straight through, unable to dock.

The man swore. 'I might have to compel her.'

Vorlyn gripped his arm. 'No, Yorg.'

Ella's mind hopped, catching memories of a time when someone meant to break the woman, violating her, like…

Gohran.

Terror blasted her limbs, jolting her back into her body, and she cried out. Where was her brother? She couldn't sense him. Had he come for her? Then she remembered.

The Curse…

She tried to speak, but her mouth was thick and gluggy.

'Hush, lass.' Yorg's weathered brown hand patted her shoulder and smoothed her straw-cropped hair.

Her hair. Where was Mara? Thyss?

She struggled to sit, and an arm slipped around her. 'Drink, lass.'

But her mind drifted.

'Just a touch more…'

Liquid slithered down her throat, and she was aware of its movement through her chest and belly, flowing along her limbs. Calming. Soothing. Each muscle releasing, relaxing, letting go.

The pounding in her head abated, as if dissolving. Relief!

She stopped fighting, burrowed into the soft bedding, sank into the fire's warm glow, as all her worries, fear, and pain melted.

Voices faded in and out as the potion carried her into oblivion.

'She's still slipping away.'

'I'll make sure her simulacrum doesn't wander.'

Hands smoothed Ella's hair and rubbed her back. Simple human touch that grounded her, until sleep came, and her mind generated nothing more than ordinary dreams.

Eight

Gohran ordered his men to separate and search in all directions. As he rode for home with a small escort, the drifting snowmelt cooled his skin. When he arrived, stinking and exhausted, his page stopped him from retreating to his chamber.

'Your Highness, His Holiness the High Priest Davith awaits in your study.'

Gohran froze. The head priest had trespassed on his private chambers. Who had let him in?

'I must clean up,' he said, offering no salutation. If Davith would not show him his due, Gohran would afford him no courtesies. He needed to change his clothes, scrub the stench of charred flesh from his hair and skin. Needed a moment to breathe before Davith accosted him.

But when he strode past his page, Davith emerged from his study and blocked his path. Staff raised; his jewel encrusted robe draped across the corridor.

'I bring pressing news, Your Highness.' Davith handed him a parchment bearing Nedran's seal. 'The dryhten's man took great pains to ensure I understood what it contained.'

He couldn't even challenge Davith, who had no business intercepting his messages. He snatched the scroll and rolled it open, poring over Venn's words as if to force them away, make them contain something—anything—other than the threat of Venn's sword.

'You must not allow your petty grievances to escalate, Your Highness.'

Gohran pivoted and ran fingers through his sweat and smoke-ridden hair. 'You think I don't know that?' Erldan could not finance a war, and could not risk losing Nedran's alliance, or the debt collectors would be at his gates before he could recite the *Ballad of Fyora and Zar*.

'You may consider treason "petty",' he spat, 'but a kingdom rests on the honour of its monarch. If an allied lord defies a king without consequence, how is a commoner to stay his hand? I cannot allow Lord Jonas to return to his brother.'

'You cannot risk open war.'

Gohran pushed his words through gritted teeth. 'My men hunt him as we speak.'

Davith's eyes narrowed. 'Good,' he said, stroking his chin. The familiarity of his gesture once comforted, but now rubbed. 'They must destroy him.'

Gohran startled. He'd expected Davith to caution him to release Jonas. To tell him the lordling was of no consequence. But their views aligned. Why? 'I have already instructed my men to stage an accident, or insist he provoked them...' *As he provoked me.*

'Excellent, Your Highness.'

The priest's deceit rendered his approval meaningless. Not a mentor, but a would-be usurper.

'In fairer news,' Gohran said, hoping to tilt Davith off balance, 'we no longer require the funds to instal additional henad courts.'

Davith's hand whipped away from his chin, his eyes demanding, and Gohran smirked. 'Dissidents on the outskirts of Erldan to the west will not trouble us. Not after my men razed their entire village.'

'Fool!' Davith hissed, spittle flying. 'Those villages provide tithes!'

Gohran flinched as if Davith struck him. 'Tithes?'

'And taxes,' he added. 'Not to mention the sourness this will spawn.'

Gohran steeled himself. 'It will inspire fear, surely. Those villagers should not have settled so far from my jurisdiction. Should not have harboured heretics, nor sheltered Nedran's younger lord.' *Or Ella.* 'I should have handled them long ago. And now, Erldan's vassals and neighbours dare not run afoul of my rule.'

'Inspiring fear is one thing. Ruling with tyranny, quite another.'

Davith's fury hovered like an ice-tipped blade at the gully of Gohran's throat. Still, the priest would not meet his gaze, nor let Gohran near him, his staff at the ready in case Gohran stepped too close.

'I caution you for a final time to seek my counsel before you act with haste, Your Highness.' His threat dangled. 'Permit my brethren to lead a more moderate pursuit. They will deal with your escaped lordling, and you need not answer to the dryhten.'

The walls closed in.

'I have drafted a response that informs the dryhten of his brother's escape. Your men had no choice but to pursue your prisoner. They intend to recover and release him on payment of the offered blood price. Should the lord never surface, it is beyond anyone's control.'

Gohran stalled. His world careened off kilter.

'Meanwhile, take to your chamber and get cleaned up.' Nose wrinkled in disdain. 'You need rest and to decide how to recoup the funds and goodwill your rashness just lost.'

NINE

Venn stalked the corridors, chasing shadows, wishing he sat like a falcon on the messenger's shoulder to observe Gohran's reaction when his threat reached him.

He tried to settle into his correspondence and accounts, but his mind skipped across his ledgers, and he could not steady his thoughts to read, nor his hand to write.

'Where is Mykan? I need to know if we raise the tariff on bound hallit, will that cover the blood price?'

But when Mykan arrived, nodding, taking notes, answering his questions and offering likely scenarios, Venn failed to absorb a thing. He sat, then stood. Pivoted and paced. Ran fingers through his hair, pulling fistfuls of strands loose like a moulting cat.

I'll kill Gohran for this. Jonas's words haunted. He wanted to curse his brother for his rashness, and yet it was he who had entangled them with Gohran. Jonas had never trusted Erldan's king.

'I'm heading out to train,' he told Mykan. Then, to his page, 'Summon my riders to the southern field.'

Though the hard ground was damp with snowmelt, he ignored the frost and commanded his men to face off against him, one by one, then two together, and by the time the afternoon light faded, sweat soaked his trousers and shirt, while livid bruises darkened his skin.

He stumbled, barely able to raise his burning shoulders or manoeuvre his cramping legs. 'Fight!' he screamed, hoarse.

'My lord! No more.' His captain sheathed his sword, and his men stepped back. Their wary eyes watched through the lengthening shadows, shields and weapons lax by their sides.

Blood pumped through Venn's temples. He did not stand down.

His captain approached with caution, ushering him aside. 'I implore you, my lord. Injured, you are no use to anyone. Go. Rest. There will be opportunity to train tomorrow.'

Defeated, Venn retreated indoors, skipped supper, and collapsed onto his welcoming mattress. Behind closed eyes, he relived every swing and strike, until his men's solemn faces crowded each victory out, willing his racing heart to slow. He wished Gohran would answer his letter and send his brother home.

He rolled over, begging sleep to silence his torment.

A gentle knock. The adjoining door creaked open. His eyes shot wide, and he sat.

There Raeyn stood, carrying a pot of salve. Her copper curls spilled around the sheer sleeves of her nightdress.

'My lord?' She inched her way inside. 'Let me loosen those muscles for you.' She padded over to his bed. 'Come, lie back, get comfortable.'

He groaned. Nowhere was comfortable.

With a forced breath, he allowed her to peel back his shirt and press the heel of her palm into the tenderest knots, easing into his flesh.

Though she warmed her hands, he flinched at every touch, remembering the vow he made before man and goddess that bound him to a witch. Not Ella, but Gohran.

'Let go, my lord,' she urged, her breath igniting the skin at his neck, and he relaxed against her. Her fingers ruffled the hair at his nape and traced his stubbled chin. Kneading and caressing in equal measure, her palms ventured across his chest, down his torso, and along his thighs. He couldn't recall another time when someone attended to his body this way.

The salve's mixture of camphor and mint at once heated and cooled, and he fought the urge to vocalise his relief, stifling each moan deep in his throat.

It wasn't Ella's touch, but it was touch. And he was starved.

'Roll over, my lord.'

He did, his flesh hungry for more.

She stroked his shoulders, his lower back, his buttocks, the tops of his legs and calves, before retracing her path to slip between his thighs. A thrill coursed through the small of his stomach and into his loins, blood flowing in a steady, tingling glow.

An untainted bodily yearning.

She continued her journey over his flesh. Palms, then lips, the heat of her breath lingering between his shoulder blades as her breasts pressed against him and her teasing hands sneaked beneath.

'Turn onto your back for me...'

He hesitated. Didn't want her to see the effect she was having on him, not when he wasn't sure he wanted to follow where it might lead, but her touch urged him on, and he complied.

Her steady gaze held his, and her curved lips enticed, deep copper ringlets framing her pale skin. She wiped any trace of salve from her palms before her fingers followed the trail of dark, curly hair below his navel. He stiffened, then relaxed.

Stroking down and then up, she encircled her fist where his arousal swelled and invited him to guide her movements to his liking—something Ella never had to do, as though she had existed inside him.

Still watching, she bent lower, her curls tickling the tender skin of his thighs and belly. Eyes locked on his, she ran her tongue along his length, and he sucked in his breath. Her lips circled his girth, teasing his tip, and he let out a low grunt as she slid him into her mouth.

His muscles tensed and another choked moan escaped, as pressure built at the base of his spine. He brushed her locks from her face, gathering them in his fist and tugging, wanting to draw her down to swallow him even deeper. Instead, he steered her to speed up and then slow, then hasten once more, thrusting up to meet her. His need mounted, readying to erupt, but before his pleasure peaked, she drew away.

Craving more, he ached to pull her back.

She hitched up her nightdress, straddled his hips, and guided him into her, sinking down and welcoming him inside her.

Gods, the heat of her! Already wet, her muscles contracted before relaxing to accommodate him. She rocked in a steady rhythm, drawing him deeper each time she lowered.

He clasped her hip, the other hand cupping her breast and caressing her taut nipple. He tugged her nightdress free. Needed to see her. Wanted to taste her, kiss her. She shoved his chest down and away, keeping him at a distance as she rode him like a steed, squeezing herself around him, rolling in a motion that catered to her pleasure.

Green eyes half closed; her lips parted when she wasn't biting down. She directed his fingers from her hip to find her peak, and she moved against his touch. No longer seeing him, but lost in her own sensation.

He tried to delay his satisfaction, not for him, but for her, because he could see how much she wanted this. Needed it. Needed him.

Her skin flushed, her muscles clenched, and she cried out, clutching his fingers still and firm against her. He paused as she ground her hips to her completion, then drew her gaze back to his. Eyes open, she willed him on.

He didn't want to withdraw from her warmth, but ached to roll her over, grip and pump himself into her.

As though she understood, she dismounted to let him out from under her and positioned herself on her knees before him. He raised her nightdress, and studied her smooth rounded buttocks, the slope and curve of her thighs. Stroking the damp darker skin of her outer sex, he delighted in the involuntary thrill of her muscles spasming against him. He clasped her hips, and thrust himself into her. Once, twice, thrice, and again, until his pleasure erupted inside her.

Spent, he collapsed, kissing her sweat-sheened shoulders, and breathing into her hair, before rolling off and drawing her to curl within his embrace.

He wanted to hold her against him forever, but she slipped out from under him, leaving him empty and cold.

'Gods willing, we'll have a son, my lord,' she said, and slid away through the dim light to her adjoining room, the clang of the bar lowering on the other side echoing off the walls.

Ten

Raeyn woke mid-morning, having enjoyed the soundest slumber she could remember. Once dressed, she meandered to the women's hall, humming under her breath.

Lynden sat with a tapestry resting untouched across her lap, gazing out the window.

'Any word from Erldan?' she asked, taking her place and retrieving her basket of needlework.

'Hmm? Oh, no, nothing.' Teeth gnawing on her bottom lip.

Raeyn frowned. 'My brother would be a fool not to back down.'

'Indeed.' Lynden's anxious fingers twined and untwined her thread. She paled. 'Bess—would you fetch me some water and salted flatbread?'

'Did you not break your fast this morning?' Raeyn asked.

Lynden stood. 'Excuse me, Your Highness…' She covered her mouth with her handkerchief and hurried outside.

Raeyn swore under her breath. The last thing they needed was an unwanted tether to her wretched brother.

Her thoughts drifted to Jaydyn, trapped at Erldan with only their handmaid, Lyrra, to help with her daughter. Gohran had proved useless at finding her a suitable match. Now it seemed she would be suitor-hunting for a ruined sister and sister-in-law.

She ran her hand along her midline, wishing her womb was as fruitful as everyone else's appeared to be. At least she knew she could seduce her husband.

Provided she did so with each turning moon, even if her brother's temper led them to war, with Venn's seed implanted, he would not banish her home.

☾

Lynden prayed to every god and goddess that nerves induced her nausea. Loath to return to the women's quarters and Raeyn's censure, she excused herself and headed into town with Bess at her elbow, armed with salted flatbread to settle her stomach.

They roamed the marketplace, Lynden mindlessly studying various wares, fending off merchants' chitchat. Bess patted her arm, and she was grateful she need not explain what troubled her.

Jonas advised her to flee to Lichen, but how could she leave Venn and her home? What would she tell Vera?

It was unfathomable. Her beloved brother hadn't just evoked the king's displeasure, he'd committed treason by making himself Gohran's fugitive. Now Venn was threatening a duel, and she was likely carrying their enemy's child.

Nausea gripped her again. She withdrew from Bess's arm and ducked into a side alley, gagging and spitting, tears running down her cheeks.

Bess followed, drew back her hair, rubbed and soothed her shoulders.

She peered around. The alley was empty, apart from a ginger tabby whose yellow eyes watched them from the steps of a wooden building. Eventually it grew bored, blinked, and turned away.

Once her stomach stopped spasming, she wiped her face on her kerchief. Gaze pitying, Bess handed her a skin of water to rinse her mouth.

'Hush, my lady, all will be well…'

Except it couldn't be. Not now. Not ever.

ELEVEN

'Letters nominating a steward, a new driver, and treasurer...' Davith pushed the parchments across Gohran's desk.

Gohran eyed them from his high-backed chair but made no move to sign. 'Until your men recover my lost prisoner, the king's coffers cannot afford three senior posts.' Not trusted appointees, but Davith's spies.

'Your Highness?' Davith's servant, an acne-pocked lad with bleached, greasy hair, stepped forward. 'Can we not request the blood price now and release the lord once we find him?'

'Fool,' Gohran spat. 'What do you suppose Lord Venn will assume if we take his money and do not deliver his brother?' He risked leaning close to his High Priest and hissed, 'It is no surprise your servants have not found the lordling if this is the measure of their competence.'

Davith's eyes narrowed. 'Leave us,' he waved the lad away.

Once the door banged shut behind him, Gohran continued. 'This is not the first time people have disappeared under your watch.'

'If you refer to your driver, it was not I who concealed the man's true destination.' He focused on the parchments, the desk, the walls, anywhere but Gohran's face. 'Nor did I choose to arrest your most important ally's younger brother.'

'Yet your servants failed to protect one man, and now they cannot locate another.' He gestured to the letters. 'And you expect me to rely on these men?'

Davith sauntered to the basket beside the burning hearth. 'Some circumstances—and people—are unpredictable.' He retrieved a rod of kindling and held it aloft. 'Others are reliable and certain.' He tossed the wood onto the fire. It sparked and flamed, slowly, then savagely, the blaze consuming it to embers.

'Enough!' Gohran thumped his fists upon his desk, spilling ink and quills over the parchments. Voice low, he said, 'You have made your point. Repeatedly.'

His chair dragged as he stood. He pushed his raven hair from his forehead and stepped nearer to the priest. Davith raised his staff between them, ever at the ready.

Gohran straightened to his full height. 'What are you waiting for? Why continue this charade?' His chest was broader and deeper than the priest's. He could use might or magic. Yet he hesitated.

A sneer twisted the corners of Davith's lips.

Do it, he dared silently. *Denounce me.*

But Davith said nothing, waiting for Gohran's outburst to resume, as he'd out-waited Gohran's fuse when he was a boy.

Davith's expression softened. 'My dearest king and overlord, I have known you since you were a child...' Davith lowered his staff and edged closer.

The heat from the fire tempered to a soothing warmth as Davith's lilting tone mollified. 'I have guided you. Cared for you...'

Gohran's shoulders crumpled. He closed his eyes, thirsting for a hint that Davith's regard was once genuine. That it wasn't all a lie. He held his breath.

'You must realise by now that a man bearing the monarch's ring is useful beyond measure.'

Davith's words sliced like steel. Sparing him was not a mercy. He remained Davith's hostage. Alive, he could hand over power. Dead, he was worthless. But if he offered no value, his life was forfeit.

He broke away, strode to his desk, and held up his seal. 'Shall I surrender this?'

Davith stood, unblinking.

'Get me that coin without Lord Jonas's body surfacing, and you shall have your men.' He slammed down the seal and stormed out.

Outside, cold air struck as he marched through Erldan's glade, and past the tree that bore Ella's memorial plaque. He trudged beyond the reinforced walls and towards his hunting preserve.

Soon, thick snow would blanket the forest floor and the road between Erldan and Nedran, preventing Venn's blade from getting near enough to cut his throat. But there was no escape from Davith's hold.

Underbrush snapped beneath his boots as he followed the trail he and Ella shared when he'd had her to himself on the cusp of winter for that brief glimmer.

The brush of her skin echoed, her familiar current shifting between them as their broken souls melded and merged. But when he reached for her now, he found nothing. She was gone. Not at Aryon. Not on the outskirts of Ycelt. So where?

If she had come to harm, he felt certain he would experience her loss as a death, killing a portion of himself. Her life breathed in his bones.

He could not demand Ella's whereabouts from his aunt. He no longer trusted anyone to deliver messages, and he could not carry one there himself—not with Davith's spies crawling all over him.

Ella's disappearance, at least, relieved the urgency and obligation of paying her dowry, and he could redeploy those funds to the moneylenders. But how was he to ensure Jonas never surfaced? Or Ella? All the while fending off his head priest.

He trusted no one to guide him.

Perhaps he should welcome Venn's sword: a clean death. He would be out from under Davith's clutches, and no one need ever uncover his heresy or reveal his twisted obsession.

But if he died, his dynasty perished with him.

Given the rift between Erldan and Nedran, he dared not count Raeyn's future children in the line of succession, which left Serrah as Erldan's only heir. An illegitimate toddler whose mother lacked wits to secure a husband, let alone rule a kingdom.

Doubtless, Ella's babe aborted after he delivered her to Aryon. And if it hadn't? The truest heir was an abomination. He sluiced the notion away.

Burdening a soul with his tainted seed rankled, yet he must assure his legacy and enshrine Erldan's future before ending his tortured existence.

A thin layer of ice coated the edges of the pond where he and his sisters skated as children. In a few weeks, it would freeze over.

He dropped to his knees, retrieved his dagger, and etched the arc of Elnora's light into the frozen surface. He had not worshipped beyond official services since coupling with Ella. But he needed the goddess now. Yearned for her guidance. Her forgiveness.

He rolled back his sleeve, and drew the blade across his forearm, slicing through old scars until his blood pooled and dripped onto the limned sun. Deep scarlet ran along the crevices, filling each line and peak of his ritual. Tears followed, diluting and extending the blood's flow. Everywhere his fluids reached, the ice melted, distorting Elnora's figure to resemble a ghoulish demon: his sacrifice rejected.

What if he stopped struggling and let go? Caved to his desire to end this torment, instead of pushing on for his kingdom and legacy, when everything he touched, he destroyed.

He stood and tiptoed across the graven image, one step, then another, then another. The melted ice cracked but held.

It would take but one more step, one more crack. The ice would give way, and he could slip into oblivion...

He stomped. Once, twice, thrice.

The pond's surface snapped, and he dropped.

Cold struck where moisture seeped into his clothing, soaking and dragging him down.

'Your Highness!' Muted shouts and cries from above.

He released his breath; the bubbles rushing past his face. Time slowed as he remained below, water blocking his ears to dampen and distort all sounds.

Through the murky lake, dirt and leaves stirred. Reeds swayed and brushed his limbs, tangling in his hair. Filtered sunlight flecked across grey pebbles and glinted off the silver scales of the startled fish teeming past. One paused to nibble at his clothing. He imagined it feasting on his decaying flesh.

Still. Quiet. What if he stayed down here? Never breathed again…

Arms crashed through the water and seized him. They dragged him above the surface, along the cracked ice, away from the pond and onto firm ground. Chill and wet collided, leaving his body trembling as dripping moisture soaked the leaves and dirt.

More arms hauled him to his feet. Not his men, but Davith's. Where were these wretched fools when he torched an entire village? Why not spare them? Why him? *Him!*

The men steered him back towards Erldan, as though he were a child. Or a prisoner.

Atop the steps to the castle keep, just beyond the old archway, Davith towered. A memory flickered. His mother the day she'd caught Ella using magic, standing in that exact spot, stern-browed and ready to scold. His spine rippled as if someone poured snow down his already icy shirt.

'Remember your duty to your kingdom, Your Highness.' Davith's voice cut through his reverie, but his features wavered, obscured by phantom smoke and haze, and when he turned and strode back to the keep, it was his mother's skirts, not Davith's robe, that Gohran saw.

Perhaps it is time he considered whether he wishes to remain the head priest for this family, she'd later said. Mother knew, even then, that Davith's interests had only ever been his own.

Davith's men closed in, ushering him inside and to his room, commanding a hot bath.

He shrugged their arms away. Growled and shouted.

His mother's agony as the priests torched her flooded him, her wails forever seared into the night. Into his soul. He squeezed his smoke-stung eyes shut, begging the images to stop. But her features wavered through the haze of his mind as her face became his: an inescapable glimpse at his future once Davith had his fill.

Twelve

Nykki! Amber sensed her beloved approaching before hearing footfalls and muffled voices. Tears sprang. No. Nykki couldn't be here, not now.

Amber peered through the light filtered from the bars above, heard grunting and dragging. A jangle and clanging of metal as Breeyan unlocked the grate, then the hinges screeched as she hefted it open.

'Here, go ahead, and I'll pass this down…'

Nykki's sandalled feet and stockinged legs poked beneath her robe as she lowered halfway, then grasped the iron brazier, which she set down on the cellar floor. A sack of coal and wood kindling followed, and then another containing food, a water-filled canteen, and an empty pail.

Amber huddled against the far corner, trying not to let Nykki get too close as she stacked the supplies.

It wasn't until Breeyan said, 'Pass me the waste,' that she realised the High Priestess meant to abandon her down there.

'No! Wait!'

Too late. The grate slammed shut.

Amber called, crying for Breeyan not to leave them—not to leave Nykki—but she was gone.

Through the shadows, she studied Nykki's face. Gods, how she'd missed her smile, her delicate, sloped nose. The one soul she kept fighting for, whose existence made her torture bearable.

Now here she was, tears of hope and joy streaming down her cheeks.

Why wasn't Nykki protesting? Why didn't she fear her?

My love... Nykki edged nearer, her yearning a lodestone tugging at iron filings.

'Stay back!' Amber stepped away.

Hurt and confusion crossed Nykki's features as she slowed, but continued closing in.

'Stay where you are.' Amber backed against the wall. 'Don't come any closer.'

'What did those monsters do to you?' Nykki crooned, her palms raised as though she coaxed an injured animal.

Amber swallowed, wanting to howl. She shook her head. 'It wasn't them. *I* did this...' The eyes she adored watched her, bewildered. 'Please—stay back. Don't make me hurt you.' Amber pressed against the dank clay.

Yet Nykki neared. 'You could never hurt me.'

Oh, but she could. The Curse of her crimes would taint and poison her beloved. 'Nykki, no...' She dropped to her knees, covered her face, and wept. This could not be happening. There was no escape. *Xenon, no...*

Nykki's arms wrapped around her, and she felt the tug of their mornings spent braiding each other's hair, the graze of her fingertips beneath a bucket of wash water, the perpetual longing to lure her closer, to catch and hold her, but she shoved Nykki off. The warmth and comfort she should have experienced in that touch scorched her.

Nykki clasped tighter, and she tried to writhe free. 'Please, Nykki... Stop.'

'We can face this together.'

'No...' Not now. Not after what she'd done.

'Everything will be well, my love.' Arms squeezing. She railed against them, but Nykki held firm, her voice low and determined. 'I'm not losing you again.'

She was already lost.

Fingers twined and smoothed her hair, but their tender sweep flashed Amber back to Erldan's dungeon, Davith tugging at her braids, his oily words slithering along her spine. Her mind screamed, wrenching away, but Nykki's grip remained solid. Resolved.

'Hush, my love.' Calming waves lapped as Nykki's warm lips pressed against her forehead. Gods, those lips! She smelled of spring wattle, not ilak grease. *Not him.*

Nykki's mind reached further. Amber craved letting her in, but needed to slam her out. *Please, Nykki. Don't make this harder.*

Nykki did not waver. 'Whatever you believe your offense, it means nothing to me.'

She grasped Amber's hands, but Amber snatched them away. 'Please stop. Let me go...' But Nykki seized and scooped her in an embrace. Amber trembled, whispered, 'No... Please... Out there, I... Oh, gods—' She covered her face.

'Out there, you did what you had to do,' Nykki said. 'To survive.'

What did that matter when she was Cursed? 'I drew from a forbidden source...'

'From Chrysanth. Her Holiness told me.'

Was that the gold-eyed girl's name? 'If you knew, why did you come?'

'Because I can't lose you,' Nykki whispered, her tears dampening Amber's hair. Tears that would drown her as the heat of those lips would tear her to pieces. And when she spoke again, Nykki's words near swallowed her. 'If the god chooses to Curse me for loving you, then let me burn.'

A cold chortle bubbled up and spilled from her. It was too late for that. They would torch Amber, but Nykki—Nykki might survive this. 'No,' she urged, swallowing a sob.

She tried once more to pull away, but Nykki would not release her. She squeezed Amber to her breast, her heartbeat steady, stroking her hair, her tender breath whispering against her forehead, 'Hush, my love. Hush.'

'I won't let you—'

But Nykki's lips were on hers, silencing, terrifying.

Thrilling.

A fiery chasm might have engulfed her, and yet... And yet those flames held sweetness and life within their agony.

Nykki took her face in her hands. 'Look at me.'

But Amber scrunched her eyes shut. She would not let—

'Look.' Nykki's mind churned, as compelling and commanding as a physical force. She was powerless to do anything but meet her beloved's gaze. *Those eyes!* The green of emerald grass, of a rainforest in spring, of a satisfied cat getting exactly what it craved. 'Breeyan told me what you did, and I chose to come here. Do you understand?'

'No...' she whimpered.

'Yes.' Nykki's lips pressed to hers, and the salt of their tears mingled, as Amber's mouth responded with insatiable hunger.

Another kiss, lips so soft she wanted to disappear inside of them. Nykki stroked her hair, her cheek. She was losing herself in that touch.

But she needed to resist. Nykki's life depended on it, or the chasm would swallow them whole, while its flames tore them apart. 'I'm Cursed,' she whispered again.

And Nykki's lips remained, their fire tracing along her throat. 'And I would live the briefest moment if in that moment I could love you.'

Thirteen

How long had Ella slept? It seemed an entire moon cycle. She sat, struggling to orient herself. Her muscles were stiff from disuse and yet ached as if she'd hefted boulders.

Her bedroll's stone recess faced a firepit that pumped steady heat. Rings of coals and hot stones extended and amplified its warmth to the furthest stretches of her surrounds.

What she initially thought was a cave appeared to be a cavern, dug out, and shaped into a spider's web of corridors and pocket-like cells. The space glowed with faint light, but she saw no lanterns or sconces.

The smell of spiced venison wafted from a steaming cauldron perched over the fire. Beside it, someone had left a cloth-wrapped loaf to prove. Its yeasty aroma reminded her of the ale barrels stacked alongside the kitchens at Erldan.

Soft voices echoed, but she couldn't see who they belonged to.

What was this place?

Footsteps neared, and then a familiar face. 'Welcome to Aeron, lass.' It was the dark-skinned man with violet eyes, Yorg. 'You might know it better as Vern.'

She frowned, trying to recall the name.

'Or not…' His laugh rumbled like a barrel drum.

Her throat clogged, and she struggled to speak. He handed her a cup of water. She gulped, coughed, and tried again. 'You're in my head…'

Another chuckle. 'As you've been in mine.'

'Should I know of Vern?'

He frowned. 'I assumed anyone porting here would know where they headed.'

'Porting?'

'Curious,' he said, his white robe swishing with every movement. If not for the gold fringed cincture gathering its waist, it would have swallowed his delicate frame whole. His garb reminded her of a vestment, but not of any religion she recognised.

Her loose trousers were of the same fabric, fastened with a gold embroidered belt, and a fitted shirt with wide-rimmed sleeves. She flushed. Who had dressed her? Where were Thymm's clothes?

'The woman who was with you—Lyn?'

'Best not call her that. She still hasn't forgiven my lapse. Around here we know her as Vorlyn, and she's hunting, but she'll return shortly. Supper is almost ready.'

He helped her off the ledge where she'd slept, and over to the fire, and motioned for her to sit cross-legged on one of a circle of cushions.

Ella reached again for her brother, for Mara and Thyss, for Venn, but most of all, Xarion, and sensed nothing. 'Why can't I feel them?' Tears welled.

'Folk in Ycelt know this place as Vern, but we call it Aeron of Nowhere, for there is nowhere we can be found.'

Why was he reciting riddles?

'Not a riddle, lass, just a truth.'

She drew heat from the fire and opened her god-sight. A net of blue light weaved along every wall and above her, embedded in the cave's ceiling. Magic shielded this entire cavern!

She swiped the scatter of tears from her cheeks with the heel of her palm. Safe from Gohran, but cut off from her babe, the flesh of her blood. She brought her hands to her breasts and then the small of her belly.

Yorg held his gaping sleeve back from his fine-boned forearm and dipped a ladle into the cauldron to fill a lacquered cup from a stack. He passed it across, and she noticed his white fingernails filed to a point.

'Broth,' he said when she sniffed it. 'It's good. Ayla does wonders with winter bones.'

Whoever Ayla was.

She blew the top to cool it, then sipped, tasting sage, thyme, salt, and spices she could not identify.

Sparkling laughter and soft murmurs as a group emerged from a corridor, all dressed alike. Most shared Yorg's deep brown complexion—or was it a midnight blue? *Indigo.* She squinted. Perhaps the glow of the shield cast by her god-sight. She could no longer tell what she viewed through corporeal eyes.

Since 'porting', as Yorg termed it, her consciousness hopped and slipped into whoever's mind she grasped, almost like her psyche had wedged open.

'We'll need to fix that,' Yorg said. 'Anchor everything back in place, or it will send you daft in no time.'

Even now, she was casting her thoughts indiscriminately, but hoped not beyond the shield that appeared embedded in Aeron's walls.

'She's awake!' a woman called.

'Welcome, lass.' A second face, with that same night sky complexion and moonbeam hair, smiled and sat on a cushion beside her.

'Ella, is it?' A third woman asked, joining them.

Yorg distributed large cups of broth as the circle filled. 'Or shall we call you Nessa?'

Ella startled. She hadn't been conscious enough to tell anyone her name. She drew her arms around her and shrank away.

A further clutch of bodies joined them, all bearing complexions so pale they were almost translucent, and tresses as dark as hers before Mara dyed it. When they looked her way, she might have been seeing her azure gaze in a mirror.

Most wore braids like the priestesses at Aryon, resembling the Ancients. Old lore nagged. *Midnight skin and twilight eyes. Hair of the moon.* Were these Myans?

'Myanai,' Yorg corrected.

But the others, with hair like the night sky, skin like the moon and noontide eyes...?

'Ancients, as you call them.'

Ella gasped.

That's why their clothing looked familiar: garb styled after the histories.

'*From* the histories, indeed,' Yorg said, and she wished he would stop invading her mind.

His laughter rumbled again. 'I do not choose to enter your mind, lass, but it seems you cannot keep your thoughts to yourself!'

The surrounding folk observed her as curiously as she examined them, but where she was wary, they were welcoming, greeting her with their fingers splayed and heads bowed, a gesture she assumed was comparable to a bow or curtsy. None feared, resented, or craved her, and it felt foreign. Their regard for her was neutral, as though her magic meant nothing.

'What is this place?' she asked again. Yet, if she allowed her mind's tendrils to roam, she knew, because they knew.

Aeron of Nowhere.

'In your time, Aeron inhabits the mortal locale of Vern.'

'In my time?' These folk appeared as the Ancients—from Ycelt and from Myan—because they *were* Ancients. *Existing in no fixed place, and no fixed time.*

'Vern sits close to the High Realm of Galliarn.' The voice belonged to the woman who retrieved her from the snow: Vorlyn. To Yorg, she said, 'I only caught a few rabbits. I doubt we'll source much else now.' She took the cup he offered and joined their circle.

Ella studied her. She didn't resemble the others. A handsome, middle-aged woman, suited to the courts of Nedran or Erldan, except she wore her unbraided honey-brown hair fastened back, and her clothing resembled that of a farmer.

Oddly familiar, Ella felt she should know her from somewhere. Perhaps because, compared to her companions, her face was most akin to those she'd left behind.

She reached for the woman's mind, searching for answers, but there was something odd about her, a quality she couldn't access—though not a shield.

'Once you've finished your broth, Yorg can help you settle back into your body,' she said.

Had she sensed Ella's probing?

Ella sucked in her breath and tried to summon a barrier around her thoughts. But while they roamed, there was no boundary to reinforce, and she felt more naked than when they'd found her wearing no clothes.

She buried her face in her cup and concentrated on drinking it as quickly as its heat permitted.

Her psyche followed a woman who took over from Yorg, distributing broth as newcomers arrived, but was also watching herself sip from the outside, eyes wide, trembling. Snippets of conversation bounced around her. Aloud, discussing the day's hunt, an upcoming celebration, gossip about this person or that. Between minds, curious to know who she was, how she had ended up here, what was to become of her. And deeper, private thoughts, of which their owners were scarcely aware.

Either they could not shield or chose not to.

But this was not her choice.

She tried to shutter them, to focus only on herself, but their minds clamoured, images blurring and merging. She was everywhere and nowhere, strong and weak, old and young, hot and cold.

'Please,' she said. 'Make it stop...'

'That's permission enough for me,' Yorg muttered, glancing at Vorlyn. He retrieved Ella's empty cup and signalled to his companions. 'Let's get you anchored.'

He held out his arm to help her up, but when she stood, her legs were unsteady as porridge, and she faltered, nearly toppling onto her neighbours. Two pairs of arms caught her on either side and propped her up. Their startled musings flitted in and out of her mind—or was she flitting in and out of theirs?

'Are you certain you've the strength to do this now? We can wait until you've rested again...'

She shook her head. 'I'm a little wobbly, but strong enough.' The sooner she regained control of—and privacy over—her thoughts, the better.

They ushered her along a narrow passage and into an inner hollowed out cell, their shadows elongating, then shrinking away. Within, a blue glow illuminated a granite bench and a ring of stone stools. She peered around, trying to locate the light's source, but found no lanterns, or cave moss. Magic, it had to be.

Someone had carved sigils into the walls and at key points surrounding the bench, which at a second glance resembled a funeral slab. She thought then of poor dead Sallyn, whose hair and skin were as pale as these folks' combined.

Behind her, someone brought a padded mat—her bedroll—and spread it flat atop the slab, gesturing for her to lie down.

She did, but she was shaking.

'Fetch her blanket, too,' Yorg said, and the woman complied, hurrying back out to retrieve it.

It wasn't a matter of warmth, Ella realised, but comfort. She wanted to tuck herself away, to feel less... exposed.

When the woman returned, she placed the blanket across her. Strangers stood on either side, at her head and hips. Their palms pressed into her shoulders, while others levered down upon her thighs. Another set gripped her face and held her steady.

Yorg peered down at her, and she up at him. Her mind swirled from seeing herself and experiencing her own sight synchronously.

Please... she whimpered, but no sound escaped.

Her vision warped, and Yorg's purple irises appeared blue, while hers turned violet, at once night and day. She was sliding away again. Could not grab hold of anything, her body as slippery to her simulacrum as oil to water.

A lodestone voice lured mind to flesh. 'Focus on the tip of your largest right toe...'

But it was so hard to concentrate when her vision was swirling, thoughts tumbling, experiencing sensations that might be anyone's.

Deep and steady. 'Just one toe...'

She breathed.

'Sense its outline, the border of nail and skin...' His breath slowed, encouraging her to mirror his. 'Notice the touch of the blanket, the temperature of the air...'

And she did. Faint at first, but his words drew her back to a single toe.

'That's it... Now take your attention to the toe beside it... And then the sole of your foot, its arch, and heel... Good... Now the other foot... Note the weight of it pressing into the mat below...' Yorg's voice lilted, hypnotic, like a Myan singing bowl reverberating through her body. It called her back to her flesh, a summons she could not ignore. Did not *wish* to ignore.

Magic hummed and the key points blazed: a vibrant blue pyramid constructed from refracted light. It was a barrier, she realised, trapping her simulacrum within.

She panicked, and her mind pulled away, withdrawing, but then that tone returned, soothing and beckoning.

Enticing.

Warmth flooded her, sweeter than any sensation, the voice captivating.

She ached to give in to its call: a siren song to her will. She would do anything, *anything*, he asked of her, to experience that exquisite warmth, not to lose it...

His irises were entirely blue now. Rounder, wider, framed by dark lashes, and as azure as the midday sky. He wore her eyes.

And their gaze intoxicated.

A slow, sinking sensation crawled across her flesh like beetles, followed by a fiery tingle.

It *was* her gaze. Her beguiling power reflected.

This is what Venn experienced, and Gohran, too. What the villagers felt when she smiled their way and commanded their attention. Its pull stronger than Amber's influence, than her mother's compulsion. More potent than anything she had encountered, except for the raw power her daughter wielded.

She could not resist, but nor did she want to. She needed to answer its call, never wanted it to end. And now she fought against embodying her flesh, to draw out the sweet agony of it, for fear once she rejoined herself, that exquisite warmth would be gone.

Yorg spoke, but she no longer heard, completely immersed in her own power.

The palms that held her down withdrew.

Someone shouted, but it was so far away. Hands reached inside the key points to wrench Yorg from her, too, but she fought them, clawing him back. He tried to tear his gaze from hers, but she captured and forced him steady.

Heat churned all around. She threw her blanket free and loosened her garments.

Where Yorg's gaze had held hers, now it was she who captivated him. He could not blink. Could not look away. It was his command, but her will.

'Someone fetch Vorlyn!' A distinct shout cut across the hypnotic trance.

Stomping and shuffling. 'I'm here—' Vorlyn halted. 'What is happening?'

Blue light weaved around Yorg like a spider's silk, binding him to Ella and cocooning him within her web. Power throbbed and pulsed, and it was the sweetest pleasure Ella had ever known.

Yorg struggled to form his own words, his voice strangling in his throat. 'Get—in—here...'

Vorlyn stepped across the key points as though they did not exist, breaking their hold. She grasped Yorg's raised and frozen palms.

'Step between us, Lyn!'

Vorlyn positioned herself between Yorg and Ella. Her ordinary green-grey eyes peered down, slicing through Ella's force.

Ella's simulacrum slammed back into her body. With the sense of a padlock clunking into place, it docked there. Home.

Pain filled the sudden void, the absence of Ella's power as intense as losing her daughter. An exhausted sob escaped.

She retrieved the blanket and pulled it around her, shrinking from this strange woman, these odd people, and that man who could enthral and channel her power back at her.

The woman smoothed Ella's sweat-soaked hair off her face, and held her tight, comforting. 'You're safe,' she whispered, but Ella caught her sharing a cautious glance with Yorg.

She stretched her mind and heard no thoughts, the quiet almost deafening for its strangeness.

Alone.

They left her to sleep. But in the darkness, she yearned for the peculiar force that thrummed within, comprehending for the first time why others feared her. But more than herself, she feared Vorlyn. A woman whose gaze held no magic yet possessed greater power than any soul in this place for its immunity.

Fourteen

How had Amber expected to fend Nykki off? To resist what she'd craved for so long. To perceive her lover fully, to embody and share and express. She had wanted to spare her. Struggled to keep her lust at bay, to tread within Xenon's bounds. But now her fortress had crumbled, and she could not get enough of Nykki's mouth, her tongue, her round, tender belly.

And Nykki's exquisite flesh yielded to hers. Gods, her silken skin was like cream against her lips, her whimpers celestial. She sought to consume every part of her. Stroking, teasing, lingering, kneading.

As Nykki encircled her and cupped her breasts, her nipples hardened to taut peaks. Her lips traced Amber's neck, and found her mouth, and her fingers, the heat between her thighs. Her centre swelled until her pleasure radiated and shivered along her spine and limbs in cascading waves, stoking a fire, which, now ignited, could never extinguish.

How had the god forbidden this? *This?* Kept this divine union from His people.

She understood why He might forbid someone like Ella, Cursed with beguilement, from joining with those powerless against her sway, but when Nykki and Amber met, it was as equals.

The High Priestess may not have intended them to spend their time this way, but the gate opened when Breeyan told Nykki she believed them both tainted and that they would share the same fate.

Nykki chose her sacrifice, as Amber had calculated the risk when survival depended on drawing forbidden power. To immerse herself in their love, however fleeting, rather than exist forever starved.

'I never asked for our gift in a world that hates and fears us,' Nykki said. 'If given the choice, I would not have come to Aryon, and with you gone, there is no reason to stay.' *No reason to live.* 'If we are going to burn, let us share something worth burning for.'

As their bodies united, their power stirred, every tingle reflected, each thought shared and amplified. More powerful than the electric thrill of drawing blood, their magic whirled, blending to merge and bond them.

Unlike using influence, where energy flowed and wound around another, Nykki's force met hers in perfect equilibrium. Each sensation a mirror for the other's, balancing, yet magnifying, as though they could move through space and alter time.

As their knowledge coalesced, Amber no longer distinguished between what they voiced or thought. She relived Nykki's childhood through visceral memories, discovered her beliefs, uncovered her feelings, as if they'd happened not to Nykki, but to her.

She tried to keep Nykki from re-experiencing her capture and torture, but any barrier left between them dissolved as their bodies became one.

The surrounding shadows gradually shifted, shortening, then lengthening, before fading into twilight, leaving stars and the moon winking. All the while, their passion rose and subsided, tumbling, then crashing over them.

A damp sheen coated Nykki's skin and darkened her chestnut braids. When she loosened them, Amber froze, recalling Davith's fingers breaching hers. For them to remain reminded her they defied Xenon, but to release them...

She choked and pulled away, trembling. Fire and ice coursed through her veins until Nykki's mind found hers again. She soothed and drew her back. *Hush, my love, it's only me.*

Between the nightmares that ripped her awake, she caught snippets of sleep, to find Nykki's arms locked around her, calming and whispering, until she settled, and her body surrendered.

Too soon, the sky brightened, the day's warmth struggling to break through to where they lay atop their blankets, but they didn't need it, or the brazier. Their coupling generated heat enough.

The haunting draughts and echoes of the cellar all but vanished, and the rest of the world with them, until she looked up and saw that wretched locked grate.

Don't think about it, my love. Down here, we are alive, and we have each other.

B reeyan slammed the volume shut. Filled with poetry and platitudes, these scriptures told her nothing. 'The Curse brings horror thrice over,' and 'It touches those around them.' What did these hyperbolic threats mean?

Season after season, moon after moon, she recited phrases by rote, only realising now, devoid of true understanding. What other lore had she consumed and regurgitated with no comprehension or analysis?

She had transgressed Xenon's decrees, yet still lived. Weary, yes, but vibrant and healthy in her middle age. Rohan had survived to see his son grow to a boy before succumbing to the festering wounds of a fall. Yet their child bore the stain of their sin. Not them. And it was Gohran who inflicted his stain upon those around him.

All she had known was the Curse carried death and destruction. A double-edged sword, because it forced those it protected to sacrifice to live by His commands.

She couldn't trouble Shira further with her research, not unless she wanted her apprentice to suspect her fears, so she wrote to Gordovyn, the head of Aryon's brethren at the Gern.

Nestled into the forests past Henctyn in the northwest, close to the twin cities of Sarrion and Ryce, the Gern sat beyond the bounds of the Cursed Realm, but with established trading partners in Ycelt and Myan via the River Arin.

Nearby priests overlooked the men of the Gern, who tithed a significant portion of their rare oilseed crops to Elnora. This afforded the Gern's inhabitants greater access to Yceltic records, through travel and trade.

Aryon could not house men within the order, so directed male refugees to the Gern, while the Gern steered women further west to the sisters at Crescent Mountain, and occasionally south to Aryon.

With Erldan's priests on Amber's trail, Breeyan dared not send word overland, nor did she trust her priestess's curiosity, so attached her message to a pigeon herself, requesting an audience with her counterpart.

When the scheduled night arrived for their meet, she waited for the midnight moon tide to turn, then crept into the Hall of Prayer.

With Xarion strapped to her breast, she knelt before the god's idol. Scrying at this distance was challenging without a powerful source, and she hated to keep channelling Xarion's unfettered strength, but ultimately, it was to spare her.

The babe's attachment to Breeyan as her caregiver created a direct route to her source, which thrummed and churned, peaking from azure to violet. Xarion was so potent, and their connection so intimate, she did not need to draw her blood and cross that forbidden line. Instead, she followed their bond to net and funnel a measure of Xarion's energy towards Xenon's replica stone, careful never to draw Xarion's power within herself.

The stone lit up, casting a glow as bright as the full moon. She breathed from her abdomen and summoned Gordovyn.

After an agonising delay, her brethren's simulacrum wavered before her. She drew more force until his mind connected with hers, but their channel was weak. Even fuelled by Xarion's source, and amplified and directed by Xenon's stone, their link churned and tugged, threatening to dissipate.

Her urgency rising, she shared her need for lore on the Curse. What could Gordovyn locate? Did any records reveal what happened once someone incited it? She waited for his response, but the tether was already dissolving.

Xarion glared, sucking power away from her with a sharp pinch.

Hush, my love... She drew the babe close, but as Xarion hungered for more, her wails ripped through Breeyan's psyche and the link tore.

Sweat prickled along her hairline, armpits, and the backs of her knees. Violet splotches sparked, and her vision blackened. She teetered where she knelt. Needed to lie before she collapsed.

Xarion's screams intensified. She placed her down and lay beside her, flat upon the cold stone. *Please. Stop...*

But Xarion's hunger built to a ravenous crescendo, extending to every mind within reach.

Shouts and footfalls approached. Someone retrieved the distressed infant, while others crowded to prop Breeyan up.

Minds murmured, their eyes questioning. Judging. What was Breeyan doing here? Why was Xarion wailing?

Breeyan thought only of Xarion's comfort. Her safety.

'Someone, feed her...' she whispered, before darkness took her and her consciousness slipped away.

Fifteen

Wails in the distance.

Amber bolted upright.

'What is it?'

She raised her hand for silence, reaching beyond their prison with her mind.

People approaching. Dozens of them, maybe more. Terrified souls fleeing for their lives. Their anguish invaded her. Images of ash-smeared faces and scorched flesh peeking through singed clothing. Their memories revealed riders displaying a familiar sapphire, green, and gold insignia: King Gohran of Erldan's men, carrying torches, setting homes alight.

Amber shielded against the horror. 'We need to help them.'

'We can't break through metal, my love.' Nykki peered up at the locked grate and folded her arms over her chest.

Pressure pounded behind Amber's temples. Distress pressed in. Desperation. Anger. Fear. 'We must try. Please—they need us...' *Can't you feel them?* Amber grappled the hand and foot holds and climbed. Near the opening, she perched beside the wall and pushed against the lock.

Nykki stood, unmoving. 'They don't want our help.'

Another series of images shoved against the first. Villagers hunting Nykki's family, waving torches through the night, shouting and cursing. *Witch! Demon-spawn! Heretic!*

Nykki had escaped, made it to Aryon, but her brother, her sister, and mother had not, and her raw grief still bled.

She supposed Nykki was right. Why risk their lives for people who would not do the same were the situation reversed? Souls who would denounce them given an opportunity.

Wait—those weren't her thoughts.

Amber exhaled, trying to clear her mind, to discern which emotions belonged to her, and which to Nykki.

'Blame the priests, not these souls for their inculcation,' she said, struggling to hold her values steady against the rising tide of Nykki's.

She reached for memories of her flight, clung to the village lad's kindness, warning her and Jonas that men were on their way. He'd sacrificed steeds for them.

Turmoil swirled on Nykki's face, a mirror of her own moments before. She wavered, unsure whose experiences were whose.

'Please, my love. It's not their fault…' *My escape brought this horror.*

Nykki faltered. She took a slow breath, wading through her confusion. Another inhale, and her mind cleared. 'For you, I'll help,' she said. *Not them.* She wiped her palms, hitched up her vestment, and climbed.

When she reached Amber, she wedged her feet inside the footholds. They locked their knees and braced against the cellar wall. Together, they shoved the grate. But it didn't budge. Did not even creak.

Frustration nudged at her, but not from the present. *'You need to draw and channel your source…'* the tutor had said. *'Xenon blessed you with the gift of movement…'* But the stubborn stone before her remained still.

At first, Amber thought the memory belonged to her, but she'd never possessed such a talent. It must be Nykki's.

The locked grate taunted. *Imprisoned again*—Amber's memories now.

Vexation and disappointment, terror and helplessness. Whose emotions were these?

Blue light churned around them. Their touch sparked the static charge of a storm, but the energy was useless. Amber couldn't follow any one thread or focus on a single power to harness it.

But perhaps she didn't need to.

Alone, Nykki lacked the strength to channel her source to move objects, while Amber lacked the latent talent. But leveraging the force their coupling generated, might Amber syphon Nykki's gift?

She caught and held Nykki's gaze. Nykki understood.

Heat stirred, radiating from every place their bodies touched, as it amassed intensity. Amber followed the whorls of blue light, gathering and weaving, ready to activate. She nodded for Nykki to engage her movement, sensing the chamber opening within Nykki's mind. She concentrated on the lock, on their muscles, on using force.

'Now!' Amber cried.

They shoved the grate.

The bars shifted and strained against the lock, only to slam back down, echoing through the cavernous cellar.

Again!

Nykki's gaze sought hers, and they wedged their torsos together, stoking and amplifying their fire through every contact until it flowed from core to limb to fingertips.

'Push!'

Force surged, and the clasp shattered. Metal bars screeched up and over, then crashed and thudded open.

Freedom! She climbed out into the daylight, then helped Nykki up. Blinking, their eyes adjusted to the sudden brightness, and they hurried towards the approaching souls.

As they neared, Amber sensed a pair of familiar minds: Shira and Felda. Breeyan must have sent them. She grabbed Nykki's hand and drew her to huddle behind the boulder that marked the cellar.

'We're going to need more bandages,' Felda muttered.

'And water.' *I've not seen burns like this.*

Thoughts toppled. Shira's. Felda's. The refugees', circulating in an anguished soup: *I wasn't sure we'd find anything out here... All those heretics had to be headed somewhere... Are these witches? Who did this? How are we going to care for them all? What if the priests come after us, too? They're more afraid of us than whoever did that to them... What choice do we have?*

Amber reached for Nykki's hand. *Shield,* she thought. Against that cacophony, Shira and Felda may not notice them.

'What should we do?' Nykki whispered.

'Nothing yet. We can't risk Breeyan locking us up again.'

'It wasn't so bad...' Nykki bit her lip, her fingertips stroking the inside of Amber's arm to distract and soothe.

Amber fought a sly smile. 'Not bad at all.'

'I think we can trust Shira,' Nykki said. 'She helped search for you, argued for your return...'

But not Felda. 'We wait.'

Voices reached them.

'Get off me! Stay away!'

'Stay still—if I don't help you, those burns will fester.'

'Drink this. It will ease the pain.'

'I'm not touching your poisons, witch!'

'Do you want to die?'

Amber risked opening her mind, but a wall of agony slammed into her. *Gods!* She stumbled back, restoring her shield.

Nykki's mouth twisted. 'Even in desperation, their hate persists.'

'More fear than hate, my love.' Her time forced inside Davith's neophyte's minds had provided new insights, and she recognised the terror at the core of the priests' loathing. Mages held a power they could not contain. And if Xenon's followers revolted against them, they would be powerless. The priests transferred that angst, instilling stigma against sorcerers, declaring them 'witches', stoking hatred among those they controlled, to shun, banish, and burn those they couldn't.

Nykki stretched her psyche this time. Amber kept hers shut and allowed her beloved to relay information without sharing her experience.

She closed her eyes to focus her mind's hearing. 'They're trying to convince those with more severe burns to accompany them to the citadel.' Nykki's eyes moved beneath their lids as she listened. She frowned, brow furrowed, mouth tight. 'They're arguing.' Her expression shifted. 'A few have agreed. Felda's taking them.'

Amber's breath escaped. 'Good.' Once Felda and her patients were safely away, they could emerge.

Meanwhile, they gathered up supplies from their stores. Amber was willing to show herself and let them Cleanse her, but no one would imprison her again.

Once Felda left, they approached. Amber's glimpses inside these refugees' minds did not prepare her for what confronted them.

Women and girls, a few men and boys, milled around the grove, many with gaping burns, some so deep they revealed bone. A few wore remnants of scorched clothing. Others stood mostly naked, having stripped their smouldering clothes away. Tormented eyes stared, faces framed by melted scalps and straggling half-bald heads. Worse than the horror she witnessed was the stench of charred fabric, burning flesh, and singed hair.

If these were the milder injuries, what did those Felda had taken to the citadel bear?

Shira worked beside buckets and bandages laid atop flat rocks, examining and dressing wounds. The order lacked the opium more commonly used throughout Ycelt, so she administered shrillan to help reduce pain. Her power soothed in limited measure. Given the circumstances, she could not rely on fire to aid her magic, and she needed to conserve her strength.

Her relief leaked from her shoulders when Amber and Nykki approached. 'See what you can do for them,' she motioned towards a clutch of wary children. There were so many wounded, yet Breeyan sent only two priestesses.

Amber searched for the shepherd who had helped her escape the king's men, but did not find him among the sea of blackened faces.

She swallowed and steeled herself, fending off the angst, the hostility, wishing they aimed where it should lie—with whoever did this, not them—and attended to the wounded.

Gruelling hours passed. A novice arrived with fresh water and bandages, and Amber and Nykki hid, shielding, re-emerging once the young priestess escorted further injured back to the citadel.

Amber wished she could silence the wails. These burns inflicted agony unlike anything she imagined, accompanied by grief for lives lost and homes destroyed.

Pain she would experience being burned alive.

Nykki eyed her sharply. 'Don't,' she whispered. 'Don't think that way.'

As though standing outside herself, Amber observed her beloved working, pushing sweat from her brow into her half-loosened braids, existing entirely in the moment of the souls before her. Her world filled with the scorch of burnt skin, fabric, and hair, the radiant heat as her magic cooled and soothed, the touch of their flesh, the cacophony of their voices, and the tang of tears at the back of her throat.

For Nykki, the future did not exist. It was an abstract concept she could scarcely imagine. When she came to Amber, she considered only what she lacked in the moment—Amber's lips against hers, bodies melding, their love realised and expressed—not what inevitably awaited.

Nykki claimed she chose but had not understood what she was choosing.

At least when they burned, the fire would extinguish their lives quickly. These folk would endure their pain for moons to come, carrying their sorrow until the end of their days.

A scream wrenched her from her thoughts. An orange-haired lad pointed at her. 'You're the one they were looking for!'

A whisper, 'When the robes came...'

Eyes on her, their censure closed in.

Shira cried, 'Go! Go now!'

Amber dropped the arm she was tending and fled.

In a heartbeat, these wretched, wounded souls could form a vigilante mob.

Nykki's mind stroked hers. *The cellar! Hide in the cellar!*

Nausea rippled through her, but Nykki was right. She ran before the mob could react and follow, weaving between trees and sparse shrubs, to face that god-forsaken prison cell. They were coming for her. She climbed down and pulled the grate closed, hoping that despite the broken lock, if she remained in the shadows, they wouldn't spot her.

The boulder! *Nykki, help me...*

At her summons, Nykki's mind fused with hers, and she focused on the stone marked with an 'X', resting beside the grate. Power surged, blue force whorled, drawn from her and directed by Nykki, as the boulder dragged across the opening, shuddering to an echoing halt, leaving her in darkness.

Sixteen

Lynden hoped her nausea would abate, but instead it gathered momentum. As her breasts grew tender, worse than their swelling before her moontime, whose absence now taunted, she could no longer blame her nerves.

When a courier arrived from Erldan, advising Jonas had escaped, she and Bess held silent, avoiding each other's gaze.

'Though the lord has rendered himself a fugitive, it is in honour of our friendship that I will pardon his misdeeds upon payment of the offered blood price,' the message read.

Gohran stipulated his men would not commence their hunt until Venn paid the coin, but Venn refused to hand over a copper until his brother returned home unharmed.

Since then, the snows had thickened and carpeted the roads. Soon, carriages would be unable to pass between their cities, and she pleaded to every god and goddess that wherever Jonas was, he was safe.

Most days, she took to her room or sat in the women's hall, avoiding Venn's volatile, thunderous moods. She tried to write to Vera, but her words stalled. If she couldn't share her heart, she preferred to say nothing at all. She considered sending a message to Aunt Servan in Mornae, far beyond this entangled mess, but even if her news reached the north, no reply would arrive before the snows melted, when it would be too late.

That day, her stomach still, she tidied her face, pinned her hair, and ventured to the women's hall.

Raeyn and Bess pored over some parchments, but looked up when she entered.

'Oh good, you're here,' Raeyn said, her smile tight.

Lynden forced a smile in return, sat beside them, and reached for her workbasket.

'Leave that,' Raeyn said, and she paused. 'I'd like your opinion on these lords.'

Her stomach sank. 'As suitors?'

Raeyn nodded.

Lynden did not wish to discuss her future husband with a stranger.

She'd expected to have Jonas here, helping plan her betrothal. She imagined his scathing commentary, pointing out those who would shun her for her affair with the king, while she highlighted the lords who would welcome an alliance with a king's mistress for the favour it might bring.

'I could do worse,' she told him in her mind.

And he would retort: *'I'd hoped for better.'*

Her throat caught.

She no longer claimed the king's influence. She was nobody to him because he could be nothing to her. Worse—he made an enemy of her by threatening her brother.

Panic gripped her, and she struggled to breathe, coughing to disguise her fear. Her grief.

'Water, my lady,' Bess said. She took it and sipped; grateful to hide her face. 'And flatbread.' Bess glanced towards Lynden's midline.

'What does my brother say?'

'Lord Venn is eager to solidify ties given the current situation, my lady,' Bess said. 'I'm happy to make inquiries in any household I can…'

She stiffened. Did Venn know? It was possible he was too blind to notice. After all, he'd not realised Ella was pregnant. And Nedran needed allies if this rupture with Erldan resulted in outright war.

'These are the dryhten's suggestions.' Raeyn handed a parchment across.

Someone had scratched out and then rewritten several names. Suitors previously passed over, whose strategic advantage negated their personal defects.

Prince Farryn of Jernot was on the list. A drunkard. Lord Steevos of Laren. A miser. Lord Ky of Rhanid. A man who had no taste for women at all.

The ring surrounding Peryndyn's overlord taunted. A man whose last wife begged the priests to intercede and annul their marriage, only for him to hang her for treason.

Had it come to this? 'I'll not marry any of these men.' She despised the pity on their faces. 'Would you?' she said. 'Any of you?' Eyes down. 'I didn't think so.' She stood, crumpled, and tossed the parchment into the fire. 'I must speak with my brother.'

The person she yearned—and dreaded—to tell was Gohran. It was his seed implanted. Him she loved, even now. Loved and feared and hated. An enigma.

As far as she knew, he remained unencumbered. No rumours of royal courtships circulated, and he had announced no betrothal. But she would not approach him.

Even if he disregarded strategy, and she overlooked his violence, she would never forgive him for forcing her brother from her. Jonas might be careless in his pursuit of pleasure, but he was no fool. He must have had sound cause to cross Gohran. And he risked himself to warn her to stay away from him—not that she needed a warning. Not now.

Her mouth filled with saliva, and her gut churned. She was going to lose what little contents lingered there.

She detoured from Venn's study and hurried to the inner courtyard, leaned over a potted plant, and emptied her stomach. Afterwards, she perched on the stone bench. Tears rolled down her cheeks as she listened to the flow of water. Curse Gohran for not taking more care during their coupling.

Once recovered, she sought Venn, but his page informed her he was training. 'Tell the dryhten I wish to speak with him as soon as he retires for the day,' she said, and retreated to her room.

She had barely settled when someone knocked at her door. She quickly powdered her red cheeks and puffy eyes.

Raeyn entered, with Bess trailing.

'What do you want?' She checked herself and curtsied. 'Your Highness.'

'Close the door, Bess,' Raeyn said. She stood upright, wooden, her clasped hands resting across her waist. But when she spoke again, her tone was gentle. 'You were right, my lady. I should not expect another to tie herself to a man I would not choose for myself, were our circumstances otherwise equal.'

Lynden remained silent.

Raeyn stepped closer. 'My lord husband crossed those names out for a reason, and no matter the present situation,' a further glance at Lynden's belly, 'it would be reckless to disregard that.' She turned to Bess, who carried a dark tincture. 'You have been unwell for some time. This should soothe your stomach.'

She took it.

Bess hovered. 'My lady, if I may?'

Lynden peered over the rim of the bitter tincture.

'With your permission, I might source something...' she glanced around, then lowered her voice, 'longer lasting.'

'Permanently so,' Raeyn added.

Lynden gasped.

Raeyn brushed her hands over her bodice and skirt as if ridding the fabric of crumbs. 'It would buy us time to find a more suitable match.'

Lynden spat the half-swallowed liquid into her handkerchief, then wiped her mouth. 'You're endorsing this?'

'As I should have done for my sister.' Her eyes sloped, but her jaw remained rigid. 'We'll need to smooth palms and seal lips, of course. I'm told the merchant who traded tonics in town has retired, but Bess has offered to travel to Rassit to make some enquiries.'

'But the snows...'

'I'll leave right away on horseback, my lady,' Bess said.

'Bess, no! This is my mess to tidy. I'll go.'

'I forbid it,' Raeyn snapped. 'People will recognise you.'

Raeyn's command rankled, but if the wardens caught her...

Still, she would not risk Bess's life on her behalf.

Bess squeezed her shoulder. 'The princess is right. I'm beneath notice, my lady.'

Wardens tended to overlook commoners inducing abortions, provided they paid the fine imposed. Ending a noble pregnancy carried a much steeper penalty, while terminating a royal one constituted treason.

The priests were another matter in the more devout regions of Ycelt—including Erldan, and therefore Nedran, now.

She shook her head, disbelieving.

'You may refuse, of course,' Raeyn said, gazing out the window at the grey sky, her tone as casual as if she had offered to take Lynden on a stroll. 'The dryhten can send word to Lord Karlos of Peryndyn this very day, offering a betrothal.'

And these were her only options.

Wind gathered, and the shutters banged.

She moved to secure them, but Raeyn's hand rested on her shoulder, pinning her to her seat.

Bess curtsied and tended to the window. Loyal, tender Bess, who had been more a nurturing aunt than a lady's maid. 'Bess, I can't let you do this...'

Bess returned to her side, rubbed her arm, and whispered, 'Hush, my lady. I mayn't bring your brother home, or change the king's mind, but this is one thing I *can* do.'

More tears escaped, and she brushed them aside.

'There is no time to dally, Lady Lynden. We need your answer.'

She noticed Bess's riding breeches peeking beneath her pinafore. They anticipated she would refuse Lord Karlos. How could she not? He was a savage beast. But surely, they could wait a few days, give her a chance to consider...

Both pairs of eyes were on her, waiting. Their pity scalded, but they would not allow her time.

Did they suspect she would waver? Not for fear of her maid's life, but for the seed growing in her belly—her last tie to Gohran. A connection that must be severed.

She recalled his scarred body against hers, his calloused hands gripping with frantic need as he thrust into her, those icy, tortured eyes that somehow warmed more than was reasonable or rational. He reduced her to a whimpering, feeble lass, grasping for his presence, for the part of him she could not possess.

Each night he had wept and cried his sister's name. Each night she had reached for him and found him needing, yet he shoved her away.

What was it she even wanted from him?

Some intangible quality he could never provide. That perhaps he had given to another, or that did not exist.

The future he offered was desolate, neither filling the other's void.

She told herself she no longer thirsted for his attention, his approval, or him. And she did not need his babe.

She straightened in her chair. 'Take my palfrey to Rassit, Bess, and have Mykan assign someone to escort you. I'll fetch my saved allowance.' *And I will do what must be done.*

Seventeen

Scraping roused Amber from where she huddled in a corner of the cellar. Two voices, then a pair of faces peered through the moonlight. They were back.

She almost wept with relief. She'd lost track of the hours spent staring through the dark, her breath shallow, her heartbeat racing, waiting without food, water, blankets, or a bucket to relieve herself.

Her trembling sigh escaped as Nykki helped her out, and she clung to her beloved.

'Most of the refugees who refused to enter the citadel are sleeping, or have fled,' Shira said.

'I never meant to bring this upon them,' Amber sobbed.

'I know, my love,' Nykki squeezed her. 'We don't blame you.'

'*They* do. And they're right to. I escaped. The priests were hunting me.'

'It was the king's men who did that.'

'But I was the one who freed the king's prisoner.' That was the glow she'd seen on the horizon behind Jonas—Gohran, razing an entire village. But it was Gohran's head priest who had put her there.

Davith's oozing tenor slithered along her spine as she recalled his stony eyes devouring every inch of her. She remembered his grasping fingers tugging her hair, and his lascivious tongue sucking his teeth and shoving against sallow cheeks. It was at Davith's behest that those neophytes abused Chrysanth while he savoured their cruelty for his voyeuristic pleasure.

As Nykki and Shira watched her, a rigid burning settled into her stomach and chest. She told Breeyan that she would not re-enter Aryon, that she would submit to being Cleansed, and she meant it. But she would not await her end as Breeyan's passive prisoner.

Xenon forbade her sisters enacting violence, lest they summon the Curse. But she was Cursed already. While she could not confront a king, she might mete out justice to his head priest. Now that she carried the Curse, there was nothing to hold her back. Let her break another vow if it toppled that monster with her.

'There's one last mission I must accomplish before I succumb to my fate,' she said with frost in her voice.

Shira tried to hide her shock, but Nykki's mouth curved into a salacious grin, her eager eyes aglow. 'A further sacrifice worth making.'

No, my love. 'I can't let you join me. It's too dangerous,' Amber said.

Nykki clasped her hands, aimed and held her gaze, her icy determination mirrored in those green eyes. 'And I won't let you go alone.'

'I agree,' Shira said, startling them both. 'You'll be stronger together.'

'I'm already as doomed as you,' Nykki said. *Please—I can't lose you again.*

Shira looked back towards the grove, and Amber sensed her grappling with something. Longing to come with them, but mindful of her duty. Her vows. She would not court the Curse. 'I swore to Ella I would look after her babe,' she said, finally.

Amber's gaze narrowed. Ella didn't trust Breeyan. Well, neither did she. Not anymore.

'Where is Ella? I thought I sensed her mind touch mine once or twice, but when I search now, I find nothing.'

'She went hunting for you.'

Amber's stomach dropped. 'And she's still out there?' The king's men razed that village, not the priests. Hunting for Jonas. But what if Gohran's intended prey was his sister? Would he destroy an entire settlement in pursuit of her?

To maintain his secret.

The thought rang true, with an acuity Amber had only recently acquired. Bedding Nykki had amplified her abilities and given her access to new ones. Together, they could manipulate the physical world, unlock steel, shove rock, gather truths, experience foresight, and the gods knew what else. Nykki's latent power was weaker, but she possessed gifts Amber did not.

With Amber's force behind her, and their capabilities combined…

She hated the idea of taking Nykki with her into Ycelt, but could not abandon her.

Nykki's thought echoed: *I'm as doomed as you.*

Amber steeled herself. Grim. Determined. When she spoke, her voice rumbled like thunder, growling across the heavens. 'If we are going to burn, let this sire of demons burn with us.'

A flicker of lightning and a deafening boom sealed their fates. The gods had answered.

PART TWO:
OPPRESSION

AERON OF NOWHERE, YCELT

Winter, 797 A.S.

Eighteen

'What *are* you?' When Ella woke, Vorlyn hovered over her.

The curl of her wry smile haunted. 'I might ask the same of you, lass.'

Lass, as if she were a peasant or a servant! Though that's what she'd been for the preceding four seasons.

Ella stood, drawing to her full height. She barely reached the woman's chest. 'You don't look like the others,' she said.

Another knowing smile. 'And yet, you do.'

Ella flinched. 'I shouldn't be here.' She strode past, following the peculiar blue light emanating from the walls to resemble fog, searching for a passage that led outside.

'Do you recognise where you are?' Vorlyn called.

The carved cells stood open, veering off the passageway on either side. She wound around, trying not to notice what went on within, but the murmur of conversation, the tinkle of laughter, and the grunt of a tryst, stalked her.

They were no longer in her mind, yet she could not escape them.

Hurrying, she sensed more than saw the people pause, their eyes and psyches observing with benign curiosity.

Why didn't they feel something, *anything*, towards her?

A gnawing settled in her chest. It was a heaviness. A loss.

A hunger.

She swallowed it down and moved on.

The passage reached a dead end, and she pivoted, backtracked, and took a different turn. The corridor curved, and she sped up, only to find herself in another cell. Navigating Aeron was solving a labyrinth.

She spun and retraced her steps, searching for a path she hadn't tested. No one followed or attempted to stop her, yet urgency pressed. A need to leave before—

Princess. Yorg's thought commanded, and she froze. He realised who she was.

As if pushed by currents from another realm, his wispy hair wavered around him as he approached. He held out a pair of common breeches, a peasant's shirt, cap, cloak, and leather boots. 'If you're leaving, take these.' *You're not a prisoner.*

Their fingers connected as she accepted the clothing, and the touch cast an echo of her enthrallment back at her. She ached, greedy for more. It thrummed in her loins, and she yearned to take this ageing man to her bed—not from lust, but to experience her magic flow between them.

'Look at me.'

She met his gaze, recalling their eyes locked and melded. Her chest rose, and her breath heightened. This time, her simulacrum anchored in place and his irises remained violet. The spell shattered, leaving that same void. A ravenous ache.

Panic tinged her relief. What if she never experienced that thrall again?

'It's called "beguilement", Princess. One of sixteen gifts that Xenon bestowed His followers. One later forbidden. Yet you somehow survived the cull...'

Beguilement. She turned the word over in her mind. The flood of captivating warmth she sampled when Yorg wound her magic back on her. Warmth she'd wanted to drown in. She'd already witnessed its effects. Now she'd tasted it.

Remembering, her body tingled, but she could not recreate the experience. Though her power lived within her, it remained inaccessible. She could only wield it on others, binding them to her will. Except it wasn't a true binding, more a thirst only she could slake. Her magic charmed and lured, so that her prey coveted whatever she desired, because they desired her.

This man standing opposite had faced it. Identified it by name. Had seen inside her soul.

Oh gods, Yorg had witnessed everything, even the violation she struggled to forget, that she fled her body to evade. She longed to claw the dirt and bury herself.

It wasn't your fault, Princess.

Hadn't she induced it? By wanting Gohran to love her again?

Not like that. Never that, he soothed, and his inner voice seemed to belong to her.

She shook his thoughts away. If her brother had been under her magic's thrall, how was she blameless?

The kindness in Yorg's expression almost caused her to weep. He saw her. Recognised her. Not with hateful pity, but compassion.

He turned and pointed in a direction Ella was certain she had already explored. 'You can exit that way.'

The passages all blurred into one as he walked on. He was leaving...

She yearned to call him back, entreat him to reconnect with her and channel her gift, craving a taste of its bliss for a heartbeat more.

That was her hollow hunger, its loss, like someone had ripped out a part of her.

Stop! she thought. She should ask him about Thymm. She should—

Yorg halted, but did not turn around. 'The man you seek resides in the surrounding village. If you wait, Vorlyn can accompany you. The villagers know her.'

'I thought you were out of my head.'

A chuckle. 'I am.'

But he'd already read too much.

She clutched the clothing to her chest and strode to where Yorg directed. The constant azure glow that seeped from Aeron's walls misted and whirred as she followed the passage, the route certain, as if Yorg had slipped that into her mind, too. *It was there all along...* What further knowledge would she discover if she searched?

Curious faces turned her way as she hastened. The corridor opened into the main cavern, and she spotted the natural light that revealed the exit. On her final dash, she emerged into a blinding glare, took a few steps, and sank into a layer of snow.

Quiet. No minds murmured within or nearby.

Frost-covered foliage surrounded her, so thick she couldn't see more than a few horse lengths deep. Behind, the cavern entrance resembled ordinary grey rock. Ivy tendrils clawed their way between ancient cracks and disappeared into the surrounding terrain. Easily missed.

Trudging between trees, she sank to her shins with each step until her feet throbbed from the cold. She leaned against a trunk to pull on Yorg's clothing. He'd tucked a pair of thick woollen socks inside the snug, fleece-lined boots with sturdy soles. She tugged them on and laced them above her calf, then drew the hood of the hardy cloak up and over her cropped hair to warm her ears and neck.

When she ported from Erldan, she'd thought only of escape. Now that she had, did she want to find Thyss and Mara's son, or should she keep moving? Already this was further from home than she'd ever been, yet it was still too close.

She looked up. Snowflakes landed on her nose, ticklish and moist as they melted, while hoarfrost coated the landscape in a weighty silence. No birds or creatures stirred. How would she survive out here? She knew nothing of hunting. When she'd camped before, she carried a bedroll, canvas, blankets, food, and a packhorse, and it was not yet the thick of winter. Now, she'd only the clothes Yorg provided. Finding and begging Thymm to shelter her until the spring might be her only option.

Just use that beguiling smile, Shira had said. Had she known of Ella's forbidden gift?

Wind whipped through the trees as the snowfall grew heavier. Clouds gathered. She trudged on, stretching her psyche to locate any trace of Thymm, his presence marking her mental map, guiding her where fellow Ycelts settled. Away from Aeron's strange folk.

From the rear, a branch cracked, and she swung around to find Vorlyn trailing. Even with her mind open, she'd not sensed the peculiar woman.

'Ella—'

Hearing her name on a stranger's lips, she bristled. 'You don't know me, and I don't know you,' she snapped.

Vorlyn inched closer, as if Ella were a startled deer.

'I thought I'd made my wishes clear,' she said. 'I thank you for your aid, but intend to proceed alone.'

Knowing what Ella was and what she had done, Aeron's people should not entangle themselves with her. Yet Vorlyn did not fear her.

She rested a hand on Ella's shoulder.

Ella summoned the heat of her beguilement—now she had a name for it—and imagined Vorlyn was someone she cared about, whose regard she desired, and sent its tendrils along her limbs to where Vorlyn's hand rested. She waited for the woman's focus to drift and her will to falter. But when Vorlyn met her gaze, her grin was natural, unaffected by her charm.

'Since you're out of Aeron's protection, you should raise your shield,' she said, the wry twist at the corner of her mouth and the quirk of her brow, gnawingly familiar.

Ella frowned. With her mind closed, how would she find Thymm?

Vorlyn reached into her rucksack and produced a strange glass sphere. 'If you won't allow me to accompany you, you might use this...' Ella took it, and the surface shimmered like flowing water. 'The glass acts as a casing for your thoughts, so you can scry without being seen.'

It hummed between her palms. A miniature world encased within revealed the home from Thyss's memories. Emotions rushed to fill her as she imagined an ordinary life. Safe from priests and their henads, away from the politicking, and the constant push and pull of being a tile in someone else's hand. Its cosiness beckoned. They would take her in. With one beguiling smile, she would own them for the winter.

Or would she carry her Curse to these strangers, too? Had she already infected the people here?

Head tilted, Vorlyn narrowed her focus. 'When we first found you, you kept repeating that you were Cursed.'

Ella stiffened, unable to influence Vorlyn, yet the strange woman seemed to perceive her thoughts.

'Yorg thinks not,' she said. 'He says something—or someone—has scarred your aura. Perhaps someone who carries the Curse?'

Ella almost dropped the sphere.

'I'd like to help, if you'll allow...'

She met Vorlyn's gaze. There was an artlessness to her manner. The opposite of Ella. Guileless.

Ella hesitated. Was she rejecting the offer from fear? Because nowhere seemed safe anymore? Because these strange folk held power and insight she'd never conceived?

Or because Yorg perceived her shame.

They were far from Erldan, from Nedran, from anyone privy to her secrets, yet her secrets followed her.

'Yorg is one of the greatest mages I have encountered, and Aeron holds some of the most treasured lore,' Vorlyn said.

She had seen it. Volumes lining the walls. No torn-out pages. Everything in the open.

'There are more like him who can aid us,' she said. 'Don't you wish to uncover the truth? To heal?'

Sixteen gifts. You survived the cull.

She wavered. What if she wasn't Cursed?

Ella slowed her breath, forcing her shoulders down and back. The cosy homestead beckoned.

A cry on the wind, and a cold, clammy hand might have grasped her throat. Out here, it was only a matter of time before Gohran detected her.

She slammed her mind shut, but not before the distant but unmistakable tug of her daughter's presence sliced through. Even this far away, Xarion's hold strangled.

The snow blustered sideways, and the wind carried ice and sleet.

In Ycelt, she would never be free. But Aeron's people welcomed her, offered her the freedom to choose. Wanted to share knowledge with her. Heal her.

Fleeing indefinitely was no option, and out here, she could not hide. Aeron remained shielded, safe.

Exhaustion settled into her bones.

'Let us help you, Ella.'

This time, when Vorlyn's hand rested on her shoulder, it was a relief. She allowed her to lead them from the wilderness and back to safety.

Nineteen

'The last refugees have headed north or back to where they came,' Shira said, carting the remaining supplies to Aryon's stores.

'Has there been word from our brethren?' Breeyan tugged at the torn skin on either side of her thumbnail. She'd been biting again.

Shira shook her head. 'Nothing, but the influx of evacuees has finally dwindled.'

A gnawing cold settled into Breeyan's gut, unconnected to the wintry chill, as she helped Shira stow empty buckets and separate bloody bandages to launder. In all her years taking in refugees, Breeyan had never buried so many.

Scarcely a handful of injured remained at Aryon. Of those, few would survive their burns in the coming weeks. Once infection set in, there was little anyone could do. Not even magic would halt the progress of putrefaction and disease.

Xarion snuffled, and she held her close, her final comfort. Her legacy.

Since contacting Gordovyn at the Gern, only Shira would help care for Ella's daughter. The others—including Felda—now refused.

Shira reached to take her, and when their hands touched, her apprentice's encounter with Amber and Nykahlia replayed in her mind. If Breeyan ventured to the cellar, she would find the grate open, and the women gone. Her stomach lurched.

'We are not your prisoners, Your Holiness, to lock up and manoeuvre as you please.'

She suppressed her urge to lash Shira's psyche. 'I sequestered them for everyone's safety,' she snapped.

'Now they are far from here. Their presence should no longer trouble you.'

The hinges on the external door creaked, then banged against the wooden frame. A bluster must be brewing outside, but she sensed no rain.

Shira carried Xarion out, and Breeyan turned her attention to her work. She wanted to scour the archives again, as though reading the repeated phrases would offer new meaning, or somehow restore the destroyed histories. Had Gordovyn understood her request before Xarion sucked all the power from her working?

She longed for someone to confide in, to seek guidance from, but as she watched Shira's back retreat, she feared their rift would never heal. Shira had not endured the poisonous machinations of a royal court and a venomous sister—her only confidante—as a rival. Nor the viperous council of her peers, who vied for power in the only domain allowed them. She could not empathise with the ruthless choices her situation compelled, nor would she, unless and until she wore Breeyan's robes.

If the Gern's records revealed a way to evade or unravel the Curse, she might instate Xarion in Shira's stead. She wished Gordovyn would send word.

A scream from the infirmary pierced her musings. She abandoned her research and followed the sound, arriving to find strewn blankets, upturned buckets, and tossed implements that would all need re-boiling. Chrysanth huddled, trembling in the corner, wielding a splint like a dagger.

Thank Xenon for blessing her with godly eyes, but no powers to match!

Felda edged closer, trying to coax her to put the wood down. The surrounding patients whimpered and wailed, the distress of one fuelling the others.

Breeyan steadied her breath. *Keep her from striking,* she thought to Felda.

Felda nodded and continued cooing to Chrysanth until Breeyan grasped the other end of the splint. While they wrestled on opposite points, Breeyan swooped and gripped Chrysanth's wrists, infiltrating her mind. She wilted, and the wood clanged to the floor.

'That's it,' Breeyan cooed. 'Quiet, now...'

Once she had control of the girl, she motioned for Felda to soothe the other patients. Additional angst would only heighten their pain.

'Look at me,' she said to Chrysanth. The girl complied, her abused skin as scarred as her mind against Breeyan's palms.

She poured power into those golden irises; her lashes darkened by glistening tears. Chrysanth had not spoken since she arrived, only screamed in fits when her memories broke through the priestesses' temporary shield.

This needed to stop. Her anguish amplified her companions', and they had suffered enough.

'Fetch the council members,' she said. It was time.

The women gathered in the Hall of Prayer, where they could leverage Xenon's replica stone to unite and direct their power. For once, they did not quarrel, joining as one.

With the girl mollified in their midst, Breeyan identified and severed her memories with precision.

Chrysanth's recollections of imprisonment and torture intertwined with other benign reveries. Chasing and playing, laughing and weeping, a fond smile, a cherished embrace, snuggling into a cushioned breast. Breeyan ignored where the boundaries blurred. If an area appeared aggravated, she encased it in a calming azure light and sliced.

As Breeyan cut each segment, Chrysanth's relief was palpable, and with it, her sisters' torment ebbed. Breeyan hadn't realised how her constant distress had irritated and set them on edge.

Afterwards, they settled her back in the infirmary. Her golden eyes clouded in confusion, and the ordinary panic of someone waking in an unfamiliar place, having forgotten for a moment where they were.

Breeyan brushed her forehead. Chrysanth did not recoil or resist as she soothed her to sleep. Her breath rose and fell hypnotically, and Breeyan drowned out the groans and whimpers of the surrounding patients. She did not wish to be reminded of their persistent pain.

She hugged Chrysanth's memories close. Stifled the pang at robbing her of them. They'd had no choice. Those reveries would have held no joy if they remained polluted. She squeezed Chrysanth's hand, and left her slumbering, before crawling, exhausted, to do likewise.

Twenty

A snap. Jonas's eyes shot open. Was that man or beast?

Quiet, then screeching above, followed by wings fluttering amongst the low-hanging branches, and the unmistakable waft of guano. Bats. There must be a cave nearby. Pity he hadn't found it before making camp beneath this dense cedar. It had to be more comfortable than sleeping on the freezing, knobbly ground.

Another snap—not the bats.

He sat and peered through the darkness. He couldn't have slept for more than an hour, but it was better than no sleep at all. His meagre fire had already extinguished, and clouds obscured the remaining moonlight. He hoped it hadn't attracted his pursuers, who he'd so far avoided by keeping to the snow-coated deer trails.

He listened, the silence only broken by his growling stomach.

Did he dare breach the cocoon he'd made of his blankets to reach for jerky from his stores? He envied his steed, who moved barefoot, unbothered by the surrounding frost or icy air, and whose nosebag of grain had satisfied his hunger.

Something rustled amongst the thick foliage. If they weren't alone in these woods, they should move.

With an inward groan, he stood to untether his horse, but the stubborn beast stomped and snorted, refusing to leave.

'I'm weary, too, but we can't dally.'

Another snort. The steed tossed its head and flicked its tail.

'Fine. We stay. But if they catch us, my last request will be to feed you to the hounds alongside me.'

He resecured the beast and crawled beneath his blankets, but left an opening, ready to scramble. Not that he could sleep now. He contemplated climbing the tree and waiting for his horse to rest, but what if he drifted off and fell?

Instead, he propped his back against the trunk, clutched his dagger, and watched for the first sign of uhtan. At least his bedroll provided some insulation from the frozen ground, but what he would give for a hot meal, a warm bed, and a warmer set of limbs wrapped around him.

The tavern owner stuck a knife into the wooden tabletop, then plonked two tankards beside it. Ale sloshed over the sides. 'It's a full house this eve, ladies.'

Nykki pulled her shawl further forward and cast her cat-green eyes down.

Amber squeezed her hand beneath the table, then jangled her coin purse. 'That's a pity.' She looked up, caught and held his gaze. 'I wonder if there's anywhere else you might suggest. We won't be staying long.'

The man leaned close, his onion breath assaulting as he brushed her cheek with the backs of his fingers. Beside her, Nykki flinched, and squeezed tighter. Amber captured his calloused hand in hers, staring him down. 'We'll pay with coin.'

He drew back, swaying, his brow furrowed, as if trying to remember something. 'Kartha,' he called to a stout, greying woman. 'Find these ladies a room.'

Kartha huffed, wiped her hands down her pinafore, and stomped upstairs. She pounded on doors and shouted. Grumbles and slamming followed. Patrons hiring the rooms by the hour, Amber presumed.

She sipped her ale and nodded for Nykki to join her, caressing her thigh beneath the table.

The tavern's main door jangled open, and a scruffy adolescent lass and two children entered. The lass didn't look old enough to be their mother. An elder sister, perhaps? They scoured the tavern for a place to sit, spotting the vacant stools beside Amber and Nykki.

Amber's smile welcomed them, but Nykki pinched her beneath the table. *Refugees*, she warned.

Amber pivoted slightly, burying her face in her tankard, grateful for the woollen cap Shira salvaged from the hordes arriving at Aryon that covered her distinctive hair.

Unease tingled outward from the small of her spine. Not hers, Nykki's.

The younger girl tugged at Nykki's sleeve, her round eyes peering up. 'Pardon, but why are you wearing Mama's shawl?'

'Hush,' the older lass said, drawing the little one back.

'But she is!' cried the girl.

The boy between them wailed.

'Hoy!' yelled the innkeeper. 'I'll not serve your cubs if you can't keep them quiet.'

The young girl joined her brother's wails in a chorus. Their faces crumpled, and tears streaked ash down their freckled cheeks.

'Here.' Nykki pulled the scarf from around her head, her chestnut hair still kinked from her let-out braids, and offered it to the girl.

She took it, and as their hands touched, Amber sensed Nykki's power surge, and the surrounding air cool, until the girl quietened. Nykki reached for the boy, whose crushed frown relaxed into a docile smile.

'How did you...?' The older girl's voice trailed, leaving her jaw hanging. Nykki's cat-green eyes flashed in the lantern light, and the lass drew three fingers over her chest and forehead in a sign of warding.

Amber's instinct was to flee. But once they started running, they could not stop, and she would not begin this crusade weakened and fearful.

She stood. 'Hush, hush,' she soothed, drawing the older lass into an embrace, and letting power bleed between them. With Nykki by her side, it flowed in abundance. She rocked the girl until her body sagged and her curiosity abated.

Nykki followed, hugging the younger ones. 'That's it, you're safe now…'

The innkeeper scowled, but backed away when the commotion eased.

Nykki released the youngsters and wrapped the scarf around the lass's slight shoulders, as Amber stepped back from the older girl.

She stacked three coppers from her purse on the table. 'I trust that room is ready?' she called to the innkeeper, then with a final touch and glance, she willed each of them to forget this entire incident, their focus clouding over and balance swaying until she was done. Her influence might not last, but it would see them on their way.

TWENTY-ONE

Yorg motioned to a wall of shelves carved into the rock and filled with books. Azure light emanated from the corners of the room, while hovering orbs cast a white-blue glow above a central stone slab stacked with parchments and tomes.

'So much material,' Ella said.

'Aeron houses the greatest collection of surviving lore outside the Place of Omens.' Yorg spoke with pride, but there was another tone Ella couldn't quite identify. Melancholy? Grief?

Before she asked, he said, 'The Place of Omens is in Myan. Once, my home. Back then, all of Xenon's temples connected. Porters, like you, carried knowledge and trained novices when overland travel became too dangerous. But that was a long time ago.'

He did not shield against her curiosity, and she sensed his throat constricting.

He pointed to a ledge carved into one wall, stuffed full. 'These mostly contain lore about various abilities, their properties, and limitations.'

'Nothing on the Curse?' When Vorlyn escorted her back to Aeron, she'd hoped for answers.

'Not as a discrete topic,' he said. 'But you may find snippets intertwined with lore and among the histories, which live on that case.' He motioned to another wall of shelves. 'Though many scribes wrote in Myanai or the Ancient tongue.'

Her stomach sank. She only read Yceltic.

'We'll share what we can, of course.' He meant everyone at Aeron. These folk did not hoard knowledge like Breeyan.

She had envisaged Yorg sitting her down and explaining why he believed she was not Cursed, what the sixteen gifts were, and what he meant by the 'cull'. Instead, he expected her to locate the answers within the largest library she had ever seen.

'If I had the information to give you, I would,' he said.

She realised she had stopped shielding, and with the weight of iron chains lifting, that she had no need to.

'My masters taught that Xenon bestowed sixteen gifts, however, not all scholars agree on what constitutes each.'

He opened a leather-bound volume, and she searched the pages for recognisable sigils, or 'glyphs' as the Myanai termed them, but the paragraphs jumped around, with passages missing, as though someone had purged or omitted certain information.

What were these authors trying to hide?

'Our kind have not always agreed on what lore Xenon's blessed should cultivate and study, or even practise.'

She recalled Breeyan removing parts of Xarion's story from the order's copy of *The Lost Warriors*.

He pushed a thick volume towards her. Glyphs inscribed along the spine showed the moon in its first quarter. 'This contains lore on porting.'

She ran her fingers over the cover. The book summoned her. Without turning a single page, its contents whorled in her psyche, showing images of Ancient priestesses, studying and scribing, much as she did now. She drew her hands away, squeezing them into tight fists.

'It has been many years since I encountered another porter, and I'm curious to learn more—if you're comfortable sharing.'

Ella said nothing, her nails biting into her palms.

Yorg rubbed the crease between his brows and sighed. 'Will you at least tell me who taught you to port?'

And reveal that she had drawn from a forbidden source? That she should be Cursed, even if Yorg believed she was not? 'Did you not discover that for yourself when you raided my mind?' She sounded petulant, but didn't care.

Yorg exhaled a weighty breath. 'No one at Aeron wishes you harm, Princess. I have ventured within your psyche, but I did not rummage through your private memories.'

She eased her nails from her palms, ignoring the half-moon indents they'd left behind, and reached for the book. The same peculiar rush of knowledge filled her mind.

Yorg's eyes narrowed. 'Those are the recollections of others who have read this tome being transferred.' His mouth twisted. 'Mine, in fact.'

He pictured a young man preparing to transport himself from one place to another. Blue light flashed, leaving a puddle of clothing and nothing else—as she'd arrived outside these caves, naked in the snow.

It pained him to revisit that memory. She should offer something in return. 'No one taught me. I—I stumbled across it, I suppose...' She'd seen no evidence that Aryon's sisters knew of porting, and she'd found no references to it while scribing.

Yorg's mouth quivered. Did he hold back tears? 'I had hoped there were others...'

'Other porters? What happened to them?'

'Ah! The exact question, Princess.'

She waited for him to explain, but silence hung between them. She turned the pages of the tome, hoping to find the answers Yorg did not voice. This time, when its contents flooded her mind, she envisaged the porter kneeling before a squealing animal. Blood flowed immediately before the flash...

She snatched her hand away.

A sacrifice.

That porter drew from the blood of a slaughtered animal, as she had drawn from Thyss and Mara. Did porting require a lifeforce?

'How did people port if Xenon forbade drawing blood?' she asked.

'How, indeed.'

'Wait—that's why there are no porters? Because they're unable to draw blood?'

'And many did not survive the cull.' Yorg's violet eyes glistened.

She shuddered. Her god-sight called, and she replaced her palm upon the tome. Images reeled, showing sorcerers being captured, tortured, and burned. Not by Elnora's priests or henads, but by other mages. They branded diagonal crosses onto faces, limbs, and backs. *Forbidden, Cursed,* a hushed susurrus.

She extracted her hand, blinked, and focused on the walls surrounding her, the musty smell of dust, ink, and vellum.

'They culled them,' she whispered. 'Porters. Beguilers.' *Like her.*

Yorg nodded, then cleared his throat. 'And removed the means to use those gifts.'

Ella recalled the map she'd found in the scriptorium at Aryon. Someone had tried to scratch it out, to hide it. Ella never should have discovered it. Not because the tunnels were secret, but because the sketch aided a forbidden power.

Would Breeyan cull her and Xarion if she returned?

Oh gods, her daughter! Through Aeron's shield, she didn't sense Xarion at all. The loss throbbed through her bones, followed by relief, which she buried even deeper. Had Yorg sensed it? Ella glanced his way, shielding with every shred of her power.

'There's no need to hide here, Princess,' he said.

But there was. She had been mistaken. She could not let down her guard completely. Not ever.

She sank onto her stool as the implications landed. There was too much to take in.

When she recovered her voice at last, she managed a whisper. 'I should be dead.' Elnora's priests. Xenon's priestesses. No one welcomed her.

TWENTY-TWO

'We should separate,' Amber said. 'To double what we discover.'

Nykki snuggled closer, her tender breath teasing and trailing the furrow of Amber's neck. 'We should stay together.' *Stay here.*

Xenon help her, Nykki felt divine.

They had barely left their bed since taking up residence at the inn. Nykki kissed her breasts, and tickled her fingertips along Amber's belly, fascinated by the pucker of her tautening skin that sent shivery tingles outwards.

'If we locate one of Davith's neophytes, we can discover his movements,' Amber said.

'Or, we could discover what happens, when I do *this...*' Nykki's words ended with her lips on Amber's and her hands cupping and squeezing her breasts.

Lust stirred, but she shoved it down. They needed to focus. Get out among the people and study the priests' routines.

She sidled away, but a wave of desire swept her up, and crashed over them both, drawing her back. With it surged a need to consume each inch of Nykki's flesh, to absorb her.

Nykki... Please... This is not some interlude for our pleasure.

Another stroke of her body, lingering at the apex between her thighs, and Nykki's will threatened to subsume hers. *Don't you wish to savour every heartbeat of this?* Nykki's fingers slipped within her, and Amber gasped.

Of course, but... 'We must end Davith.'

A further wave crashed. *We only have these moments, my love. Finally, we are free.*

No longer able to surface above the rising tide of longing, Amber could not distinguish which sensations, thoughts, or desires belonged to her, and wasn't sure she wanted to.

But must.

'*Stop!*' she cried, with voice and mind.

A blast of sleet and snow as Nykki withdrew and shielded, retreating to the other side of the bed.

Amber ached to claw her back. She hadn't meant to cut her off. To push her away. 'My love...' *Please.* But she couldn't reach her. She struggled to find her breath, to speak. Explain. 'I want this as much as you...' Gods, she yearned for it more than she'd yearned for anything in her paltry life. 'But we're not risking ourselves in Ycelt to satiate our passion.' *We came here for a reason.*

Nykki's shoulders shuddered, then stilled. Were her words getting through? Not knowing almost ended her.

When Nykki spoke, her voice cracked. 'I am aware of why we are here.' Mouth hard. Eyes like stones. 'But this path can only lead to our deaths. Forgive me if I intend to make that sacrifice worth the time we have left.' She stood and moved towards the door, clutching her clothes to hide her body.

Amber wanted to howl and wrench her close. Close the gap between them. Her absence was unbearable.

In the shadow of that loss, Amber was a girl, watching her mother retreat into the distance, leaving her with the peculiar strangers at Aryon. Witches. Never safe or cherished again, forever frightened and alone.

Privation tore her heart. A wound she feared she would not survive. More painful than the torture she endured at the hands of Elnora's priests, because someone she loved and trusted more than herself delivered it.

A sob caught in her throat. She swallowed, trying to stay afloat, to form words. She was drowning, reason beyond her grasp. 'Please, my love...' she whispered over and again, but Nykki's back was impenetrable, a wall she could not read, unable to interpret her body without sensing the mind within. She faced away, arms hugging her chest—where *she* should be.

Amber whimpered, wailed, and begged. *Let me in...* All she saw, thought, heard, was that she needed Nykki to love her again.

She was a terrified child.

Loathed who she became. Hated what Nykki reduced her to, that someone had so much power over her. Despised Nykki for revealing how helpless and pathetic she was when faced with her engulfing *need.*

She wasn't this snivelling, pleading girl.

Through the haze of panic that she might lose her beloved, a part of her knew this wasn't Nykki, either. Two wounded children, who perceived any deviation as rejection.

But knowing and feeling were not the same, and she needed to get away. Leave of her own volition before Nykki hurt her further, or she used magic to persuade and force their rift closed. A path from which they might never return.

She withdrew, and painful as it was, she shielded.

With a decisiveness that stole her fire, she dressed, pulled on her boots and cap, strode past Nykki, and slammed the door behind her.

She stomped along Harnal's streets, willing her heart steady, letting the heat of her anger thrum through her muscles. Gravel crunched underfoot and her breath formed ghostly puffs in the wintry air.

She passed refugees, recognisable by their singed clothing, loitering outside doorways and lining the cobbled road, begging for food and shelter. These folk had fled east, rather than west, or perhaps changed direction once they realised what Aryon was.

Compared to them, the gods blessed her.

She reined her hurt back in. All would be well. This was a temporary breach, a misunderstanding, and Nykki would forgive her. There was too much at stake to begrudge any wound.

Her pounding heart slowed, her breath steadied, and she focused on the road ahead.

Around the next corner, a horse-drawn cart wheeled slowly towards her. A local priest and his neophytes were at its head.

The world tilted, and her vision turned black. She stumbled. Reached for the nearest building and leaned flat against its wall. Cold, uneven stones pressed into her shoulders and hips, crevices indenting her fingers. She breathed until she saw only the streets surrounding her.

She was in Harnal. These were not Erldan's priests.

She must ground herself. Eat. This rift with Nykki had rendered her fragile.

The idlers nearby fell quiet to watch the priests. Refugees lined up beside the cart, waiting patiently as neophytes distributed flatbread and jerky. Others handed out woollen blankets and old shirts and trousers, but no tunics or kirtles for the women who made do with men's clothing.

'Come nightfall, you may sleep on the floor of Elnora's temple. All are welcome in Our Lady's house,' the priest called.

The refugees whimpered and wept, some reaching out to touch the robes, or falling to their knees in prayer.

A thought slid into her mind: *Those who pay their tithes receive Our Lady's blessing.* Her shield must have slipped.

She waited until the cart bumped past and then searched for a stall selling fare. She wouldn't return to the inn to eat. Not yet.

She purchased a stodgy, grain-filled loaf from a bakehouse, but found no ilak grease or butter, only milk to wash it down. Her stomach growled. She and Nykki had barely eaten since arriving in Harnal. But when food hit her gut, it churned. Only her magic calmed her nerves enough to keep it down, and she hoped no passersby noticed the strange chill surrounding her.

At least among the milling strangers, no one paid her much attention. Nonetheless, she tightened her shield and avoided meeting anyone's gaze.

Within a few hours, she had explored the entire town and noted the layout, listening and learning. Apart from the priests, the residents of Harnal held no compassion for the refugees.

'They chose to live all the way out there. Why should we take them in?'

'My uncle ventured out there once and found them trading all sorts.'

'Trying to evade taxes, I heard.'

'And now they'll be wanting what little work is on offer.'

She had learnt all she might. She hurried back towards the inn, ignoring the skip of her heart and queasiness in her stomach at seeing her beloved, praying the time apart would have calmed them both, and that Nykki had forgiven her. With a deep breath, she headed indoors.

B etween kisses and sobs, caresses and tears, there was no need to apologise, justify, or explain. Amber swept Nykki into her arms, letting the heat of their fight ignite the fire of their love. Minds, hearts, bodies, united. They would not—could not—differentiate again.

'With you gone, I didn't even make it past the door,' Nykki choked. 'What if someone outed us? What if I lost you?'

Amber allowed herself to treasure each touch. Stopped fighting her desires and let Nykki's yearning feed hers as they clung, hungry to escape themselves in the other, the threat of loss and imminent doom heightening their fervour.

Between bouts of passion and hiatuses for food and drink, Nykki focussed on their mission, helping Amber plan, listening to all she had learned while wandering the town. Yes, their sin doomed them, but their sacrifice might end Davith's stronghold.

'Harnal appears free from henads,' she told Nykki. 'I encountered only charitable priests. Though I doubt their kindness would extend to any villagers who did not pay their dues.'

Nykki smirked. 'Without question.'

'But most importantly, I learnt the henads from Erldan hold hearings in Harnal to try heretics on each new moon,' Amber said.

Nykki's voice rose in panic. 'That's a few nights away.'

Amber frowned. She was right. She'd lost track of the days passing since the night she escaped. They needed to hasten their plan. 'It will be time enough,' she assured.

Nykki wept. 'It will never be enough.'

Amber drew her close, inhaled her neck, her hair, her essence, her body reassuring where her words could not. It must suffice. It was all they had left.

Twenty-Three

Ella rubbed her eyes and refocused on the far wall. She had combed through these pages for days. The sheer volume of knowledge overwhelmed her, but she preferred to work alone. Tucked away, no one questioned her or delved into her forbidden past.

Apart from a single tome, she'd located almost nothing on what Yorg termed beguilement, or on porting, and as Yorg warned, found no discrete references to the Curse. Instead, she discovered vague depictions of Xenon's laws entangled with descriptions of His powers.

She saw what he meant about scholars disagreeing. While some abilities shared obvious names and universal definitions, others contradicted each other. Several translations were incomplete or missing, while authors quarrelled over interpretations of various terms and traits.

One source described each power aligning to the seasons of the sun, based on a translation of the glyph for 'orb' or 'light', while another argued it referred to the phases of the moon—which made more sense, given these were Xenon's gifts.

As she teased apart what she discovered, she charted and defined individual abilities, augmented by what she experienced and observed.

'I see you've been hard at work.' Yorg appeared at her shoulder.

Alignment	Sphere	Power	Description
New Moon	Sourcing Energy	Drawing	Absorbing power
	Directing Energy	Channelling	Directing Power
Waxing Crescent	Ethereal Perception (Received)	Foresight	Receiving omens or portents
	Ethereal Perception (Directed)	Vision or God-Sight	Receiving through ethereal sight
First Quarter	Physical Manipulation of Objects	Movement	Manipulation of objects
	Physical Manipulation of Self	Porting	Transferring ethereal and physical body
Waxing Gibbous	Thought Manipulation (Received)	Sensing	Receiving sensory information
	Thought Manipulation (Directed)	Transference	Direct transfer of sensory information
Full Moon	Ethereal Perception (Received)	Scrying	Spying via a charged surface
	Ethereal Perception (Directed)	Travelling	Scrying in ethereal form
Waning Gibbous	Perception Shared	Thought	Reading and sharing thoughts
	Perception (Shielded)	Shielding	Protecting thoughts from another's perception
Third Quarter	Manipulation of Mind	Influence/Alteration	Manipulating thoughts or feelings (temporarily/permanently)
	Manipulation of Memory	Severance	Severing memories or emotional ties (permanent?)
Waning Crescent	Manipulation of Soul	Beguilement	Manipulating feelings towards the wielder
	X	X	X

Startled, Ella shuffled her parchments to conceal her notes. When had he arrived? Without windows, it was easy to lose track of time. She'd found only two places within the caves where natural light broke through: the main entrance leading to the forest, and an opening above the crystal pools where they bathed, though there might be more amongst the passages she had yet to explore.

'There's no need to hide here, Princess,' he said, clearing the parchments to reveal the catalogue of powers she'd created.

He tapped his pointed fingernail at the top of her notes, where she had scrawled her name for each power, its function, alignment, and sphere.

Thus far, she had identified and defined fifteen abilities. The rest she determined were combinations of others, or their specific applications. Each shared an alignment with one other, forming complementary pairs, though she hadn't discovered the counterpart to her own gift: beguilement.

'I'm surprised something like this doesn't already exist,' Ella said.

'Oh, I'm sure it did. Probably still does, just not in Ycelt.' He cast his eyes across her chart, nodding slowly and rubbing his beard. 'A solid foundation.'

His admiration warmed, and she yearned for more. 'I wasn't sure about alteration and severance,' she said, showing the rest of her notes to him. 'Some of these texts describe them interchangeably with influence, but that doesn't seem right. At Aryon, my aunt used both, and they were permanent.' She assumed he already knew who Breeyan was.

Yorg sucked in his breath as a shadow crossed his brow. He forced his voice steady, but she sensed a tightness in his throat. 'Mages should never employ these gifts without permission, and only as a mercy.' He looked at her with a strange mix of angst and pity. 'Xenon's havens should be places of sanctuary,' he said gravely.

She scoffed. 'Aryon was no haven for me.'

'I see that.' Not pity, but compassion, she realised, as his understanding carved its way through her shattered casing.

She swallowed the hardness in her throat. 'I have found nothing yet on why beguilement and porting were forbidden,' she said, focusing on her notes.

'I feared that would be the case.' Yorg sighed.

She read the one passage she'd located aloud: '*"Should a man draw the life-force of another to fuel his power, he shall be Cleansed or those he touches shall be Cursed thrice over."* It looks like a scribe has translated from the original Ancient tongue into Myanai and Yceltic in the margins, but the glyphs for "curse", "cull", and "cleanse" all look alike to me.'

Yorg peered over her shoulder at the glyphs resembling various versions of a flaming hook. 'So they do.'

'And over here—does the word "draw" appear shadowed to you?' Beneath, she saw traces of a word beginning with 'bl' that someone had scratched over, as though they scribed the new moon glyph for 'draw' over the sigil for 'blood'.

'Probably a palimpsest, Princess—'

A cry of pleasure erupted from a nearby room, followed by distant grunting. Would she ever get used to the openness of Aeron's inhabitants? They shared everything: resources, thoughts, and bodies. Their only real privacy was to defecate.

'Yorg, why are Aeron's people permitted to act out their lusts?'

He startled. 'Why wouldn't they?'

'Why *would* they?'

'Culling the beguilers removed any risk from enacting desire.'

Ella reeled. 'But the lore says anyone touching a sworn priestess in violence or in lust...'

'Do you see any sworn priestesses here?'

'Are you saying Elnora's priests could raise an army to rape and murder without threat of the Curse?'

Yorg shook his head. 'That might be how Aryon's priestesses interpreted the scriptures, but Xenon forbade violence against His people, sworn or no. If an Yceltic fool raises a hand against Xenon's own, he will doubtless suffer.'

'Then how can your people...?'

'Aeron's inhabitants share willingly. The circumstances are not comparable.'

Ella sank back. None of this made sense. 'Then porting is only dangerous with blood and beguilement only dangerous with sex?'

'So it would seem.'

She tightened her shield, for she had done both, drawn blood to port, and beguiled with sex, yet Yorg insisted she wasn't Cursed.

If that were true, why did horror befall everyone she loved?

Since leaving her old life, she avoided scrying on those she left behind, not wanting to relive the pain she caused—what she'd witnessed before porting here. Most of all, she did not dare spy upon her daughter. Not because she worried Xarion was hurting, but for fear she wasn't. Observing Breeyan nurture her is what allowed Ella to leave, but she did not wish to be reminded of the many ways she had failed her.

'Yorg, why are there no children at Aeron?' Her brother's seed had taken root the moment he raped her, while Aeron's inhabitants coupled daily but seemed to bear no fruit.

'When you're ready, I'll ask Mayel to show her device to you.' A woman of perhaps twenty summers, Mayel was one of Aeron's younger folk. 'When coupling with arrow to quiver, it stops seed implanting. Or, if you prefer, you can sheath the arrow to catch its seed before it enters the quiver. Much easier to prevent a seedling from taking root than to expel unwanted fruit.'

What would Elnora's priests make of that?

As though Yorg summoned her by speaking her name, Mayel appeared in the doorway, her oval eyes peering out from her deep indigo complexion surrounded by a halo of ghostly braids.

'I brought you some stew.' Such a lovely warm voice, as she smiled with the most beautiful lips Ella had ever seen.

She took the offered bowl, in awe of the way these folk used their connections to attune to each other's needs.

Mayel's head tilted to expose her fine chin and graceful neck, and Ella's beguilement stirred. She tore her gaze away and spooned the stew, letting it burn the roof of her mouth and tongue. Anything to rip her attention from what all this magic surrounding her awakened.

The woman crouched beside her and grazed the backs of her fingers against Ella's cheek. An invitation, in the easy way these folk exchanged their desires.

But sex was hazardous for Ella. Did she not realise?

Yorg stepped between them. 'Mayel, I think Ella needs more time on her own.'

'Of course.' Her voice sounded musical through her wistful smile, and with another brush of Ella's cheek, she was gone.

Ella let out her breath and fanned her burning tongue.

Yorg sighed. 'If you're to couple with our younger folk, we need to learn more about your beguilement.'

She flushed. While Aeron's people shared their bodies as freely as food or clothing, without shame or attachment, it unnerved her for him to speak so openly, so perfunctorily. As though being here, she would inevitably meld into their customs and behaviours.

Cold rippled down her spine. She had the strangest sense the god was laughing at her, for why would He offer his people gifts and then forbid using them?

TWENTY-FOUR

Jonas couldn't take another sleepless night in the woods. He needed sturdy walls, a barred door, and a soft bed. After a few days exchanging labour for lodging in farmsteads, he risked staying in a tavern where people wouldn't notice a lone traveller.

It was mid-afternoon when he rode into the township of Marlin. Rather than traders, the town was abustle with artisans and labourers rebuilding stone and timber walls. They hammered battlements and palisades, reinforcing the archway around the main portcullis under the scrutiny of robes, not men of his lordship's guard.

Jonas sensed people watching. Their sombre mood reminded him of attending Gohran's coronation, and he pulled his hood further forward to shield his face.

Normally he avoided the towns this close to Galliarn, the High King's city, and now he remembered why. Marlin's nobility was among the interbred rulers constantly vying for dominion. The town wasn't large or prosperous, but positioned within Galliarn's reach—wealth enough for any lord.

These townships often underwent rival sieges, spending winters repairing damage before the spring brought fresh riders and skirmishes. So far from home, no one should recognise him, and amidst this commotion, he could disappear.

He made his way to the seedier part of town, keeping his hood raised and avoiding meeting anyone's gaze. Surrounded by miscreants and the poor, he would be safer than in any respectable tavern where his peers might shelter.

He paid a full silver to the wardens to stable his steed, then slipped into a smoke-filled inn which reeked of sweat, sex, and sour hops.

Inside, the revelry was almost frantic. Minstrels recounted bawdy ballads to fire up the crowd. Patrons of all ages, shapes, and sizes entered, some for a meal or to drink. Others for a tumble. Despite the season, women paraded exposed skin, bared shoulders and thighs, deep cleavage, and naked midriffs, and the men, muscled chests and sheer braies. Several mimicked the Ancients, dressed in loincloths and shifts, with hair in elaborate braids, and faces masked or painted to resemble wild beasts.

Equally underdressed workers served drinks or food. Many loitered, trying to entice clients upstairs, only to return shortly afterwards to pair off again.

Someone clapped his back, handed him a tankard and a mask bearing the features of a wildcat. He fitted the disguise, which framed his eyes, and concealed most of his forehead, nose, and cheeks, but left his mouth free to drink.

His hired room and padded bed beckoned, but despite his lack of rest, his nerves fired. He imagined lying awake while the clientele's grunts and groans emanated through the corridors. Instead of heading upstairs, he called for ale. Perhaps if he consumed enough, he could forget the mess he'd got into and get some sleep.

As he drank, the lurid atmosphere intensified. Carousers didn't bother hiring rooms, having their fill against the tavern walls or atop the benches.

A server brought a tankard. 'You'd best drink up before the Dark Sun claims Marlin's soul and its court.'

Before Jonas could ask what he meant, two others swept the man into a tryst.

All around, revellers imbibed, feasting on one another as much as the free-flowing food and ale. He waited for the stirrings of lust that might urge him to join in, but felt neither tantalised nor repulsed. He was numb.

A woman sidled up beside him, her light brown eyes sparkling as her mouth curved into a sultry smile. Her hands warmed his chest and her breasts pressed against him. He drew her dark curls away from her neck, and his lips caressed the tender skin behind her ear. He imagined the curves of her waist and rounded hips wrapping around him, making everything disappear, but his lust would not stir.

Jonas grasped another tankard and gulped half of it down, needing to silence the noise inside his head. The room lurched and spun. He should eat.

But when he opened his mouth to call for food, his words were as slurred and nonsensical as Venn's when he'd blurted that Ella was alive, fixating on regret.

'They said she was dead...' He swayed in his seat. 'And I believed them...'

'But she's not?' the euphony of his companion's voice reminded him of Ella's.

When he didn't reply, she leaned close, peering through darkened lashes, and whispered, 'I can keep a secret.' She bit the corner of her bottom lip.

He shook his head, trying to steady the room. He'd already said too much.

'Perhaps I can distract you...?' Her fingertips traced the edges of his mask. 'You have beautiful eyes...'

He closed them and inhaled. She smelled of jasmine, like Ella... He opened them again and studied her face.

'More green than hazel...' she sighed.

Once, he would have taken her upstairs, dimmed his lantern, and focused on the available pleasures. But not now.

He swallowed another mouthful of ale.

'That won't take your mind off your troubles like I can,' she whispered hotly and pried the drink from his hands. 'I guarantee it.'

He stared at the near-empty tankard and the others on the table beside it. *I'm as bad as Venn.* And what good did that do?

'What's your name?' he asked.

She perked up. 'Syrena.'

'Well, Syrena,' he said. 'You are lovely, and your offer is tempting, but I must rest...'

A second woman, pale where the first was dark, appeared, with an attractive man in tow. 'Why don't you join us?'

He shook his head. A strange desperation permeated this orgy, and he wanted no part in it.

The other leaned in, too, unbuttoning his shirt, while the man slid his hand towards Jonas's crotch as he stole a kiss.

Jonas edged back, raising his palm to stop them.

The first woman, Syrena, tried to peel off his mask. 'You're not some stuffy henad hiding under there, are you?'

That's what was off, what reminded him of Gohran's coronation following Queen Prya's death. Henads riddled the streets, while robes, not noble servants, oversaw the town's repairs.

He wanted to slip away, find somewhere else to spend the night, but he'd already paid for his room, and he needed rest.

He tossed some coppers onto his table and brushed past, ignoring his companions' dropped jaws. Grateful to have a bed, he staggered upstairs, finally drunk enough to sleep despite the noise.

TWENTY-FIVE

Jonas's head pounded. Images of the previous night played behind his eyes, of too much bared flesh, and drunken, stinking revellers, himself among them. He glanced around to check he was alone, and let out his breath. Despite the ale, he'd exercised some prudence. When he sat up, the room spun, and he barely retrieved the chamber pot in time.

A knock. 'I hope you're not messing up the place in there!'

He groaned as the footfalls retreated.

The chamber stank, and so did he. He wrinkled his nose at the rotting straw littering the floor and rummaged through his pack for some clean clothes.

More footsteps outside before his door opened, and Syrena leaned languorously against the frame. He felt her eyes devour his naked arms and torso and hurried to pull on his shirt.

'You look like you've seen tamer nights,' she said.

'Do you always enter your patron's rooms uninvited?' In his drunkenness, he'd forgotten to bar the door. He was lucky no one had robbed him.

'Only when Pa sends me to check in what kind of state they're leaving his lodgings.'

He looked pointedly at the threadbare sheets, the putrid straw, and grimy walls.

She flushed. 'It suited you last night.'

He picked up the chamber pot. 'I'll take care of my mess if you can fetch me a hearty meal and direct me to a public bath.'

'Wouldn't you prefer to use our one?' She caught her lip between her teeth and trailed a hand along her cleavage. 'I could join you...'

'Just the food and directions, my thanks.'

She straightened. 'As it pleases you,' she said, then strode away.

Perhaps he should line his stomach elsewhere, too.

Dressed and fed, Jonas counted his remaining coins and sauntered to town in search of the bathhouse. He couldn't afford another night like that, but at least he'd slept.

Along cobbled streets, he encountered a mob marching towards the lord's castle with fists and voices raised. Some wielded halberds, pitchforks, or spades. Their protests seemed aimed at the inhabitants of the keep, where someone had erected podiums before the walls and posted stakes, as though preparing for Cleansings.

At their front, people tugged and ripped what appeared to be a length of cloth. Jonas squinted. Was that a priest's vestment?

Dressed in the same fabric, robed men rang bells, shouted, and shoved them back. It was chaos.

He ducked down an alley and slipped away in the opposite direction, weaving between smithies, cobblers, stores, and houses, until their cries faded behind him.

Eventually he located the stone bathhouse, constructed close to the major river, where staff pumped or carried water as needed. The building adjoined the town's bakery for shared warmth, and the yeasty smell of fresh bread wafted.

The attendant held out a chary palm to collect before letting Jonas in. Like the communal stables, wealthy travellers and merchants paid a hefty fee to bathe somewhere clean and warm, while the poor plunged into the icy river beside it. Normally when he visited public baths, he requested a haircut, shave, and occasionally a massage, but forwent these luxuries to save coin and maintain some disguise—the scruffier, the better.

On the ground level, a trio of men soaked within a long, tiled bath. Steam rose around their urgent whispers, hugging them close, but when Jonas entered, they fell silent.

'Don't stop on my account,' he said. 'I'll be on my way once I scrub my travel's stench off.'

Wary, they studied him, before resuming their conversation.

He ignored them and stripped off, eager to slip beneath the cleansing water. If only he could scour the grime from his memory as thoroughly as his skin.

Between each splash and dunk, he heard, 'Lady Shelby', 'heirs', and 'heresy', whispered countless times.

His curiosity itched. 'I don't mean to eavesdrop, but I can't help wondering what the townsfolk protest?'

Narrowed eyes peered through the rising steam, watching, watching.

'I'm passing through, and—'

'Then why do you care?' said a half-bald man with a carpet of wet, curly hair sprouting from neck to navel.

'Curiosity feeds a bored man's soul,' he replied.

The blond man seated beside him chuckled. 'It does indeed.' With a cautious glance toward the attendant, he said to Jonas, 'Throw some more coals in, will you?'

Jonas complied, eager to keep outside ears away. Once the steam stopped hissing, he returned to the water and settled closer to his companions.

'If you plan to leave,' said the first in a low voice, 'I wouldn't dally. With all this unrest, they'll likely shutter the town for the winter.' He tossed Jonas a hog bristle brush.

'Oh?' Jonas set to work scrubbing his grubby nails.

The thrill of bearing gossip triumphed over caution, and all three leaned in to include Jonas in their circle.

'I expect they won't reopen Marlin to travellers before the spring, once the handover is complete,' said the second.

Jonas scrambled to recall the local lord. 'What happened to young Marnos?' Hadn't he only recently inherited Marlin?

'The robes have forfeited all his property.'

'What? Why?'

'Lands stripped by heresy belong to Elnora's servants.'

Puzzled, Jonas frowned.

'Lord Marnos accused Lady Shelby of aborting his sons to leave him without heirs.'

'How is that heresy?' Jonas asked.

'He claimed she employed a witch to rid her of her pregnancies.'

'Superstitious nonsense,' Jonas said, scrubbing every inch of flesh within reach. And yet, Alina was undoubtedly a mage who trafficked in abortifacients until her fear of the priests outweighed the potion's profits. 'Why would she try to leave her lord with no heir?'

'They say cankers covered his ballocks,' one man said.

'And pus,' added another.

'Blisters, I heard.'

'Probably all three,' said the first. 'And when the lady refused to let her husband's pus-filled spindle near her, he had his men tie her down and force her.'

Jonas felt sick.

'After her third miscarry, his lordship's servants caught her buying a witch's potion to take care of the fourth.'

'And that was that.'

'What of the damage to the fortifications?' Jonas asked.

'Her brother raised an army, seeking vengeance against the lord.'

'Some justice, then,' Jonas said, the brush idle in his hands.

'But no mercy,' the man sighed.

Jonas frowned. 'How so?'

'Her family laid claim to the title of Marlin, but after staking the lady, the Dark Sun Cult staked their claim on Marlin, too.'

'Lands made forfeit by heresy.' Jonas nodded as the markers fell into place.

'Precisely.'

The previous night's revellers seemed desperate because they were. Once the priests commandeered a town, they would shut the inns and brothels, maybe even outlaw them.

These men were right. He'd best escape Marlin while he could.

Alina had said she thought Ella was in the forest between Rassit and the High City. He'd already veered north of Galliarn along the Gythyn Run to avoid the towns where folk knew him. If he ventured further south, he would reach Wernad and encounter the same problem. His only options were to follow the northeast running road towards Narldan, the next major town, or cut across the fields to the east before circling back to those woodlands.

The latter option seemed safest now, especially while unrest brewed in the region.

'My thanks for the entertainment and advice,' he said, drying off. 'Before I head out, I'd like somewhere quiet to winter, away from conflict and politicking. Know of any settlements in the woods backing onto Rassit, between the town and the High City?' He described the scenery Alina showed him.

'None, unless you want to join an outlawed crew.'

Without his brother to keep him sheltered and fed, he might have to. 'My thanks,' he repeated, then dressed and hurried to the gates.

Twenty-Six

Lynden's nose wrinkled at the foul brew.

'The tonic should bring about your moontime and expel any seeded matter—or so the apothecary assured,' Bess said.

She brought the cup to her lips, sniffed, and gagged.

Bess rubbed her shoulders. 'All will be well, my lady...'

She kept saying that, when it wasn't true. Couldn't be. 'I need to be alone.' Lynden's voice cracked.

'Of course, my lady.' Bess dropped a curtsy and hurried out.

Once swallowed, this putrid liquid would sever her final tie to Gohran. She set the cup down on her dresser. Stood and paced, one hand resting on the small of her belly, the other pressed across her heart. Expelling his seedling meant expelling him.

Sweat prickled her armpits and the backs of her knees. Beyond her window, the sky was a wall of grey.

Returning to the dresser, she sniffed the tonic, then replaced it. Like lode-stones repelling one another, she struggled to bring the liquid near enough to drink. Every inch of her protested at ingesting something so vile.

She reached for the cup once more, but her mind blanked. Why had she come to her dresser? She stared at the scattered items across its top. A hairbrush, a hand mirror, some jewellery the maids hadn't stowed away, a quill and ink, but no parchment—she must have run out, and a strange tonic.

The tonic! That's right, she needed to drink.

But why? What was it for? She squeezed her eyes shut. *Remember...*

Don't be lumbered with stray seed, Lynny... Who had taught her that? Vera's Aunty Lee?

Had Gohran lumbered her with his seed?

If so, Bess had risked her life to fetch this, for if anyone discovered who the tonic was for...

Wait—who was the tonic for...? It must be her, but why?

Gohran's seed. She carried Gohran's seed.

Again, that peculiar skip and her thoughts slipped away, like waking from a dream she couldn't quite recall...

Or a nightmare.

She struggled to focus. What was that cup of foetid brew upon her nightstand? Had the servants not cleared her old dishes?

She felt ill.

She picked it up and brought it to her window, levered the panes open, and tossed its contents outside.

A gentle knock at her door. Lynden roused as Bess entered, carrying a tray of hot, milky tea sweetened with honey, a bundle of rags, and a cloth-wrapped, warmed flat stone.

'For the spasms, my lady.' She set them down.

Was it her moontime?

No—it couldn't be. Could it? What phase was the moon?

Bess must have read the confusion on her face. 'They can take a while to come on, so I'll leave these by your hearth.'

She laid more wood and stoked the fire until it pumped out a steady heat.

Why was she certain it wasn't her moontime?

She opened her mouth to protest, but her thought slipped away.

The last time she'd felt this confused was when Ella returned unexpectedly from Erldan, covered in bruises.

Those bruises...

Had Gohran done that? Jonas said Ella's brother hurt her. So why hadn't she intervened? Why had she taken the king to her bed?

Because his eyes drinking her in warmed in a way that obliterated everything else. Remembering that feeling made her woozy.

'Can I fetch you anything?'

She shook her head. 'My thanks.' She wished Bess would leave. She was weary, and Bess confused her.

But when Bess stood to exit, Lynden panicked. *Don't go...* The words stuck in her throat.

She lay back and closed her eyes, letting her bedding swallow her. So heavy. So tired.

'Try to rest, my lady,' Bess said, but she need not have worried. Sleep had claimed her before the lady's maid reached the door.

Twenty-Seven

Raeyn retreated from Venn's chamber the moment their coupling concluded, as had become her habit, leaving him panting and hollow. He rolled over and stared into the dark of his empty bed.

Once, her expectant smile peered across their common table. Now, they were lucky to share a meal. When they spoke, it was of mundane matters, always staid and practical. Like him, Raeyn had been orphaned while relatively young, inheriting the oversight of Erldan's household in her brother's court.

The burden of responsibility weighed on them both, and he realised how much he had coddled his siblings, relying on Mykan and Bess, rather than Jonas and Lynden, to help manage Nedran's fiscal, political, and domestic spheres.

Even now, he left Lynden in Bess's care, fretting over Jonas, and enduring her heartbreak in private. Her lady's maid would provide her greater comfort than he could, and once the snows melted, he would send her to Lichen or invite Vera to stay, sparing the awkwardness of never knowing what to say.

He hadn't yet sent word to Lichen. He wasn't sure what to share while Jonas was still missing. Vera and Jonas should have been finalising their betrothal and planning a wedding. She probably assumed Jonas would resurface in the spring after a last winter of irresponsible carousing.

But each day that passed with no sign of Jonas eroded Venn's hope. Neither his men's searches, nor Gohran's, had uncovered any traces of his whereabouts. Jonas had seemingly vanished into the night.

He prayed his brother had convinced a friend or ally to risk sheltering him until Gohran's temper cooled. It was the only circumstance he dared contemplate.

Through the winter snows, negotiations for his recapture continued via horseback. Venn urged Gohran to declare Jonas a free man, and make his pardon known, while Gohran insisted Venn first pay the blood price.

'Let no man mock my authority,' Gohran wrote. 'He who dishonours a king, forfeits his life.' He added, 'Out of respect for our familial treaty, I shall consider commuting your brother's sentence upon payment of the offered blood price. However, once pardoned, Jonas of Nedran remains exiled from my lands.'

Jonas of Nedran. No honorific. And Venn noted Gohran included Nedran in *his* demesne.

Venn replied: 'Until the Princess Elder of Erldan delivers a son, Lord Jonas of Nedran stands as my lawful heir, and is thus permitted on all Nedran's holdings. I shall exchange no blood price before the lord returns to his rightful home, unharmed.'

Not trusting Gohran's magical influence, Venn's couriers dealt with Erldan's priests, not the king.

Raeyn repeated her offer to speak with her brother. 'Gohran can be irascible, but I have experience talking him down,' she said. Venn refused. If Gohran could arrest and then disappear Jonas, what might he unleash on Raeyn?

Neither side mentioned Ella, though her existence was at the dispute's heart, instead referring to Jonas's insult in vague terms.

Privately, he strived to forget she was still alive, that he had visited her, willing it a dream. A nightmare. Tried to deny he'd ever touched her with lust and therefore erase any risk of invoking Xenon's Curse.

He should have realised something was awry. Ella's lure blinded him to reason, to duty. He saw it clearly now that she was gone and her spell broken, and Gohran's with it.

He contemplated denouncing Gohran, or at least leveraging his knowledge to secure Jonas's pardon, but held back for Raeyn's sake. Erldan would not evade the priests' forfeiture a second time, and Raeyn would lose her remaining family and home, leaving Nedran with a religious stronghold on its doorstep. Given Venn's tie to Raeyn, the ramifications of a heresy trial for Nedran were unclear.

A darker fear lurked: that no one had found Jonas because he had located Ella after all, and become embroiled in her haven of heretics. Ensnared by Ella's strange magic, they might hole up for the winter, disregarding the threat of Xenon's Curse as superstitious nonsense.

As Venn wished to do.

When he imagined them together, anger surged. Resentment.

Jealousy.

Ella might have been his.

The odd thing was, Venn never considered himself devout until he discovered Ella's heresy. Upon recognising her vestment, his gorge had risen in a crashing wave of sickening realisation.

He immediately recognised why her thrall entrapped him as the pull of opium. Why he'd sickened with desire for her. Why loving her felt like poison.

When he believed her lost, death hovered. His strange fever, not caused by any malady. The medic blamed grief, but he knew it was greed: hunger for Ella's power.

Venn wanted to put the entire sordid business aside and focus on building a life with his new wife. Try for an heir, find a worthwhile match for his sister. Give Nedran a powerful alliance, independent of Erldan.

Yet each time Raeyn left him spent and barred their adjoining door, he drew his wash basin near and scrubbed his flesh raw, as if he could rid his body of heresy's stain, as his soul sought the constant aching hollow that he knew only Ella could fill.

TWENTY-EIGHT

Mayel looped her elbow through Ella's, laughter in her eyes as her velvety lips brushed Ella's cheek. A man around the same age, Jurn, slipped in to join her on the other side, and a third, the eldest, Freesa, led the way. Though all three were older than Ella, they moved with the playfulness of adolescents.

When they reached the narrowed passages nearing the crystal caves, they detached to form a line, with Freesa at their head. Ella remained between Mayel and Jurn, enjoying the ease of their arms coiling around her.

She'd grown used to these meandering corridors, Aeron's rooms branching on either side, like pockets or pouches, or perhaps bubbles within blown glass. She no longer noticed the constant blue light unless she stepped outside, when for a brief period while her sight adjusted, amber tinged her view.

Ahead, water purled along the rocks, where it seeped through the walls from the surface above. Had it rained, or was the snow already melting? Surely not this early.

Steam rose around the pool's edge, curling and dancing, capturing and reflecting the light, warmed by the same source that heated the floors, as if some fiery current flowed beneath the caves. Perhaps naturally occurring, perhaps fuelled by magic.

The walls grew slick with condensation, moist tendrils running in rivulets along the rock, as if the heat caused the stone to sweat through the constant blue glow.

Jurn, Mayel, and Freesa stripped bare, peeling their clothes away to form a puddle in one corner. One by one, they dived beneath the crystal water, laughing and splashing like undines frolicking, liquid beading and glistening where their bodies surfaced.

Her heart skipped, giddy with longing. She loosened her shirt and trousers, slid the fabric from her shoulders, and froze. She could have sworn she saw Thyss in her periphery, averting hungry eyes as her beguilement stirred. Her cheeks flushed and her pulse raced.

Ella recalled standing proud, defiant, in his and Mara's hut, daring him to watch and for Mara to seethe, so she could net the energy surging from their emotions.

She faced away, but echoes of the priestesses' whispers thrummed, their spiteful minds crawling over her as they had in Aryon's communal washroom when they sensed Xarion growing inside her womb.

Eyes closed, she breathed. *That was in the past. You're safe now.*

Steam caressed her neck, but in her mind, it was Venn's hot breath nuzzling, luxuriating in her body like a man losing himself in white smoke, not noticing her laying beneath him, cold and broken.

'Ella?' Jurn touched her arm, beckoning. His black hair fell over blue eyes that turned pitch. Ravenous. Hateful. Needy.

Gohran.

Panic rose, and she slammed her mind shut, desperate to lock them out, to flee. 'I—I shouldn't have come...' She refastened her shirt and belt, stepped away from the pool—from them.

'Wait!' Mayel called, water dripping down her luscious midnight skin.

'I need to go...' Ella stumbled over a rocky ledge, steadied herself, and kept moving, fleeing their naked flesh and enthralling smiles.

Heart in her throat, blood thumping, she did not stop until she reached the library, where Yorg dusted and re-shelved volumes of lore beside a series of reading glasses and scrying spheres.

He turned, unsurprised, and let out a slow puff.

She swiped her tears, swallowed her nerve, and steadied her breath.

Yorg's fingertip rested at the crease where his brows met.

'Don't,' she said. 'Don't pity me.'

Another exhale. 'It's not pity. It's sadness.'

She shook her head, the corners of her mouth crumpling as she fought tears. 'Not for me. I don't deserve it.' She brushed past and pulled out a volume she'd been working from earlier.

'Princess—' he reached for her.

She shrugged him off. 'I'm well.'

He lowered his hand and drew his shoulders back. 'If that were true, you'd be bathing with your peers.'

She turned the page, and a slab of unfamiliar glyphs confronted her. 'Is this a Myanai dialect, or some other tongue?'

'Ella.' Yorg covered the text with his palm.

She snatched it away and reached for her quill. 'This work is important.'

'So are *you*.' His expression was earnest. Caring. Not swayed by her beguilement, but from genuine regard.

'I—I can't do this. I can't—'

'Princess, what he did to you—*to* you, you understand—was not your fault. Even if he was under your beguilement's influence, he still had a *choice*.' Yorg rocked back on his stool.

Mouth tight. She swallowed. 'I *chose* to use my power, to win him over...'

Yorg seemed to mull over something, delivering his words deliberately. 'Have you always used your powers judiciously? No. Have you made some poor decisions? Certainly. But you were also a *child*.'

'I was marrying age!'

'I forget how young Yceltics are when you assume your adult roles,' he said, and she wondered again how old he was and how long Myanai lived.

'It wasn't only Gohran...' She studied the crinkles around his brow and mouth, searching for any twitch or crease that might betray his censure. 'I beguiled the man I loved until he became...' She couldn't finish her sentence, but Yorg's expression told her she didn't need to.

'Another weak mind,' he tutted.

'No. Venn wasn't like that. He was strong. A beloved leader, until I...' Venn's horror at the grove as he realised she had magic crashed over her. She pictured him backing away as if she would poison him, as if he would burn just by looking at her. She gasped. 'Until he...'

Yorg offered a gentle soothing warmth, but let her decide whether to receive it.

He cleared his throat, picking words like treading on uneven rocks to cross a rapid. 'I won't justify all the ways we use our power that might not be... ideal. But when Elnora's worshippers corner us, and force us into hiding, when they persecute and burn us alive, we find methods to protect ourselves. To survive. Why would we not employ the gifts of the gods?'

'Gods?'

'You think Xenon is the only deity with magic?'

'The only one who bestowed it upon His people.'

A wry shake of Yorg's head. 'There is so much for you to learn, Princess.' He pointed to the stack of manuscripts. 'But I begin to wonder whether you will find the answers you seek in these pages.'

Footsteps approached. 'Ella, are you well?' Mayel popped through the archway, trailed by Jurn and Freesa. The trio had dressed, hair wrapped to prevent it dripping, concern splayed across handsome faces as they spilled into the library to surround her and Yorg.

Mayel tucked Ella's cropped locks behind her ear, and Jurn squeezed her hand. Only Freesa hung back, wearing a knowing frown.

Power stirred between them, warm and inviting. Coursing from core to limb, it swirled in a vortex around them, unmistakable yet invisible against the already blue light.

Ella's body stiffened, on guard.

Like Yorg's, their magic didn't venture far, or force itself on her, remaining present between them: an offering.

Tension only slipped from her muscles once she was certain no one would invade. Her breath eased, but she stopped short of accepting their gift.

They watched her, eager to help, and she fought her urge to push them away, forcing her psyche to remain grounded in her body.

Mayel sought her gaze. 'Take all the time you need. You are always welcome to join us.'

'Whenever you feel ready,' added Jurn.

Freesa smiled reassuringly. 'Always.'

The trio exited, and as their footfalls faded, Yorg turned to her. 'Most of Aeron's people have never existed beyond this haven, haven't encountered Ycelt's cruelty as you and I have.'

Ella stayed silent.

'Given your history, I'm not surprised you froze, and your peers won't be either. They don't think you're daft or strange. They want you to be well,' Yorg said. 'As do I.'

'You were spying on me!'

'I was watching over you.' He twirled his wispy beard. 'I worry.'

She hugged her mind and body close.

'With your permission, I'd like to seek Vorlyn's help. Searching for lore might answer your intellectual questions, but won't heal that scar upon your aura.' His gentle eyes studied her. 'Or that fear response.'

Ella frowned. 'Why Vorlyn?'

'She and you have more in common than you realise.'

Twenty-Nine

That night, Ella woke tangled in sweat-drenched clothes and bedding. Indistinct images of flames and smoke hovered. A metal flash and a spill of blood caught her in a wave of terror, hopelessness, and loss, and she stared panting through the eternal dim blue light.

As she emerged from her recess, unease crept along her limbs and settled in her belly. This was her first dream since arriving at Aeron, as though the seal placed over these caves kept her nightmares out.

Tucked into catacomb-like hollows, her bedfellows did not stir, their steady sleeping breaths humming through the corridors. She had learnt to open her mind to their collective knowledge to navigate the labyrinthine passages. She gathered her blankets and shuffled them towards the laundry. Once there, she slipped out of her nightclothes and dumped them along with her bedding atop the rest of the soiled items, then crept to the nearby bathing pools.

Cool air puckered her damp skin, while azure steam rose before her like low-hanging clouds trapped in a steep valley. She slid beneath the warm depths, dipped under the surface, and pushed off from the wall to glide from one side to the other. It felt so good to bathe after she missed out earlier that day.

She surfaced, and rested against a smooth bench-like hollow, watching the water's rings expand outwards. Vorlyn told her the water contained minerals that cleansed and soothed, and as the liquid fizzed against her, she believed it.

Something tugged at her mind. Not a summons, but a nagging discomfort that settled around her heart, and she was certain it related to the dream that brought her here. The surrounding water swirled and shimmered, beckoning. Might she scry through Aeron's shield?

She looked up. Far above, a slight opening revealed the night's stars: a crack in Aeron's shell.

Power charged along the water's surface, but when she pictured those she left behind, the images appeared muffled, blurred shapes and muted colours that refused to resolve into anything concrete.

She lay back, resting her head on the rocky ledge, which time had smoothed into a neck-shaped indentation, and closed her eyes. Cool air from the opening brushed her skin. A relief from the otherwise stifling heat.

She envisioned Xarion sleeping and imagined the warmth of the water as the temperature of her snuggling body. She reached for her daughter's mind to share her blissful dreams, but Xarion fretted, and slammed her out.

Ella's thoughts flitted, and she pictured Xarion grown into a girl on the cusp of womanhood. She stood before a library of tomes, pulling out one volume after another. She pointed to a passage containing glyphs that blurred and morphed between languages Ella couldn't read, then tore the pages out and tossed them with a whip of raven hair.

Her heart lurched. She was so like Ella. But when she turned back and caught Ella watching her, she glared, resentful. Ella sensed some other emotion, too, that eluded her.

A further breath, and Xarion altered again. Not ageing, but transforming. Her features blurred, melting and melding into a faceless monster. Beneath, malice writhed: the feeling she'd been unable to grasp.

Ella cried, but no sound came out. She must have fallen back asleep, and yet she seemed wide awake.

She tried to run, but her body froze in a leaden weight, and she couldn't move her mouth or throat to utter a noise.

The creature strode towards her, something inside it shrieking, and for a moment, Ella recognised her terrified child trapped within the monster's mask. Desperate, she reached for her, but the demon swallowed the last of Xarion's features into its fleshy, faceless mound.

It neared, pulsing raw power. Ella needed to move, but couldn't.

Another silent scream.

'Ella?'

She woke with a gasp and looked up. Vorlyn stood at the entrance to the pools, rubbing her eyes.

'My apologies,' Ella said. 'I must have fallen asleep…' She summoned deep breaths and splashed water on her face. She was lucky she hadn't slipped and drowned. 'I was trying to be quiet…'

'You were, but your dreams were rather loud,' Vorlyn said with a wry smile.

Ella flushed.

'Something troubles you.'

An invitation.

She climbed out, and Vorlyn handed her a towel, then drew her close, rubbing her shoulders with a warmth she'd scarcely experienced. She shrank away.

Vorlyn laughed gently. 'Am I that frightening?'

To Ella, she was, when her presence rendered Ella's only power useless. She pulled the fabric tighter around her.

Vorlyn tilted her head, eyes narrowed. 'You know, seeing you just now reminded me of your mother.'

Ella startled.

'I met her once. Before you were born, of course.' Another wry smile. 'Finish drying off and meet me in the library. I'll brew us some tea.' Her eyebrow quirked. 'Or perhaps something stronger.'

Ella took a moment to still her heart, pulled on fresh trousers and a fitted shirt fastened at the waist, and wrapped her hair to dry.

She found Vorlyn perched before the volumes Ella had been reading and accepted the steaming cup she offered. Ella sniffed. Spirit of some kind.

'It's good,' Vorlyn said, and sipped hers.

Ella did likewise, a burning heat flowing down her throat and warming her chest, grateful as the images of her nightmare faded.

Vorlyn motioned for Ella to sit.

She had so many questions she couldn't fathom where to begin. 'You said you knew my mother?'

'Met, yes. And it was long ago.' Vorlyn refilled her thimble-like lacquered cup. 'You know what I miss about living in Ycelt? Wine, not ale, or this Myanai spirit. Liquor from fermented fruit, rather than grain.'

Ella gestured to their caves. 'Don't we live in Ycelt now?'

'Physically, I suppose we do. In this time. But Aeron's inhabitants tend not to follow Yceltic customs.'

Ella sighed, impatient.

'My apologies,' Vorlyn said. 'Meeting someone from near my childhood home brings back memories.'

'You're from Erldan?' Yorg had said they had much in common.

'Near there, yes.' Her eyes misted, but there was a tight twist to her mouth. 'I still recall being introduced to your mother and her sister at one of Erldan's notoriously lavish balls.'

Ella sucked in her breath.

She sensed Vorlyn mulling something over. Wait—why did she sense her? 'Vorlyn, why can you read my mind, and sometimes share thoughts, but seem immune to my beguilement?'

'Immune to all influence,' she said. 'Those with magic can't draw from me or manipulate me. If you catch my thoughts, it's because I let you, because you're not forcing me. I hear when you're not influencing or beguiling.'

Was that beguilement's counterpart—its inverse? The sixteenth gift.

Ella frowned. 'Like the captain from the story of Xarion in *The Lost Warriors*,' she whispered.

'Do you know, I've never read that work? We hold no copy here.'

And Ella had left Amber's back at Nedran.

'I'm getting diverted again,' Vorlyn said. 'Tell me about your dream.'

Ella flinched, not wanting to remember or share the nightmare that flashed behind her eyes, except...

Her gut gnawed. She would get no answers if she continued to withhold. Could she trust these people? This strange Yceltic woman who had known her aunt and mother?

She rummaged through the parchments strewn across the bench until she retrieved the page she'd seen in her dream—the only one she'd found that referenced drawing lifeforce and invoking the Curse, a passage quoting an excerpt from *The Lost Warriors*.

She angled the text towards Vorlyn and read: "'*Should a man draw the lifeforce of another to fuel his power, he shall be Cleansed or those he touches shall be Cursed thrice over.*' Is that why they culled the mages?'

'From what I understand, the priests feared the Curse's contagion spreading throughout Ycelt and rounded up supposed witches—what we see as Cleansings today—and culled those within Xenon's havens using forbidden powers.'

Her vision had shown priestesses, not priests, murdering their own. Porters. Beguilers. Anyone drawing lifeforce. 'The priests may have initiated it,' she said quietly, 'but Xenon's disciples carried out their wishes with relish.'

'Xenon's blessed have always Cleansed those Cursed before its tentacles could spread,' Vorlyn said.

'But there is nothing here about porting or beguilement being forbidden.'

'Both gifts require lifeforce,' Vorlyn said. 'Porters and beguilers must draw from a forbidden source.'

'But I drew blood to port here, and Yorg says I have not invoked the Curse.'

Vorlyn sucked a breath between clenched teeth.

'And I can beguile without drawing lifeforce.' She had captivated long before she understood what she was doing. Without *doing* at all. Provided she had full access to her power, if she liked someone, and wanted them to think well of her, then they did. 'So which piece invokes the Curse? Is it using a forbidden gift, or drawing lifeforce? And why, having done both, am I not condemned?'

Her nightmare echoed a flash of glyphs merging and distorting. The text before her glowed blue as the words blurred and bled into each other.

She ran her finger over the translation in the margins and settled on a glyph that resembled the new moon: the sigil for 'drawing'. But instead of the usual circle, with two puncture wounds on either side, and an upright cross in the centre, the top and bottom arcs of the moon didn't quite align. The lower arc sat flush against the dots, while the vertical stroke of the cross extended above the moon. Almost as if someone had combined 'draw' with 'life'—or perhaps overwritten one with the other, like the palimpsests Yorg mentioned.

'Does that resemble the glyph for "draw", or "bleed", to you?' she asked, pointing.

Vorlyn peered over her shoulder, comparing the original to the scratched translation in the margins. 'It could be either,' she said, then read, '"Should a man *bleed* the lifeforce of another"?'

Ella's vision blurred again. She blinked and tried to focus on the page before her, studying the glyph pair depicting 'lifeforce'. 'That is undoubtedly the symbol for "life,"' she said, indicating the horizontal dots nested between mirrored overlapping waves. 'But that looks like the glyph for "power", not "force" to me.' She moved her finger to the second sigil, which showed a horizontal line crossing two dots within waxing crescent arcs.

'That's because there is no glyph for "force,"' Vorlyn said.

'And yet, no equivalent exists in the source text.' Ella pointed to where the missing word ought to be. Directly translated, it simply read 'life'.

Vorlyn leaned closer, comparing the marginalia to its source. 'You're right. Whoever transcribed this added the second glyph…'

She stumbled. 'What if it was supposed to read, "*Should a man* bleed *the* life *of another*"? Punished for committing bloodshed. Nothing to do with drawing lifeforce.'

Vorlyn frowned. 'A mistranslation, perhaps?'

Pressure built behind Ella's eyes. 'I—I'm not sure…' She winced and took a breath, trying to hold steady. The strain intensified, like a storm brewing in her temples. 'If someone added that glyph…'

A suspicion was forming. One she didn't dare believe. Wasn't sure if she should voice. Her temples throbbed. What if Xenon hadn't Cursed porters or beguilers? 'Suppose Xenon's gifts weren't prohibited because they required blood, but forbidding leveraging lifeforce prevented people using those abilities.'

'Are you suggesting Xenon's *followers* outlawed drawing blood?' Vorlyn paled. 'But why?'

Ella pictured her dream-daughter grown into a powerful demon and a smirk twisted her mouth. 'To keep us small.' How would women like her aunt and mother, who coveted knowledge and power amongst the strongest individuals, ensure they maintained their positions? 'Priests disempower women by declaring us witches, but women diminish other women by making us compete for the meagre crumbs we're afforded.'

The histories flashed before her. 'Porters once drew lifeforce without consequence...' And the old warrior priestess Xarion had once beguiled, like her... 'If Xenon has not Cursed me...' She recalled the missing pages from Xarion's story at Aryon. Manuscripts purged and altered, but to hide references to forbidden powers, or the original lore? 'You said we have no copy of *The Lost Warriors* here?'

Vorlyn shook her head.

Then Yorg had been right. She wouldn't find the answers she sought at Aeron.

'Let us speak to Yorg when he wakes.'

The shadow of Ella's nightmare had faded, but when she stepped across the library's threshold, she caught her reflection in a reading glass atop a shelf beside the door, and the haunting image of the faceless monster stared back.

Thirty

Jonas jerked awake to find an icy dagger aimed at his throat. Its point pressed into his skin, and he gasped, then stilled, his breath rushing through his nostrils. Without turning his head, he counted at least five ruffians. No insignia on their shabby clothing. No obvious engravings on their crossguards or blades. Not any lord's men, but bandits.

He sneaked his palm towards his ribs, searching for the small pouch beneath his shirt.

'Looking for this?' A mangy bearded man jangled his purse containing his precious coin—the coin he'd camped out here to save. A short-sighted frugality, under the circumstances.

How had they nabbed it while he slept? He inched to sit, pressing against the trunk where he'd taken shelter, keeping as far from the blade as he could. If they were going to slay him, he'd be dead already.

Beside a blond man whose diagonal scar marred both halves of his handsome features, his steed contentedly devoured grain from a nosebag. *Traitor,* he thought.

'If you wouldn't mind getting off that mat, we'll be taking it as well.'

He swore. 'My blanket, too, I suppose?'

'More than a pretty face, lads. This one has some sense.' Snide tittering.

The man wielding the dagger—*his* dagger, Jonas realised—edged aside, allowing him to stand, while the others moved closer, crowding him in with their raised weapons.

Even if he ducked out from one, and took down maybe two, he'd have three more blades in his chest before he'd escaped through the first row of trees.

The bearded man, who seemed to be their leader, fingered Jonas's cloak, before examining the tatty one he wore. 'I think that's about the right size, don't you, lads?'

'Certainly a hue to complement your fair complexion,' Jonas smirked.

A second blade came at him from the side. 'Don't get impudent, lad.'

'Can't even flatter a man in these troubling times.' He removed his cloak and handed it across.

Their leader peeled off his threadbare coat and tossed it aside, then pulled Jonas's on, and posed for his men, who nodded and grunted approval.

Chill seeped through Jonas's shirt and gnawed into his bones. 'If you're not using that...' He pointed to the discarded coat.

The leader trod it further into the snow, grinding the mud below, then stepped back and hacked a gob of phlegm on top.

'Perfect, my thanks. Spit always adds a glistening flair, don't you agree?'

'Move.' The second dagger prodded his rib, and the troop turned and started walking, each trampling the cloak deeper into the dirt on their way through.

Jonas stooped to retrieve it, brushed off the debris, and pulled it on. It could be worse, he thought, remembering Amber's putrid robe.

A further jab at his ribs. 'I said, move.'

He fell into line as they trudged through the snow. How had he escaped one set of jailors only to wind up captured by another?

Considering how much gear the bandits pilfered, their camp was rather shoddy. They covered their makeshift lean-tos with frayed canvas and left soiled and tattered bedding and blankets to rot against damp trunks during the day. Come mealtimes, the men fought over scraps of roasted squirrel, a pheasant, if they were lucky, and whatever tubers and edible roots they scrounged.

Jonas watched them feast, ignoring his growling hunger. No one offered him any, and he did not ask.

The handsome man with the gruesome scar seemed the most benign. When he sat beside Jonas to eat on the second night, he introduced himself as Jarl. 'I'd offer you some to stay those ravenous eyes, but you haven't yet earned your keep.'

'How am I to do that? You've robbed all but my shirt and braies.' He didn't want them to maintain him. He didn't want to be here.

'Fighting, of course,' Jarl said.

Jonas frowned. 'Surely your purses brim with gold.' They were mercenaries in a region that had seen a glut of conflict these past seasons.

'Ha!' Jarl tore a chunk of meat between jagged teeth. Grease dripped down his chin. His mouth full, he said, 'Men like us only grow fat when fighting is sporadic.'

'Sporadic, eh?' Jonas eyed the scruffy crew, surprised that an outlaw grasped the word. How many had been educated nobles before ending up here? And how had they become impoverished? Was Jarl right? Overlords often hired mercenaries to bolster numbers during a conflict, then released the survivors—their purses full—over the winter. While none looked too closely into a man's history in urgent times, no decent lord would swear an outlaw to his permanent army. And when war dragged, overlords invested in sworn recruits.

'What about you?' Jarl wiped his chin on the back of his hand. 'You look too pretty to have ever sold your sword, so what takes you off the major thoroughfares in the thick of winter?'

'I didn't realise the task demanded a degree of ugliness.' He surveyed the bandits pointedly. 'But perhaps that's a requisite for *this* troop.'

An elbow clipped his ear. 'Shut it.'

'The pretty one thinks he's clever.'

'If he was clever, he'd know where his next meal was coming from.'

If he had been clever, he wouldn't be here. He kicked the heels of his worn and flimsy boots—a pair bequeathed him after a scrap over his thick-soled ones.

'They won't fit your ogre feet,' the smaller one vying for the boots had goaded his colossal opponent.

'They'll hug my sturdy hoofs better than your puny stumps!'

After some extended posturing and a brief skirmish, the ogre had claimed Jonas's shoes. But when he'd struggled to squeeze into them, he'd delivered Jonas a hefty cuff. Then he dropped his thin, misshapen boots beside Jonas's feet, loosened his trousers, and doused them in piss.

Jonas had skittered aside, trying to avoid the splash. Urine leaked out of the left boot through a split in its sole. The right he had to upend to empty, staining the snow a dark amber.

Now as Jonas crouched, his feet protested the foreign indentations of the ogre's old shoes and cursed himself again for ever confronting Gohran and demanding Ella's whereabouts.

The feasting over, Jarl nudged him. 'Get up, Pretty One. It's your turn.'

Jonas groaned. His turn for what?

'Up.' Someone thrusted a rusty, child-sized dagger into his palm.

The other bandits formed a ring around the boot-thieving ogre.

One of them elbowed Jonas's ribs and shoved him forward. 'Fight!'

'Pardon?'

'Carrying a fancy blade doesn't mean you know how to wield it.' A hand gripped his jaw and savage eyes inspected him. 'The skin like a baby's rump under that beard says you've not seen many scraps. If we're to feed you, Pretty One, we need to see your mettle.'

Apart from the small scar near his eye that Jonas had earned falling from a tree, his otherwise unblemished features had only known mock combat. Between Venn and his father, he had learnt to deflect close-range strikes, wrestle in confined spaces, and drilled with Nedran's army from the time he could carry a sword. But all that training had been in well-fitted shoes, wearing his own attire, and wielding a familiar blade. These ruffians were used to making do with scavenged clothes and weapons, with makeshift armour, and bore scars that evidenced their survival.

'Let's see if you're worth your winter keep.'

Their circle tightened, leaving no gaps for escape.

He eyed his opponent. The ogre stood a clear foot taller, with the shoulders of an ox. 'I have no quarrel with this man, or any of you—though I'd rather you hadn't pissed in these shoes, stolen my cloak, my bedding, my steed, my weapons, my coin—'

'Shut it, Pretty One.' The ogre's grunt thundered through Jonas's chest. He towered, his bulky shadow looming.

'I've naught to prove here, and there's no need to feed me. I was on my way to find some caves...'

'I said, shut it!' A cuff.

Hungry eyes demanded entertainment.

'You'll do better with us than that witchy lot.'

Jonas's ears perked.

'So, fight!'

Someone shoved him forward, and he landed in the ogre's meaty paws. A further grunt, and the oversized man flung him off.

'Get on with it!'

'Fight!'

A chorus of shouts and jeers.

Melted snow seeped through the cracks in his shoes. He grimaced, shuffling his feet to reduce the squelch.

The ogre's fist clipped his jaw, pitching blood and spittle sideways. Stunned, he stumbled back. Another fist to his gut stole his breath, and he doubled over, winded and gasping. A boot—*his* boot—smacked his shin, before a knee plunged into his stomach. He groaned.

Their laughter and jeering intensified with their escalating appetite for violence. He hadn't escaped his brother-in-law's clutches and outlawed himself only to end up a target for these thugs' amusement.

More blows landed, lifting and knocking him, propelling him towards the ground and dragging his face through the snow. So far, he'd not managed a single strike. A jut to his ribs shot pain through his chest. His jagged breath pinched and squeezed. Another kick sent him careening, and he staggered to his knees, crouching on all fours.

'That's it, Pretty Swine! Squeal like a piglet!' Jeers swam around him as his vision reeled.

He rubbed the hilt of the childlike, rusty dagger. Once, he'd told Ella that without size on her side, she must be nimble, use her wits, and leverage whatever she had to hand. He sneaked a glance at the ogre's giant legs and ale-barrel waist. The man had bulk, but he was slow, each movement lumbering, and after a time, predictable. One fist, then the other, a kick, followed by a knee. A pause for adulation, before his actions repeated.

The next blow took out Jonas's eye. He felt it swelling closed, blood and sweat trickling down his face and hair, but he rolled away before the subsequent one connected with his ribs.

When the sequence restarted, he waited for his opponent to raise his paws, and he dived for his shins, slicing the dagger through the tendons at the back of his knee. The ogre yelped and buckled.

Jonas aimed his next strike upwards and punched through the ogre's bal-locks. A howl to rival a banshee left his ears ringing, before enormous arms plunged, threatening to crush his skull.

He wasn't ready to die. Not today. Not ever.

He rolled and skittered away, then scrambled to his feet. He would have one opportunity to land his next blow. If it didn't take the ogre out, the burly man would quash him.

His opponent staggered from where Jonas's swipe crippled his knee, his beefy arms swinging like pendulums.

Jonas ducked, crouched, then leapt, grappling from behind. His elbow cir-cled the man's neck, and his calves wrapped around his waist. He yanked the giant's hair and stabbed the dagger through his throat. The blade stuck, skew-ering the ogre like a chicken.

Blood spurted from where it poked out at a sickening angle, and the ogre gasped and spluttered. He flailed at the dagger's hilt, tried to claw it free, but failed, and Jonas felt the hitch and shudder of his gurgling breath as he struggled to swallow and breathe.

He clung to the ogre, who swayed like a felled tree, ready to topple. More terrifying rasps and his shoulders juddered to a deathly halt. He needed to jump off and find a safe place to land before—

Too late, the ogre tilted and crashed to the earth, with Jonas still attached. Pain screamed through his ankle beneath the ogre's crushing bulk.

He writhed and shoved. 'Get him off! Get him off me!'

Hands gripped the oversized man and rolled him onto his side. Crimson blood pooled and soaked into the snow as further arms drew Jonas out from underneath and helped him to his feet.

He took a few tentative steps and cried out as fire burst through his ankle. The swelling throbbed and ached. He staggered, then stumbled. Wiped the blood and sweat from his eye and mouth. Each breath squeezed. But he could breathe.

The ogre lay flaccid, unmoving, the thirsty snow absorbing his seeping blood, while his chest remained frighteningly, permanently, still.

Jonas had delivered a lethal blow to a man twice his size with a child's rusted dagger. He choked on a sob, the tang of blood haunting the back of his throat.

One by one, the men knelt and touched the ogre. Some kissed and sprinkled dirt across his lifeless bulk. Others stroked his shoulder, rested a hand on his cheek and whispered his name. 'Better fortune in the next life.'

Jonas hovered, not knowing where to look, grateful for every cursed breath.

Someone handed him a wooden staff to prop him up. 'If you can walk, you can stay.'

Another clapped his back, and he winced. 'Welcome, Pretty Swine.'

Further thuds and muttered congratulations followed, though no one was more relieved than him, that he'd triumphed and survived.

The pixie man who the ogre defeated retrieved his shoes from the corpse and dumped them at Jonas's feet. 'Seems they're your boots, after all.'

THIRTY-ONE

At the new moon, a cavalcade of henads and priests arrived from Erldan to assist with the proceedings in Harnal, but Davith was not among them. Amber released her breath. *He's not here.*

Aren't his neophytes privy to his movements? Nykki squeezed her hand. *We only need one...*

She drew Nykki close, reassurance flowing through their touch. It would take a little longer, but their plan could work.

As the noontide hearing approached, they waited inside the tavern until the townsfolk stopped milling. Many had crammed within the temple for the trial. Others hovered by the doors, listening and awaiting verdicts. Harnal's local priest, the one Amber observed distributing supplies and offering shelter, was notably absent.

Once the court was in session, Amber and Nykki emerged. They ducked between buildings until they spied the temple. Amber's earlier meanderings guided them towards its rear, where they could advance without being seen.

A guard kept watch beside the cart that imprisoned the accused: three women of varying ages, shoved together. Bound, as Amber had been, but with no hoods to cover their frightened faces. Intermittent snivels, sobs, and prayers seeped between the bars of their shared cage.

Not one captive possessed magic.

Should we release them? Nykki thought.

Not yet. Not until we have what we came for.

Won't that be too late?

Amber raised her palm. *Listen. They're coming.*

A pair of neophytes emerged from the temple, and Amber and Nykki ducked behind the western wing, senses primed.

The voices grew louder as they neared.

'Let's start with the scold.'

'Ah, yes, the comely one,' added the other, eager.

That voice. Amber stifled a gasp. She didn't need to see his greasy hair, to smell his acrid breath, to know who he was: the neophyte from Erldan's dungeon.

'I heard you cursed your lord husband when he kicked your quiver for refusing him.' A snide chortle.

'Useless to him now, aren't you?' goaded the other.

'I'd wager a full silver we could part those thighs.'

'I cursed him, and I'll curse you,' the prisoner spat. 'May both of your spindles rot!'

'That's the way, lass,' said the older accused. 'Let them stay limp, in this life and the next, for a steed who can't service his mare might as well be a gelding!'

'Quiet!' a neophyte banged on the cage.

'For shame!' said a third woman, her thin voice breaking. 'Calling yourselves sons of Our Dark Lady.'

'Get her out and shut them up,' said the neophyte Amber recognised.

It took all her fortitude to remain in the here and now, and not back inside her crate, cowering alongside the prisoners. *She was them. They were her.*

Nykki gripped her hand. *You're safe.*

Eyes closed, Amber leaned against the temple, sucked up Nykki's warmth, and breathed. She struggled to block out the squeal of the cage door opening. The shouts and wails, a gob of spit landing, a slap, and a thud. Someone groaned, and metal jangled as a lock clunked shut, followed by heavy silence.

They're gone. Nykki tugged on her wrist, and she reluctantly opened her eyes and sneaked a look.

The guard had accompanied the prisoner inside, and the wagon stood unattended beneath Elnora's lengthened shadows. *Go now!*

They hurried towards the cage, and with a heated glance, shattered its lock. The door swung open, and Amber prayed no one would notice its telltale whine. Finger to her lips, she signalled to the captives, and she and Nykki helped them out.

Loosen their bindings, Amber thought to Nykki. *Legs first.* That way, the prisoners could run.

The flesh surrounding their stiff twine appeared bruised, and Amber's wrists and ankles ached in sympathy, her memories raw.

Nykki's fingers worked to untie the priests' knots. *It might be faster to break the rope.*

No... It was too risky. The women would realise they had magic. They were lucky none had noticed them snapping that lock without tools.

'What about Freyda?' said the older prisoner, whose rheumy eyes dominated her weathered face. 'We need to find her.' Freyda must be the third woman, whose trial had already begun.

Amber signalled again for quiet.

'We can't leave her,' the prisoner's voice rose.

Nykki pinched her arms. 'Look at me,' she whispered, and let her power flow. The woman stilled, falling silent. Compliant. For now.

The other woman's eyes widened, agog, her sallow face framed by cropped auburn hair. She dropped to her knees, bound hands signing a warding. 'May Elnora shine and prove me true to Her Light before Her servants...'

Amber tried to clasp her wrists and use her magic to persuade, but she thrashed and writhed, her blunt locks whipping across her cheeks as she evaded Amber's grasp and continued her drone.

'May these witches perish in Her Darkness...'

Leave her, Nykki thought. *She can burn.*

They ushered the first woman away. Her hunched bones jutted, wrists so frail Amber feared they might snap.

We're not taking her. Amber wouldn't lumber them with a helpless prisoner. Not again. She held the woman's gaze. 'Hide until you're able to sneak past the guards. Then travel west.' She slipped the route to Aryon into her mind. The woman nodded slowly and then headed away from the temple. Amber hoped her influence lasted.

She's condemned either way, my love.

The devout woman remained kneeling, her bound hands aimed at the sun, as she rocked and prayed. Amber didn't attempt to influence her again; her wails would provide a diversion.

She and Nykki ducked behind the building and awaited the neophytes' return. Her breath felt thick in her chest as she forced her heartbeat to slow. The delay was agonising.

Within the temple came cries and jeers. They should have intervened right away, confronted the two neophytes and spared this torture...

Don't think that way, my love. We can come back for her following the trial. There was no stopping her conviction, but they wouldn't Cleanse her until eventide, under Xenon's light.

Shouts erupted, and the temple doors banged open. A stolen glance from around the corner revealed the neophytes shoving their convicted prisoner, her round face bloated and bloodied, towards the wagon, ready to trade her for the next. Amber ducked back.

'By every demon...!'

Beside her, Nykki tensed. They must have spotted the empty cage.

Wait, Amber thought. *Not yet.*

'Your Holinesses,' the devout prisoner called. 'Please, I beg you, I am no heretic! Witches came to release us, but I remain loyal to Our Dark Lady...'

'Fool,' spat the condemned prisoner, Freyda.

'Elnora will set me free. She will—'

A sickening thud. Then another. Then silence.

'Lock them back up. I'll search for whoever did this.'

The neophyte's familiar voice chilled Amber's blood, sending ice through her veins and fire to consume her belly.

Nykki's mind stroked hers.

Footfalls neared, and she steadied herself. *Now!*

The greasy-haired neophyte rounded the corner, and they pounced, grabbing him on either side until he dropped. The fool carried no staff. Didn't bother to shield his eyes. The priests had not expected to encounter genuine sorcerers.

I have him. Take down the other.

Nykki hesitated.

Go! Before he summons help.

Nykki skittered off, and Amber hefted and rolled the neophyte face down. Her knees pressed into him as she bound his hands behind his back with salvaged twine.

She leaned in close and slid into his rancid mind. *I've dreamed of this moment...* Let him experience the power he despised. Let her savour the ripple of his fear.

Once she had him secured, she listened for Nykki. It was quiet. Too quiet. Either she'd captured and forced him still, or—

Nykki's silent, terrified cry flooded her psyche.

And then someone shouted, 'Escaped heretics! Hurry!'

Turmoil erupted into a wild commotion.

No. No-no-no-no-no-no-no-no...

She surged her power through the greasy-haired neophyte to keep him docile on the ground, before she rounded the corner. People spilled from the temple, pointing and shouting as they scattered to search.

Where was Nykki? *Where was her beloved?*

Ahead, the wagon's wheels rolled with a scrape and crunch. The neophyte must have hitched it back to its steed and tied the cage door shut. He was wheeling his prisoners away.

Nykki! Nykki!

Cat-green eyes peered through the bars, pleading and helpless. Alone, Nykki's magic wasn't strong enough to escape.

A lean man spotted Amber, and then the unconscious neophyte on the ground behind her. 'What's happened to the priest, lass? Why is he—?'

Amber caught his gaze. Without Nykki, her reserves were low, but the moment he touched her arm, her power flowed, slipping into his mind's chambers to sway him to her will. 'The escaped prisoner did this to His Holiness. Leave me to care for him. Quick, join the others. Don't let the witch escape!'

The man complied, and trembling, Amber sank back to her knees beside the neophyte. She needed food or a fire, or both.

'Come, my greasy little pet. Let us eat, and then you can show me where Harnal hides its prisoners.'

THIRTY-TWO

Yorg had confirmed the discrepancies Ella saw between the source glyphs and their translations, but offered no explanation. 'It is consistent with my rusty recollections of the Cull occurring later,' he said, rubbing his weary temples, 'following the Great Upheaval. But the translated passage is the only version I learnt, first in Myanai, and then in Yceltic. It seems the source language predates even me, Princess!' A rumble. 'Though it would solve the mystery of why your aura does not reflect the Curse.'

But it didn't explain why she poisoned the lives of those around her.

'I suggest you work with Vorlyn as we discussed, and I shall monitor any changes in your aura.'

Vorlyn had designed a series of exercises to calm Ella's nerves and lessen the panic that drove her to flee her body and help her remain in control of her power.

'Years passed following my ordeal, before I could accept loving touch,' she'd told Ella when they commenced their work. 'Until I felt safe in my body'—a cautious glance—'and trusted myself.' A memory hovered, but when Ella stretched her mind, Vorlyn's thoughts remained sealed. 'With a measured approach, you may see results much sooner.'

Ella hoped she was right. Already she had experienced a shift, as if starting this work opened a floodgate. The previous day, when Mayel invited her to swim, just the two of them, she had stripped naked without hesitation, and entered the water alongside her with ease, though Mayel was careful not to touch her.

'There is no pressure,' Mayel had soothed. 'Not from me or anyone here.'

But there *was*. Ella needed to be well. Wanted to experience desire free from fear. To accept and offer love and pleasure, not as an exchange of power, or a manipulation, but something shared. A gift.

And when Ella's beguilement had stirred with her longing, her panic forced her to turn away to hide her tears.

Now, Vorlyn sat opposite her, cross-legged on the floor with her palms resting open on her knees, her chest rising and falling, steady as she waited. 'Remember, I am *inviting* you,' she said. 'Your curiosity is *welcome*.' It was the same relaxed tone Mayel had used, but Ella squirmed.

The hollowed-out room was one in a series of communal spaces dressed in plush carpets and littered with square silk-covered cushions hugging a closed-in brazier. Smoke escaped the cave's surface via a pipe, and Ella wondered how locals failed to notice Aeron's presence among Vern's surrounding woods.

Vorlyn was still speaking. 'My hand, expression, and psyche, lay open for you to explore as much or as little as is comfortable. Tell me when you've had enough, and we'll stop.'

Ella examined the stranger's features that seemed hauntingly familiar. As though Ella should recognise her from somewhere. But how? She'd left Erldan before Ella was born.

'When you're ready, reach for my hand...'

Ella curled her fingers along Vorlyn's palm until her mouth curved from the ticklish touch, but Ella felt nothing. Sensed nothing.

The creases around Vorlyn's eyes and arch to her brow suggested a mischief that belied her darkness, just as she masked her pain in wry humour. As she invited Ella beneath that mask, behind her wicked grin, Ella reached tentative tendrils outward, but grasped none of Vorlyn's thoughts. She chewed on her lip. She could not penetrate Vorlyn's mind, but might she receive a projection?

Summoning courage, Ella sent her request without force or influence.

Vorlyn complied, and cast a series of still images, letting Ella's imagination complete the detail they represented.

The first showed Vorlyn's limbs entwined with a stranger's, her vacant stare not caring who he was. Next, she sucked at an opium pipe, chasing oblivion for days on end. Between times, she visited inns and brothels, downing carafe after carafe of wine as she danced and caroused on a peak of sensation. The images looped, showing new settings, different people, while Vorlyn's behaviour stayed constant.

Then came the inevitable crash, plummeting her into an oppressive quiet, haunted by inescapable memories and crippling shame. This phase never lasted, for she sought another body, the next substance, losing herself not for pleasure, but to forget.

She rarely experienced joy. Rather, she chased numbness. An escape from the aftermath. From reality and loss.

Ella withdrew and shielded, struggling to articulate her thoughts.

Vorlyn opened her eyes and exhaled.

She need not reveal the details of what she'd escaped for Ella to know how acutely she had suffered, nor the torture and grief that led to such excess.

Ella's instinct was to cast magic to soothe, but doubted it would reach Vorlyn through her strange immunity.

Vorlyn swallowed. 'That all happened before I came here,' she said. 'Before I found a new home and realised safety was possible.' Her voice cracked. 'I believed I was reclaiming my autonomy. Repossessing what my captors tried to break and steal. But I only re-enacted the same pain, over and again, compounding my shame. I want to spare you that.'

Ella's ordeal was nothing to Vorlyn's. Why did she think they were alike?

'We were both violated,' Vorlyn said. 'In different ways.'

And to differing degrees. But the question that plagued her sat unspoken on her lips. *By whom?*

Vorlyn smirked. A bitter and cruel twist that turned her eyes hard and her mouth ugly. 'A young neophyte by the name of Davith.'

Ella gasped.

'I believe he subsequently found a calling in your late father's service.'

Ella whispered, 'He became Erldan's head priest.'

Another smirk. 'By all accounts, King Rohan grew increasingly devout following his fall. There's nothing like a man's frailty to lead him to seek the solace of the gods.'

Ella thought back to her father's later years. He'd been her entire world before his injury. Doting on her, accompanying them while the equerry taught her to ride. A proud and robust fighter and huntsman, his gruff drunken laughter filled Erldan's halls as he entertained courtiers from every province south of Galliarn.

The day he'd been injured, his horse had startled for no cause she or anyone else determined. Spooked, it reared and bucked like an enraged bull, and when it threw him, the crack of his shattering femur resounded through the forest, along with his scream. And a heartbeat later, Ella's.

She had stared at the blood pooling where fractured bone jutted through torn breeches, noticing the detached elation that followed.

Her father had looked at her, squeezed her hand until she was numb, until his features softened, woozy, treasured warmth passing between them.

Oh gods. She had used her magic on him.

She shoved the memory away.

'What is it?' She had forgotten that Vorlyn couldn't see into her mind to learn what reveries played behind Ella's eyes.

'I was there when Father's steed threw him off,' she said. 'The medics set the bone, but he never fully recovered.' A chill crept the length of Ella's spine. The break had healed, but Rohan's fear festered, along with a gash to his foot no herbalist could treat. And as time passed, the wound ulcerated, forming a blackened crust that the chirurgeons had to slice away.

Rohan had raged when his proud gait turned lame. He refused to rely on a staff to walk where anyone might see, insisting his servants carry him on a litter, his festering leg hidden beneath his sapphire-encrusted cloak.

Before his fall, Ella had often sneaked into his study to show him her dolls. He would set aside his ledgers and scrolls, delighting in her captivating imagination.

After almost falling to his death, his demeanour changed. Having realised he was not invincible or immortal, whenever she peered around his door, Ella found him praying to Elnora.

Mother had rarely visited. Perhaps she already acted as regent. Those memories were hazy. But her older siblings attended upon him, though his eyes never brightened for them as they had for her. To them, he was curt. Gruff. Distant.

'You shouldn't play-act with your sisters and nursemaid,' he'd scolded Gohran. 'With dolls. People will assume you're a witch.'

She had squeezed Gon's hand against their father's crushing condemnation.

Then came the day when Rohan sent Gohran to the temple. 'Your Holiness,' he'd said to his newly appointed priest. 'Watch over my son. He needs guidance if Our Lady is to save his tainted soul.'

Another gasp. Rohan had put Gohran in Davith's path. Encouraged him to worship Elnora, to prove himself worthy.

To avert suspicion.

Did their father realise what Gohran was? Or her?

What about his wife?

She was supposed to be attuning to Vorlyn, but the mention of Erldan's priest had hijacked her thoughts.

She wrenched her attention back. 'My apologies, I...'

'Let your mind wander where it needs.' Vorlyn squeezed Ella's hand. 'This is for your healing.'

Ella had adored her father, but he was not a good man. Not to her siblings or her mother. She'd not seen it before.

Rohan had carried his whims like a halberd at their throats. The slightest displeasure ravaged and sliced.

Because he'd been gentle with her, she never recognised what his demeanour did to her family. Queen Prya had always seemed ruthless and cold, even when she acted kind. But she was shielding. Surviving. As Ella was forced to.

She pulled her attention back to Vorlyn once more. Steadied her voice. 'What was Davith doing with you?'

Another wry twist. 'He pursued the very thing that eludes you.'

'Your immunity,' she whispered. Of course. Davith wanted to protect himself from magic's influence. In the service of a witch queen's family, he sought to render mages as powerless as he.

A further scene played, though Ella wasn't sure Vorlyn meant for her to see. She hugged her cushion to her chest and squeezed, as she pictured a babe wailing inside a pannier. A wail that shattered Vorlyn's heart in a manner Ella recognised all too well.

When they captured Vorlyn, they abandoned her infant because it wasn't immune like its mother.

Horrified realisation struck. *Davith wanted Vorlyn because he hoped to breed immune servants.*

'May I ask something?'

'Of course.'

But Ella's words stuck in her throat.

'I promise, Ella. It's fine. Ask your question.' She set the cushion in her lap.

Ella swallowed. 'I wondered if... If there were others. Like you, I mean. Were you the first that Davith...?' her voice trailed. 'How did he know?'

Vorlyn's eyes turned cold, hard. 'There were,' she said, her fist strangling the cushion's padded corner. 'Before and after. And he knew, because prior to serving your father, he served Nedran.'

Ella sucked in her breath.

'He couldn't gain a stronghold, however. Nedran's overlord refused to appoint a head priest to enforce—or even endorse—any cult. That's when he set his sights on Erldan.' She picked a loose thread and tore it free. 'But women frequently went missing from the surrounding woods. Supposedly abducted by bandits, but too often, the women were presumed witches. The Lord of Nedran would not abide sectarian persecution, but many suspects disappeared—myself among them.'

'You were suspected of witchcraft?'

'Not exactly. My capture served a myriad of purposes. Political and religious, and eventually, experimental. Davith sought to learn all he could about sorcery and how to defend against it. Imprisoned alongside me was another with magic. When he chose not to torture her by touch, for fear of the Curse, he used me to get to her. Though she could not influence me, nor I her, I could not shield her from my suffering when they tried to break and then breed from me.'

Ella feared to ask if they succeeded.

'I am certain his quest did not end when I escaped.'

Was that why Davith had captured Amber?

Ella had not experienced an omen since her nightmare, but this notion resounded in her mind like a singing bowl. A truth, then. When Amber had gone to fetch her dowry from her brother, she had ended up in Davith's clutches—with or without Gohran's knowledge. She hoped without.

Had Davith experimented on her? Tortured her? Is that what Ella had witnessed through the fire when she camped between Aryon and Erldan?

She shoved the notion aside.

Vorlyn had been one of Davith's successive victims. Ella studied her green-grey eyes, her curved lips, her arched brow. And when she looked up, Ella imagined it was Lynden staring back. The pannier she'd left behind... That's why she appeared naggingly familiar. Vorlyn reminded her of Lynden. Abducted, not killed.

Yet, she referred to Nedran's overlord by formal title.

It could be coincidence. Regional characteristics were common. Many villagers surrounding Erldan and the southern provinces resembled her father and sisters, and no one accused Rohan of siring them all.

Ella's cropped locks were growing out. Soon she could not hide her midnight hair and midday eyes. Attributes she shared not only with her mother, brother, and aunt, but with a quarter of Aeron's inhabitants. The irony did not escape her, that the famous Erldan royal line's unique colouring did not descend from the High King, but the Ancients. Had Erldan's priests ever visited Aeron, they might have recognised their heresy. Ancient characteristics that bore Ancient magic.

An Ancient rule Davith sought to infiltrate and vanquish.

Something in Vorlyn's demeanour prevented Ella from voicing her suspicions. After all, Yorg had said she forbade him from calling her Lyn. If Ella's hunch was correct, perhaps it distressed her to be reminded. But studying the wry twist to her mentor's mouth, the inkling that Vorlyn of Aeron and Lynette of Nedran were one and the same haunted.

Thirty-Three

Amber took advantage of the commotion to shuttle her prisoner back to the tavern. With her elbow hooked through his, she willed him inside and they sat near the hearth. His long sleeves obscured his bound wrists, though their odd posture earned them curious glances. She would worry about unwanted attention once she replenished her power.

With her free arm, she motioned to a lass who served watery stew and a hunk of grain-filled bread. She devoured the meal, and soaked up the fire's warmth, until its flames dimmed and flickered. Beside her, the neophyte dozed.

The lass cleared Amber's empty bowl. 'Ale?' She looked the neophyte up and down, and Amber heard her thinking he'd already drunk plenty. Aloud, she said, 'Is the hearing over?'

Amber captured her gaze, and with a rush of renewed energy, directed her nosiness elsewhere.

'Upstairs,' she hissed to the neophyte.

'Grogan,' he croaked. 'My name is Grogan.'

'I don't give a demon's sweaty ballocks what you're called.' She imagined wrenching his innards with her bare hands.

He winced and let her shuffle him up to her room.

She pushed him onto the bed. 'When is the Cleansing?'

'You think I'll help you?'

Another searing glance, and she pictured yanking and castrating his privates with a dagger until he squealed like a pig. 'I can make you...'

'Never, witch!' But she sensed his whimper.

She searched for somewhere to secure him, but the room barely extended beyond the wooden bedframe. Amber and Nykki had stuffed their supplies beneath: a bedroll, blankets, preserved vegetables, and now-stale flatbread, wrapped in a canvas sheet: all Shira spared before they left, scavenged from refugees and Aryon's stores.

Pain pierced her. *Nykki!*

Her focus adrift, she sensed her beloved, but saw only darkness. Bound and hooded, as she had been. *Hold tight, my love. I am coming for you.*

She yanked the neophyte's greasy hair, forcing his gaze to meet hers. If he would not help her, she would raid his mind like a bandit.

Nykki couldn't understand how it had happened. She hadn't sensed the guard sneak up behind her. Usually, she was aware of surrounding minds, even ones she could not see. He'd clapped her mouth shut, grasped her hands and bound them before she reacted, before she could scream.

Though her power churned, he might have been a leaking vessel. None of her gifts held any force. She'd launched her distress toward Amber like a beacon, but by the time her beloved emerged from behind the temple, the priests were already carrying her away.

Normally she would have detected something amiss, but unease had surrounded her since they made this foolhardy plan, and so she had noticed no portents.

Why hadn't Amber fled with her? Together they might have evaded the robes and their henads and travelled far from here. Lived as many days as the gods allowed in peace.

The Curse brings horror thrice over. That's what the priestesses taught. Is that what this was? Was she being Cursed?

Freyda, the feisty woman the priests had already condemned, raged beside her, while the devout one, whose name she didn't care to learn, prayed.

'I hope they burn you and your demon-spawn accomplice,' she spat.

Quiet! Nykki needed to think. She hadn't the strength to break her bindings, not without Amber to amplify and focus her gift.

Eventually, the wagon halted, and rough hands grappled the women out of the cage. The guard's impenetrable gaze met hers.

'Here—take this,' said his companion, and he covered her with a hood, so that even had her magic affected him, he'd cut off her access to use it.

She reached for Amber and felt her waves of anger seethe between spikes of distress. She clung to the unique pattern of her psyche, and let it circle and soothe. Amber would come for her, she was certain.

The guards shunted the prisoners. Blinded, she listened and waited.

Around her, implements shuffled and clanged. She sensed a few minds: her fellow captives, and at least one guard whose mind she could penetrate.

Heat pumped from a fire, and she sucked on its power to remain steady. What sounded like a poker being lifted from a rack sifted through burning coals, stoking the flames. Her magic must be drawing them lower.

More poking and prodding.

Something wasn't right. Her heartbeat lurched and her breath hastened.

Metal ground through ash and coals, and a crawling dread seeped through her skin and along her limbs, boring into her soul.

A loud, prolonged sizzle accompanied the stench of charred flesh, and an agonising, unrelenting scream.

Her heart thrummed, and she thought it might burst through her chest as she writhed against her bindings and bit down on her gag, her breath so short she struggled for air.

She knew. Before they removed her hood, she had seen.

Atop the fire sat an iron poker. Attached to one end, someone had fashioned a symbol: a ring surrounding a diagonal cross. An X. The mark of Xenon. Buried in the smouldering coals, it glowed a fiery vermillion.

By all the gods and every demon, they were going to brand her.

Smoke and charcoal filled Amber's nostrils, accompanied by the acrid stench of burning meat. Flames danced, and the world tilted.

The scream that tore through her mind was disabling. Time ceased. In the agonising moments that followed, she was deaf and blind.

She was pure pain.

The ground beneath might have cracked and swallowed her, and she stumbled.

Beside her, Grogan cried out, his face and body contorting as he struggled to block the sensations she had channelled reflexively.

Finally, Nykki's wail ebbed to a dull whimper. But it was no relief. They had broken her.

Thirty-Four

'Why did this freezing panic only begin after I arrived here?' Ella asked.

Vorlyn's hazel eyes darkened. 'Like you, I didn't exhibit symptoms until I felt safe again.'

Ella had spent many afternoons with Vorlyn, practising exchanging thoughts and touch, remaining grounded, then separating from her body, which she termed 'travelling'.

Was that true? Did she finally feel secure? Protected? She knew only that she wanted to heal, and that meant learning to trust—them and her. So, when Vorlyn co-opted Mayel's help with the exercises, she complied.

Jurn, who shared Ella's colouring—the same as her brother—also offered, but Vorlyn suggested that might be more challenging. 'For now, it's best to work with no one resembling individuals from your past.'

Though his skin was paler, almost translucent, his familiarity and his sex quickened her breath and tensed her muscles. Vorlyn was right. Mayel was a better candidate.

She directed Ella and Mayel to face each other, cross-legged on a pair of cushions before a covered brazier in one of the more secluded recreation rooms. At first, they sat apart, edging closer with each session, until their hearts met, and their legs entwined.

'Seek permission,' Vorlyn instructed, 'to give and receive without expectation or demand for anything beyond curiosity and acceptance.'

Opposite, Mayel's glorious smile and vibrant amiability captivated with no need for beguilement or magical influence.

Her throat dry, Ella swallowed. This deliberate touch seemed transactional, even mercenary.

'I want you to,' Mayel coaxed, and Ella pushed herself to explore, reaching a tentative hand to lips she longed to kiss, meeting eyes she could lose herself in. Mayel waited before her, patient, beautiful, and she imagined caressing her graceful limbs, sliding hands along her thighs...

Her beguilement stirred, an awakening beast, and she inhaled, smothered her magic, and shielded.

'Relax, Ella. There is no danger here. Mayel is learning to protect herself from you as much as you are guarding from her.'

But what if Mayel couldn't, and Vorlyn didn't intervene in time?

These exercises were not about pleasure or lust. She sought nothing except a shared and healing experience, curtailing each stroke to the inside of a forearm, a cheek, a palm, knowing Mayel's gentle soul would never hurt her. But she could not be certain her magic wouldn't bring Mayel harm.

'Let us continue tomorrow,' Vorlyn said, and Ella withdrew with relief.

Yorg appeared wordlessly at the room's threshold, as he did after each session. He approached, focus adrift, and captured Ella's gaze as he viewed her aura using god-sight. With a sage nod, he released her. 'Your scar appears less aggravated today.'

Initially, it had worsened, and Ella feared she would never be fixed.

'It is the natural progression,' he assured. 'Like a scab forming, or a bruise darkening in the early stages of healing.'

Yet each time he examined, she braced, certain he monitored for signs of the Curse—and afraid he would find them.

'Come help me prepare supper,' Vorlyn said, her familiar hazel eyes disarming. Ella followed her out, grateful for the distraction.

Within the sparse kitchen, Ella chopped vegetables onto a wooden board, while Vorlyn skinned a freshly killed rabbit over a copper pot, pushing her grey-streaked hair from her face.

The pooling blood formed a siren song that thrummed from limb to core, settling as a steady heat in her loins. In its wake, memories of experiencing her thrilling—and terrifying—beguilement edged and shoved closer to the surface. She reached further through time, for recollections that predated her brother's shaming of her, from before she wounded Venn, to when she'd first discovered a yearning fleshy ache that lived apart from her magic.

Another surge of force, and through half-closed eyes, she settled on Jonas's image, and the passion he'd awakened. Back then, danger had fuelled her excitement, her anticipation. Now, the memory of his hot breath and daring touch ignited a deep throb that radiated from the apex between her thighs and tingled outwards.

She blamed all the power surging around her, using her magic, the exercises with Mayel... Everything converged as a swelling need within her body for pleasure and release.

Once, she would have slipped to her room and ridden that wave to completion, but she was cognisant of Vorlyn's patient presence. Instead, she ripped her attention back to chopping vegetables, and willed her crimson blush to fade, grateful Vorlyn did not live inside her head like the others.

'Sometimes, a change of environment helps us recover during this work,' Vorlyn said once they'd set the stew to simmer. 'Shall we venture outdoors?'

No doubt Vorlyn was right. She missed Elnora's rays on her skin and breathing air free from dirt and moss.

They left their dishes to soak, pulled on their outdoor hats and cloaks, and headed through the winding corridors to the widened communal space, then outside via the main ivy-covered entrance.

'Remember to shield,' Vorlyn said as they stepped over the threshold and into the dazzling light. Ella squinted, protecting her sight as much as her mind. She fingered the bleached ends of her cropped hair, poking beneath the woollen cap that concealed the darker roots regrowing around her scalp.

The snow seemed to have eased already, giving way to crusted ice that crunched underfoot as they weaved between barren branches.

They hadn't got far when a gnawing unease crept under Ella's shield, along her spine, and settled into her belly. Apprehension gripped her, as billowing smoke and roaring flames rushed her vision and pressure throbbed behind her eyes.

She winced and faltered.

'What is it?' Vorlyn asked.

'I—I'm not sure. Maybe nothing.'

'It's never nothing.'

Whatever it was, it penetrated her shield, but wasn't Xarion, or her brother.

In the distance, a collection of small huts peeked out from the forest canopy—the settlement where Thymm lived.

Another stab.

'Let's get you back,' Vorlyn said.

'Not yet.' She halted. 'It's like something wants—no, *needs*—me to know.'

'To know what, Ella?'

'I—I'm not sure...' She scrunched her eyes shut. The knowledge beckoned yet slipped away—a revelation over a horizon she could never reach.

Fire flashed, followed by scorching heat. Smoke. And screams—screams of burning agony.

She spluttered and coughed. 'I need to let down my shield.'

Vorlyn took her by the elbows. 'Are you certain?'

She nodded. 'What about the glass sphere?'

Vorlyn shook her head. 'That won't help you receive an omen.'

Ella swallowed. What if Gohran sensed her?

The pounding intensified, like a thousand screams inside her mind.

'If it's too much, we can go back to Aeron,' Vorlyn offered.

'There is something the god wants me to learn...' Ella's nightmare had broken through Aeron's protection. This portent would be no different. She would have no peace if she ignored it.

She braced, reminding herself that Gohran could not reach her before the spring, and lowered her shield...

A wave of sorrow engulfed her. It clawed and swallowed, tugging her down. She dropped to her knees and howled.

She was back in Erldan's glade, making daisy chains, Gohran twirling her around with her doll squished between them. Witch.

On the next breath, Gohran was denouncing their mother, sending her to Nedran, putting her in the path of hope, before snatching it away...

Another inhale, and Jonas was robbing her future, letting her believe Venn didn't care, that her brother would deny them.

Like water topping a dam, it wracked through her body, and she sobbed, uncontained.

With the next shift, she was wooing Gohran to befriend her again, to salvage her fate. And afterwards...

All she had lost, everything she had left behind and destroyed, was crashing debris over her. What she'd done to Venn, to Lynden, to Thyss and Mara and everyone in that village. Her beguilement and Curse. Her needy, greedy babe, who she wanted to love but could not endure. Who she abandoned. Gohran's daughter.

The portent did not feel like her loss, her pain. And yet, it chiselled into a grief she'd never processed, never owned, as it flashed her bodily to her past.

Eventually, the wave subsided, and she whispered, 'Gohran killed them. Tried to burn them all...'

Another flash. In his wake, the Cleansings continued to sweep Ycelt's people in a vortex of terror.

Everything intertwined. Leading back to that day in the glade.

Her surroundings came into focus. Thyss and Mara's son's settlement loomed. 'Thymm's parents are dead,' she said, as the knowledge seized her. So were most of their neighbours. She'd fled Erldan's outskirts to save its inhabitants, and Gohran burned them anyway.

Flames rose again behind her eyes, beyond Thyss and Mara's village... Throughout Ycelt...

Vorlyn waited for whatever was happening within Ella to complete, for her vision to subside and her grief to run its course. Then she scooped Ella into her arms and let her weep gentle, exhausted tears.

'I should tell Thyss and Mara's son, I should—'

'Hush, Ella, hush.'

'But—'

'If you front up to a stranger and claim a god revealed his parents are dead, you might as well climb onto a henad's stake and light the fire yourself. The news will have to wait. We'll make sure the report reaches him with the melting snows.'

Ella sobbed against her chest.

She knew the omen held a further message. The images reflected past events, yet she experienced a portent of her future, or perhaps something happening in the present that she could not see. Was it tied to her dream of Xarion? She had surrendered her daughter to Aryon to protect her from the flames that etched themselves into her soul, but was she still at risk?

'It's more than that... It's—henads—they're burning. Vorlyn, they're still burning!'

'Who, Ella?'

Ella's vision faded, indistinct, along with a wave of helplessness, knowing her loved ones were in peril, and there was nothing she could do.

The Curse brings horror thrice over. Yorg said she was not Cursed, but had she evoked the Curse, nonetheless? If Aeron's vast library didn't contain the answer, where would she locate it? If she was to deter whatever horror she had inadvertently unleashed, she needed to find out.

Thirty-Five

Nykki drifted in and out of consciousness. Was this real? Was she still alive? Her shoulders and hips ached from being propped and bound to a diagonal wooden cross.

Why hadn't Amber come for her?

Staked to her right, the loathsome, pious woman howled, 'Burn them, not me!'

To her left, Freyda sobbed and wailed as the priests tied her to another X.

The scattered clouds surrounding Elnora's sinking light blazed like the embers that had branded her face.

Amber wasn't coming for her.

She was about to die among these strangers. Before a mob who despised and feared her. Unable to cry or shout or fight.

She wasn't there. She was floating in a dream.

And she felt nothing at all.

The cage where the priests had housed their prisoners stood empty.

'You lied,' Amber spat.

A cold, gruesome grin spread across Grogan's features. They had crossed town with little quarrel, and he had sneaked them past a surprising dearth of guards, but now Amber understood why. Usually, Elnora's priests tried heretics when Elnora was at her peak, and burned them beneath Xenon's light—an affront to his dominion. But they must have moved Nykki's Cleansing forward.

'Where are they?' she shrieked.

Grogan's sneer widened as he delighted in her anguish. Leaving her mind open rendered her vulnerable, but she needed to locate Nykki.

Her focus drifted. Where had they taken her? She didn't sense her. Oh, gods. Amber couldn't find her!

'Where do they Cleanse them?' she hissed.

Another sneer.

'Where?' She grasped his wrists and imagined wrenching his tongue from his throat. He sputtered and coughed, and she released him.

'In the field behind the temple, witch,' he croaked.

'Come.' She wrenched him along beside her.

Nykki's simulacrum had never travelled apart from her body before. She had not thought it possible. But when the torture became too great, for a time, the god showed mercy and permitted her escape.

She hovered beyond her physical form: a child again, watching flames consume her mother and brother. Back then, eager spectators cheered the blaze on, relishing their screams.

At that moment, seeing herself staked alongside two other women, the surrounding field stood eerily quiet. She heard only the roar and spark of fire enveloping the anguished cries of its victims. The people of Harnal did not hunger to watch those they condemned burn.

Hovering outside her body, there were no sensations. No pain. Merely the knowledge that she was alone.

Smoke filled her nostrils, careening her simulacrum to reunite with her flesh. Intense agony near swallowed her.

Haze billowed. She coughed and choked, blinking the stinging tears away.

And then she sensed her. Amber. Amber was coming.

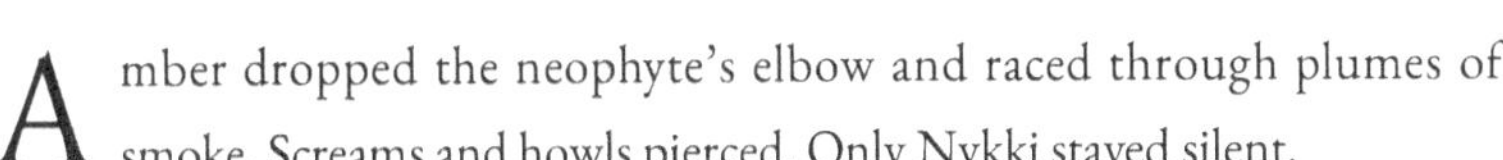

Amber dropped the neophyte's elbow and raced through plumes of smoke. Screams and howls pierced. Only Nykki stayed silent.

The women spied her. 'Please! Please, help us!'

Flames rose between her and them, and she had no water or sand, nor wool with which to smother.

Behind her, the neophyte wriggled, entangled in his robe and unable to stand. *His woollen robe.*

Amber sped to where she'd left him and summoned her force until he lay flaccid at her feet. She peeled his vestment from his pasty, pudgy body, but the sleeves caught on his bindings. She swore.

Nykki, help me. She reached through Nykki's pain. *Use the fire and focus. Draw all you can and find me...*

Nykki roused, and their minds brushed, but only for a heartbeat, before her beloved slipped away.

Please, my love. Please...

She worked to untie the ropes. Each time Grogan struggled, he'd forced her knots tighter.

She needed that robe. *Nykki!* But she couldn't reach her.

I'm going to create a haven for you... For us.... If Nykki remained conscious, Amber might access and direct her power. She summoned memories of their limbs entwined, lips merged, as the rest of the world receded. The two of them, sharing their deep, intimate connection.

It wasn't enough. Nykki's mind slipped into its detached cocoon.

When Amber had fled from Erldan's dungeon, she'd constructed a soothing chamber for gold-eyed Chrysanth, to protect her from her pain.

Which she'd created using blood.

Grogan's pudgy belly glowed orange against the fire's light, and his sinewy, hairless limbs sprawled across the grass.

Might she draw his lifeforce?

She splayed his bare forearm over her lap. His blue veins darkened to purple and then bright crimson beneath the pyre. Her god-sight hungered. A gnawing ache. She dragged her thumbnail to bite into his flesh. But his skin resisted. Refused her penetration.

His blood throbbed and pulsed, merging with the women's screams inside her mind. Her mouth watered, and she brought his wrist to her lips and bared her teeth. Pressure built until she found a weak point. A vulnerability. She pierced.

Liquid burst and flowed over her lips, her teeth, her tongue. She spat, and swiped the copper tang from her mouth, then sucked the magnetism from his lifeforce to summon Nykki back.

Their minds connected with the sweetest sensation of her existence.

Use the fire, Nykki. Draw its heat and help me.

A tingle rushed from the tail of her spine, through her torso, and out through her limbs. Energy erupted through her fingers and snapped the rope like a dried twig.

Heart pounding, she tugged the vestment free and ran.

When she reached the base of Nykki's dais, its flames roared, drowning them in smoke. She pounded the woollen garment against the inferno, slamming it down, over and again. The pyre flared between each beat, fighting to remain alive.

Keep drawing. Drive the fire lower!

Ash stung her eyes and burnt her throat. She coughed and spluttered, pounding on the robe, stomping it down to suffocate the blaze.

Suck more power...

Nykki stirred, and her neck lolled. Sweat sheened her forehead and cheek. The flames were shrinking, but she was drifting away...

Amber called her again, and her head rolled the other way, answering.

That's when Amber saw it. The angry, welted X seared into the left half of Nykki's face. For a moment, she couldn't breathe.

Why? Why brand their victims? Wasn't it enough to cage and shackle them, force them to endure these farcical trials, and burn them alive? Did that not satisfy their brutal hearts? Was their goddess so ravenous for cruelty?

A fire ignited in her soul to rival the inferno before her, but it was a cold, savage blaze.

She drew more power until the pyre lowered sufficiently for her to lay the neophyte's robe down and climb to her beloved. The dimmed flames licked up and around the fabric but could not touch her.

Finally, she reached Nykki and a sob caught in her throat. With a slow exhale, she directed her beloved's mind to snap the ropes that tied her to the cross. Legs first, then one hand, then the other.

Nykki collapsed into her arms, weighty and solid, and she clasped her with desperation and hunger. Clinging to each other, they stumbled out of the fire's grasp, but their fight wasn't over. Two women remained staked, and their pyres continued to roar.

She left Nykki to recover, retrieved the vestment, and pounded the blaze of another dais.

She willed Nykki to keep drawing. The flames before her flickered and dimmed, but not enough. Fire ravaged the staked women's clothes, their hair, their skin, accelerating faster than she and Nykki could draw. Already sated from Grogan's blood, Amber couldn't channel the excess, while Nykki struggled to focus and soothe herself. Even if they freed the women from those stakes now, and they survived, their residual burns would torture.

Exhausted tears streamed down Amber's cheeks. With a jagged breath, she channelled all she could, rendering the remaining victims unconscious. If they were going to die, let it be painless, at least for a while.

Behind them, Grogan stirred. His eyes widened as he took in the surrounding scene. He gasped and staggered to his feet. 'Help! The witches have escaped!'

Stop him! Amber sent her shriek to Nykki's mind, but her beloved froze.

Grogan backed away, beyond her grasp. There was no time to recapture him. If they stayed to hunt him, they would become hunted. If they lingered to rescue the other women, they would all die.

She helped Nykki stand. 'Run!' she shouted. 'Nykki, run!'

PART THREE: ESCALATION

The Kingdom of Erldan, Ycelt

Spring, 797 A.S.

Thirty-Six

Gohran trained his focus on an underfed deer who was foolish enough to wander into a clearing between the budding trees of his preserve. He nocked his arrow, squinted, and, ignoring the sweat beading his forehead, loosed it.

The arrow zinged past the beast and thudded into the wood.

He swore.

'Beans and tubers for supper again,' young Ganno groaned.

'You might have to sleep in the stables, Gan!' said the much older Tarraen.

'I'm changing cots,' added Farlos, a recent recruit whose darker complexion hinted at Myan heritage.

Gohran's men continued their jibes. 'Settle, lads, before I regret letting you accompany me.' After a while, their mocking and jesting grated.

It was better—safer—than venturing out alone, for standing apart from the other men, his newly appointed steward, Arhys, watched, stiff and staid. Gohran did not trust him one iota. *Davith's spy.*

At least his men did as he asked—as they were told—and kept their mouths shut.

But they were right. There would be no roasted meat again for supper, and he was as tired as they of fasting like peasants.

'Better that one got away, Your Highness,' said Tar. 'It's barely a yearling. Give it a few seasons to spread its seed, and there'll be more prey in the springs that follow.' To the others, he said, 'Learn to stay still *and* quiet, lads, or we'll all be stuck in our barracks until the summer.'

Gohran appreciated the sentiment, but blamed his nerves. Ordinarily, a battle could rage around him, and he would have homed that arrow straight through the stag's heart. He only found peace in his chamber by night, and even then, Davith's guards hovered on the other side of his barred door.

The snows had retreated, but the wildlife was shy to emerge, and Gohran refused to waste effort chasing them. He signalled for his men to gather up and ride back.

Near the castle keep, they dismounted, and Gohran tossed his reins to Ganno and the others. With Arhys and Tarraen trailing, he trudged along the cobblestones, wishing they would leave him, too.

From the direction of the market stalls, a rabble milled. They spotted him, shouting and pointing. Mostly vendors, judging by their embroidered tunics.

A merchant's guard he recognised waved. 'Your Highness! They turned our wagons away again.'

'They?'

He confronted Arhys. 'Again?'

The steward gave a sage nod. 'Nedran's men are stopping every cart and carriage to search for the dryhten's younger brother, Your Highness.'

'You were supposed to take care of that,' he growled.

'They're doing more than searching, Your Highness. Nothing originating from Erldan is getting through,' Tar said, keeping his voice low.

Not low enough—the merchant's guard must have heard him. 'How are we to exchange our goods if we can't get them out, Your Highness?'

Gohran swore.

The winter had been tough, and Gohran was relying on the spring trade to replenish supplies. Even routing goods via Harnal, Nedran controlled the Gythyn north of Rassit, while Herron regulated passage to the east, isolating them.

He cursed Venn. Though neither side had raised a sword, they were at war just the same.

Beneath his breath, voice slipping like a knife's edge, he addressed Arhys. 'Get this sorted.'

J aydyn pushed her spiced venison—cured and dried from the previous sea-son—and pureed tubers around her plate to make patterns in the watery gravy, wondering how Raeyn fared with her wealthy new husband in Nedran.

'Are you not hungry, Your Highness?' one of the few remaining ladies-in-waiting asked. Most had returned to their families. Maintaining an army was Gohran's priority, not occupying the womenfolk.

She hadn't bothered presenting to the dining hall. Her brother would be plotting with Davith or drilling his men, and the long table's oppressive silence carried haunting echoes of her family's absence. Instead, the servants brought her meal to the women's quarters. Next door, Lyrra settled and fed Serrah in the nursery, giving her a few moments of respite.

Serrah tended to be at her most unwieldy from twilight until dusk. That day, she'd been fussier than usual, her distress threatening a furious crescendo. Jaydyn pushed her dish aside and went to relieve poor Lyrra.

She picked Serrah up, despite her flailing protest. 'Hush, my love.' Ordinarily, the more Serrah writhed and squirmed, the closer Jaydyn held her until she settled. But on this occasion, Jaydyn could not console her.

'Why don't I take her for a stroll, Your Highness?' Lyrra asked.

'Let's all go.' Jaydyn felt as restless as her daughter.

When they entered the grounds outside the castle, peasants, merchants, and nobles milled, gathering on the cobbled streets, some beside covered wagons, others herding poultry and livestock, as if the city were under siege. What, by every demon, was going on?

'It looks like the guards have shut the external gates,' Lyrra said. The closure meant many couldn't return to their homes following the day's market, leaving those outside clamouring to get in, and those inside anxious to get out, for even with her brother's recent fortifications, Erldan's walls were too small to house all its people.

A crowd had gathered around the portcullis, waving torches and shouting. Erldan's riders paced the walls, urging the dissenters home.

She glanced at Lyrra. 'More protests? What for, now?'

Warm and heavy in one arm, Serrah wriggled against her hip. With the other, Jaydyn brushed the copper tendrils from her damp nape and hitched up her skirt to step over a pair of sleeping dogs, trying to find a path through the crowd to the western glade where they could walk. 'Let me pass!' Her nose wrinkled, wishing for a third hand to hold her pomander.

'Make way for Her Highness!' Lyrra called.

A grey-haired woman with a gap-toothed grin hunched over to herd her hens out of the way.

'My thanks,' Lyrra mouthed to the woman.

Jaydyn placed her daughter down to stretch her back, trying to see what was up ahead.

The protestors had dressed a stake in a black wig and sapphire-blue cloak. Someone set the effigy alight, and flames roared along the wood until the hair and fabric smouldered. She shuddered and reached to collect Serrah, but she was gone. Her throat tightened.

'Sess? Sess! Where did you go?' Gods, where was she? The crowd pressed in, blocking her view with a wall of brown and grey. 'Sess!' Her heart plummeted, ears ringing as her vision narrowed. 'Someone has taken my daughter! Find her!'

Stinking torsos closed in. She couldn't breathe.

A faint wail. 'Mama!'

She froze, listening, willing the rowdy mob to quiet.

'Mama!' A sob, followed by a horrid hacking cough.

Oh gods. What had they done to her? 'Serrah!'

'Your Highness,' a woman appeared beside her. 'Your princess is just here.'

Jaydyn seized her daughter. Tears coursed down her cheeks, and she gulped for air. She had never clasped Serrah so tightly.

'Ow!' Serrah squirmed and whimpered.

Her forehead was hot. She was burning up! Yet her skin was so pale. 'Darling…'

Serrah's tiny shoulders quivered before she heaved all over Jaydyn's dress. Had she eaten their rotten food? 'What did you feed her?' Jaydyn screeched.

'Anything she ate, she stole, Your Highness.'

'Like your family steals everything else,' the man beside her muttered into his beard.

'What did you say?' She swung around.

Serrah wailed. She needed her away from here. 'Lyrra, take her.'

Lyrra held out her arms and Serrah snuggled into her chest, smearing snot across her pinafore. 'I've got you, my little dearling. Let's get inside...'

Jaydyn glared at the peasants, studying their indifferent faces. If any of them had harmed her daughter...

'Your Highness,' her brother's rider appeared at her shoulder. 'The king demands you and your womenfolk head within the keep at once.'

'You can tell him we're already on our way. We have no desire to be among all of this.' She snatched up her skirts, pivoted, and stomped home, her gaze fastened ahead, ignoring the peasants' stalking eyes.

Safely inside, with the doors barred behind them, they hurried upstairs to Jaydyn's private chambers.

She peeled Serrah from Lyrra and clutched her to her chest, sank onto her bed, and sobbed. Between juddering gasps, she struggled for air. She'd almost lost Sess in that crowd. What if someone had taken her? The resentment and disdain in those peasants' eyes! As though she didn't suffer alongside them. As though she were as much to blame as her brother.

She rued the day he denounced their mother. He soured everything he touched. What did it matter if the dryhten's brother insulted him? He'd doubtless deserved the slight and more! Now Lord Venn was threatening him and Erldan was on the cusp of war.

'Why let it come to this?' she blurted. One sister lost to the Afterworld, and the other to become an enemy. Did he think for a heartbeat of a single soul beyond his own? 'He can be so like Father. Stubborn, obstinate fool!'

Lyrra glanced around. 'Hush, Your Highness. You should not speak so.'

'What does it matter? Out there, in here, we're all tired and afraid, and for what?'

'The people will grow weary of their remonstrations, Your Highness. Now spring is here, they'll have more to distract them.'

Serah snivelled and whined, then heaved again.

'Let us hope that's purged whatever filthy food she took from the peasants outside.'

'She was sick earlier, too, the poor dearling.' Lyrra hurried to fetch clean rags and a bucket.

'And you didn't tell me?'

'Toddling children often purge and it's of no consequence.' Lyrra frowned at Jaydyn's dress. 'Let me take that off to launder, and I'll fetch a medic.'

Jaydyn scoffed. 'You imagine my brother will spare the coin?' She set her daughter down and turned so Lyrra could help her undress.

'What about Ellyn?' Lyrra said, tugging at her laces. Ellyn was one of the few remaining chambermaids. 'She studied herb craft before taking up her post here. All the servants go to her.'

The same crone who tended to the common folk was now to care for her daughter. Is this where Gohran's stubbornness steered them?

'Ma...' Serrah grizzled.

Jaydyn stepped free of her overdress and picked Serrah back up. Her flesh scalded, yet she trembled as if from the cold. What choice did Jaydyn have?

'Send for her.'

She sank onto her bed, with Serrah close to her chest. She didn't want to let her go. As her whimpers dwindled into the even snuffles of sleep, she brushed Serrah's ringlets from her clammy forehead.

Sometime later, Lyrra woke her to announce Ellyn's arrival. She reluctantly made room for the maid to examine her on the bed.

Fretful, Ellyn shook her head. 'See this rash?' She lifted Serrah's nightdress to reveal tiny red blisters covering her belly and chest. 'If a fever has taken hold, Your Highness, your daughter's fate lies with the goddess.'

Another grizzle, and Serrah vomited again.

Ellyn screwed her nose and stepped back.

'I'll clean her at once, Your Highness,' Lyrra curtsied, hurrying to fetch more rags and a fresh bucket.

Ellyn glanced towards the door. 'You should sequester her in case it is a contagion.' She leaned close. 'And you'd do better to save her rations for folk who'll keep them down.'

It took all Jaydyn's resolve not to slap her. 'That's it? That's all you offer?'

'The gods choose whose fate to favour, Your Highness. Were the city gates not slammed shut without notice, I could procure willow bark to help break her fever...' She handed Jaydn a strange charm and curtsied. 'An offering to whichever deity you honour. Sometimes the old ways are all we have.' She hurried out before Jaydyn could chastise her further.

She rubbed the charm's pale, smooth surface. In Ancient times, when a child died, a mother would salvage the bones to ward off whatever took the child's life. The babe the bone belonged to must have perished from a fever. Perhaps the same malady that killed her sister.

She shook the morbid thought aside. Childhood fevers were common. This would surely pass. But if it didn't, and the city remained shuttered for the spring, with a feverous contagion trapped inside...

'Hush, my love.' She kissed Serrah's forehead. 'All will be well.'

This was no siege. Not yet. But Nedran's blockade had halted trade and isolated Erldan, with no recourse but to declare outright war, which her brother was loath to do.

With Nedran's treaty teetering, Erldan needed other allies.

Serrah looked so pale.

Might she contemplate a betrothal to putrid-breathed Kerr after all, if it offered her and Serrah an escape from this demon's den? Or might her brother set his prejudices aside and make his own match? It was time Gohran considered someone other than himself.

THIRTY-SEVEN

'How does she fare?' Raeyn asked when Bess arrived in the women's hall without Lynden again.

Bess picked up her workbasket, rummaged for her needle and thread, and spoke in a hushed voice. 'My lady wishes to remain abed, Your Highness.'

Raeyn's other ladies-in-waiting busied themselves to offer some semblance of privacy. Venn had invited her to select her own serving women. She contemplated asking Jaydyn, but that involved approaching her brother, and Venn would never agree, so she made do with Lynden and Bess's suggestions. That Nedran's lady trusted them did not deem them trustworthy, however, so the only person she dared confide in was Bess.

Raeyn sighed. The moon had completed a full cycle since Lynden retreated to her room, sulking. *Grieving*, she reminded herself. She stood and brushed the creases from her skirt. 'I'll check on her.'

'I don't imagine Lady Lynden will welcome—'

Raeyn raised her palm. Lips pursed, head high, she did not care for Bess's reminder that the Lady of Nedran held her no affection. Grieving, sulking. Whatever it was, it must stop.

When she creaked open Lynden's door, with Bess trailing silently, she found her sister-in-law atop her bed, doubled over and moaning. Sweat stuck her honey-brown hair to her drawn forehead and cheeks.

'Fetch a medic,' she ordered.

This wasn't brooding. Lynden whimpered as a fever gripped her. Raeyn wanted to approach and soothe, but dared not get close enough to inhale the foul humours of her miasma.

Bess hesitated. 'Your Highness, what if it was the…?'

Raeyn's scowl silenced her. 'Go, Bess.'

'Yes, Your Highness.' The lady's maid scurried away.

More whimpering, and Lynden threw off her blankets. Her nightdress clung as she writhed and twisted, as though unable to find comfort. Then, shivering, she crawled back beneath her bedding.

Had Raeyn imagined the swelling in the small of Lynden's belly? Her chest tightened.

The window rattled and banged in the blustering wind. Someone had left it ajar. She held her breath, covered her nose with a pomander, and hurried to close it and draw the blinds.

An empty flask stood discarded by the sill. She retrieved it and raised it to the light. Dry remnants crusted its base and sides. What if it was the remains of the tonic Bess had fetched from the apothecary? It must have perched there for weeks. Why had the maids not cleared it? She would have words with the chamberlain.

She shoved it between the folds of her kirtle, glanced once more at Lynden, who had rolled over, secure in her bedding, and closed the door between them with her heart thudding in her throat.

When the medic arrived that afternoon, Raeyn hovered by the entrance to watch him examine Lynden. Bess moved to reopen her blinds, but Raeyn pulled her back. 'What if her fever is infectious?' He could work by lantern light.

Eyes solemn, lips pinched, the physician ran hands along Lynden's limbs, her breasts and belly, before slipping his hand beneath her nightdress.

Bess gasped, and Raeyn clutched her arm to stop her intervening. 'Let him do what we hired him for.'

'But it looks like—'

Raeyn glared the lady's maid into silence. There was no disguising whatever was happening inside Lynden's body now.

Painful moments passed as Bess's breathing laboured beside her.

Eventually, the medic withdrew his hands, wiped them and his instruments on a cloth, and with a resigned exhale, trod over, and ushered her and Bess outside the door.

Eyes shadowed, voice low, he said, 'Several seasons ago, I attended upon the dryhten with a similar affliction—a fever with no sign of contagion. The lord recovered without lingering malady. However, I fear in the lady's case, the goddess may not be so generous.'

'What did you assess to be the cause in my lord husband?'

'Grief, Your Highness.'

Raeyn frowned. Mourning her sister. 'And in the lady?'

'I surmise the child distresses her humours.'

Raeyn steadied her breath as he confirmed her fears. The abortifacient hadn't taken. 'What can be done?'

'The babe weakens the lady's constitution, and she withers.'

Bess baulked. 'My lady has eaten all our cook's hearty meals these past weeks.'

'I intend no insult, Mistress Bessandra, Your Highness. It is not a question of quality. Rather, the child fights its mother for the sustenance available.'

Raeyn clasped her hands over her waist and forced her shoulders back and down.

'It is a rare occurrence, and one for which there is no cure. The mother can consume, but the babe continues to hunger. I shall not lie. I fear for the lady and her unborn child. Summoning a midwife is the best course now...' To bring on the babe, who would surely die.

'Out of the question,' Raeyn snapped. A medic's visit she could attribute to illness, but a midwife's, she could not explain. Even if people assumed it was for her, when a child did not materialise, they would doubt her ability to carry a living heir. After the raven's curse at her wedding, she could brook no further rumours. The medic must suffice.

'Nedran shall provide any medicines you require, but beyond these walls, Lady Lynden suffers from a fever.'

He nodded. Had she imagined the barest twitch to his brow?

'I trust I can rely on your discretion.' She mentally calculated the coin already paid to the charlatan apothecary, and now for the medic's silence.

'Let us pray for Nedran's lady.' The crease between his eyes and pucker to his thin lips told Raeyn he believed prayers necessary.

She turned to Bess. 'No one enters this room. We must isolate the contagion. Do you understand?'

Bess nodded. 'I shall inform the household at once.'

'Lyn...' Venn brushed his sister's sweat-soaked hair from her face and pressed a damp, cool cloth to her forehead. 'Oh, Lyn!'

She opened her eyes and smiled weakly before they fell closed again.

'I didn't realise...' He assumed she was hiding away, worrying about Jonas, nursing her wounded heart over Gohran. He had respected her privacy, focusing on training, trying to bolster their finances, plotting for his brother's return, but most of all, not dwelling on the vulnerable state he'd put them in.

She looked so frail. Like their father during his final days. He shoved the memory down.

'Now spring is here, Jonas will doubtless meander home, as he always does...' A hollow assurance. Without paying the blood price, he could not count on Gohran to retrieve his brother. Instead, he'd ordered his men to search every horse and wagon leaving the king's jurisdiction, but so far, it had only escalated matters.

Lynden struggled to find her voice. She was so pale.

'Hush, Lyn. Save your strength.' He squeezed her hand and leaned to kiss her forehead.

'My lord!' Raeyn burst into the chamber. 'You should not be in here.'

'I won't abandon my sister.'

She drew near and hissed, 'You can't afford to fall ill, my lord, not with your brother exiled—'

'To be pardoned.'

'Yet still missing.' She would not utter her suspicion. What they all feared. They did not know if Jonas lived.

Raeyn was right. It was risky for him to be by his sister's fevered side, but she needed him.

Lyn groaned and threw off her blankets. Her loose nightdress clung to her slick skin and there was no hiding her bulging middle.

'By every...' Venn's voice trailed off.

Raeyn brushed past and pulled the covers back over his sister. He gripped his wife's wrist. 'Don't.'

She tugged free and continued drawing the blanket up and over Lyn's torso. Her eyes accused him of indiscretion. She had not feared him catching a fever, but of discovering—and exposing—his sister's pregnancy.

How had she kept this from him? He forced his voice low. 'Is it Gohran's?'

Raeyn shot him a foul look.

'Forgive me.' Of course it was. His sister had taken no other to her bed. He asked, not from censure, but hope it was otherwise. 'Why did no one inform me? Seek my counsel?'

Raeyn fronted him, defiant. 'It is a woman's matter, my lord.' Not staid, nor compliant, he had not known this side to his wife.

With clenched fists, his breath drew ragged, and his voice emerged as a low growl to rival her brother's. 'She may no longer be the lady of this house, but she is my sister, and that is a royal heir in her womb.'

'Precisely why we kept this from you.'

'We?' Had Lyn been party to this secrecy? This treachery? Why hadn't she trusted him? He choked back the desperation rising in his throat.

Raeyn tugged his elbow, tried to draw him away, but he would not budge. Would not leave Lyn's side.

She perched beside him, keeping her voice lowered, but firm. 'We sought not to trouble his lordship at present. You forget, my lord, I have experience in these matters.' What her brother failed to do for Princess Jaydyn. He had not considered such an action, nor would he have contemplated…

Raeyn continued: 'Since Nedran's entanglement with Erldan, the local herbalist has ceased dealing in abortifacients for fear of the priests. We had to source an apothecary in the next town, yet it appears the tonic did not take.'

He stared at Lynden's wan complexion. 'Did not take, or poisoned her?'

Raeyn shook her head. 'We would have seen the effects of a poison immediately, my lord. This fever has erupted recently. The medic believes since the babe took root in her womb.'

He stood, towering over his spouse. 'Why haven't you fetched a midwife?'

She rose to face him. 'Do you want people knowing your sister is with child? Once she recovers from whatever ails her, we still need to make her a good match.'

'*If* she recovers.' He ran his fingers through his hair, staring down at Lyn.

'*When* she recovers, if the babe survives, I'll arrange to foster him or her.'

He folded his arms over his chest. How could she focus on propriety when Lyn looked like *that*?

'Leave your womenfolk to tend to her with the medic's aid and concentrate on your people and restoring relations with Erldan.'

Treaty be damned. Did his wife care only for her brother? How could he trust her with his sister's life?

'Your rivals must believe you strong. Cannot suspect Lady Lynden of indiscretion. The sooner we commence negotiations for her husband, the better.'

Even while Lyn remained abed, Raeyn thought only of strategy and politicking.

'I propose we approach King Sardin of Herron, whose youngest son remains unwed.'

'That would ally us with Erldan's rival.'

'Indeed.'

Lord Sheevan of Creywmm, erstwhile friend to Nedran and Erldan, had since made himself and his family Erldan's enemy by breaking off his betrothal to Jaydyn, following Queen Prya's denouncement. Now he was marrying Herron's Princess Elder—a slap to Gohran, sure enough. If Nedran also allied itself with the rival kingdom, enemies would surround Erldan.

Any lingering doubts about Raeyn's loyalty vanished as she revealed her political acumen. She knew how to wound and weaken her brother.

'Let us pray your sister recovers soon,' she said, squeezed his shoulder, and departed.

Thirty-Eight

When Gordovyn's message arrived with the melting snows, it was to inform Breeyan he would not send a courier bearing the Gern's manuscripts while political unrest abounded between their havens. Turmoil had taken root between Nedran and Erldan, and goods were being embargoed and wagons searched.

Meantime, she could only pore over the passages sequestered from *The Lost Warriors*. They told her only of beguilement's nature, warned of its snares, not what to do about it, or anyone Cursed.

She abandoned her parchments and joined Xarion on her rug. The child crawled and played with smoothed sticks and rags, bringing them to her mouth to explore. Her delighted squeals, contented babbling, and wide azure eyes captured Breeyan's attention, eliciting more joy than she imagined possible.

'Your Holiness?' Chrysanth appeared in the doorway. 'Shall I take her?' Since her severing, Chrysanth had rediscovered her voice for something other than anguished screaming and availed herself as Breeyan's eager servant.

As she collected Xarion, her golden eyes glowed with warmth. Chrysanth's ease around her was a blessing. Unsworn and ignorant, she did not fear the Curse. Without magic, didn't notice Xarion's peculiar aura as she blissfully absorbed her charms.

Xarion circled her neck and giggled, pleased to hold someone new in her thrall.

Her focus adrift, Breeyan sensed Chrysanth chasing an elusive memory of another time she'd held a babe this way, followed by a frown of confusion.

'I—I have the strangest sense...' She grimaced, sucked in a breath, and forced her features to soften and relax. 'My apologies—I thought I'd remembered something, but it must have been a dream...' She wiped her nose and stared down at her finger. Blood.

Breeyan's conscience bit. When she'd severed, she had prioritised expediency and certainty over preservation, slicing deeper and wider than necessary.

She shrugged off her guilt and studied Xarion's captivating smile. It was safer for them all this way. Chrysanth's trauma and volatility had threatened their peaceful existence.

The surviving refugees' fates hung over her. Several were well enough to leave Aryon's infirmary. By rights, she should direct those without magic, who could not swear to Xenon, north, where they could rehabilitate in the more permissive towns surrounding the Gern. From there, they might emigrate via the Gern's trade routes to Myan.

This system had suited Aryon for generations whenever refugees sought asylum from religious persecution. These folk did not worship Xenon, however, and many considered His priestesses a threat. Under different circumstances, they would have denounced Aryon's inhabitants to Elnora's priests. Would she and her sisters need to sever them all?

Chrysanth was another matter. She held no spiritual qualms or doctrinal beliefs. Her severance prevented her recalling the specific events of her captivity, but she understood Elnora's followers had persecuted her. That back in Ycelt, they would target her again.

A perfect candidate for Xenon's sequestered existence, but without magic, she could not swear to the god, and therefore, should not remain. Yet she had eagerly pledged herself to the Dark Sun Cult's enemies.

Seeing her take to Xarion's charms, Breeyan hoped she might stay as Xarion's nursemaid. If she studied Xenon's lore and swore her life to Him, if not her source and soul, did it matter that she lacked His gifts?

Already, she pictured her sisters' protests. It was the same argument she had presented to Ella when her niece did not wish to swear her vows. Xenon only afforded sanctuary to those who were Moon Sworn. To do else made a mockery of His mercy. It had been so since the time of the Ancients.

And yet, Chrysanth demonstrated consistent loyalty and a willingness to care for the babe they feared.

She gathered up the pages that recounted the tale of her granddaughter's namesake, grateful to the god for sending her an omen all those years ago. Hiding the old lore bought her time to unravel the Curse. And she must unravel it if she was to spare Xarion.

Without that story, her sisters remained ignorant of what Xarion's inverted and twisted aura represented. Thrice Cursed, for inheriting her mother's beguilement, her father's Curse, and for being born of rape and incest.

She ran her finger once again over Ynad's words: *Only if you let it be.* She drew her nails to her teeth, willing peace and reason to prevail, and Gordovyn's courier with it.

THIRTY-NINE

'I f we're to verify your mistranslation theory, we need to locate the source text,' Yorg said, frowning before Aeron's library. 'It's the only way to know what Xenon intended.'

'But Vorlyn told me you hold no copy here.'

'Indeed, we do not,' said Yorg, with a poorly concealed grin. 'However, my former home houses one of the greatest depositories of doctrinal history upon the known continent.' He paused to study her reaction. 'Including the only completed manuscript of *The Lost Warriors* scribed in the author's native tongue.'

'And how does that help me?'

'It will help you once you sight it with your own eyes, Princess.'

'Are you suggesting I journey to Myan? How do you suppose I get there?'

'The same way you arrived.'

Ella blinked. 'But I don't have the strength to port without drawing blood.'

'Which is why Vorlyn's hunting crew have offered you their fattest boar.'

He proposed she do the very thing that condemned her predecessors. What if she was wrong about the translation, or Yorg was mistaken about her aura being scarred and not Cursed? What if drawing blood invoked the Curse after all?

She clamped her thoughts down. 'I don't want the poor creature to suffer.'

Yorg's laughter rumbled—a sound she'd come to adore. 'We must butcher and bleed the beast to fill our bellies, so you might as well profit from its lifeforce.'

How could he be so sanguine, given all she destroyed in her wake?

'I have been studying the changes in your aura,' he said.

Her nails bit into her palms. Her shield must have slipped.

'I appreciate your fear, but you forget, I knew a time when drawing lifeforce was commonplace. After all, it was lifeforce that brought me here.'

'But you're not a porter...?' Yorg had never explained how he'd come to reside so far from his home.

'A young mage whose powers rivalled yours ported me here.' He continued shuffling books, his back to her.

'How? When I ported here, I carried nothing with me—not even my clothes.'

The transferred lore had shown the same situation: porters arriving naked in their destinations.

'That's a skill we can work on.' He seemed to mull something over. 'A skill I'd *like* you to master.' He remained facing the shelves, running a pointed nail along various spines.

She caught glimpses of his private recollections, of Yorg caressing a youth's lilac skin, the shy smile of his golden eyes. 'The mage was your lover.' Voice low.

'He was. And he did not survive the cull.'

'Leaving you stranded here,' she said. Cut off from his former life, grieving alone. 'I'm sorry.'

'You'd think time would have eased that wound, but it feels as raw as the day it happened.'

Ella squeezed his arm, and his intent became clear in her mind. He wanted her to port him home.

Yorg pat her hand. 'Sweet lass.'

There was a bitter aftertaste to his words, and she sensed him wondering how she had not succumbed to the wiles of her aunt and mother. Oh, but she had.

'How many decades ago was the cull?' she asked.

'Centuries, Princess. Not decades.'

'Then you must be...?'

'Ancient.' Another rumble. He retrieved the volume he'd been searching for and turned, a glint in his eye.

She caught the book's cover, and though she could not translate the Myanai title, she recognised the illustrated glyph of the first quarter moon.

'*On the Physical Manipulation of Self and Objects*,' Yorg read. He spread the tome open, stroking each page like an old friend. He pointed to a passage of indistinguishable foreign glyphs. 'To carry something—or someone—other than yourself, combines porting with movement,' he explained.

Tension crept across her shoulders, a prickle of excitement and trepidation. Her fear of the Curse aside, she wasn't confident in her ability to do either.

'Let's begin by moving a simple object,' Yorg said, placing a polished moonstone no wider than a silver coin atop the nearby bench. 'See if you can move it to that shelf over there.' He pointed.

Focus adrift, she envisioned the bench, the books, the ink and quills, beside the moonstone, detecting the unique hum of each. She imagined using force to drive the stone sideways, but it stayed stubbornly motionless, as if her hand passed through air or water.

She tried again, with the same result. Then thrice more, to no avail. Why couldn't her mind connect with it?

After a score of unsuccessful attempts, her frustration rose, and the gem quivered. But when she tried to leverage the momentum, the stone rattled and jiggled, then stilled.

'Remember to breathe, Princess.' Yorg rested his palm over hers—a gesture meant to reassure, but whose heaviness bore down. To him, a simple object and a simpler manoeuvre, but to her, it carried the weight of his hope and her risk. Their need for her to succeed.

She expelled her irritation with a puff, closed her eyes, and tried again. This time, her power tingled, radiating outwards, beyond the gem, until the volumes trembled on their shelves.

Her chest tightened. Memories crowded like haunting echoes. She was back in Ycelt, terror gripping her as she fought to quiet what her roiling emotions had inadvertently stirred: crockery rattling, cups shaking, and tack jangling, before the ugly red welts that her dream's magic had lashed across Vera's creamy cheeks filled her vision.

Her eyes shot open with a gasp.

Yorg clasped her, his violet irises beseeching. 'Breathe.'

She mimicked the slow rise and fall of his breath, and as her respiration slowed and deepened to mirror his, the pressure stilled and eased, and the books steadied and fell silent.

He drew a thumb over the creases in her forehead. 'Release those poor tortured worry lines, Princess. It's not their fault you don't trust yourself.'

She forced her muscles to loosen and relax.

'Better,' he declared. 'Work need not be all grim.' He padded over to the shelves to reset a couple of dislodged volumes.

Was Yorg right? As a girl, long before she'd understood what she was doing and the risk it posed, she had created fantastical illusions from her physical dolls through imagination and play, and she had delighted in her magic. A period that seemed at odds with every tragedy that followed. But was lightness—her joy—the key to unlocking her power now? She scarcely recalled the last time she'd felt playful. Probably at Nedran, when Jonas and Lynden's relentless banter punctuated their interactions.

She wrenched her attention back to the task at hand, drew another breath, and pictured the gem as a toy. On her next inhale, it grew weightless, and so did she, and she captured it in her envisioned palm. Her surroundings appeared as she once experienced her doll, Nellie's world. Crystalline. Ethereal. She carried the stone and settled it on the shelf, then returned to inhabit her body. Her mystical vision faded with a rush of chill and burning hunger.

He watched her, stunned. 'I don't know whether to be impressed, or aghast, that you travelled in your ethereal form to move a simple object.'

'Is that wrong?'

Yorg's words stumbled, and she sensed the grind of him collecting his thoughts—the pattern of his *process*, rather than his mind's content.

'Not *wrong*, but potentially dangerous. Travelling unintended can put your simulacrum at risk.'

She knew that fear, the tension between the physical and ethereal, its tether stretched and ready to snap, and the deadly suck of energy suffocating as it depleted. Is that why Yorg had dragged the lidded furnace in here, to pump out a steady heat for their work?

'Try directing your mind using your god-sight, *without* involving your god-body,' he said.

She frowned. 'If I'm porting, won't I be travelling, anyway?'

'Not if you're doing it correctly,' he said. 'Porting and travelling are discrete skills, and you should master both.'

His tone reminded her of her early lessons with Amber, before her life careened off course, and she bristled.

With a deep breath, she employed her ethereal sight to search for the stone's vibration. But as before, when she attempted to pick it up, her simulacrum passed through, as if the gem was liquid, not rock.

She reached again, focusing on moving the stone while remaining within her body, and the gem trembled at last. Her mind clutched at its edges, trying to locate the point where its circumference began and ended, but it stayed fixed in place. She could not gain a hold.

Time crawled as her hunger and weariness gnawed.

'Keep going,' Yorg said. 'A mere hand span in any direction will do...'

She grasped and shoved, but it would not budge. Why did such an elementary task seem impossible? 'Hrrrah!' she cried, half grunt, half groan.

'It's only a pebble, Princess. Almost weightless.'

He might mean to reassure her, but his words reverberated in her mind as the mocking of Aryon's priestesses. Like pressure. Her fists balled, nails biting into her palms, leaving a row of half-moons. 'You think I don't know that?'

Yorg remained quiet, his eyes unreadable and his thoughts shuttered, but the weight of his hope, his expectation, transformed the gemstone into a boulder.

Her stomach grumbled, and her limbs dragged.

'Shall we rest for the day, Princess?'

She forced her hands open, wiped the sweat over her trouser leg, and shook her head. 'I can do this.' Yorg needed her to conquer this. And she needed to prove to herself, to her aunt, and to every wretched priestess that she could.

Through narrowed eyes, she directed her force until the stone blurred and trembled, almost humming, as though it might shift at any moment.

And then it stilled.

It was hopeless. *She* was hopeless. A failure. She couldn't do this.

'So close, Princess!' Yorg's chest rose and fell. Steady. Even. But the slightest frown had etched into his brows before he smoothed them, and his disappointment sliced as a dagger through her heart. His hope had seeded and taken root, but she felt the burden of its need to grow, to bloom, like a vine strangling.

'You want it moved?' She collected the stone between thumb and forefinger. 'Here!' She hurled it across the room. It thudded against the wall and dropped to the floor.

Yorg's breath sounded heavy. 'Pick it up, Princess. Try again.'

Her cheeks burned, and she lowered her face to retrieve the gem, ignoring the pale streak marring the smooth limestone.

Emotion trembled and percolated through her fingertips, and the stone quivered in sympathy. She raised her palm and studied its shimmer; the way its vibration mirrored her irritation. Her god-sight revealed the faint blue line of her magic stirring to resemble tentacles wrapping around the rock.

Instead of fighting her frustration, she fed it, letting it grow, and channelled the feeling outward. The surge of power grew stronger, more solid, and she risked taking her hand away. The gem remained suspended, and her mouth curved into a smug grin.

Once, she'd incited emotional currents in her prey and netted their charge as a source for her beguilement. Now, she stirred those reactions in herself to shove against the moonstone, letting them roil and simmer and burn.

With a burst of savagery, the moonstone hurtled towards the opposite wall.

Yorg ducked aside just in time as it whipped past and smashed into the ledge behind him, colliding with a scrying sphere in a satisfying explosion of glass and light. Their tingle reverberated off the walls and through her ears, sending shivers along her skin.

She imagined the shards piercing every person who had tried to shame or control her. *Odd little Ella.* Pictured Aryon's priestesses' hateful ire. The priests dragging her mother to be persecuted, tortured, and burned. Her brother's ravening eyes...

The shattered fragments peeled away from the shelves. Suspended before the wall, they formed jagged, pointed blades surrounding Yorg. In a heartbeat, she could direct them to become treacherous—grievous—weapons.

'Princess...' Yorg's deep baritone cautioned like ice slithering down her back.

She reined in her anger, expelled it along with the air inside her lungs, as a long, slow exhale. With her next breath, her rage subsided, and so did her power. The shards dropped to the floor and shattered.

She winced and covered her ears.

After a moment, she heard the heavy crunch of boots trudging over glass, before a solid arm rested on her shoulder. She recoiled and stifled a squeal.

It was only Yorg.

Not angry or disappointed, but a quiet, calming presence to contain her. 'Well done, Princess. You now know how to find and move an object,' he said, as if she hadn't just wreaked havoc across his precious library. Or threatened his life. 'Take a moment, then clean up those shards without relying on your emotions.'

She drew from the brazier to ground herself, then tried again, focusing on a single sliver of glass. Yorg instructed her to draw and direct the furnace's heat. Through her mind's eye it blazed, and she syphoned its energy to wrap around the shard. *Breathe. Just breathe.*

She imagined sweeping the fragment up in a blast of hot air, rather than grasping it, and for a moment, it hovered. She gathered more power, keeping her thoughts benign to avoid whipping up her emotions, but the shard wavered. *Why was this so difficult?*

'It is merely a different source of energy,' Yorg said.

But it wasn't. Moving the glass using the fire felt *intangible*, as though some element was missing.

Yorg rested a hand on her shoulder. Heat stirred, followed by a rush of cold. His magic thrummed through her. 'Focus on the glass.' He raised his other palm, and with eyes half closed, directed his power through her. The force vibrated along her veins, through her muscles, and without leaving her body, she lifted every piece of the shattered sphere, as though attached to strings.

Was that it? Was movement simply imagining her source as a thread, or fabric, weaving in and around the fragments?

Yorg withdrew, creating a chilling absence. But having identified the distinct sensation in her mind, her focus held firm. With a surge, she deposited the shards in a neat pile to be swept away.

'Excellent,' Yorg said, and despite herself, pride put down roots alongside Yorg's hope. 'Now the stone.'

On an inhale, she drew and channelled the furnace's heat until her power's weave solidified. She envisaged it encircling the gem, then carried it like a spider's thread blown in the wind, until it settled on Aeron's bookshelf.

'Very well done, Princess!' Yorg's words hummed through her, warm rays nurturing the first shoots of her burgeoning pride as he retrieved the stone, fastened a strip of leather, and tied it around her neck. 'For love and protection,' he said.

With a smile, she examined the stone's faint azure glow, and tucked it beneath her shirt, close to her heart.

FORTY

'Let's see if you can view and manipulate my simulacrum as an object using your ethereal form,' Yorg said.

Ella had spent countless days mastering her movement. Finally, after she relocated the gemstone from one end of Aeron's caves to the other without leveraging her emotions, Yorg deemed her skill 'sufficient'.

'Take my hands,' he said, and motioned for Ella to join him on the rug.

His rough skin crinkled like parchment against the pads of her fingers, and when they connected, the echo of her thrall pulled, as though her psyche could blur into his at any moment.

She slipped away, but he clasped her tighter. 'Let the merge happen, Princess. It won't consume you, not now that I understand how to remain separated.' Understood her beguilement would devour him if it could.

He caught and held her gaze, and power bled through their touch, through his violet eyes, until the boundary between their minds dissolved and her surroundings appeared awash with indigo. A surge of energy propelled her vision to take on its ethereal form. The objects before her became crystalline, the cave walls glittering like veins of quartz.

She did not float far, aware of Yorg's simulacrum carrying—or rather, guiding—hers, through the viscous currents that divided mind from flesh, what Yorg termed 'the soup of the gods.'

He released her, and she drifted, searching for him as the ethereal tide bent and shifted, tugging at her like a lodestone pulls at iron filings. Separated, she saw no body, only a man-shaped shadow resembling a darkened void: a reverse light, unlike any simulacrum she had encountered.

With a draw of heat, she stretched her mind to its edges, trying to perceive the dark shape not as an amorphous shade, but weighty and solid. A siren's song, it called to her. The deepest crevices of her heart and soul yearned to secure it.

View my simulacrum as an object, he thought to her.

But where she had woven her power like fabric around glass and stone, the nearer her god-form reached, the less substantial his appeared, dissipating. Not even scattered dust, but smoke through the wind, leaving her aura's tendrils dangling, helpless and needy.

He winced as her ethereal claws shredded.

Yorg—I—

Don't stop, Princess.

'I can't—' She was hurting him.

She withdrew and edged towards her body. Her flesh sucked and pulled, intensifying as she drew nearer.

Careful!

She fought the urge to let go, which would spring her dangerously within her body's casing, easing until she sensed the telltale click of a puzzle piece sliding into place.

Her heavy muscles pressed into smooth rock. Cold air rushed to fill the gaps where her torso and limbs curved away from the rug beneath. Aeron smelled earthy, like moss after the rain, amid the eternal blue glow.

When she spoke, her throat felt gluggy. 'Why can't I reach you?'

Opposite, Yorg looked weary. 'I sense your longing to merge, but whenever your psyche reaches for mine, it becomes...' He rifled for the exact word. 'Prickly.'

Not just prickly. Sharp, like knives. 'It pains you,' she said. 'Yorg—My apologies. Please...'

He shook his head. 'It's uncomfortable, but tolerable. I will tell you if it grows too much.'

She recoiled, drawing her arms over her chest. 'Why let me hurt you?' Like she hurt everyone she cared about.

He sighed. '*That* is the prickliness I experience, reflected in your psychic form.'

She sensed it, too. The part that ached to join him, desperate to connect. Yet the moment he was within reach, that same part became barbed, clawing and shredding. Keeping him distant, and her safe.

'I don't mean to...' She hugged her arms tighter and clamped her mind down.

'It warrants no shame, Princess,' he assured. 'Your psyche merely seeks to protect you.'

'But I *want* to merge. I *want* to trust—'

He drew her against his chest and stroked her hair, his heart and breath pulsing a steady beat. 'I know.'

As much as she yearned to fall into that rhythm, allowing it to flood and soothe, she slithered from his grip. He let her go, and she sensed his grief. For her. For him. She wasn't sure.

After a moment, he spoke again. 'Until you can find and hold me in ethereal form, porting with me in tow isn't safe.'

She withdrew even further.

'I suspect why you struggle to grasp my simulacrum is akin to you not tolerating playing naked with your peers. Why you startle and flinch.' He frowned.

Was he right? Was this less about mastering her magic, and more about conquering her fear?

A sigh. 'There is nothing to conquer, Princess,' he said, having perceived her thought. She could not grasp his simulacrum, yet her mind remained open. 'And this isn't your fault.' She sensed *his* frustration now, but not at her. 'You won't be able to trust until you learn to trust yourself.'

He kept saying that, as if she wasn't trying. 'How do you propose I achieve that?'

'I'd like you to continue working with Vorlyn. I'm already seeing signs of your aura recovering, and I'm beginning to wonder if carrying another while porting is not a matter of improving your skills but of healing your psyche.'

Forty-One

'Stay still, you pesky beast!' Nykki's arms skimmed past the duck. With a honk, it fled her groping, and a cloud of feathers erupted. Teasing her, it hovered out of reach, then flapped in a startling flurry. Nykki stumbled backward, tripped on a protruding rock, and tumbled, hair and shirt flying, to land on her rear with a thud.

'Fine!' she called, as the duck glided to safety across the pond. 'But we're taking your eggs, and your fat mate's, too!'

Watching on, Amber laughed until her chest hurt, and tears streamed down her cheeks. She laughed because she could. Because they were free. Because the terror that propelled them here was so far removed from this absurdity.

It was liberating.

She helped Nykki up, brushed the grass from her trousers, and pushed her locks behind her ear, before catching sight of the raised and welted flesh that branded her a heretic. Her breath hitched.

'Oh gods.' *Your beautiful face.* Day after day, Amber poured blessed power through her fingertips to soothe and heal, but nothing would remove the puckered skin that had melted Xenon's mark over one entire cheek.

'Hoy! You there!' A farmer's gap-filled maw hung open from across the field. A straw hat shaded his angry white brows.

Nykki rolled her eyes and let out an exaggerated sigh. 'We're not stealing your poultry, good sir.' *It's not our fault if it wants to be eaten.*

Though it clearly doesn't!

Nykki pinched her arm. *Don't make me laugh!* She held up her empty arms. 'Your foolish birds are safe from us.'

He removed his hat to wave at the gathering flies and squinted. With the warmer day, Nykki hadn't worn her usual cowl to hide her incriminating scar.

If he comes over, turn away while I talk to him.

Nykki nodded, already retreating behind Amber, in case his rheumy vision saw that far.

'Just know I have my eyes on you.' He replaced his hat, leaving white tufts of hair poking beneath, waved a pointed finger, and ambled off.

Nykki and Amber shared a glance. *Let's collect the eggs and go.*

The man, Tobyn, had only come close enough for Amber to influence him once but that was all it took for him and the surrounding farmers to leave them alone. It was unnervingly easy to persuade passersby to aid or ignore them.

On rare occasions like that morning, a local inhabitant would grumble about interlopers helping themselves to crops they hadn't sown and poultry they hadn't raised, but there was no shortage of pasture out this way. More and more, folk abandoned the land in favour of work in the towns or in a lord's—or priest's—service, where they didn't slog and punish their bodies, only to be taxed and tithed to near starvation.

Spring meant recruitment, with many younger men and older boys taking up arms. This year, another seasonal fever ravaged, so Amber and Nykki found vacant land and shelter with ease.

Eggs in hand, they loped through the thigh-high grass and nettle, picking their way between brambles towards a poorly thatched hut. Chickens clucked where they roosted—those not hunted by bandits or foxes—while geese and ducks skirted the farm's old pond.

Inside, they set the eggs down and sprawled languidly across the straw mattress they'd salvaged, thankfully, free from fleas.

Nykki's kiss stole Amber's breath as heat surged between them.

'We should clear some of the larger weeds before the days grow too warm...' Nykki sighed.

Amber caught her lips to silence her, but mostly to distract from the truth edging its way forward: they wouldn't be here when the days lengthened.

Nykki let Amber's mouth sweep her up, tracing the sweet hollow of her neck, her clavicle, continuing beneath her shirt, to claim her breast.

A moan escaped, thieving reality, and for a time, they could pretend they weren't doomed.

Nykki smiled through her pain, soothed by Amber's power, and in each other's arms, they could forget. Amber would not begrudge her beloved these moments, though tinged with grief. By immersing herself in Nykki's immediate pleasure, Amber caught glimpses of hope. Brief glimmers, where their torture—and her guilt—disappeared.

By some gift from the gods, Nykki did not blame her.

But overshadowing their bliss, they fought in circles about whether to stay and fight or run and hide.

Nykki's words echoed from when they first took shelter in the abandoned hut. 'This crusade is over. It's too risky. Let us winter here. The priests will assume we've given up, and we can traverse east with the spring. I heard in Myan they don't even care if you have magic...'

She was grasping, desperate to keep what they'd newly discovered, what she treasured, what they'd sacrificed.

It hadn't seemed a sacrifice when she was giving up a life she despised, but now... Now there was so much to lose. Now, she knew what death's flames tasted like as they licked her flesh.

Amber wanted to fight. Needed to take down the men who inflicted such horror and delighted in their subjugation and torture.

After those first few searches, the king's henads had retreated, deeming the souls they had scorched sufficient to appease the goddess, but with the melting snows, they would doubtless reemerge. Would not give up. But neither would she.

'Why, after this...?' Nykki gestured to her brand, red and angry.

'More than ever after this. I vowed to take Davith down—and Grogan, too—but I can't without you.' She needed Nykki's power to bolster hers.

'How are we to get near this wretched head priest with our heresy branded across my face?' she choked.

'Yet you imagine we will make it east as far as Myan?'

'We'll stay out of major towns or anywhere the priesthood thrives. The common folk won't care to embroil themselves with strangers. We can use our influence and move on.'

In moments like these, playing house by Nykki's side, a future Amber had not believed possible seeded. Not as a sequestered priestess, but a freehold farmer, as ordinary as any other peasant in Ycelt. A glimpse of what freedom might afford. 'You make it sound so easy.'

'Easier than a hopeless crusade to stop men more powerful than two women alone.'

'Two formidable women wielding our combined magic. Together we can bend their will, and with your movement—'

Nykki pressed her finger to Amber's lips. 'No, my love. Not all of them. One of those priests—I couldn't influence him. Couldn't read or affect him at all. It was like he was immune to sorcery.' Amber sensed Nykki's throat constrict and her chest tighten. 'I've never felt so helpless. So afraid...'

Amber squeezed Nykki's hand and let her soothing flow. She recognised that terror: the moment of realisation when the only weapon afforded them was rendered useless. No one had taught them that such folk existed.

'While fleeing my captors, I met another who was impervious to our power,' Amber said, picturing Lord Jonas of Nedran's arched brow and remembering his wry wit. She sucked in her breath. 'His blood was like...' She searched for a descriptor. 'Like, water, I suppose.'

It was the first time she had confessed her crime of drawing from a forbidden source: the true reason Xenon Cursed her.

'Even if we can't influence them, they fear touching sworn priestesses.' She recalled the lengths Davith's neophytes went to, keeping her blinded, addled, and distant.

Nykki shook her head. 'Those priests in Harnal didn't realise I was a sworn priestess to fear harming me. Our vows are worthless. Let the Curse follow its natural progression and flee this hellscape. Leave them to rot. They've done nothing but hurt everyone I've cared about.'

Amber's gut twisted. How could she make Nykki understand? 'If we're to die, I need to take Davith with me.' Her voice a whispered growl. When they marked her beloved, they branded Amber's soul with flames so black they consumed every iota of her compassion and solidified their fate. 'Him and his neophytes.' She would burn them all. 'Our sacrifice must mean something...'

'It means *this*.' Nykki placed Amber's hand over her heart and slid the other beneath her hair to grip her nape, and drew her close until their lips collided. A newfound hunger fuelled her kiss, but it was a hunger Amber could not meet, polluted by shame and guilt. She withdrew, slipping out of Nykki's grasp.

Nykki slumped back against the straw and Amber swallowed a wooden lump, aching, knowing the fight had evaporated from Nykki's eyes. They had broken her.

'If I help you, promise me—swear to me—we can flee afterwards. I won't return to Aryon,' Nykki said.

'I promise.' Amber's throat caught.

If they survived. If the priests didn't hunt them before they were hunted.

That night, when Nykki's foresight woke them, sending her screams ringing, they both knew they were out of time.

FORTY-TWO

E lla's vision broke off and the glass sphere's hum fell silent, dampened like the weight of a blanket between her palms. She'd seen enough. Amber and Nykki were walking suicides.

Vorlyn rested a hand on her shoulder. 'They believe themselves Cursed, as you did.'

She met Vorlyn's hazel eyes. 'But if someone enacted violence on them, why would they endure Xenon's wrath?'

'Regardless of the truth, belief is a potent and deadly force.'

It had been Vorlyn's idea for Ella to spy on her old life. 'Try to recall your past with moderation and control,' she'd said. 'Not free from natural emotion, like anger or sadness, but with no urgency to flee.' Without shutting down or escaping her body.

'How does scrying on the present achieve that?'

But Vorlyn didn't need to explain. Observing her former companions would stir up painful reveries. After the hours they'd spent helping her tolerate touch, she couldn't allow her reactions to derail her.

She squinted behind her raised palm at the verdant green of the landscape surrounding Aeron. How long had it been since she ported here? Surely not time enough for spring to emerge. Her vision of Amber and Nykki offered no clue—it could be any season inside their hovel.

Where were they? Not Aryon. They had freed their braids, and wore singed and tattered trousers and tunics rather than robes. When Nykki had turned her cat-green eyes to face Amber, raised welts marred her cheek where someone had seared an X into her flesh.

Marked like cattle.

Amber had escaped Davith's clutches, so why was she hiding in a barn with Nykki? Had Aunt Bree refused her return? She swore she would not sever her, but did not promise to take her in. Ella's gut twisted.

What if she believed them Cursed, too? If not for violence, perhaps lust. Though willingly shared, both had sworn to the god.

Ella inhaled sharply. What kind of deity would Curse His people for enacting their love?

When she'd last seen Amber, it was on the road, accompanied by Jonas, and the synchronicity resonated like the overlapping melodies of a fugue. Amber, tortured by Davith, who had also tortured Vorlyn, who had been with Jonas, who might be Vorlyn's son.

Her curiosity itched. If they had parted ways, where was he?

The sphere in her hands taunted, its surface already blurring with potential.

Vorlyn's brow arched. She was laughing at her.

'Is *this* part of my healing, too?'

'Trust yourself, Ella.'

'You sound like Yorg.' She sighed, then filled her lungs and gazed into the orb, following the play of colour and light. The fawn of straw and peasant clothing, and the whip of saffron locks entwined with chestnut hair, distorted and fogged.

On her next inhale, the subtle movement sucked her mind within the glass casing, and she heard the whir and clash of steel, and the clang and thud of metal on wood. Shouts like battle cries crowded. Anxious fear and trepidation—not hers—coupled with a violent thirst, unlike anything she'd encountered. Her breathing hastened, thudding in her throat as the thrill of a skirmish gripped her.

Amid that chaos, she spied Jonas's unmistakable hazel eyes, and her breath stalled, heart skittering. His hair was grimy, his face unwashed and un-shaven—almost unrecognisable—and he wore the scruffy leathers of a merce-nary.

Dread settled in her belly, and she searched the surrounding faces, but recognised no one. Not an army, or a proper battle, but ruffians scrapping over paltry supplies.

Who were these bandits?

When she widened her vision, the terrain was indistinguishable from the woodlands and occasional clearings common in this region. Not Nedran, Erldan, or anywhere that far south.

Why would Jonas be out there? No matter how much he and Venn clashed, she couldn't imagine him outlawing himself. Abandoning his home.

In the flash of a blade, it seemed their eyes met, and the world tilted as familiar green and grey seized the air from her lungs. A heartbeat later, Jonas ducked and weaved, avoiding a strike, and she tore her focus away.

She shoved the sphere inside Vorlyn's satchel.

Vorlyn exhaled. 'You did well. Your emotions didn't hijack your nerves until that last moment.'

'This was a test?'

'Of a kind.'

An exercise to provoke and judge how she would react, to determine whether she would spiral.

'Those woodlands are close to here,' Vorlyn continued. 'This area is renowned for bandit crews.' *As my home once was*, her unvoiced thought followed. 'A side effect of all the political instability.'

'You saw?'

'The glass contains the vision,' she said. 'Which allows you to scry with your shield raised and lets me observe what you see.' An ordinary, physical manifestation.

She studied Vorlyn's expression. If she recognised Jonas, she didn't show it. Perhaps Ella was mistaken about her identity.

A moment later, Vorlyn's words landed. Jonas was nearby.

A flurry in the surrounding trees disturbed a conspiracy of ravens. An explosion ripped through her torso and whorled down her legs. Squawking, all but one bird took flight. A lone creature that hesitated, then travelled in the opposite direction.

Ella pictured the conspiracy as those bandits, and the solitary raven as Jonas slipping away. Fleeing his flock.

Vorlyn wore a curious expression, as if Ella puzzled her. 'If you're worried someone you know will find you, by "close", I mean anywhere between Wernad and Rassit along the Gythyn Run.' Her frown met Ella's. 'You've done enough for today. Let's get you back inside.'

Relief leaked from Ella's muscles. Part of her had wanted to reach within the glass and pluck Jonas from that brutal scene, while another longed to shatter the sphere and her past with it. To soar like that raven, far beyond anyone's grasp.

Jonas could be anywhere, and the safest place for her in that moment was deep within Aeron's shield, before hers slipped entirely.

The copper tang of blood ripened the air, and the clash of steel reverberated against a backdrop of cries and curses. Sweaty, stinking torsos shoved, shields thrust, while weapons struck and parried. Spittle, sweat, and blood flew. Another hit. Another block. A push and a shout. This close, there was more wrestling, jostling, even biting, than weapons deployed.

Jonas ducked and weaved between falling bodies, climbed across the injured and dying, then dived and rolled beyond his opponent's reach. Hefting his sword in time to parry a strike, his side twinged from twisting to favour his sprained ankle, which hadn't completely healed.

He rose to his knees, only for someone to shove him back to the ground. He spluttered, coughing up blood and dirt. How had he got embroiled in this skirmish, defending unwilling allies against this rival band? Doubtless, they sought a finer pair of breeches or a braided leather jerkin, and instead of teaming up and hunting for a shared supper, they tore each other apart.

He'd no quarrel with, nor loyalty to, any of them.

Metal glinted as a shield caught the light, and for an agonising moment, he imagined seeing Ella's blue gaze staring back. He had the unnerving sense she watched him, reminding him of Amber's thoughts slithering into his mind.

The world fell silent as his breath ceased. Was she nearby, after all?

Something hard struck the side of his head and sent him reeling. Ears ringing, he swore and scrambled on hands and knees between dense foliage. Cries faded beneath the scrub, and he crawled further into the woods.

Ella's moonlit smile became a soothing echo behind the pounding ache. He dragged himself deeper, ignoring the mud caking his hair and clothes, the stones and sticks scraping his shins. Let these fools bury each other in this wilderness. Nothing mattered except getting away, locating Ella, and freeing his home.

Stars winked between clouds. Or were those shadows from branches? The wind carried the frost of melting ice, and Jonas's teeth chattered with aching numbness. Fire stabbed him somewhere—everywhere—he couldn't tell anymore. The ground was cold and wet, and so was he.

Dragging himself on his elbows, he needed to get further, deeper. Stay hidden. Pain pierced his shins, throbbed in his hips, and ran down his spine, but nothing compared to the wretched hammering in his skull.

The forest was quiet. No shouting. No clanging or fighting.

Peace.

Just a little further out of the clearing.

He shuffled his elbow forward and crawled, copping a face full of dead leaves and moss. It would do. He rolled over, and covered his legs and torso with foliage, burying himself from the cold as much as potential predators: not animals, but the fellows he left behind.

No stars now, only darkness.

Blessed darkness.

Forty-Three

'Why won't you marry Layla? She told me herself she desires the match.' Jaydyn rarely sought her brother, and certainly not for counsel. With Raeyn gone, his only advisers were his unctuous priest's lackeys. But that evening, she hunted him to his study and barged her way in. 'If she's not to your taste, when you're not producing an heir, the dryhten's sister might warm your bed.'

Gohran stood before his desk, jaw twitching. Jaydyn sucked in her breath and eyed the exit, already regretting speaking up.

'Allying with Rynwood is no longer viable.' His voice chilled, and he shuffled parchments as though searching for something.

Jaydyn's eyes widened. 'She refused you, didn't she?' The words escaped before she could stop them, and she braced, awaiting the sting of Gohran's knuckles across her cheekbones.

He turned and paced, jaw muscles quivering, fists clenching. He halted, swallowed, then exhaled. Jaydyn could only imagine what it cost him to remain calm.

Eventually, he spoke. 'It seems the alliance no longer benefits Rynwood.'

Rynwood's overlord had hungered for a betrothal with Erldan since their families were first introduced. Rynwood was a lesser province, nestled between wealthy Saellyn, close to the High King's city of Galliarn, and the ranges that straddled the Rialden River.

Lord Kerr of Rynwood saw benefit in allying with a higher-ranking kingdom with free passage to the Gythyn Run, which would open new trade routes in the west. For Erldan, the alliance offered a stronghold near Galliarn, with access to Halbar and Myan in the far east.

At the time, Jaydyn was relieved Lord Kerr had set his sights on Ella, freeing her to pursue that spineless lordling Sheevan, whose bronze skin and light green eyes had long since lost their lustre.

Kerr's sister, the young widow Layla, was another matter. Layla's daughter was around the same age as Serrah, and the pair had become friends when she and her brother stayed at Erldan—before Gohran chased Kerr away from pursuing Ella.

Had their families united, Jaydyn and Layla's daughters could have grown up together. While Jaydyn did not see the appeal of her brother as a husband, he besotted Layla, and their union would benefit them all.

So why would that match no longer be an advantage?

'Surely Venn has not offered Lynden to Kerr?' she said.

Another tight swallow. 'Not to Kerr, no. To Sardin,' Gohran said.

King Sardin of Herron, the nearest rival king. Sardin was a widower with grown children. 'Isn't he a little old?' What was the value in procuring a young mare he couldn't service?

'Not Sardin himself. His youngest son.'

'From night to day!' Adyn was an acne-pocked lad, barely riding his own steed.

Well. Not a match she expected, but a strategic one, sure enough. Gohran had broken at least three pitchers when he heard Herron had allied with Creywmm. It had been a slap to her, also, knowing her former lover would marry a rival princess. Now Venn intended to tie his sister to the king himself! A move calculated to rile her brother. Meanwhile, Kerr no longer found benefit in tying his family to Erldan, the monarchy who had repeatedly rebuffed them.

Gods, what a tangle!

As complicated as one of their mother's schemes. Raeyn must have had a hand in this. Well, Jaydyn could play her own game of Foresight and add a further piece to the board.

'How does Lady Vera of Lichen please you? I seem to recall you favouring her company.'

The candles flickered and the space between them grew cold, as if someone had opened a window or door. The changing light shadowed and then illuminated her brother's puzzled frown.

Confusion gave way to an icy, satisfied sneer that was a sight to behold. To marry his rival's beloved would be delicious vengeance, sure enough.

But for Jaydyn, it meant security. Lichen would defend its own fiercely. Proximity and history, not blood or law, tied their family to Nedran. With Jonas missing, there was no betrothal and no alliance, leaving Vera abandoned, and free to marry.

She first met Vera when her parents introduced the comely blonde to Gohran, before he denounced their mother. Following Queen Prya's condemnation, Vera's family had retreated from cultivating a relationship with Erldan.

But Vera and her aunt recently attended Raeyn's wedding, and with the priests' presence rooting out the least whisper of heresy, a betrothal to a king was a worthy prospect once more. After all, if the Princess Elder of Erldan was a desirable enough match for the dryhten of Nedran, Erldan's king must be deserving of a lady of Lichen. With Lichen backing Erldan, Nedran might hesitate before letting whatever rivalry existed between Jonas and Gohran escalate to war.

Gohran appeared to wind the idea around his teeth and tongue. Doubtless, he pictured the threads they were weaving: a tether Nedran would not wish to break. A moment later, she saw the slightest quirk of lip and brow. Admiration.

She might be the brazen one. The impulsive one. But she understood people, their loyalties and rivalries. She knew how to manoeuvre them as her mother had cast them all like prized game pieces.

'Fetch the scribe,' he said.

'I can't do that to Lyn.' Vera scrunched the letter between tightened fists.

Lichen's women huddled in the parlour while the men hunted for the first of spring's yield. When the courier arrived from Erldan, Vera's aunt and mother accosted her—not even waiting until they were within the privacy of the women's hall.

'Of course you can,' said her mother, Selmyra, pushing an invisible strand of fair hair back into her perfectly braided roll. 'If she bedded a man she could never wed, why should you wear her veil and wimple?'

Vera rolled her eyes. 'That's hardly comparable.'

Aunt Leena leaned in close, her firm hand on Vera's. Sympathy inhabited her eyes, but conspiracy possessed her tongue. 'Think of it this way. Would she rather he marry a rival? Better her oldest friend than someone she despises.'

'I assume she would prefer to hate whoever he weds,' Vera retorted. She would detest the woman who stole Jonas. If he ever settled. Where was he? She expected him to winter with her here. They were to plan their wedding. Formalise and seal their betrothal.

There was no betrothal.

After every smile, whisper and touch, all the intimacies they shared, he still made her no offer.

Is that why she'd not heard from Lyn? Not a single reply to any of her letters since Venn's wedding. The last she knew, Jonas had dropped his sister at Nedran and disappeared. He'd sent no message, just left. Fled from responsibility.

From her.

Years she had waited, refusing to consider other offers. Who knows how many lords her father had chased away on her behalf, despite her mother's insistence that she contemplate someone—anyone—else. Of course, Ma adored Jonas. They all did. But she'd warned her daughter countless times. Jonas was a wanderer. She might wear his brooch, but she would never possess his heart. Not fully.

Jonas would meander as her father had strayed from her mother's bed, always seeking some intangible quality no woman supplied.

'If your father can't source the perfect stone, he will turn over every other pebble he finds,' Ma once said.

Jonas was no different, substituting perfection with novelty.

She tried to convince herself his looks and charm, his affection and friendship, would somehow suffice. That once sealed to her, he would change. But it was a lie. She now recognised what her mother had always known. Wedded to a man like her father, she would forever wait for Jonas to find his way home to her, never feeling she was enough.

Well, she was done waiting.

The last of her hope died when, instead of riding to her door, brooch in hand, waving their betrothal contract, he disappeared into the night the moment circumstance stole his final excuse to delay.

What had he to offer her, anyway? A younger lord, with no title or extensive holding, no army or castle, who failed to choose her, over and again.

Now she could marry the monarch of one of the oldest dynasties in Ycelt. She would be his queen, head his household, clothe his army, raise his children: heirs to a throne.

She would never again weep over a man who would not offer her his heart, or his brooch. 'Tell the king it is my honour to accept.'

Forty-Four

Breeyan arched her back, ignoring the crackle in her knees and her stiff joints, as she left Xarion to Chrysanth's care, and retired to her chamber, barring the door.

Sleep captured her quickly, but in its clutches, she could not rest. Her dream body hovered over blood-soaked battlefields strewn with corpses, ravens circling, hungry for their fill. A warrior with hair as dark as the birds and ice-blue eyes leaned upon his sword and met her gaze. Was it Gohran, or, in the way of dreams, did the soul belong to another?

Her vision altered, and she observed through the bird's view, soaring above blood-soaked mud and trampled grass, above razed village huts, forests, and pastures, over the walls of a city and towards its keep, only to settle on a windowsill.

Within, a woman laboured, sweat-damp hair clinging to her cheeks as she howled. Her companions encouraged and soothed, but what finally emerged was barely recognisable as human. Not a babe, but a monster, unable to take a single breath.

The raven cawed, and the mother looked up, staring through eyes Breeyan did not recognise.

She startled awake, ghostly shadows dancing across her walls.

'Begone!' she banished them, before laying back down and pulling her covers tighter around her.

Fire poured along Lynden's limbs, and then ice, and then fire again, as she fought her legs free from the tangled, blood-soaked sheets. She wanted everyone to leave her. Go!

She drew her tiny, lifeless babe closer. So cold. So still.

Her mind heard its phantom wails, tugging at her breasts and womb, though not grown large enough to form lungs that could cry, a voice that could speak. Eyes shut, she pictured miniature arms and legs, a pink torso, an oval head. Imagined black curly hair resembling his, but hazel-green irises like hers.

Yet, the unformed creature her body expelled bore none of those attributes.

'Is it—human?' The speaker had not intended for Lynden to hear. The words whispered so quietly, they were almost inaudible.

A curious, cruel gaze examined the peculiar lump her womb had produced. Purple and bloodied and faceless.

A cancerous flesh that ate her heart.

'Should we burn it?'

'No.' Raeyn's response came fierce and firm. 'We'll bury it.'

Lynden clutched it tighter, unswaddled. She needed it against her bare breast.

It would never suckle. It would never breathe.

'My lady, we need to take the babe and let you recover,' Bess said. 'The medic will be in to tend to you shortly.'

Lynden rolled it away from their grasping hands.

Raeyn sighed from where she hovered above the bed, her shadow looming. She hissed to Bess, 'We can't allow the medic to see it.'

'Do you think the tonic caused this?' Bess asked.

Another exhale, and Lynden pictured Raeyn's stony eyes and grim mouth judging her. 'We may never be certain. Either way, the authorities won't hold the apothecary to account—not unless we admit to procuring an abortifacient.'

'I suppose the gods can never guarantee the tonic's success...'

A click.

Stomp. Stomp. Stomp.

The medic's spindly frame crossed the floor, his fingers marking a sign of warding.

Raeyn drew the damp sheets up to cover Lynden and her dead babe, but it was too late. He had already seen. Eyes narrowed, mouth tight.

'I am pleased you are here,' Raeyn said with false brightness. 'Lady Lynden requires your expertise.' A pause. 'And your prayers.'

The medic said nothing, nearing Lynden's nightstand, where his medicines perched.

'It is some comfort to find a devout physician,' Raeyn continued. 'Most men who worship the goddess rely solely on Her prayers, but prayer and medicine combined—that is a boon.'

Silence.

'My maid was relaying the rising accusations of witchcraft among herbalists and apothecaries who procure tonics to end unwanted pregnancies. Our Dark Lady blessedly took this life without such intervention.'

His eyebrows shot up. He signed another warding and finished packing his medicines.

Raeyn squeezed Bess's shoulders, as they rose and fell with a hastened breath, and confronted the medic. She gestured to the bloody mess, to Lynden's frail and trembling body, to the still foetus clutched to her chest, but the man made no move to assist.

'Do you refuse to attend to his lordship's sister?'

'I believe I must, Your Highness.' Stiff. Upright. 'Had I known such unholy practices were taking place in the dryhten's home, I would have declined my service before now.'

Beneath her hand, Bess flinched. Unblinking, she said, 'The gods surely condemn a lack of mercy over your pretence of piety.'

'I honour Our Lady of the Dark Sun—not whatever impiety has occurred here.' He brushed past Bess and Raeyn and peeled back the sheets to reveal Lynden's deformed foetus. 'Prayer is all that remains for you now, Your Highness.' He clutched his packed case to his chest and strode away.

Raeyn hissed to Bess. 'Send a page after him and offer more coin. Let us pray he values wealth over the purity of his soul.'

Lynden shrank back into her mattress in a haze of confusion, not sure what had just occurred, but certain it was not good.

'I feel for your loss,' wood coated Raeyn's voice. 'Say your farewells, and I'll have the servants make a grave for it.'

It. Not him or her.

She peered at the amorphous shape of her babe, her mind searching for its humanity. It looked like someone had replicated the wrong pieces of a developing foetus, over and again, then stitched them together in arbitrary places. Chaos spread amok.

She didn't care. It was hers. It had grown inside her from Gohran's seed, and she had loved it, even as she felt it drain and poison her.

Raeyn pried it from her arms, and she recoiled, hunched and whimpering, clutching her empty womb in its stead.

'I am sorry,' Raeyn said again, and she and the babe were gone, leaving an aching void she feared nothing could ever fill.

Forty-Five

S unlight burst behind Jonas's eyes. He groaned and rolled into shadow. Somehow, no one had hunted him. Not ally or foe, animal or human, and he'd survived the night.

He tried to swallow, but his tongue stuck to the roof of his mouth and parched throat. His temple itched, and when he wiped his hairline, half-crusted blood smeared the back of his hand. He sucked it clean.

He should rouse to search for water. His gnawing hunger he might disregard, but the thirst he could not ignore. Yet when he tried to stand, the forest floor spun, and he sank back down before awareness escaped him.

W hen Jonas woke again, it was to the distant laughter of lads whose ballocks hadn't attained their full breadth. Gods, how was he still alive? Once or twice, during bouts of consciousness, he'd hobbled west, balancing against trunks and branches, or crawling on hands and knees, but did not know how far he'd travelled.

The sounds of lads playing in a field continued. No bandits or nobles.

He dragged his body, trying to sit. He needed to draw their attention. Noise formed in his throat, but at most, he emitted a garbled croak. Even if the boys looked his way, they wouldn't see him through the long grass.

Stand up. Come on. You can do this.

He grasped a nearby boulder and grappled to his feet. Upright, at last.

He'd re-injured his ankle in that final skirmish, and as he tried to walk, its fire surged through him. It had not healed from the ogre's crushing weight, made worse when he'd had no opportunity to rest. He couldn't even begrudge the ogre, who'd paid for the damage with his life.

He waved, but the boys weren't looking, and his call caught in his throat, ending in a cough.

Sound enough, for the lads shouted, pointing. They'd spotted him.

With arms flailing, he hobbled towards them, staggered, swayed, and then dropped to his knees. The last thing he remembered before losing consciousness once more was the smack of hard ground against his cheek and chin.

Forty-Six

With the babe's passing, the strange confusion that had clouded Lynden's thoughts lifted. Winter retreated into spring, and her fatigue and nausea passed like a fog dissipating to reveal a lush valley. Her breath grew steady and her voice strong. She feasted on Bess's bone broth and salted flatbread and was soon asking for meat and pulses. She gained weight, filling out until her dresses no longer hung off a bony frame. The shadows circling her eyes brightened, and her hair regrew from where it had fallen out in clumps.

'Let us head to town, my lady,' Bess said that day. 'Get your strength back up. Perhaps we can shop for some cloth for your wedding dress?'

'What wed—?'

'Lady Lynden,' a courier called and made a curt bow. 'A letter for you.' Another bow.

She turned the message over to see the green spray of Lichen's seal and cracked it open. She'd not written to Vera since Venn's wedding.

My darling Lyn,

I write to inform you directly, before official reports reach Nedran, of my impending betrothal to the King of Erldan. Know I intend no ill will, but I can no longer await your brother's false promises. Even if he were to make me an offer now, I would refuse. I cannot rely on his word, for his meandering heart has shattered mine too many times. I get no younger and must consider my future and my family. Please believe that I love and honour you and your brothers always.

—V

Her world cracked. Vera was marrying Gohran.

She swallowed and braced, waiting for the blow of imagining her oldest friend in Gohran's bed. She felt nothing. No—not nothing. A tether stretched to breaking point, springing free. Vera could have him.

She hunted for memories of his gaze falling lovingly on hers and found none. His eyes had been lustful and needy, drinking in her body, but never her. She had been right there, forever unseen.

His tenderness and vulnerability were moments of grief and longing for those he'd lost, and all she pictured were his bloody scars and hateful tears as he thrusted into her in the dark, and then his arm raised to strike her as his maddening anger flashed, consumed by his tempests.

'No! No—she can't!'

She looked up to flag the courier, and send a message straight back, but he was gone.

'Bess, she can't. She can't marry him.'

'He was never free to wed you, my lady.'

Bess didn't understand. She no longer desired him. Not now. 'I need to warn her—'

A memory stirred. *'Stay away from Gohran, Lyn.'* Jonas beseeching. *'Our demon king has a way of influencing people...'*

Oh gods, where was Jonas? She'd almost forgotten her brother had fled. It was possible Vera wasn't aware that he was missing. Outlawed. She assumed he'd abandoned her.

'I promise a trip to town to focus on your wedding shall lift your spirits, my lady.'

Why did Bess keep talking about a wedding? What wedding?

'I know Prince Adyn is still young, but he'll be a man soon enough, and that will give you time to heal before you're expected to provide his heirs.'

'Wait—Prince Adyn of Herron?'

Not a name from the list they'd presented her, and that she had refused, but a prince from a neighbouring kingdom. Why would she be marrying Gohran's rival? Wouldn't that signify the end of Nedran and Erldan's treaty?

Bess looked as confused as she felt. 'Of course. Don't you remember? The draft contract for your betrothal should arrive any day now.'

What betrothal? Had she been in a daze this entire winter?

Under Gohran's spell. Is that what Jonas meant? Did he believe Gohran was a witch?

Recollections toggled through her mind. Fragments she had attributed to being lust-drunk, the heat between her thighs warping her will.

Warping her will.

What if it wasn't lust, but witchcraft? Sorcery.

Fever had clouded her, but that did not account for the preceding weeks—moons—that she could not recall.

Did Venn know, too? Is that why he forbade anyone from trying to intercede directly with the king? Venn spoke of Gohran's undue influence. His ability to sway. Not by the inherent power of his rank, but unholy means. Heresy.

She realised Bess awaited her response.

'You're right,' she said. 'A pleasurable diversion will do me good.'

L ynden and Bess idled away the warm afternoon in the market square. Stall holders and customers eyed her. She supposed they hadn't observed her in town all winter. Well, let them gawp!

Soon, she spied a luscious cream silk sample that was finer yet more robust than any spool she had seen. She rubbed the surface, then tugged it taut. 'Is this from Myan?' she asked.

'Indeed. A new supplier, my lady,' the mercer said.

Lynden's brow creased. 'Oh?'

'Since the blockade, we've had to source our fabrics further afield.'

'Blockade?'

A commotion erupted behind them.

'There! She's over there!'

Arms pointed, aimed at her.

Bodies shuffled and shoved, and the crowd parted to let a pair of robed fellows through. Neophytes.

The holy men marched like soldiers, backs upright, mouths grim, then halted.

'Mistress Bessandra of Nedran?' said the taller one.

Bess turned. 'Yes?'

His hair was half-shaved, and he'd bleached, greased, and fastened the rest to resemble a horsetail. He unfurled a scroll with an exaggerated flourish and read. 'By order of the High Priest, Davith of Erldan, I hereby arrest you for heresy.'

'Pardon?'

'Did you say heresy?' Lynden swivelled to confront them. 'That's absurd! Bess is my lady's maid, and lady-in-waiting to the Princess Elder of Erldan.'

'Stand aside, my lady.' The robed men seized Bess.

'Get off!' Lynden prised their hands away. 'You have no claim here. Release her!'

Behind the neophytes, two burly guards appeared, dressed in full armour, halberds at the ready.

'My lady.' It was Mykan, her brother's steward. Why was he here and not with her brother? Where was Venn? 'It is in your best interest to let the priests do their duty.' Did she imagine him glancing down at her midline?

'All will be well, my lady,' Bess said. 'Go with Mykan and get yourself back to the keep.'

Mykan drew her away from Bess and the priests. Away from the guards.

'The henads will try her, and she can plead her case like every honest citizen,' Mykan said, as if lulling a child.

'Under whose authority?' her voice rose. 'Whose?'

But they were already carting Bess away.

FORTY-SEVEN

Raeyn woke to distant shouting. She crawled out of bed and hurried to the window, forgetting that her chamber overlooked the inner courtyard, not the keep's exterior. It was still dark.

Where was that noise coming from? Its rising hostility reminded her of the mob protesting at her wedding. Her chest tightened and for a moment she couldn't breathe.

She listened at the adjoining door. Silence. Venn must be up already—unless he had not gone to bed. What hour was it?

When she opened the entrance to the corridor, she expected to see Nedran's inhabitants abustle, but the hallway stood empty. Where were the guards? The servants?

She pulled a cloak around her nightdress, slid into her woollen slippers, and followed the commotion until she reached an external window. Below, a crowd gathered. Clad in white, they chanted the same three syllables, over and again. It took her a moment to discern their rallying cry.

Wit-chez-spawn! Wit-chez-spawn!

Witch's spawn. Her.

More shouting and jostling, this time originating from the town centre. She hurried towards a window on the other side of the keep. A second horde marched, dressed in the ordinary brown and grey of peasants, yelling a rival chant. A different three syllables. She listened, waiting for their words to resolve into something that made sense.

Hen-ads-out!

Still in her nightclothes, she scurried downstairs as further cries and the jangle and clomp of armed riders added to the melee. She rushed to the main entrance, where guards stood with halberds raised before the bolted door, ready to fend off protestors should they batter their way through.

Where was her husband?

'Your Highness, please, stay upstairs.' A lady-in-waiting appointed to her court caught her arm and ushered her back.

'What's going on?' she asked, brushing her off.

Another appeared at her side. 'Let us escort you to the women's quarters, Your Highness.' Still no sign of Bess, Mykan, or Venn.

'I'm not leaving until I know what is happening. Where is my lord husband?'

'With his riders, Your Highness,' called a guard. 'You'll be safest upstairs with the other women.'

More arms urged her back. She shrugged them away.

Outside, Venn's voice cut through the commotion, commanding, then beseeching, then commanding once again.

Brief quiet settled. Raeyn stared at the door as if caught in a daze. Heart beating. Frozen.

Another cry and the crowd erupted. This time, their battering force shoved and strained against the metal bars and hinges.

'Come, Your Highness. Quickly.' The words cut through her trance, and she let the women and guards usher her upstairs.

'All shall be well, Your Highness. Do not trouble yourself. Your lord husband will placate his people, he always does.'

Our people, Raeyn thought. But Nedran's citizens would never view her as such. They wanted her gone. She and her ties to her family. Well, she wished to cut Erldan loose, too.

The ladies-in-waiting continued to reassure, but they remained strangers to her. She didn't know who she could trust besides Bess, who she had not seen since last evening.

During the henad raids following their mother's execution, she and Jay had cowered in the women's hall. Why hadn't Erldan's folk protested like Nedran's? Those traitors had lined up to be examined, eager to display their piety.

Back then, she had been frightened. Numb. Beaten and shamed. Resigned to the omnipresent threat, the fight trampled out of her.

But not now. She would not see her new home replicate the carapace she left behind. While the other women fussed and cooed, she plotted.

Mykan, not Venn, brought Raeyn news that the clash concluded with several arrests and an urgent public hearing set for the following day. Her ladies were right. Venn had calmed his people, and she was grateful that, in his diplomacy, he was unlike her brother.

When she enquired after Bess, Mykan looked more troubled than she had ever seen him.

'The priests have arrested Mistress Bessandra for heresy, Your Highness.'

'No...' she whispered.

'It seems someone caught her trafficking in poisons...' He drew a breath. 'Abortifacients, to be precise.'

The floor dropped away, and the walls closed in.

'It's part of what prompted the remonstration earlier. Her brothers rallied to beg his lordship to intercede.'

But the protestors had been denouncing her, not Bess.

He must mean the second group, those decrying the priest's mounting influence. But she had been the one to send Bess to procure Lynden's tonic.

'He will pardon her, won't he?'

Mykan looked away.

'Won't he?'

'Other factors complicate the matter, Your Highness.'

Because the babe belonged to Venn's sister. And Gohran. *Treason.*

'Bess is common born, is she not?'

'As I said, Your Highness, the situation is complex...'

'Explain it to me. Even if Bess procured such a tonic, why arrest a commoner? They should issue a fine and let her go! We shall pay what is owed, and that should end the matter.'

Mykan's forehead creased until his thick brows almost touched.

She exhaled slowly and faced him with hands clasped below her waist, as staidly as her mother—but with no monarch's ring to distract her worrying fingers.

'This might explain matters more thoroughly than I can, Your Highness.' Mykan handed her a parchment bearing Erldan's seal.

She took it and glanced up, trying to weigh his demeanour. Brow still creased, he sucked on his teeth, jaw muscles pulsing. He feared her response.

She unfurled the scroll and read. It was a deed of passage granting Erldan's priesthood access to oversee the 'religious wellbeing of Nedran's souls,' whatever that meant. Her brother's initials beside his seal created an odd tightness in her chest. The rest of the proclamation was not in his hand. Davith's, no doubt.

Her brother was always too devoted to Erldan's head priest, trailing him like a stray dog might its master after showing the least kindness. If Davith hadn't manoeuvred Erldan's coin from his devotee, she would be settled on her own estate, managing a household that need not succumb to the whims of a spouse or sibling. Instead, that betrothal contract and her womb were being weaponised.

Elnora's cult didn't want her for her perceived ties to her heretical mother, while Nedran's secular citizens rejected her for her ties to that cult. Meanwhile, her husband and brother tried to render her powerless. Well, neither would defeat her.

She handed the scroll back. 'My thanks, Mykan. You may go.'

FORTY-EIGHT

'I did not authorise this, and the King in Erldan had no authority to do so.' Venn could not believe Erldan's priests had the audacity to detain one of his citizens—a loyal member of his household.

How could Mykan remain so sedate?

The guards had made several arrests under the priests' direction—not his—and now Elnora's servants had commandeered the great hall where Venn conducted his people's court for their trial.

Upon his dais stood the priest who officiated, a slithery man with a greased strip of hair fastened with a bone clasp, the sides and back shaved to reveal pasty, oily skin. A pair of beetle-like henads and a scribe perched on stools beside him. Prostrate and bound, Bess cast her eyes to the floor, resigned.

Venn lurched, pressing through the rabid crowd—more souls than at any ordinary hearing—but before he could interrupt, Mykan stopped him.

'My lord, if you intervene, you implicate your wife and sister.' He kept his voice lowered. 'They have accused Bess of *heresy*.'

For procuring an abortifacient. For Lynden.

If he interceded in a religious matter, it could quickly become one of state, and it wouldn't take long for someone to cry treason.

His fight abated. Bess was a commoner. The priests would make an example of her, issue a fine, and release her.

Defeated, he hung before the dais beside Mykan, and let Elnora's robes drone about the sanctity of life—the foetus's, not the mother's, and certainly not the maid's.

His breath squeezed, hot and tight in his chest, as he caught Bess's gaze across the crowded room. Her brow fierce, she stared straight back and gave a slow nod. She would sacrifice herself for his sister, for their family. She always had.

More speeches and sermons, declarations and accusations. It took every iota of restraint not to rap the pommel of his dagger on the lectern, raise his sword, and bid them to cease this farce. But Bess's nod contained him. She knew what would happen if he did.

He wished his aunt Servan were here. She would guide him through this.

Outside, remonstrations started up again. He'd calmed his populace yesterday, but that was when he believed the priests would yield. Before they waved Gohran's proclamation in his face.

Was this retaliation for the blockade? Or would Erldan's priests have infiltrated Nedran, anyway?

Now, he let the people vent. Eyes shut, he silently joined their chant: *he-nads-out!* until in his mind, it became, *Goh-ran-out!*

A clang and a thud as the double doors swung open and slammed into the walls. Armed guards marched, their halberds parting the crowd to allow someone through.

Raeyn.

Head high, shoulders back, she strode towards the dais as if she was Nedran's queen. She handed a signed and sealed parchment to the presiding priest.

His grey eyes narrowed as he snatched it from her and read. Without uttering a sound, he met Raeyn's gaze, crumpled and discarded her message.

'Dare you disregard a royal pardon?' she demanded.

Tall and spindly, though commanding, he stared her down. 'This is a spiritual matter, Your Highness.'

'Yet you have made a secular arrest.'

'By royal decree from the King of Erldan.' He remained unmoved.

'The King of Erldan is Nedran's *ally*, but holds no jurisdiction in this affair. As Erldan's Elder Princess, and wife to Lord Venn, your dryhten, I authorise Nedran's court to pardon Mistress Bessandra.'

'You hold no authority over the priests, Your Highness.'

'The priests in *Erldan*.'

'Over *any* priests.'

'Your Highness,' Mykan coaxed her back and away from the dais. His voice low, he said, 'As I informed you yesterday, your brother the king authorised the subsuming of Nedran's clergy to Erldan. Both his head priest and Nedran's agreed.'

'Don't listen to the witch's spawn!' someone shouted.

'Mistress Bessandra is *your* lady-in-waiting,' called another.

'Acting under your authority!'

'Charge the witch-princess, too!'

The previous day's chant of 'witch's spawn' started up again, like a vortex whirling, toppling, roiling.

'Stop!' Venn raised both arms. 'All of you, be silent!'

A cloak fell over the room as every pair of eyes turned towards him.

'Much as it pains us, the priests have the right to investigate claims of heresy. Princess Raeyn is my legal wife and rightful lady of Nedran, a union sanctioned by the gods. When you dishonour her, you dishonour me and Nedran. Let the henads conduct their hearing in peace. If found guilty, Mistress Bessandra won't—'

The crowd erupted again, shoving and jostling around the dais.

Arms grabbed him—Mykan's—and dragged him beyond the mob's reach.

Atop the melee, he shouted Bess was a commoner, that she wouldn't face execution, but Mykan wrenched him back.

'They can't hear you, my lord.'

They didn't care to.

Mykan stayed Venn with an outstretched hand as he surged forward and whispered to Raeyn, urging her to retreat to safety.

She shrugged him off and hissed. 'I am no fool.' Her eyes were harder and colder than Venn had ever seen, the grim line to her mouth enough to turn a man's heart to stone. Her voice cut across the uproar as she addressed the presiding priest. 'My royal pardon stands. Should you choose to ignore it, I defer the matter to my lord husband.'

She broke off and stormed out the way she had come, leaving the room aghast behind her.

◯

'W'hy make yourself a target?' Raeyn hissed when Venn followed her back inside the keep.

He seized her arm before she retreated to the women's hall. 'I was defending and protecting *you*.'

'And now Nedran's people recognise where I stand.' Raeyn clasped her hands until her knuckles turned white.

'They know you tried to wield authority as a Princess of Erldan and undermine *me*,' Venn said.

'I deferred to your rule.'

'Provided I agree with you.'

'Had you not desired a wife with her own mind, you should not have married one.'

He exhaled. 'Raeyn, please. Neither of us wants Bess to come to harm. Our interference only increases the priests' determination. They will want to set a precedent. Make her case an example.'

Bess was unlikely to be proved innocent. Witnesses had attested to her crime, and the medic refused Raeyn's bribe. It would be best for them all if the priests convicted her. They could accept the royal pardon or offer leniency and issue a fine. Even banishment. Anything but the fate of a condemned heretic.

Another weighty breath. 'Bess would have known the risk she took, and I know you would not have forced her.'

Hoped, she thought. She wondered what she would have done had Bess not volunteered to fetch the tonic. Lynden had refused any of her proposed matches—the only betrothals Raeyn could execute swiftly enough, and who would not challenge a premature pregnancy.

Venn reached for her. 'Weren't you the one who told me our goals align? We're fighting for the same thing. Let us work together.'

He was right. They were. It was an unfamiliar feeling. Even Jaydyn, her closest childhood companion, had been her rival, vying for their father's affection, uniting only against a common enemy: Ella. She sighed. It should have been against their brother. Ella's only crime was to be beloved, whereas Gohran worked against their interests to pursue his own.

'Please...' Venn's face crumpled. It had been selfish of her to go around him to issue that pardon, but Lynden begged her, and it was the only authority she had. It might not change the outcome, but Nedran's populace would know she had tried to defend one of them.

As Venn *had* defended her.

'We're aligned,' he repeated, and she let him unpeel her clasped hands, draw them around his neck, and pull her close, his heart pounding against hers.

He stroked her hair, and she softened into his chest. He smelled of sandalwood. Of *him*.

She longed to weep into his shirt, melt into his embrace. Allow someone to care for her. But she withdrew, hardened. This fight was not over.

Yet that night, Raeyn left the interior bedroom entry unbarred, and once she heard Venn settle next door, slipped within the adjoining chamber.

Venn glanced at her, wide-eyed.

She'd loosened her curls and slid her nightdress down to bare her shoulders. Her moontime had just finished, so Venn's seed was unlikely to bear fruit, but she wasn't trying to conceive an heir.

She wanted him.

At first, he hesitated, but her hands and mouth encouraged, making small, mewling sounds that signalled her willingness and pleasure.

'Do you desire this?' she whispered, her hand sliding between his thighs to cup and stroke him.

He moaned, 'Yes...Yes!'

When she pleasured him with her tongue, he grunted his enthusiasm. 'Ahh! Raeyn!'

He pulled her back to meet his kiss. 'I want you close, like this.' He peeled off her nightdress and clutched her bare breasts to his naked chest. His arms wound around her, tugging the hair at her nape, kissing her neck, her nipples, her belly, her sex, then finding her lips once more.

He positioned her to straddle his hips, and she felt his eyes drink her in. She eased herself down to welcome him inside her, and he watched her with lustful wonder, as though she were the most beautiful creature he'd ever seen.

She sought his lips, needing to close the air between them, as he moved to meet her. Her thighs squeezed around him, and he rolled them over, laying against and within her.

Between whimpers, his mouth found hers with tender passion, as he guided her hand to the apex of her sex, and whispered, 'I want you to take your pleasure while I'm inside you.' He rocked above her in a steady rhythm, not too fast, nor too slow, savouring yet building their mutual satisfaction.

She loved feeling all of him against her. The weight of him. His sandalwood scent, and the smell of his sex, the taste of his mouth, and his deep grunts as he whispered her name, over and again.

'Oh, by the goddess, Raeyn!'

She felt his muscles tense, saw him fighting his release, waiting for her to find hers. But at that moment, she didn't want or need it. She wanted *him*.

'Venn!' And then it took her, peaking in waves that radiated from her core all the way out across her torso, to shudder through her shoulders.

His mouth stifled her cries as he erupted inside her. 'Raeyn!'

He collapsed atop her, and she clung to him, their sweat-sheened limbs entangled.

Curved within his arm, head rested on his chest, she listened to his breath slow and his heartbeat ease and found herself still curled in his embrace when Elnora rose the next morning.

FORTY-NINE

Lynden's howl rose to a fevered pitch. 'You told me they would fine Bess at worst. Do something, Venn!'

Raeyn and her brother accosted her in her chamber following the impromptu hearing. She couldn't bring herself to attend the women's hall. Not with Bess gone. Instead, she'd embedded herself before her dresser and mirror, making up her face, as if painting over her anguish might conceal this nightmare.

'He's tried, my lady. We've all tried. And Bess knows that.' Raeyn squeezed Venn's hand—defending him to her.

This attempt at gentle compassion, the farcical amity between them, did not suit her.

Lynden snapped, 'It wasn't the tonic. There was no baby. Only a monster. I felt it in my bones. It was draining me.'

Raeyn's eyes bored into her like stones. 'Never speak of this again, do you understand?'

'Venn?' Desperate now.

But Venn's focus locked on Raeyn, looking at her with—what? Affection? Love?

'Raeyn's right,' he said, addressing her, but leaning against his wife. Yellow light from the window formed an aura of dust motes over them. 'The summons accuses Bess of poisoning, following a failed abortion. The priests claim the malformed foetus is proof of demonic intervention.'

Elnora disappeared behind thickening clouds, and the aura dimmed. Lynden turned back to her mirror, and picked up her horsehair brush, studying her reflection so she didn't have to see their pity. Their strange new intimacy.

'The medic has agreed to remain silent about whose baby it was, provided Bess pleads guilty to heresy.'

Not treason.

'What does the charge matter when the outcome is the same? Either way, Bess's life is forfeit.' She ripped the brush from her scalp to her tousled ends.

Raeyn clasped her wrists away from her face, her hair, and held her gaze. 'But yours is not.'

Nor hers.

Frost consumed her, and she snatched her hands back and resumed brushing. 'You were the one who bid Bess to source the tonic!' she lashed, stunned by her callousness.

Raeyn sighed. 'Bess volunteered. It was her idea. I had you married off to Lord Karlos.'

Had she not known Bess's heart, she would have accused Raeyn of trying to make Bess her scapegoat. That didn't stop her every fibre from screaming in protest. How could this happen? How was this just?

'Bess told them the tonic was for a common-born cousin. I doubt they believed her, but provided we say or do nothing to contradict her tale, they can't prove otherwise.'

But Lynden would always know.

'I have issued a royal pardon,' Raeyn said. 'And your brother has begged for leniency...'

'But as a religious matter, the henads must decide Bess's fate,' Venn concluded. 'Meanwhile, you don't have to stay. Raeyn and I will see to the priests, and you can be safely away. I'll send you to Lichen, or—'

'Not Lichen,' she snapped, pivoting to face them.

Venn frowned. 'But you and Vera—'

'It seems Lady Vera has agreed to marry his highness, King Gohran of Erldan.'

Venn sucked in his breath. 'Have the priests sealed the betrothal?'

'I presume not, if the official proclamation hasn't arrived.' Bess's arrest and the protests had Venn too distracted to stay abreast of his correspondence, but surely, he would have paid attention to that.

He paced, the thick carpet dampening his heavy footfalls.

'I know what you're thinking,' she said, 'but Vera's letter made it clear she's given up waiting. Were Jonas to propose now, she would refuse him.'

Venn paused. 'Curse Jonas thrice over!' He swore and tugged at his hair, then resumed his strides. 'We'd best hasten the negotiations for your betrothal to Adyn of Herron. I need sufficient leverage to pressure Gohran to bring Jonas home.'

Lynden tossed her brush down. Her voice flat, she said. 'The king can't bring Jonas home.'

Lightning flashed, followed by the distant rumble of a spring storm.

Another halt. Venn's throat bobbed with an anxious swallow. 'What do you mean?'

'Gohran doesn't have Jonas. He rode north at the start of winter.'

All the air seemed to flee Venn's body at once. 'But Gohran said when Jonas escaped, he headed west... That's where he and his riders tracked...' His eyes darkened beneath the shadow of his brow.

'Where Gohran's men torched every hut and hovel between Erldan and The End of the World?'

Another series of flashes lit up the room, casting strange shadows across their features.

'How do you know that?'

A low, persistent rumble.

'I saw him.'

'Who?'

'Jonas.'

'What?' A clash and a boom. The storm neared, the air growing thick.

'He sneaked home before he fled north.'

Venn's jaw dropped, then clenched as he scrambled to process this information. 'By the hells.' His whisper almost a hiss. 'Why didn't he—? Why didn't you—?' He pinched the bridge between his brows, swore, then composed himself. 'Lyn, we've been wasting our men blocking off the passage from Erldan when they should have been searching up north.'

She paled.

'And our blockade is probably the reason Gohran's priests are exerting their power over Nedran.'

Ice rippled along her spine. Her entire body tingled with cold. Oh gods. Was he right? Had she made things worse by keeping Jonas's counsel?

'Venn—I'm sorry, I—'

Lynden poised for his rage, for him to castigate her stupidity, her selfishness. Instead, he pulled her into his chest, and smoothed her tresses, the way Jonas used to. 'None of us wants this,' he spoke into her hair. 'Bess was like my mother, too.'

She waited for her tears to come, but his warmth couldn't penetrate as the hardness settled in her throat. Trapped. Rigid. When she contemplated relaying Jonas's warning to stay away from Gohran, calling him a demon king, she hesitated. She wasn't sure if it was because Venn would think her foolish for believing in sorcery, or because Raeyn still hovered, watching.

'We're in this together, Lyn,' Venn whispered, reassuring, forgiving. 'We've each of us mis-stepped along the way. At least now we know we can send men north.'

Another flash and boom resounded, and her heart shattered like brittle glass.

If Lynden was right, Vera's betrothal changed everything. There was no time to wait for Jonas to make a leisurely journey back. He needed to be home and formalise his prior claim now.

Venn provisioned two small cohorts to search north and east, and unofficially, spread word of the deal he'd brokered with Gohran to offer him a pardon.

What Jonas told Lynden may have been a decoy, so he suggested another troop head for Creywmm, in case he sought refuge with his good friend Sheevan.

He wanted Lynden to join them. There was no reason she couldn't formalise her betrothal to Adyn from Creywmm. Or, if she preferred, the second contingent might escort her to Mornae to stay with Aunt Servan. It was a long way from home and from Herron, but Lynden would be with family. Away from Gohran, and away from this farce of a heresy trial. With any luck, the priests would accept Bess's plea and enact Raeyn's pardon, and Bess could leave too.

It wasn't just Bess's life at stake. If Erldan's henads condemned her, let alone Cleansed her, he would have an insurrection on his hands.

Which is precisely what Gohran wanted.

'Curse it!'

But once he'd sealed Lynden to Herron and its vast army, Gohran wouldn't dare risk a war with Nedran, and he could scorch that treaty to dust.

FIFTY

Lynden spent the morning choosing dresses, jewellery, and cosmetics to pack, trying to imagine the members of her prospective husband's court. She wasted an hour searching for the exact ribbons to match the dried flowers for her hair.

'I think this one will go nicely, don't you, Bess—?'

Her heart dropped through the crater where Bess should have been.

She swallowed the wooden lump in her throat, choking on a sob that she refused to let escape. Bess would be back soon enough. This nonsense would be over, and she would be by her side, deciding on the exact style of sleeves for her dress, speculating about Vera's fate at Erldan, wondering how Sheevan of Creywmm managed to secure Adyn's older sister.

Venn had arranged for her to bid Bess farewell before setting out to Mornae, and eventually Herron, but if they dallied an afternoon or an evening more, her trial would be over, Venn would have convinced the priests to pardon her, and she could travel with them. Surely her new husband wouldn't begrudge her bringing her own lady's maid...

Shouting erupted outside. More protests.

She slammed her window shut and drew the curtains.

The silence crushed as Bess's absence pressed in. The air was thick with it, squeezing her lungs.

She flung open the door, and the flickering sconces cast distorted shadows down the looming corridor. The empty women's hall taunted, so she pivoted and headed towards the kitchen, then hesitated. The servants may not welcome her.

Another turn, and she padded her way to the drawing room. Once inside, she hugged the muffled quiet. No shouts, no sidelong glances or whispers, and no reminders of Bess.

She pulled out the embroidered silk bag that housed their set of tiles—a gift from her father—and tipped the pieces onto the table before her favourite settee, each one smoothed over years by dextrous fingers. Until that moment, she hadn't realised how much she missed her family's languorous evenings reading and drinking, or the boisterous ones spent gaming, with accusations of cheating. Never Jonas, though, with his rotten luck.

She turned over the High Lady tile to sit face-up beside the King of another suit. Between them, the minor lord tile, the Cynnelic, had landed upside down. She stuffed the tiles back in their bag for when she visited.

Why hadn't she told Venn about Jonas at the start of winter, when the entire household palled with worry?

Her mind skipped in its peculiar way as she chased her memories of the preceding moons. Images morphed and blurred. She recalled Jonas leaving before a pervasive dread settled on her. Nausea and fatigue had eaten into her bones and did not release its grip until they carried that bloodied bundle away from her...

What was it? She tried to remember...

A picture formed, but it was so faint now. *A creature expelled from her womb. Swaddled and silent. A mass of teeth and bone and hair amid amorphous flesh...*

Her heart lurched as she hurried towards the door. She hurled the contents of her stomach onto the hardwood floor.

'My lady!' A chambermaid arrived and almost stepped into her pool of vomit.

She drew back Lynden's hair and ushered her down the corridor. 'Let's clean you up, and then you must go.'

'What about Bess? I haven't...'

The maid shook her head, pitying eyes sloped as though she were a child. 'There's no time for that, my lady. The lord dryhten has ordered his men to leave right away.'

Her vision blurred, and her ears rang. 'No! We need to wait for Bess!'

Yet she knew. Had always known, from the moment the priests pointed their greasy fingers at her in the marketplace.

Bess wasn't coming.

The carriage tilted and jerked. To think Lynden had dallied, preening and packing. Avoiding. Now, there was no time.

Venn would remedy the situation. He had to. Then, Bess could follow on horseback. She would catch up to them, and—

But as they drove into the night, the crunch of gravel echoed around the lonely carriage and screamed in her ears.

She drew the velvet curtains closed, but nothing could disguise the fiery-orange glow that haunted the sky and clawed its way into her soul.

Raeyn retreated to her chamber and barred the door, unable to stop trembling. Outside, the rabble's competing chants fused into a wordless cacophony that she needed to drown out.

Not her mother. She wasn't in Erldan.

But it was under Erldan's direction that the priests would burn Bess, as they twisted every argument to justify their conviction.

Earlier, she had watched Nedran's servants load Lynden and her belongings into the carriage and carry her north and east to safety. Gohran would not be foolish enough to hunt her down. If he suspected the poison was for his child, he would want Lynden gone.

The same did not hold true for her. She was the one who had authorised—and encouraged—Bess to procure the tonic.

She wrung her hands, twisting a knot in her kirtle.

A rap at her door. 'Raeyn?' Venn called.

He must not see her like this. She pinched her cheeks, fastened her curls back from her face with a sapphire-encrusted clasp, and straightened on the tail of a robust breath. 'What is it?'

'May I enter?'

Another inhale. Steadfast. She could do this.

She unbarred and opened the door.

Venn's dark hair fell in lank segments across his forehead, overshadowing his troubled eyes, whose surrounding flesh was pink and swollen. He stepped inside and collapsed against her breast, heaving juddering gasps. She drew him close and squeezed him tight as his tears soaked through her bodice.

'I—I didn't think—I didn't believe—Oh gods...' His voice choked off in a howl that burrowed into her chest.

Raeyn let him weep where she could not, her throat and heart a desert where nothing would grow. Barren. Like her.

As Bess's screams cut through the night, and the people's anguish rose to banshee wails, they clung to one another in the shadows.

FIFTY-ONE

Eager hands brushed Jonas's overgrown hair from his face, then rubbed his beard. He stirred, blinking until the room—and a pretty smile—came into focus.

'You're awake,' the smile's owner said with an unfamiliar, clipped accent. She sponged a moist cloth over his forehead and cheeks.

'Where am I?' And who, by every demon, was she?

'Let me fetch Ma.' Her skirts swished away with her padding feet, and out through a dropped curtain.

He propped himself up on this stranger's bed. A dim lantern cast a flickering yellow glow across the small wooden table beside him, shadows dancing over the crowded walls.

He pivoted his bare legs over the side of the straw mattress. Where were his clothes?

When he tried to stand, his muscles wobbled, and his head spun, forcing him to sink down atop the scratchy blankets.

'Our Lady help me, what were you thinking?' A rounded woman in her middle age pushed past the drape. Her hands grabbed his legs and hefted them onto the bed. She straightened his torso and tucked him back against the feather-stuffed pillow, then pulled the blankets to cover him, her thick waist and thicker bosom a padded barrier against his escape. 'You're in no state to be strolling around the village.'

She turned to the pretty young woman—presumably her daughter. 'Our guest needs some water, Milla.'

Russet irises studied him, the same colour as the girl's, but harder, suspicious, while her deep brown skin spoke of Myan heritage.

Milla reappeared, carrying a pitcher and a wooden cup. She shared her mother's complexion and padded hips.

'My thanks,' he took the offered water and drank greedily, flashing the girl one of his charming smiles.

She blushed and sucked in her bottom lip.

'Out, Milla,' said her mother. 'Tell your pa to serve your supper. Now.'

Milla skittered off, casting a further glance at Jonas on her way.

Lips pursed. 'Don't even think about putting those paws near my girl.'

Jonas nearly spit out his mouthful. He spluttered and coughed until he could breathe again, then took another gulp to hide his face.

'Milla will sleep in with me and her pa.' She drew the drape away to reveal a second bed. 'Should she find her way back here, this curtain is very thin.'

'I'm in no state to feel the least bit amorous, I assure you.'

Eyes narrowed. 'I know your kind,' she said. 'If you'd honourable intentions, you wouldn't be scrounging a living out in those woods. And you'd have found a spring hire.'

Spring. Gods. How long had he been out here? His fingers combed his thickened beard. It exceeded the stage of itching and now irritated.

'Do you happen to have a blade I can borrow?' He searched the room but saw nothing resembling a dagger.

She scoffed. 'You think I'm going to hand you a weapon?'

'Well, my excellent lady, I could ask you to do the shaving for me...'

A puzzled frown. 'You don't talk like most mercenaries.'

'Probably why no one would hire me.'

She snorted. 'I doubt it was your accent.' She appraised his muscular frame in the same manner as her daughter, earlier. The curve forming at the corners of her mouth told Jonas she was just as appreciative.

She set the basin and cloth within reach on the mattress beside him. 'I'll leave you to get tidied up, but no blade—the beard stays. Milla will bring you supper when you're done.'

It was no bath, but after camping alongside animals who called themselves men, this warm soapy water was liquid gold.

Soon, a potted stew wafted, and his stomach growled, clenching and cramping in protest. He drank to feel a substance enter his mouth, throat, and belly, until Milla arrived carrying a steaming wooden bowl. 'Finally, the gods shine my way!'

Milla removed the basin from the bed and perched in its stead as he ate, watching with that same coy grin.

'Milla! If he's conscious, he can feed himself! He doesn't need you hovering,' her mother called.

She giggled, cleared his empty bowl, and left him to rest.

Between the pair of them, Jonas preferred the elder woman. She could hold a conversation and had navigated her way around a man's body at least once.

He lay back and stared up at the wooden beams and underside of thatch. Despite himself, he grinned. He must be recovering if he was contemplating anything beyond his next meal and surviving the freezing night.

Fifty-Two

The new moon brought a fresh heresy trial, and though only one woman awaited condemnation, it was enough for Erldan's neophytes to return to Harnal.

Amber and Nykki milled outside the hearing, alongside the curious, morbid, and grieving, using this window to thieve from the onlooker's minds.

Thick with anxious sweat, the afternoon air was unseasonably warm, and Nykki scratched at the edges of the cowl that concealed her brand. Despite the heat, as they inched through the crowd, Amber drew her shawl tighter to cover her distinctive hair.

Two burly guards in bland tunics carrying halberds shuffled the accused from the hearing to her cage to await execution. Still no sign of Grogan.

The young woman's sweet, round face, and symmetrical features sobered, and when she looked up, grey streaked one brown iris through her tears.

Nykki wailed, mimicking the bustle of spectators trailing the alleged witch. To anyone watching, she and Amber appeared as her loved ones.

'Stand aside!' A guard raised his halberd and bid the bystanders to disperse as they disappeared with their captive behind the temple.

Amber and Nykki weaved their way forward. It was surprisingly easy to manoeuvre their collective will through these heightened psyches, enchanting via a casual touch or the brush of an arm, until their neighbours peeled away and created a clear path.

A distant screech and a clang sounded atop a steady whimper. They rounded the corner as the guards were locking the prisoner within a cage.

Once close enough, Amber lurched forward and gripped a guard, while Nykki grabbed the other, their force surging through that touch until the men's thoughts fogged over.

'Let us see her!' Amber cried.

'Please—we need to bid her farewell,' said Nykki.

The first guard nodded slowly; his voice wooden as he echoed the request. He turned to his fellow. 'Go back inside. This won't take long.'

Confusion clouded his companion's features before resolving when Nykki squeezed his arm tighter. 'Very good,' he said, and Nykki released him to head back towards the temple's entrance.

Power buzzed through Amber's contact, and tension slid from the first guard's body. Nykki stepped in close to help prop him up before he wilted to the ground.

Open it, Amber commanded, directing his movements.

Metal screeched as the door swung on its hinges.

Free her bindings.

His hands moved haltingly under their command to untie the prisoner.

Step aside, Amber thought.

Aloud, Nykki said, 'My thanks, good sir. May Elnora bless your compassionate soul.'

Amber reached for the round-faced accused and weaved a tether of force through her psyche. *Give me your kirtle.*

Head swimming, she did as Amber asked.

Now you, she wound another around the guard. *Hand me your cloak and tunic.*

Amber quickly undressed, and the three of them swapped clothes.

Hide, Amber ordered the freed prisoner, who wore Amber's borrowed garments.

She hesitated, glancing back at the neophyte clad in her ill-fitting kirtle.

Go. Flee. Amber applied more pressure, and she skittered into the dark, away from the village crowd and temple, while Amber and Nykki secured the disguised guard within the cage, gagged him with a sock, and tied his hands and feet with twine.

With the guard's cloak pulled up over her hair to shadow her face, Amber stood sentinel, while Nykki huddled behind the cart's wheels and waited.

Nykki's mind tingled from Amber's grip. *Whatever happens, promise you won't leave my side.* Amber would not lose Nykki again.

From a distance, the guard would appear as his prisoner, and Amber as the guard, but the masquerade would not hold once anyone known to either neared, and their enchantment wouldn't influence the onlookers to stay away for long.

Whenever the guard roused, Nykki slipped her hand between the bars of the cage to pinch him quiet, and he slumped, his head lolling.

Twilight faded. Frogs croaked through the thick air, along with the occasional rusty squawk of a nighthawk, and still no one reported to collect the accused.

Thrice, footfalls approached, but never the ones they sought and when stars winked through the violet night, Nykki rattled the cage and hissed under her breath.

Hush, my love. Grogan will come.

What if he didn't? Worse—what if the fellow immune to their influence arrived in his stead, or another like him? They wouldn't know until they were close enough to touch him, when it would be too late.

My skin itches. We should go... Nykki's jittery muscles twitched.

Amber's reassurance came in waves. *Be patient.* They could not afford for either of them to panic and freeze.

Then she felt it, the unmistakable slither of Grogan's craving.

By Xenon, he had lagged in his duty to savour his anticipation. Amber's stomach churned, but she could not risk shielding against his lascivious thoughts. Keeping abreast of his intentions was the only way to keep them safe.

He's coming.

Her fear and anticipation were as ripe as Grogan's, reflected and amplified in Nykki's psyche.

Steady. We won't have long before—

Grogan appeared from behind the temple, and pushed a palm through his greasy hair, then wiped it on his robe. He barely glanced Amber's way as he reached for the cart, his pudgy eyes eager to torture another prisoner before the finale of her death.

Now!

Nykki leapt out and seized him.

His surprised cry caught in his throat as Amber and Nykki's power silenced and paralysed him. Nykki's azure light threaded and weaved to secure his arms behind his back.

Amber stepped forward, and his already pasty complexion paled gratifyingly. *Two powerful witches to a lone neophyte. I'd wager that stiffens your puny rod.* She directed her thought into his defenceless mind, relishing the moisture beading at his temples and across his upper lip.

He writhed in Nykki's clutches, his mouth and tongue torpid as melted butter, unable to shout or scream.

They dragged him from the cage, between buildings and down alleys, away from the township until they reached the river's edge that marked the village border. At least he knew now to remain compliant. Knew to fear Amber's torturous imagination.

His acrid sweat stank of dread, and Amber contemplated pushing him underwater to wash it off and then plunge in after, to scrub the stench from her, too. But there was no time. They needed information.

Share Davith's movements, his routine. Show me when he is most vulnerable...

A slow smirk. Even now, he sought to resist them.

Do you want me to torture you, fool?

His groin twitched, and her memories crowded. Every licentious slither, each cruel thought, the hands he laid on Chrysanth.

She imagined wrenching his kidneys, squeezing his liver, clawing at his heart.

He gasped and gurgled, his tongue too lax to speak.

Another wrench, and she forced her way into his mind, a puppeteer tugging and twisting on strings. She trampled through his recollections, saw the high priest at Erldan conducting rites and sermons, preaching, but also politicking with King Gohran, who grovelled and seethed.

When is Davith next away from the king?

Another silent sneer.

She imagined contorting his intestines, coiling and knotting, and he tried to scream. She eased off but did not let go, until his thoughts grew too muddled to decipher, when she allowed him control of his tongue.

If your voice rises above a whisper, I will rip your guts from the inside to the out.

'Nn-Ne-Nedran... He's in...'

He gurgled again, but this time, blood sputtered up from his throat to stain his lips.

How?

She let go—briefly. Just enough to detect a second mind gripping him.

Oh, gods.

Nykki's cowl had loosened, and when Grogan spied her brand, a callous, libidinous grin spread across his features and his stiffening rod spasmed.

Nykki sensed it, too, and her loathing seethed.

More blood gurgled from the priest. Agony pierced every fragment of his body, and his eyes rolled back into his head.

Nykki—stop!

Another twist wrenched through him, devoid of pleasure now, as Nykki's brutal torture overrode his taste for pain.

Amber fought to extract her mind, to shut Nykki's unbridled fury down, but she could not break free. Entangled through the bond of shared lust, her power was Nykki's to wield.

'Nykki!' she cried. 'Nykki—No!'

Her thoughts remained embedded in Nykki's, knotted and trapped. She could not withhold her source, nor shield herself as Nykki contorted Grogan's organs, then sliced through his innards, her imaginings as visceral as knives with Nykki's movement and Amber's strength behind her.

Amber grasped the neophyte to her, tried to fend Nykki off, but it was too late. Welts appeared and more blood spilled out of him, soaking his robe and coating his lips.

An icy hand clutched her chest and throat as the light extinguished from the neophyte's eyes, and her hope with it, when his final breaths juddered to a halt. A few sickening twitches, and then nothing but the sound of Nykki's rasping sobs, and the silent scream inside her mind.

She choked down the wooden lump at hearing Grogan's last words: *Nedran. What about Nedran?*

Grogan lay flaccid and sprawled over her lap, his blood spattered across her dress, her face, her hair. Her only avenue to trace Davith's movements and claim her true prize, gone.

Opposite, Nykki lapped the crimson spatter from her fingertips and her eyes blazed before she realised what she'd done.

'I—I'm sorry...' Nykki wept. 'I didn't—'

Grogan was the means to an end. Nykki's fury stole his value.

Her vengeance.

A dampened sob—she wasn't sure whose—tossed into the night.

Amber dragged herself from beneath Grogan's corpse and drew Nykki close, listening to her heart throb and bracing against her violent shudders.

'Hush, my love. You're safe. We're alive. That's all that matters...'

Distant shouts. The villagers and their holy men would soon be upon them. She wrenched Nykki away from Grogan's body. Lifeless, and yet...

Raw power thrummed like the static of a storm, heightening her senses. Intoxicating force weaved around and between them, summoning a carnal, savage hunger that overwhelmed her grief. Its thrill buzzed along her limbs and set fire to her core.

Nykki's cat-green eyes glimmered, alight, as her appetite rose to match, reflecting and amplifying the charge that danced through her veins.

Laughter bubbled up her throat and erupted out of her lips as Grogan's life had spilled out of him.

She craved more.

Amber drew beyond what she could contain, blotting out every other emotion. Each fragment of pain.

Satiated. Drifting. Dreaming. Bliss!

The villagers' cries grew louder and keener, but her intoxicated haze dampened their alarm and muted their terror.

Something shifted. Grogan's source seemed to coagulate, leaving a rancid aftertaste. Thickening like tar, his blood rotted as the last of his lifeforce extinguished.

Nykki's eyes darkened to inky pools, her veins blackened, and her skin paled. Breath rasping, she appeared to age. Grogan's lifeless blood was draining her! Killing her.

They were drawing from a dead source.

Stop drawing, Nykki! Stop! Her cry snapped Nykki's mind alert, breaking the blood-force's spell.

Nykki blinked and gasped. As she ceased drawing, colour restored to her cheeks, and her irises returned to their usual hue, aware of the surrounding scene: two ravenous, ecstatic women hovering over a butchered priest, stained with the evidence of their crime. Encircling them, three score villagers and their priests thirsted for vengeance.

They turned and stood back-to-back as Harnal's inhabitants encroached. Torches flamed like beacons against the dark, casting ghoulish shadows across hostile eyes and grim mouths. Too many bodies to sway at once. It would take just one immune to their influence to render them powerless and allow their capture.

Amber's vision flashed to Erldan's dungeon. Its dank, musty odour flooded, and cold earth pressed in, accompanied by the sour tang of metal bars, stale excrement, and vomit. The guard's clothing, and Grogan's corpse, reeked of it.

She squeezed Nykki's hand, and the souls before her dimmed and flickered. She felt oddly weightless, drifting from her body as in a dream.

Lend me your power, Nykki begged, and Amber let her magic flow. Grogan's depleted lifeforce was no longer a weapon but a liability, yet traces of viable blood lingered, soaked into their clothes and his.

Nykki's other hand gripped tight, carrying her, lifting until they floated up and out of their bodies, the stars appearing as bloated orbs surrounded by a viscous indigo soup of roiling currents.

Keep imagining, Nykki urged. *I can see a way out... almost reach it...*

Amber couldn't rid her mind of the same memory repeating: a cot on the other side of iron bars, and a dense wooden door, locked and bolted. In one corner, a girl with golden eyes whimpered. In another, a handsome man with a self-deprecating grin huddled.

Cold shivered across her limbs, her hairs prickling upright as though naked under the night sky, where Xenon's shadow formed the barest sliver in its invisible phase. Strange echoes overlaid the image with silhouettes of iron bars flickering along stone walls.

She blinked, and the cells stood empty.

Don't stop...

Strangers' hands grasped, but as she drew more, her body became ghostlike, and they passed straight through.

Screeching erupted. Horrified eyes and gaping mouths cried, 'Witch!'

Another breath. Power tugged her mind and tore her flesh, like a tether stretched to break.

Draw more, my love... Keep going.

Fear surged, and the flames rippled closer. 'Witches! Burn them!'

Blood, fire, and rage churned: an amalgam of raw force creating a glowing azure haze. Amber sucked it within, weaving a net of ethereal substance to surround them both, but there wasn't enough.

Oh gods, I can't source more!

A torch slashed forward, then another, and her tunic whooshed alight.

She braced for the flames to scorch her, but she was already naked.

Had already fled.

Except...

'Cleanse the demon spawn!'

Her clothes aflame, she still stood by Harnal's lake, straddling the priest Nykki murdered as villagers seethed.

One more draw... Amber, please!

Choking plumes rose on and around her, scorching heat so close and yet...

She was burning, and not; she was there, and gone.

Through the suffocating haze, Nykki's scar blazed, no longer pink puckered flesh, but an ice-blue sigil.

Keep picturing...

But she saw only dirt and excreta, blood and pain, while before her, scores of souls ravened to enact their wrath.

Elnora might take their fool priest into Her arms as a martyr, but for Amber and Nykki, there would be no Afterlife. The villagers' fire would extinguish them.

This fight was not over.

Amber let go of Nykki, fusing back with her corporeal form. Pain seared as the flames licked her. With a cry, she grasped the guard's halberd, then slashed and hacked through flesh, hungry for blood.

A crimson spray whipped across the crowd, then another, and she tossed the weapon aside to clasp Nykki again. Energy surged, and she sucked up its raw power. Nykki's eyes glowed. She clung to her beloved and braced as their simulacrums slid along her imagined cord until it tugged and strained.

On her next breath, the tether released and propelled their bodies with them, plunging through the ethereal currents and careening them away from Harnal.

Azure light flashed, and icy air rushed to fill the void where the two sorceresses had stood. Pitchforks skewered uninhabited smouldering clothes that dropped to the ground before horrified eyes. Torches ignited the space surrounding Grogan's butchered corpse while howls of rage and terror rose into the night.

Fifty-Three

Ella continued her training, practising relying less on wild emotion, and more on controlled and calculated direction, until her mental muscles strengthened and she could move objects with ease. On one occasion, she connected with Yorg's simulacrum and carried him a handspan. Yorg had been right: her work with Vorlyn helped.

'You grow stronger,' he said, when she no longer needed to feast between attempts, and her clumsy grasps stopped slicing him.

That evening, when Mayel and Jurn invited her to swim, not for work but to play, she didn't hesitate.

Before they reached the pools, Mayel led her to a side chamber where Aeron's people groomed, while Jurn went on ahead. The chamber housed troughs, brushes, and soap. Beside one basin sat a pair of shears. Instinct told her what Mayel intended.

'I like your hair shorter... like this.' She fisted Ella's locks above her ears. 'Let me cut it for you.'

How long had it been since Mara hacked off her treasured tresses, taking to the remains with her harsh dye? A brutal necessity. But when Mayel sliced away the dead bleached ends, leaving her raven dark silken roots to frame her face, it seemed intimate. Tender.

'It suits you.' Mayel tickled her languorous fingers through the tips of Ella's hair, and a spark traversed her spine. She cupped Ella's cheeks and kissed her nose with a warm azure cloud that hugged her soul.

'Shall we wash these stray strands off?'

Mayel's smile glimmered, sending an eager thrill into the pit of Ella's belly as she tugged her towards the pools and into the steaming water.

A dense mist rose around and between them in a moist veil. Jurn was already there, and he swam near, catching Ella between them, stroking one arm, and Mayel, the other. Heat swelled as Mayel snagged her gaze, her soft hand trailing her cheek, gripping her nape, and pulling her close, until her lips found Ella's. Mayel's tongue stroked hers. Gentle and inviting. Her kisses trailed Ella's neck, and down her throat towards her breasts, as she peeled Ella's sodden shirt away.

Snowmelt trickled along the rock face, sending icy currents to swirl against her skin, but nothing could cool the heat rising within her core.

Jurn's hand steered her mouth to his and then he was kissing her, too. His hands explored her waist and hips, then lower, venturing to secure her against him until his arousal pressed into her.

Her beguilement stirred, and she panicked.

Breathe, Ella. You're safe. A soothing stroke of her mind.

This wasn't the roiling, inverted current of her brother's corrupted power, nor the drunken vessel for her influence she found in Venn.

She relaxed against their flesh, hard and soft, yielding and exploring, allowing the tingle of her pleasure to remain corporeal. She welcomed their magic while containing hers.

Their minds sought permission before their bodies united, not spoken, but felt and known. As their power wrapped itself around her, it filled the cracks in her fractured soul.

This is what she had longed for. She eased into their touch, their flesh melding as her desire reflected in their thoughts, and theirs in hers.

The blue currents of their magic swirled and rippled along her limbs, through her centre with a pleasure so intense it threatened to engulf her.

An icy tremor stirred the surrounding water. She shuddered.

'Ella...' Mayel's palms traced her shoulders and spine while Jurn feasted on her neck, and she slipped back into the chasm of their bliss, emitting a low moan.

The sound cut off in a cry as a piercing stab clanged behind her eyes, and they shot open.

Far above, the tiny breach in the cave's defences formed a tunnel for her vision, but instead of the sky, she saw plumes of smoke and flame. Blue spears of force shredded a pale, hairless belly into a savage, bloodied mess. A brunette woman, spattered in gore, and another with saffron hair, screamed and wailed. Nykki and Amber.

The surrounding arms suffocated, their lips like acid. She wrenched away.

'Ella?'

Her vision clouded and concealed the image again, but when it cleared, a bearded man with green-grey eyes stared back: Jonas.

'I—I need to go...'

She climbed out of the pools, tugged a cloth around her, and retreated with her heart thudding in her throat. Cold struck her bare neck and quivered over her skin as she rushed through Aeron's corridors to the snug cavern where she and Vorlyn worked. Huddled in a corner, she hugged a padded cushion, waiting for her pulse to slow.

That was the second occasion the god had shown her Amber and Jonas—not together—yet entwined, and the third time the god's warning had penetrated Aeron's shield. Why taunt her with these visions when she could do nothing about them?

Power churned and she coiled it around her, a blanket to soothe, until she could expel the images and settle her heart and breath into a steady rhythm.

Fifty-Four

'We've collected abundant fungi from the caves this season.'

An unfamiliar voice roused Jonas from inside the hut where he rested. He peeled the drop curtain back to spy a middle-aged woman dressed in trousers and a tunic, opposite the hut's owner, Thyla.

The guest pushed her grey-streaked, honey-coloured hair aside to sip her tea and reached into her satchel to hand over a cloth parcel tied with wool.

Thyla loosened it and examined the contents. She held up an assortment of long-stemmed mushrooms of varying shapes and sizes. 'Excellent! How much?'

'Consider them a gift,' the woman said. 'And a consolation.'

Thyla glanced up. 'Oh?'

'I bring sad tidings. Tragedy befell your brother Thyss's village at the start of winter. The king in Erldan razed the buildings, searching for escaped prisoners he believed sheltered there. I can't say how many survived…'

A sob caught in Thyla's throat, followed by a horrid, wracking note that wrenched Jonas's gut.

He dropped the curtain back. Hells.

She knew of Gohran's attack. Harvested fungi from nearby caves.

Could they be…? Could she know…?

He hauled out of bed and dressed in the leathers and tunic his host had kindly laundered, favouring his good leg. By the time Thyla and this honey-haired woman—Vorlyn was her name—finished trading gossip and tea, he'd fashioned a crutch from a broomstick and was ready to hobble after her and find out.

The women bid farewell, neither turning back, as Vorlyn retreated towards the forest escarpment with a single wave, and Thyla headed to the main clutch of huts, presumably to share her new wares and ripe news.

Jonas ducked outside, half weaving, half hopping between the last homesteads and into the thickening woods, keeping a steadfast watch on Vorlyn's path. Each step fired through his ankle, but he pushed on. He couldn't risk losing Vorlyn's tail.

He tottered between branches, ducking beneath the tree canopy, careful not to trip on the uneven roots poking through the grass. Ahead, the landscape shifted as rocks emerged—the same kind he'd seen through Alina's glass sphere, covered in ivy and moss, and promise caught in his throat.

But as Vorlyn picked up speed, turned again, and disappeared between a rocky outcropping, that hope dissipated.

He swore, trying to match her pace, to catch her before her next turn took her out of sight forever, only for his boot to clip a concealed tree root. The trip tipped him onto his injured ankle. It twisted, collapsing under him. He screamed and toppled to the ground.

Winded, he stared at the blue sky peeking between leaves and boughs. He wasn't sure whether the pain of his ribs on each inhale was more intense than the stabbing in his joint that would not abate.

He cursed himself for his clumsiness, for losing Vorlyn too far from the village to hobble back, unless he crawled out the same way he'd arrived. Was he doomed to die out in this wretched forest, so close to where Alina told him he would find Ella, yet never close enough?

'Look!' a deep voice called.

Another replied in an unfamiliar tongue.

Two pairs of eyes peered down at him. One cinnabar; the other, a silvery blue, embedded in faces resembling night and day.

'You're hurt,' the first said.

'Let's get you inside,' said the other, whose accent thickened his clear Yceltic words.

Jonas thanked them profusely as they hoisted him by the armpits and knees and carted him in the direction he'd been headed—following Vorlyn—all the while conversing in that same melodic tongue.

The indignity of being hauled like a sack of grain rubbed, but he was too cursed grateful to have someone move him without putting weight on his ankle to protest.

When they carried him within what was undeniably a cave, hope rose in his chest.

Inside, the walls glowed, casting strange shadows, but he saw no lanterns or sconces. Perhaps from fungi or insects. They set him down on a rug before a dim brazier and propped his head and feet up with silk-covered cushions.

'I'll fetch Ayla,' said the cinnabar-eyed one, whose pale skin appeared ghost-like in the constant white light.

The darker-skinned fellow studied him curiously. 'Ayla is our best healer.'

Jonas wasn't sure anyone could fix the repeated damage he'd inflicted on those wretched bones, but he would take whatever help they offered.

Sure enough, when the woman, Ayla, appeared—another odd-looking soul, with dark skin, white hair, and luminous eyes—his injury confounded her.

She repositioned his calf across her lap and pulled off his boot and sock, and he grunted. She pushed up his trouser leg, placed her hands on him, and closed her eyes, as if she expected that to affect him.

With a frown, she turned to her fellow. They exchanged some chatter in that same strange language. The only word he recognised was 'Vorlyn'—the woman who he'd encountered at the village. The woman he'd followed here.

Ayla set his leg down, smiled shyly, then left him staring after.

He expected the caves to smell damp with rot, but found the hint of moss and the fecund soil of forest undergrowth refreshing. Glittery veins threaded through the strange rock and that same pearly glow coated every surface.

Whispers at the entry. Vorlyn arrived and peered down her nose at him, then approached.

'May I?' She sat beside him and plied his leg as the other woman had, balancing it across her thighs.

She examined the swell of yellow and purple, twisting and applying careful pressure while studying his face.

'Does that hurt?'

He winced.

'What about this?'

He grimaced through gritted teeth. 'It's fine.'

Her eyebrow quirked.

'I'm going to rub salve on the swelling, but we may need to re-set the bone against a splint. Do you understand?'

'Do I look like a fool?'

'More like a lost child.' Her mouth curved. The barest movement. Nurturing. Wistful. Troubled.

Her brow creased, and she applied the salve, firm but cautious, all the while monitoring his reactions. Her voice reminded him of home, and he fought his tears.

'How did you find this place?' she asked as she massaged the muscles and tendons surrounding his ankle.

'I didn't know it was a secret.'

Another quirk.

He'd never been a good liar. 'I followed you.'

She frowned.

'I was staying with Thyla and her family.'

'And you hobbled here on that?' she nodded to his injury.

'I've survived worse.' Like an entire winter wearing salvaged rags and piss-filled boots, eating roasted lizards and squirrels, while fending off bored, stinking thugs.

'Is that a south-western accent I detect? What brings you this way?'

He swallowed, trying to stop his mouth twitching, for she sounded no different from him. 'I journey through many places... And you?'

She didn't answer, pressing down and digging her thumb into an intense knot that earned her a cry.

She turned to the second woman. 'Fetch the liquid opium.'

'Ale or spirit will do,' Jonas said.

Vorlyn raised her brows. 'You're sure?'

He nodded. 'I've never had a taste for the wretched smoke. I doubt the milk will suit me any better.'

The women eyed each other.

'Spirit it is,' Vorlyn said. She examined his ankle. 'Gods willing, this manipulation realigns your bones and joints, and it heals with no need to re-break the bone.'

'I'll drink to that!' He took the offered spirit and swilled it down.

She pressed into another knot, discomfort radiating and then easing. 'That's it, just breathe...'

Vorlyn steadied his limb while the second woman cradled his heel. She tugged and a series of sickening cracks sounded. Fire sparked through his ankle, and he howled.

The woman refilled his glass thrice more until the edges of his pain blurred and he relaxed back against the pillow.

As the walls swam, and his body melted into the cushions, Ella's tormented gaze watched from behind his eyelids. 'I'm coming, El...' he slurred, drifting to sleep and dreaming of home.

Fifty-Five

Everything stilled, and deadened silence filled a blue abyss for what seemed like forever and no time at all. Then slowly, the colour resolved into the dim grey of a darkened room, the muted echo of moisture dripping, and the all too familiar smells of dank dirt and rot: Erldan's dungeon.

Every inch of Amber ached, as if someone had dropped them from a great height, and patches of her flesh stung from where the torches scorched.

She reached for Nykki. Naked and shivering, they clung to one another, hearts hammering, jagged breath rasping. They'd survived!

'What is this place?' Nykki asked, meaning, *why here?* Why did Amber's mind lead them *here?*

She winced. She had tried to expel her memories, purge the images that flashed unbidden, yet in her panic, Erldan's dungeon was all she saw.

The surrounding cells stood empty, but for how long? 'We need to leave,' Amber whispered, scrambling towards the exit, but found it bolted from the outside. She turned back to Nykki. 'Whatever you did to get us here—do it again.'

'I—I don't know how...' Nykki's trembling didn't stop.

'You knew to draw more power to fuel... whatever that was.'

'I saw a path leading out, and I... followed it.'

Nykki frowned, struggling to describe her experience, but Amber sensed what she couldn't articulate. Her mind's machinations had resembled their powers merging when Amber directed her movement. Then, when the strain overwhelmed her, she'd summoned Amber's strength, and somehow, she'd moved *them*. Relocated them as she had shifted a boulder, snapped a rope, and carved Grogan's flesh to pieces.

Amber's mind provided the path to follow and amplified their power, but it was Nykki's gift that transported them. 'We can do this,' she said. 'Concentrate, and I'll try to imagine a way out…'

Faint tendrils tugged at her psyche.

'I can't. I've nothing left…' Nykki shook her head, weeping, exhausted.

She was right. They were depleted, and there was no source to draw upon.

Except…

'Give me your arm.'

'What?'

'Your arm.' She grabbed Nykki's wrist and pressed her nail down. Crinkled pink burns marbled her flesh and Nykki's terror flashed and caught in Amber's throat. She couldn't do it.

But there was no one else.

Tears sprang.

Nykki swallowed her fear. 'Do it,' she said. 'Cut me.'

She shook her head. 'I—I can't.'

'Amber.' Nykki clasped her hands. 'Look at me.'

She had never seen Nykki so determined.

'We did not endure this torture to rot in a cell.' Nykki peered around, then captured Amber's gaze. 'When I agreed to help you on your quest, I knew I sacrificed my life, but by every demon, I'm going to fight to live it first.' She thrust her wrist forward, her abused flesh taunting as her chest rose and fell. 'Take my hand, and slice.'

'I—I'm sorry…' Amber choked.

Distant movement and voices echoed, threatening to draw near.

'We don't have time for you to feel sorry.' Nykki slashed her nail across her bare skin, once, twice, thrice, then applied pressure until her blood welled.

When she looked back up, her green eyes glowed.

The electric thrill of raw power churned. *Now, get us out that door.*

But Amber couldn't see past the dense wood, the irons dangling from the dank walls, the stench of piss and decay.

Nykki clutched her close and willed the floating sensation that would signal their simulacrums detaching from their bodies, but everything felt leaden. Blue light swirled as they experienced the slightest hover, teetering on the edge of the physical realm. A line of force stretched, but it was too fragile for either of them to grasp.

Amber's mind tilted and swayed, her vision distorted, and Nykki appeared in tiny fractals like the reflection in a broken mirror.

'I'll bleed more…'

'No—stay with me.' Amber pinched Nykki's arms.

'You said we must go.'

'Yes, but we're drained.' Nykki's blood had provided a source for them to share, but they needed a clear destination to move towards, and Amber was too ragged to concentrate. They were both too weary.

Nykki forged ahead, battling her fatigue to drag Amber onward until pressure built behind Amber's eyes and the fraying tether sucked at her flesh: a thousand lodestones tearing her in all directions.

Stop! 'Nykki, stop.' Cold certainty clutched her. If they continued without a solid path to follow and the strength to complete their relocation, the cord would snap. 'Look at me.' She projected the god-sent knowledge.

'You received an omen,' Nykki whispered, surprised.

'It's you, my love. All these gifts are yours.' Until she'd shared Amber's strength, Nykki had barely accessed her impressive suite of abilities.

'And you bring them, and me, to life.'

Nykki's words filled her heart like a nightingale's song. 'Come,' she beckoned Nykki into her arms. 'You can stop fighting. We'll find another way out.' She kissed Nykki's unmarred cheek and squeezed her tight.

They huddled together, listening to the shuffle of servants moving through the kitchen and cellar beyond. Eventually, the distant sounds dwindled as the household retired to bed.

When the silence seemed like it would last, Amber motioned towards the bolted door.

Nykki understood. She dragged her nails back over her cuts where the blood flow had waned and dried, and clawed the wounds open.

Shoulder to shoulder, with Xenon's power behind them, they directed their force at the metal bolt and threw their combined weight against the door. The bolt snapped, and the door swung loose on its hinges.

They shared a grin and emerged through the dim, empty corridor.

FIFTY-SIX

With the help of a pair of muscled fellows, Ayla deposited Jonas in what appeared to be a public bath: a series of natural ponds carved from flowing water leaving impressions in the rock. Vorlyn said it would take weeks to regain the strength he'd lost in his ankle. Meanwhile, he was stuck living among strangers... again.

'These pools contain healing properties,' Ayla told him, and left him to soak. Steam condensed against his cool skin, forming rivulets that trailed his face and chest. He lay back in the soothing warmth, emitting a sigh that was almost a moan.

Near the cave's entrance, someone laughed playfully, and he bolted upright and peered through the rising mist. A trio of cave-folk appeared, wearing their distinctive white shirts, gathered at the waist with gold weaved belts.

He recognised Vorlyn, but not the beautiful dark-skinned woman with ghostly braids who stood opposite, nor the one beside her with close-cropped black hair facing away from him.

The women leaned in, voices low, and then the shortest pivoted, and he caught her profile.

For a moment, time ceased.

Could it be...?

'Ella...' he whispered.

Wearing a shirt like the others, she turned, and in the peculiar cave light, her azure eyes shone brighter and more luminous, almost violet. She smiled in a way he'd never seen at the dark-skinned woman, who slipped her arms around Ella's waist, grown slender, along with her cheeks.

The sight caged his heart and lungs.

Was it truly her? She looked so different. Older. Less naïve. More at peace.

Curse his wretched ankle. He wanted to rush to her, scoop her up, and absorb her breath. Inhale her very soul. He imagined exploring her cropped hair, tracing her neck, tasting her lips...

But then... Her lips were brushing the dark-skinned woman's, noses touching in an intimate whisper.

His chest tightened as something in him stirred. Not jealousy, exactly. Envy?

He longed to be the receiver of that kiss, that twilit moon smile, but it was also... What? Warming? Gratifying? Seeing her look so... *alive.* Free.

He swallowed and cleared his throat as he struggled to find his voice. To form words. 'El? Is that you?'

Her entire body stiffened like a startled deer.

'Oh gods... El...'

Alarm—or was it anger—flashed across her features.

His chest ached. *Breathe.*

Vorlyn stepped forward. 'My apologies. We didn't mean to disturb you. Ladies, this is...?'

'Jonas,' he said, and his voice cracked, before he gathered himself enough to offer a nod. 'It's an honour to make your acquaintance...' He looked up and caught Ella's gaze. 'And to find you at last, El...'

Her complexion grew even paler, and her eyes chilled. 'You must be mistaken. My name is Nessa.' She turned to the other women. 'I don't know this man.'

'El, please...' He rose from the ledge, forgetting he was naked until brisk air struck his damp skin. The women glanced down, and he ducked back beneath the warm water.

'I'm sorry,' she said. 'I don't know you.'

He tried to stand again, and his ankle buckled, tipping him backwards to plunge into the pool. Crystalline currents rushed and fizzed, heat rising and swirling, mingling with the cooler depths below.

He swam to the surface and heaved a breath. But she was already leaving. Walking away, surrounded by these mysterious people with their luminous skin and gemstone eyes, wrapping her in their arms and whisking her away. Away from him.

'Do you truly not recognise him?' Vorlyn asked. 'Is he not the man you spied through the sphere?'

Ella had seen the way Vorlyn watched him. Wistful. Hungry. Wary.

'I—I—need to go... Yorg says I am ready to port.'

Ella didn't know why she denied Jonas. Voided him, as if she could void her past. But the moment she spotted him soaking in that pool, her body froze, and all her progress unravelled. Heart racing, breath pounding, she saw pain and fire and ash.

Why had he come here? Did he mean to drag her home? Not for Venn—he had married her sister, and certainly not for Gohran. But he had encountered Amber. Had she persuaded him to find her and haul her back to Aryon? Is that why she kept seeing them both in her visions?

She needed to flee. Port far from here, as she'd ported from Erldan.

But then Jonas was hooking his finger to raise her chin, their eyes locking. 'El, swear to me that if ever you need, you'll come to me. Promise?'

Before he left her at Nedran, Jonas had suspected her brother hurt her. Had wanted to take her away, to elope. Shun his family and his responsibilities.

To rescue her.

She didn't need rescuing. With no overlord, priests, or priestesses, to control her, with full access to any source, she was powerful.

Except... Except he was like Vorlyn. Like the captain from *The Lost Warriors.*

Impervious. Immune.

He rendered her powerless.

Now, tucked away from him, with Vorlyn and Mayel beside her, she tried to ground herself, focusing on the library's shelves, and the smell of ink and vellum.

'Ella, what aren't you telling us?' Vorlyn asked.

She wanted to retort, *'What aren't you telling me?'* but forced her voice steady. *Breathe.* 'That man holds no love for my brother, but now he's seen me, knows I'm here...' What if Gohran finds out? What if the priests come for her?

'He's not going anywhere, not for a long while.'

Mayel said, 'We'll make sure he doesn't remember you...'

Ella shook her head, and to her surprise, so did Vorlyn.

'You know, don't you?' she whispered. 'That he's like you.' She wouldn't speak her gnawing suspicion.

Vorlyn nodded. 'But if we can't influence his mind, nor can the priests, or your brother.' Ella waited for her to say more, but Vorlyn's mouth pinched, and her eyes sloped with pity. 'Are you certain your past isn't urging you to flee?'

She startled. Was Vorlyn right? Was this her old fear, resurfacing, out of proportion with the threat he posed, injured and soaking benignly in Aeron's pools?

'He's already seen you. At least speak to him. Find out why he's here. Then leave if you wish, and we'll make certain he keeps your secret.'

Ella hesitated. *Swear to me, El...*

Jonas had only ever brought her pain.

And pleasure. Fun. Freedom.

But also, danger. Castigation. Destruction.

Vorlyn's hand rested on her shoulder. 'It's your choice, Ella.'

She winced. A hammer pounded through her temples. The room darkened and her vision narrowed as a single thought resounded over and again, as certain as if the god had etched the words into her heart and bones: *he would bring her death.*

FIFTY-SEVEN

The familiar passage through the cellar and kitchens tormented, and if Nykki hadn't been beside her, dragging her forward, keeping her grounded, Amber would have frozen, retreating within the dungeon to huddle in the dark.

The pair feasted on Erldan's meagre stores, devouring jerky, preserved vegetables, and stale bread, likely set aside for stuffing, or animal feed.

We need to find clothing, and get outside, Amber thought, though hesitant to wear anything against her fresh burns.

Nykki's hands shook as she returned a jar to a shelf. It dropped and shattered on the floorboards.

Footsteps shuffled, and a swinging lantern bobbed shadows along the walls.

Wait. She grabbed Nykki's wrist and pulled her to crouch behind a bench.

A bleary-eyed kitchen maid rounded the corner. 'Who's there?' She raised her lantern, squinting through the dim light. 'Cursed rats,' she muttered, then set the lantern down and reached for a broom.

Now.

They seized the maid, and she sagged into their arms before she could scream.

More footfalls approached, followed by a gruff cough. 'Nelda? Is that—?' The guard froze, confronted by two burned and naked women holding an unconscious maid. 'Who are—?'

'Thank the goddess you're here, good sir!' Nykki cried. 'This kind lady fainted... Please, will you help?' She pulled her hair to cover her cheek.

The guard stuttered and fumbled. 'Of-of course...' His cheeks flushed as he averted his eyes and edged nearer.

Nykki took his arm, and pressed against him, guiding him closer, leaving Amber to support the maid's weight, whose head lolled as she groaned.

'I fear she has swallowed a poison...' Nykki said.

He hunched over the maid, and Nykki reached behind him, clasped Amber's hand, and their power flowed. A line of blue force wound around him, visible only to its bearers, and he crumpled, too.

Quick, help me undress them.

Nykki hesitated. *There's no point. We'll only end up naked.*

She was going to attempt to relocate them again.

Imagine a place for us to arrive, Nykki thought.

But Amber's memories crowded, anxious and hazy. It was too long since she'd resided within these walls and nowhere seemed safe. Apart from Ella's tower room, she had almost never been alone, living among the servants.

It's no good. Let's take their clothes and run.

Nykki untied, unbuttoned, and tugged every item of clothing within reach, indifferent to the guard's head slumping to the floor, and the side of the woman's face shoving into the bench.

Amber took more care, undressing them and pulling on what fit.

Don't forget their shoes. They were too large, but they would offer some protection from the shattered glass and whatever else they might encounter.

She pulled the guard's shirt over her head, and when she looked back down, Nykki had grabbed a paring knife from the bench, and sliced into the man's thigh.

Nykki! Stop!

We need blood.

Even without using Nykki's gift to transport them, she was right. Blood was the richest source available.

As the guard's wound welled, static energy teemed and thrilled along her limbs and traversed her veins. The power shuddered through her, radiating dreamlike bliss, almost as pleasurable as the passion they shared. Oh gods, it felt divine!

Then Nykki's lips were on hers, eager. *I want to take this feeling with us.*

Amber staved her off. *We must go. Now.*

But Nykki was slicing into the woman, too.

Stop, Nykki!

Yet when she inhaled, fire ignited her entire body in a heady rush of sensation. There was no pain, no fear, only weightlessness. She longed to lie back and drink in every morsel of pleasure.

Nykki caught her lips again, and this time it was she who pulled Amber from the intoxicating source. 'Let's go.'

Amber tucked her hair beneath the shirt, but Nykki stopped her, still gripping the knife. She tugged the ends loose, then grabbed a fistful and hacked her long tresses away.

Let Elnora's pets find this. They'll know what it means.

Leaving a trail of orange-yellow locks sprinkled over two unconscious, naked, and bleeding bodies, they fled.

FIFTY-EIGHT

'So, you know me now,' Jonas smirked.

Ella found him resting in Aeron's infirmary, in the cavern where Yorg fixed her simulacrum within her body. He looked strange, bearded and gruff, tucked into the small bed. But that grin, and everything it promised, liquified her core the way it had when Venn first introduced them in the main hall at Erldan.

With the aid of a wooden staff, he staggered to his feet. 'El...' He reached for her, and she remembered how he used to brush her cheek, imagined him ruffling her hair, and recoiled.

Jonas dropped his hand by his side, and whispered, 'Gods, I scarcely recognise you...'

In her mind, his fingers trailed along her neck, and she longed for him to tug her close and find her lips. She stepped back, out of reach.

His tears welled. 'It is you, isn't it? When Venn told me he'd seen you—'

His coarse shirt and unfamiliar leathers made him look like a thief or mercenary.

'Please...' He propped on his staff, and drank her in, but let her maintain her distance.

She adjusted her gold belt to keep from stroking his strange beard. Touching him. 'Why are you here?'

His face crumpled, his pain finding a crack within her shell. She looped the belt's end around her palm.

'Listen. Your brother...'

'What about him?' She coiled the belt tighter.

'The illustrious *King Gohran of Erldan* has exerted some sort of—force—over Venn.' Her brother's name always sounded bitter on his tongue.

She stiffened. 'A monarch *should* exert force.'

'No, El, you don't understand.' He fought to find the right words. 'This is... Something else. Something sinister.'

'How ominous! Have you not outgrown your fanciful embellishments?'

'I wish that's all this was.' He looked grim. Earnest. Exhausted. He cleared his throat. 'Whatever happened between you and Venn is your business—'

'By every god and demon, it is.' She strode to the infirmary's shelves. Vials of tinctures, packets of dried herbs, and jars of powders sat beside a set of scales, a mortar and pestle, and a scrying orb. She busied herself rifling through the various medicines.

Jonas sighed. 'Hear me out. I need you—'

She swivelled to face him. 'You *need* me?'

Eyes beseeching. '*Nedran* needs you.'

She imagined Yorg's voice. *Breathe, Princess.*

'Venn told me you and he swore to one another before the gods.'

'What of it?'

'And you consummated that betrothal?'

'*My business*, you said.' She turned back, repositioning the orb. Its surface shimmered. 'My *private* business.'

A louder exhale. 'With *public* ramifications.' He stalled. 'This isn't the most comfortable topic for me, either. I ask because it's the only way to invalidate Venn and Raeyn's marriage.'

'Why would you want to do that?' She sniffed some acrid herbs.

'To free Nedran from Erldan's king.'

She froze.

'Proof that you live will force the priests to annul Venn's marriage to Raeyn.' He hobbled closer.

'Your brother chose to ignore any such promise and wed my sister. What he does now is not my affair.'

'A foolish choice he made under a false premise, and under your brother's duress.'

'He made a match to everyone's advantage.' Except hers. She had only ever been a tile in someone else's hand. In a game she never wanted to play.

'Not to Nedran's.'

She glanced back. 'How so?'

'El...' He scratched his foreign beard. 'Do you need me to speak it?'

She stood firm and waited.

'You know what Gohran is.' The familiar scar near his eye twitched.

'An ambitious, irascible man, who pursues his goals as ruthlessly as any other.'

Teeth gritted. Eyes cold. 'A murderer. A monster.'

'And no concern of mine any longer. He made that clear when he announced my death to the whole of Ycelt.' She motioned to her very much alive presence.

'If you testify Venn had a prior engagement, we can prove he established his betrothal to Raeyn under a falsehood...'

'Leaving him bound to me—and still tied to Erldan.' She forced her voice steady. 'You haven't thought this through.'

He swore. 'But the priests never sealed your betrothal.'

'Rendering it invalid—and therefore no basis to void Venn's marriage to Raeyn. Either way, your reasoning is flawed.'

'El, don't you see?' He edged nearer. 'Venn's subsequent infidelity offers grounds to annul your betrothal. But he forged his marriage to Raeyn on a lie.' Again, he reached for her. 'Once you reveal you're alive...'

'No,' she snapped. 'I can't.' She faced him with arms crossed.

'Please—without legal cause, Nedran is irrevocably bound to Erldan.'

Still out of reach, she left his arms dangling in the space between them, but when she spoke, her tone softened. 'I didn't say I won't. I said I can't. What do you imagine will happen if I reappear, alive, given Gohran is the monster you claim?'

'You think he'll denounce you...?' His voice a whisper.

She sucked in her breath. Did he realise? Had Venn told him?

Jonas limped beside her and picked up the orb.

Ella snatched it off him. It danced to life, light and colour playing within.

'Can't you use your powers to...' he waved a hand over it, 'perform whatever you do to stop them?'

Stunned silence. He knew.

'When we escaped, your friend took out multiple guards. She glanced their way, and they... dropped!' He mimicked releasing his staff, catching it just in time.

Amber! 'Where is she? What happened to her?'

'She made it back to her home, I presume. But when I headed north, your demon brother razed an entire village searching for us.'

Ella's breath caught. That's what she'd seen in her vision. Only he hadn't ravaged the village looking for them, but for her.

'Don't you see?' she said. 'That's why I can't return. He'll destroy me and annihilate anyone who gets in his way.'

Jonas's eyes locked on hers. 'But he's like you.'

Ice in her veins and venom on her tongue. 'He's nothing like me.'

'By the hells... My apologies, El...'

He reached for her, but she shrugged away, pacing faster than he could follow on his staff.

'I can't do what you ask. You're not only seeking my death, but my daughter's. How do you propose I prove my betrothal was consummated without alerting the priests to her existence?'

'You have a daughter...' he whispered. 'I didn't think...'

'No. You didn't.'

He swore, sagging onto his staff, as his brows knitted together.

'"We escaped", you said...?' Had Jonas been captured, too?

He groaned and gestured to the orb. 'Can't you read my mind, or whatever it is you do?'

She said nothing. He must see her seething.

'Your brother arrested me,' he spoke at last, a flush travelling up his neck to stain his tanned cheeks behind his beard. 'I may have told him Venn believed you were still alive...' He sucked on his lip. 'And that I wanted to know where you were.'

Oh gods. 'Don't you see what you've done?' The colour drained from his skin as quickly as it had appeared. 'Gohran wasn't hunting you, he was hunting me. And he will silence anyone he suspects knows about me.'

Jonas closed his eyes, as if to hide from her words. When he finally spoke, his voice strangled. 'I didn't realise... Hells, I'm so, so sorry.'

She ached to comfort him. To bury herself in his chest and reassure them both that all was well, but it wasn't. None of this was.

'Who else has Venn told?' So cold.

'Probably no one.' Jonas swallowed. 'He didn't intend to tell me. He was drunk, and I'd just revealed that I uncovered your empty grave...'

Jonas placed his hands atop hers, still clinging to the orb. His touch sent a thrill along her arms, and the glass hummed between her palms. He lay open to her, and she saw his memories reflected. The upturned cairn amid a valley of clouds where she'd met Venn through her dreams.

He pictured the inside of Erldan's dungeon, witnessing Amber take on those guards, then flames rising against the night.

She swallowed and shrugged him off. 'Your mistake was expecting my brother to act rationally.' She replaced the orb on its shelf.

Jonas choked back a sob. 'I would never knowingly put you or your daughter at risk. But I beg you, for Nedran and my family, help me find another way to prove that your pre-existing betrothal is as alive as you...'

She took in his beard and leathers, his injured ankle, the small nicks and scars that peppered his handsome face. He *was* a bandit. An outlaw.

Gohran had arrested him. Had he threatened her brother? Surely, he was not that foolish. But the king might not view it that way.

Oh, by every demon. She realised then what he wouldn't say. Jonas was a fugitive.

He came here to save himself. To beg her to sacrifice her life for him, because returning home would cost his life, too.

E l was right. Jonas had assumed Gohran would see reason, despite all evidence to the contrary. Why would he destroy a village to hide her, when he could just denounce her like he had their mother? He'd escaped suspicion then; he could do so now.

Unless… Unless she had some leverage over him. Something he feared her revealing before they torched and silenced her.

He tried to stand, but his ankle gave out under him, and he collapsed back onto the bed. Curse it, he never should have come here. He'd thought only of himself and Nedran. Not what this would mean for her: a sorceress in Ycelt.

'Give Ella time.' It was Vorlyn. When had she arrived? 'She needs to work through the implications of what you ask.' She handed him a lacquered cup of their strange, distilled spirit. Unlike the others, she wore the regular trousers and shirt of an Yceltic peasant.

Jonas sniffed—his eyes watering as it punched like sweetened rubbing alcohol—and gulped it down. 'What do you know of it?'

'More than you realise.' She refilled his cup, and then her own, and perched on the edge of the bed beside him.

He tried to read her hazel eyes, the same colour as Lynden's, as his. Did she know who he was, and that Erldan's king had declared him a fugitive? She had known about the village Gohran torched…

'Most of us are exiles,' she said.

He frowned.

'They call this place Aeron of Nowhere, because here we can cease existing and disappear. Like you, we can't go home…'

Her gentle, haunting fingers brushed his cheek, and a piece of him shattered. He wanted to weep, but gods, he was sick of needing to.

'I wish this was only about me. But I've done this to my family, to my sister, Lyn...' His voice cracked. 'I wouldn't ask if it wasn't for them.'

'I know.' Her tone was soft. Kind.

'Does Ella?'

Vorlyn sipped her spirit. Swallowed. 'You're asking her to return to her death.'

'How so? When you—all of you—are stronger than the whole of Ycelt! With your powers against—'

'You want us to wage a war? You are aware of how that ended last time...?'

She meant Xenon's War and the Great Upheaval. 'If you believe Elnora's priests,' he said. 'It need not lead to battle if even a few of you—'

'Have you looked around? Most of Aeron's inhabitants wouldn't make it to the next town without being accused of heresy.'

The priests had arrested the gold-eyed girl alongside Amber. She'd had no magic, was no heretic, and they tortured her just the same.

'You could pass in Ycelt,' he insisted. 'You could be my aunt or mother!'

She spat her mouthful of spirit and coughed. 'I have no powers that could help you.'

'If none of you intervenes, there will be war, and not one that either side can win.' Jonas lay back and closed his eyes. He saw it playing out. Gohran had bankrupted his kingdom to make Erldan impenetrable. While his army flourished, his people hungered. Nedran was economically fierce, but militarily weak. Even with Venn's skill in swordcraft, he was but one man. That's why Venn sought to ally with Erldan to begin with.

Could they rely on Lichen's support?

Oh, hells. Vee probably still waited for him. Surely Venn or Lyn had explained... Explained what? That he'd chosen to insult the king of Erldan rather than follow through on his proposal?

Curse it! He should have ridden to Lichen and sought refuge. Teegan and Selmyra might have interceded on his behalf where Venn couldn't.

He naively believed Ella would rush back to save her beloved Venn, if not him.

Venn. Who rejected and betrayed her.

Him. Who let his pride and sibling rivalry govern his silence, instead of defending her to her monstrous brother.

He was proving as worthless as Venn always claimed. Even when he tried to take responsibility and be selfless, he messed up.

When he next opened his eyes, Vorlyn was gone.

FIFTY-NINE

Yorg was almost ready to journey home. He'd selected his favoured texts and mementos to carry in a satchel and planned his farewells, while Ella wasn't sure what, if anything, to take. The more she risked carrying, the harder the task to port them would be.

'I wish you'd reconsider going to Nedran first.'

Ella glanced up to see Vorlyn hovering in the library's doorway. She continued sorting through the manuscripts she wanted to verify.

'Jonas said something that puts his request in a different light...'

'He has a convincing way of colouring things,' Ella said, not looking up.

Vorlyn sighed. 'Whatever happened between you back in Ycelt, he made a valid argument just now. He reminded me of how powerful sorcerers are. I've lived among Aeron's people for almost a score of years. Here, magic fades into the walls like the brightest tapestry one no longer sees.'

Vorlyn strolled closer. 'My gift isn't like yours. When Davith captured me, I was defenceless, but for *you*, porting and beguilement are *weapons*.'

Ella froze.

'You're so much more powerful than the priests or your brother.'

Beguiling her brother is what brought this hell upon her.

'I understand you fear what you left behind, but back then, you didn't appreciate your capability. Nor could you control it. Now, with porting mastered, you can prove your prior betrothal *and* flee to safety.'

Was Vorlyn in earnest?

'*If* they believe me. *If* I can access a potent enough source before they arrest and disable me.' And *if* she didn't invoke the Curse after all, which she couldn't confirm until she ventured to the Place of Omens to verify her hypothesis.

'You underestimate your strength, Ella.'

Through the fire, Ella had seen Amber, a powerful sorceress, drugged, hooded, and helpless. Yet, she'd gotten away, and if Jonas's memories were accurate, she'd felled the guards like a scythe through hallit.

'You said Jonas needs time to heal before he heads home. I promised Yorg I would carry him to the Place of Omens. Once we conclude our business, we can return...'

The light flickered, casting a shadow over Vorlyn's features. 'By then, it could be too late.'

'I won't dally.' Provided there was sufficient source and no one seeking to cull her in Myan, she could travel back and forth, like her predecessors.

'This is greater than him and greater than you. He's asking you to prevent a war between Nedran and Erldan.'

'Jonas loves to exaggerate.'

'Maybe so, but this threat is real.'

She rifled through parchments, searching for her notes on the mistranslated passage. 'I don't see how my presence changes anything.' Even if the priests annulled Venn and Raeyn's marriage, Gohran now knew Venn and Jonas realised she was alive. Venn might keep her counsel, but Jonas had proved untrustworthy in that regard. She would jeopardise her life—and Xarion's—for nothing. She hefted another book onto her pile.

'Please, Ella. Think what you risk by delaying.'

'Your divided loyalty clouds your judgement.' The whip of her tongue might have come from her aunt or mother.

Vorlyn didn't deny it.

There was no point in hiding her suspicion any longer. 'Your sons have done me no favours.' Vorlyn was asking her to die. For Jonas. For Venn.

For Lynden.

The thought didn't belong to her, but it sliced to her core.

Hadn't she fled to keep them all safe when she believed she carried the Curse? Now, she knew better.

Hoped, not knew.

'If I can prove I'm not Cursed, I can prove my child is not either. I won't abandon her.' *Like you.*

Vorlyn's eyes filled not with anger, but with pity. 'When I shared my memories, I spared you the savagery of my torture. Trust me, your daughter is safest when you are far from her.'

'You still haven't told Jonas who you are, have you?' What must it cost her to conceal her identity when he was within her grasp? When she could love and hold and know him, not as a refugee, but as a son?

'My children believe me killed.'

'Missing. Your children have never had the certainty of your death.' Ella retrieved another volume with a thud.

'Davith cannot learn that Jonas is like me.'

She thumped the pages open. 'You don't trust Jonas to keep secrets, either.'

'It is safer for all my children if they don't discover what I am.'

She set her work aside and met Vorlyn's gaze. 'Then you understand why I must go to Myan first,' she said. If Myan's archives revealed the Curse was a lie, she would claim her daughter and leave Aryon—and Ycelt—behind.

Pain in Vorlyn's eyes, her swallow tight; she nodded. 'I only wish it were otherwise.'

'Are you ready, Princess?' Yorg arrived, his cheeks flushed with tears. He'd waited so long for this.

She stood and clutched her handful of scribed parchments.

'Ella, please—'

She brushed past Vorlyn. 'I'm sorry.'

Yorg frowned, and the weight of his concern pressed on her.

'It's fine, Yorg,' Vorlyn said. 'I understand why she needs to go.'

They shared a glance, and Ella sensed the stir of their minds excluding her.

'Tell Jonas I'll hurry back, I promise,' she said, remembering she hadn't bid Mayel or Jurn farewell, either. But if she delayed, she might waver.

Aeron's community was what Aryon's should have been, and it was far too tempting to remain hidden among folk like her. Worse, she feared what Jonas stirred in her, a flame she thought she'd extinguished, burning still. Most of all, he represented a past she did not care to return to. Not now. Not ever.

It was time she carved out a fate of her choosing.

She turned to Yorg. 'I'm ready.'

'I see Ayla has constructed a medicinal shoe for you.' Mayel passed Jonas practising walking through Aeron's corridors, wearing a rigid leather boot reinforced with wooden splints.

They eyed one another warily. Curiously.

'I'm impressed with her ingenuity.' Jonas extended his foot to admire the handiwork.

'Ordinarily, Ayla uses magic to heal us from the inside out, but your injury tested her.'

'I suppose my mind doesn't work the right way?' His eyebrow quirked.

Mayel took his measure with a smile that hid a thousand secrets. 'I can see why Ella desired you,' she said, her alluring lips curving into a laugh, while her eyes sparkled like gems.

'Likewise,' he said, returning her grin. 'Is it strange for you, me being here?'

'Not at all. But I suppose it is for you.'

He cocked his head. 'In countless ways.'

'I am sorry for your predicament,' she said. 'But I wish you had not come here.'

Did everyone know his business? 'I'm no threat to whatever you and Ella share,' he said, wishing it weren't true. Wishing Ella had shown an inkling that she felt something for him still—assuming she ever had.

'You are, but not for the reasons you suppose.'

'Oh?'

'You are why she's leaving,' Mayel said.

His breath eased, a visceral loosening of the muscles across his chest. Ella had changed her mind. 'Then I am sorry for *your* predicament, but I will do everything within my power to return her safely.'

Confusion knitted Mayel's brows together. 'I always expected she would go, but at the end of spring or summer, perhaps before the next winter. Not today.'

'Today? But—' He gestured to his boot. 'I'm not ready.'

More puzzlement. 'Excuse me, I'd like to send them off.' Mayel turned and scurried toward the cave's exit.

He stared after, wondering what she meant, then resumed his exercise.

He hadn't got far when two others bustled past, offering polite nods. They raised and pointed their fingertips to touch in what he now recognised was the local greeting.

'Where are you headed?' he called after them.

A tall, slender man turned and said, 'To bid Ella and Yorg farewell.'

Ella and Yorg?

His breath seized as his guts dropped through the floor.

Oh gods.

Ella hadn't changed her mind. She wasn't leaving *with* him. She was leaving *him*.

'Wait!' he called again, but they were already gone.

SIXTY

'Shall we, Princess?' Yorg asked, hefting his satchel over his shoulder. Ella nodded, and they clasped hands. She carried only her parchments, stuffed within a skin pouch and tucked beneath her shirt.

She glanced at the handful of onlookers who had prepared a bonfire, with their beast tethered and ready to slaughter, noting Vorlyn's absence.

Mayel skipped forward, wrapped her arms around Ella's neck, and found her lips. Her cheeks were moist. 'Return to me quickly, please.'

Ella's breath hitched, and she stole a further kiss, mouthing, 'I will.' Not wanting to let go, her whisper grazed Mayel's cheek. 'My thanks—for everything.'

Jurn squeezed her, and kissed her forehead, and they both stepped back to join the others, whose dissonant chanting swelled as they sang Ella and Yorg on their way.

This was truly happening. After countless exercises, she was finally embracing her magic to port Yorg home. She took a deep breath.

'You know what to do,' Yorg assured her.

She nodded, concentrating on the sound and escalating rhythm as she sucked up the fire's heat, basking in the power flowing between her and Yorg. Flames danced and flickered, and smoke clouded her vision. The creature snorted and snuffled, clawing at the dirt, oblivious to its fate as its executioners enchanted it to experience nothing but calm bliss.

Song and light swirled, and she captured and weaved its magic to surround them, as she had netted the moonstone during their lessons.

Yorg's thoughts lay open. His vivid memories formed a sketch in her mind of moist, dense air, lush rainforest, and the harsh squawk of unfamiliar birds. Yet through Yorg's lens, they sounded of home.

A dark-skinned family with moonbeam pale hair smiled her way. Tears welled in the violet eyes of the wrinkled woman. *Mayora.* Mother. Her image faded, long gone, and others appeared in her place. A lad and lass with matching white braids and Yorg's strong nose. Behind them, a man's laughter rumbled. Faces she'd never seen yet recognised instinctively. They drew her towards them, and her simulacrum tugged away from her flesh, intertwining with Yorg's, just like they practised.

Nostalgia settled into her bones, her joints creaked, and her muscles ached. She was wearier than she'd ever imagined. A deep-seated fatigue that no amount of sleep could restore. His, not hers.

Soon, you can rest.

She concentrated on the route they were constructing from Yorg's memories. Then she scooped the fiery heat until it thrummed through her veins. The tether widened, forming an azure tunnel of swirling light: a whirlpool, sucking them along its vortex.

Aeron's song rose, vibrating in her chest, drawing her on, but the following cadence pounded in her temples, yanking her back, and she winced.

'Princess?'

She refocused on the sound, on Yorg, yet instead of his home, her next breath revealed hazel eyes, beseeching. *'Promise me, El...'*

Even now, behind that scruffy beard, Jonas's cursed smile liquefied her core. He pleaded for his family. For Nedran.

She shook the image away and clung to Yorg, following his mind's path.

They each drew more power, and the tunnel glowed, expanding and solidifying. When she glanced down, her simulacrum wore her clothes, and Yorg's his, though his satchel remained fixed on the forest floor.

'Leave it, Princess. Keep moving.'

Chanting rose atop the beast's squeal as the butcher sliced its throat.

A collective breath held silent before an excruciating howl screamed through her mind and clanged behind her eyes. Blood tore and spilled, soaking into the earth. More than could possibly belong to the boar.

Their song resumed, its rhythm frantic, as the faces of Yorg's vision contorted, crying and screaming. Crimson spray spattered and stained their crisp white shirts.

What if she was wrong and drawing lifeforce carried her Curse to Yorg's home?

'Princess—we must go while the source is fresh.' Yorg's voice cut through the chaos, urging her on. He'd examined her aura countless times. Scarred, not Cursed, he'd assured.

A sharper clang hammered, more insistent, and she let out a cry.

'*Mama!*' a child wailed behind her. Xarion! She swivelled towards the sound, but the grass stood empty. Out in the open, with her shield lowered, Xarion's perennial need seized her.

Yorg squeezed her hand. 'Don't lose sight of the path, Princess. Follow my lead.' His attention didn't waver.

More details came into focus as they neared, and the tether stretched with them inside their shared tunnel.

Lush green foliage surrounded rainbow-hued plants and the most vibrant flowers she'd ever seen. Crystalline water reflected the pure blue sky, while brightly coloured buildings with columns and sloped roofs lined the paved streets.

Laughter pealed. Children kicked small grain-filled sacks back and forth, and a pointed-faced cat with elongated ears slinked its scent against a marble statue.

'We're almost there...'

The scene was so close now. Sounds ringing, smells clamouring, the moist air dampening her skin...

Another step, and she would caress the cool marble...

'Don't! Stay back!' someone shouted, before hands gripped her, wrenching her from her ethereal path.

Startled, her heart thudded, and her breath drew ragged. She stood in the forest outside Aeron's caves. Folk chanted before rising flames, and a pair of hazel eyes caught hers.

'El, please, don't leave...'

Those words sliced through her vision, Jonas's plea a siren song to everything she feared leaving behind. But through the haze, Aeron's bonfire became a pyre, revealing flashes of women fighting with magic, like the Ancients.

Agony. Terror. Heartbreak.

A warning to stay? Or a portent impelling her onward?

Smoke filled her lungs, and she choked back a cough.

He would bring her death.

She shrugged Jonas off with violent force, but the jolt caused Yorg to slip from her grip.

'Princess! No!'

The tether she'd painstakingly constructed flung her along the tunnel, un-controlled, as if released from a trebuchet.

Behind her, Yorg's cry faded, getting farther and farther away, while she flew forward.

Her ethereal body accelerated, dragging her corporeal one with it. Azure light writhed and swirled, and she struggled to control her momentum, searching for something—anything—to cling to, to slow her passage and reconnect.

'Help me, Yorg!' she cried, but the sound dampened, swallowed by the whirling currents.

The azure vortex sucked and propelled her, as the path she'd travelled disin-tegrated in her wake, leaving Yorg on the other side. She was losing him.

She pictured Aeron's caves, Mayel and Jurn, even Vorlyn, willing their forms into being. But she could not gain purchase, and their imagined bodies dispersed like fog.

The surrounding tunnel cracked and broke into pieces, as if solid, liquid, and gaseous at once. It crumbled and fell along with her.

Oh gods. What if the ethereal path into Myan dissipated before she reached her destination? Would she be stranded between realms, or nowhere at all? She could end up shattered between existences. The guiding passage must remain strong.

She stopped envisioning Aeron and fought to remember all the details of Yorg's memories. When she tried to recall Yorg's mother, she couldn't resurrect her crinkled face, while the children he'd pictured aged and vanished behind an indistinct veil.

Desperate, she visualised the cat scenting a statue in the market square. A tail winding around a pillar. With her next breath, it manifested before her, its coat changing from fawn to striped and grey. Green eyes peered and offered her a blink. A different cat amid what was now crumbling ruins.

Another inhale, and a marble sculpture emerged, chipped and surrounded by faded columns. The years since Yorg visited this place had etched and worn into the stone and wood, while roofs sagged, and the fecund scent of rotting vegetation forced its way through cracked pavers.

Between the ancient remnants, newer buildings rose. Streets bustled with fresh-faced citizens browsing wares, while the aroma of Myanai spices wafted.

But as the image grew denser, clearer, she sped again. Her vision blurred and the currents of the vortex sucked her deeper into their web. She grasped and clung but there was nothing to hold. Nothing to break her fall as she hurtled nearer to the town square.

The one detail that persisted through the whirling stream was her daughter's omnipresent and insatiable need. Where Xarion's demand once shackled her, now it offered hope, snagging her heart. She cast her ethereal net towards it, feeling the drag as her momentum slowed.

She continued to fall, clutching at Xarion's presence with the friction of a metal rod inserted into a wheel's spinning spoke. Crushing tension grated. Its weight bore down, and she screamed into the void.

The bond yanked and heaved, tearing her in a third direction, threatening to alter her trajectory. What if she careened off course? She needed to let go.

Another whir of sound and light, and a force that was both and neither.

Azure flashed, blinding as it encompassed her. Hard ground punched through every inch of flesh as she landed, and her simulacrum jarred like lightning striking her psyche.

Then, it was gone. The last of the tether and tunnel evaporated.

She emitted a low moan. She couldn't move. Struggled to breathe. Her head pounded and her vision swam, and she battled to remain awake and alert.

Xarion's presence vanished, along with Aeron's souls, leaving her utterly alone.

Her final memory, before consciousness slipped away, was the resounding echo of Yorg's rusty tears, and the cold clutch of foresight that told her she would never see him again.

PART FOUR: LIBERATION

The Kingdom of Erldan, Ycelt

Spring, 797 A.S.

SIXTY-ONE

Gohran's promised wife stood before him in Erldan's foyer. Golden tresses, arch smile, and perfected demeanour. A known beauty. A renowned wit. Attractive, well-mannered, and wily. For once, Jay showed sound judgement. The wife she suggested for him would serve his kingdom well.

Most importantly, perhaps, Davith approved. In fact, she delighted him.

'I'm pleased you finally heeded my advice to tend to your own garden,' he'd said with an imperious sneer.

Except Gohran was no gardener, but a cuckoo fertilising eggs in another man's nest. Regardless, Vera would raise his hatchlings—his heirs.

She curtsied and looked up appealingly through wide blue eyes. Pleasure curved her small, pretty mouth, yet the only desire she roused in him was from the vengeance anchored to his heart.

He left his servants to settle her into a guest chamber. Once the deeds were finalised, and their promises sealed, they would instal her in his mother's former room, where he would perform his nightly duty. After Lynden, he would not allow another into his private chamber.

Vera's surviving brothers offered testament she would likely produce a son, but he prayed Elnora would not forsake him on that score.

Meanwhile, greater concerns occupied him, such as the apparent murder of one of Davith's neophytes attending a trial and Cleansing in Harnal.

Earlier, two messengers had accosted him with their extravagant tales.

'Witnesses swear a pair of witches sliced him to pieces and then vanished into the night!'

'And when they tried to burn the sorcerers, their torches passed straight through.'

'Others claim the witches addled their minds, Your Highness.'

This did not bode well. Regular Cleansings created a bedrock of order and stability, of piety. Conducted under his jurisdiction, they instilled a useful measure of fear, while demonstrating his devotion to the priests and Elnora Herself. Rumours of sorcerers running rampant eroded that same foundation.

Palms raised to settle them, he said, 'Even witches cannot disappear.'

'But Your Highness!'

'Why would the villagers' torches not have set these heretics alight, when Our Lady of the Dark Sun would want them to burn? Now, I must consult with His Holiness.'

'High Priest Davith has not yet returned from Nedran, Your Highness.'

'What?!'

'He was there to oversee a Cleansing. That is why His Holiness's servant conducted the rite in Harnal.'

Heat surged. He captured the lad's wrist and pierced his gaze. When he spoke, ice coated his words. 'What Cleansing in Nedran?'

Venn woke to a pounding head and a dry mouth. He peeled back his bedclothes and reached for the dregs of his water pitcher. He still could not quite believe the priests had followed through and executed Bess.

If not Bess, they would have come for Lynden.

Or Raeyn.

He rolled over to find her gone, the bed already grown cold. How late had he slept?

Pushing to his feet, he peered through the dim light. Not his chamber, but hers. He padded to the window and drew open the heavy drapes. Elnora's rays pierced his eyes.

His world had steered off kilter, and he needed to set it right.

Father always stressed the importance of staying out of religious matters, of focusing on secular rule. Likewise, Erldan's priests ought not to trespass on his jurisdiction, regardless of their king's proclamations. He was Nedran's lord and ruler. Erldan's priests had overstepped, and now they would answer to him.

He stepped out into the corridor to summon a page. 'Send for the priest who oversaw the Cleansing.'

The lad hesitated, frowning. 'My lord?'

'Tell him the Dryhten of Nedran will see him at once.'

'Yes, of course, my lord.'

As the boy scurried off, Venn promptly dressed, splashed cold water on his face, and with grim determination, strode to his study. He would not falter.

By the time Davith and a pair of robed servants arrived, he was ready, his mind clearer than it had been for a long, long while.

'Lord Venn,' Davith nodded—not quite a bow, eyes unreadable, an imperious twist to his mouth. 'You wished to consult with me?'

Davith, the same head robe who had conducted his marriage rite to Raeyn. Who urged him on, even after seeing the bloodied raven bearing the heretic's mark, hurtled in protest amidst a violent remonstration.

'I sense no binding evil here, only petty malice. You may pin the brooch.'

Gohran's hand had persuaded, but Davith's endorsement reassured. Lent validity.

Did he know what Gohran was?

Surely not, or his erstwhile friend would have burned long since.

'I hereby rescind your right of passage to enter my lands without prior permission. You and your servants are stripped of all undue authority bestowed by the King of Erldan.'

'My lord?'

Venn raised a hand for silence. Stared this slithering robe down. 'You are to vacate Nedran immediately. Should your king seek access in the future, he must apply as a supplicant through my court.'

Chin tilted, a slight sneer to his lip as his eyes narrowed. 'Forgive me, my lord, but I answer to the King in Erldan, and so do you.'

Was this grovelling robe in earnest? 'King Gohran is an ally,' he snapped. 'Not my overlord. And you can remind him of that upon your return.'

He signalled to his guards to usher the priest and his neophytes out. The holy men could forge any hierarchy they pleased within their spiritual domain, but access to his lands was a secular matter. While Gohran outranked him, this robe was mistaken if he believed his marriage to Raeyn afforded the king any more than a brother would under the law.

He closed the door behind them, and buried his face, wishing he'd had the wherewithal to act sooner. For Bess, it was too late.

At least if Gohran retaliated, and their clash escalated to outright war, Lyn was safely out of reach. With her betrothal underway, Nedran would have Herron's backing and need not crumble beneath the weight of Erldan's might.

He hoped Vera's words to Lynden were hyperbolic vitriol scribed from anger, and that he could convince her to reject Gohran's proposal and forgive Jonas. The only thing he needed now was for Jonas to return.

'**F**ool!' the old man called Yorg hissed at Jonas.

One moment, Ella had clasped the man's arms, but when Jonas begged her to stay, with a blinding flash, she'd vanished, leaving Yorg howling.

'You've sent her helpless into a foreign land, lad.' Yorg's shoulders trembled with tears that did not fall.

Lad. A reckless, idiotic boy. He deserved much worse.

He stood agape as the elder retreated, shuffling weary bones too heavy for his muscles to carry. The others dispersed, trailing after with their heads bowed, carting the remains of the slaughtered boar past the dwindling fire.

Vorlyn rested her hand on his shoulder. She must have followed him outside. 'Yorg's anger is raw, but it will pass. He needs time to grieve. He was returning to his home in Myan for his final season.'

Jonas swore. What more could he ballocks up? 'Can't someone go after her? What about Ayla? Or Mayel?' He scrambled for names of powerful individuals he'd encountered.

Vorlyn shook her head. 'Ella was our only porter.'

'Porter? As in...?'

'Able to transport herself from one location to another using her magic. She intended to carry Yorg with her to Myan.'

He swore again. She hadn't merely cloaked herself like a conjuror, creating illusions to amuse children in the market square, but vanished from Ycelt. These sorcerers were more powerful than he had imagined.

Using that power, having finally reached her, in less than a heartbeat, she was gone. Beyond his grasp.

'She will return, won't she? Ycelt is her home. She has a daughter—Nedran's heir...' He clutched at desperate hope. 'At least until Raeyn...'

Vorlyn's eyebrow quirked as though humouring a child.

The bonfire's flames caught and flared behind them before fading away. It occurred to him that Ella's babe was not with her, and that he'd not once seen or heard her—in fact, he'd observed no children among these caves. 'Where is Ella's daughter?'

'Somewhere safe, for now.' Vorlyn patted his arm, eyes sloped. 'I need to head into the village, but I'll ask Ayla to check on you while I'm gone.'

'I'm not staying.'

She sucked in a breath. 'Where will you go?'

'Does it matter?'

'Please—don't leave. At least wait until your ankle has healed.' Her hand grew heavy. 'In time, Yorg will forgive your ignorance. He, of all people, knows how easy it is to make mistakes.'

He shrugged her off. 'Why would I care what a stranger thinks of me? And what is it to you if I leave?'

She flinched. 'I—It—It's been a long while since I... Well, since I met someone like you.'

There was something she wasn't saying.

'Don't mistake me—I am grateful to your folk for taking me in, but there is nothing for me here.' With Ella gone, he was an unwelcome guest, biding his time. Without her, he had no legal recourse to remedy Nedran's situation. But that did not mean he should laze about, waiting for someone else to solve his dilemma.

He turned to depart and pain stabbed his ankle. He cried out. Would this wretched wound never heal?

Before he could take another step, Vorlyn was by his side, propping him up.

'Tell me this,' he said, as she helped him hobble inside. 'Your companions can use magic to influence?'

'As you've seen.'

'And they—spy—would you call it? On people and places from afar?'

'Scrying, yes.'

'As well as moving objects, or using force on them, or... some such?'

'To varying degrees.'

He halted, leaning on the wall of the cave, then pivoted until he faced her. 'Come with me. Disguise some of your sorcerers. Help me free Nedran.'

She scoffed. 'We've talked about this, Jonas. You know what happened the last time people employed magic in battle.'

'Using sorcery would avoid a war by infiltrating peacefully.'

'That's how you define peace? To compel individuals to act against their will?'

His shoulders slumped. 'When you put it that way...' The notion sat like being served a plate of rancid meat.

'We'll find a solution, Jonas. Be patient.'

But there was no time for patience. Every day his brother remained embroiled with that witch-king was a day of freedom lost, and a day Nedran's people lived under the influence of a villain.

SIXTY-TWO

'Your cook has done wonders with this venison, Your Highness.' Vera tried to hide the twist on her tongue at the inundation of salt. Chewing on the morsels of aged meat drowned in watery gravy, she kept her jaw movements small and washed it down with the only palatable item on the table: the wine her family loaded onto her carriage to gift her promised husband.

'My thanks.' Gohran glanced her way, and she smiled coyly, running a delicate fingertip over the silver edge of her brooch. Its sapphire accentuated the marigold of her silk brocade gown, the sleeves tapered in a style lately adopted by the women in Galliarn.

'Wherever did you source that stone?' Across from her, Princess Jaydyn tugged absently on her sapphire earrings in an ornate gold drop setting. Old-fashioned and garish, they matched her outdated woad dress with overly wide sleeves. Perhaps with a young child to tend to, she'd neglected her apparel.

Vera ignored the stab in her chest at remembering Lynden's sly grin when she presented her the brooch, never knowing she would sit beside Gohran, instead of Lyn. 'It was a gift, Your Highness.' Erldan's royal dynasty boasted its collection of fine sapphire jewels, and the stone embedded in her brooch matched the cut of the monarch's ring, and even the earrings worn by his sister.

Jaydyn's eyes narrowed.

Had she miscalculated? Did Jaydyn think her vulgar, wearing jewellery to imitate that of the monarchy? She wanted to signal that she belonged. And it *was* similar—perhaps too similar.

She turned to Gohran. 'How was your hunt, Your Highness?' She sipped her wine, hoping he didn't notice how much of her meal she'd left untouched, and that this wasn't a sample of what lay ahead. Once instated as queen and head of Erldan's household, she could oversee the kitchens.

'It's early in the season yet,' he dismissed with a wave, gulping wine from his goblet as if it were ale or mead.

Vera frowned. They were deep enough into spring that game should be plentiful, but she didn't contradict him. 'I'd love to accompany you on the next,' she said, and a shadow crossed Gohran's features. 'With the other ladies, of course.'

Whenever she'd begged Pa to let her ride along with his party, he'd dismissed her. 'One day, Vee, you'll attend so many of your husband's hunts you'll find them as tedious as your mother, and be grateful for a time before your seat ached from the long hours atop a palfrey.'

Jaydyn snorted into her wine. 'Erldan's men don't care to cater to the whims of bored womenfolk.'

'I see. Then perhaps you and I could ride while the men play, Your Highness?' She assumed Jaydyn rode like her late sister, Ella.

Gohran signalled for more wine. 'You'd do better to stay within the grounds of the keep, at present.'

This wasn't going well.

When Aunty Lee—who was supposed to be her chaperone—left her to visit an old friend in nearby Harnal, she'd said, 'My absence will give you and the king an opportunity to become acquainted.'

'My thanks.' Vera kissed her cheek and whispered, 'Your subtlety is remarkable.' Now, she wished Leena had stayed.

Vera was used to captivating the room with her wit, receiving the king's attentions with grace, but Gohran seemed distracted. Worry creased his brows and forehead. His eyes appeared darker, and mouth tighter, than when she'd last seen him.

She supposed she shouldn't expect him to court her when their marriage was all but certain. What was flattery, after all, when he offered her a kingdom?

Following their supper, no one suggested a game of tiles or an evening stroll. There seemed to be a dearth of ladies-in-waiting, who might have accompanied her even if Princess Jaydyn had not wished to play. Once established, she would prioritise reviving Erldan's court, formerly renowned for its extravagant balls.

When she retired to the guest chamber, Gohran bid her good night with a chaste kiss upon her cheek—not her hand, and certainly not her lips. 'I shall see you at breakfast following the dawn worship.'

But instead of heading towards his room, a pair of advisers ushered him away with urgent whispers.

She lay awake in the strange bed, listening to the unfamiliar evening sounds of the household's routine. She wouldn't sleep in the queen's chamber until after the wedding.

Lantern light passed through the moth-eaten holes of the heavy drapes hanging from the canopy. She rolled over and pulled the thin, worn bedclothes tighter, but the empty place beside her taunted.

She closed her eyes and slid her hand beneath her nightdress, remembering the heat of lips on her neck and breasts, the fire of a tongue at the peak between her thighs.

Her mind pictured Jonas's wretchedly alluring smile. Kept hungering for his mouth on hers. His palms caressing. His need inside her.

Curse him!

She placed her hands back atop the covers and stared at the shadows flickering along the walls.

Gohran wasn't Jonas, but having a man in her bed would surely distract her. Should she try to seduce him? Lure him to her chamber, or slip into his? Let him know how eager she was to make this union succeed?

What if he was leaving her alone because he'd changed his mind? The priests were yet to seal their betrothal.

Footfalls outside. She sucked in her breath, sat, smoothed her hair, pinched her cheeks, and straightened her nightdress, waiting for them to approach. At any moment, a servant would knock and summon her to the king's chamber.

The steps retreated.

She lay back down, heart thudding.

Hushed and agitated voices echoed before bodies thundered up the stairs and along the hall, knocking on door after door, but not hers.

More whispers, a gasp, and someone weeping. What was going on?

She rose and pulled a cloak over her nightdress, grabbed her lantern, and peered into the corridor to find Jaydyn clutching her daughter and pacing.

'Hush, Sess. Hush.'

'Is everything well, Your Highness?' she asked.

'There's been an incident,' Jaydyn said. 'You should stay in your chamber.'

Is this how her life at Erldan was to be? She would not be coddled in a darkened room. 'Tell me what happened, Your Highness.' Her tone, commanding. The king's sister should be mindful that Vera would soon out rank her.

'Someone took to a scullery maid and night watchman with a paring knife.'

'By Our Lady!' she gasped.

'Thank the goddess, they're both recovered, but the culprits rendered them unconscious and stole their clothes.' Jaydyn leaned in close. 'And scattered strands of hair over the bodies.'

'Scattered *hair*?' Incredulous.

'My brother's men are searching for the offenders now.'

What, by every demon, had she got herself into?

SIXTY-THREE

'Halt! We need to search all covered wagons,' Erldan's guard called, as Amber and Nykki queued to be let through. They'd not expected to encounter other travellers at this hour, but rising tensions, haphazard blockades, hunger, and boredom seemed to coalesce into a hum of activity that persisted through the night.

'We venture north to visit our aunt, who lies dying,' Amber said, hoping no one would recognise her through Xenon's light from the seasons she spent as Ella's tutor.

Suspicion passed over the guard's lopsided brow, and he scratched the fair whiskers that only partially concealed his askew chin. 'Urgent business only.'

'Please, good sir!' Nykki clutched him. 'Our aunt might pass into the goddess's arms at any hour.'

His eyes widened at the blood spattering her tunic and smeared across the exposed side of her face. He opened his mouth to shout, but then his focus drifted, and his jaw dangled without uttering a sound.

A second guard left his post to investigate the commotion, and Amber seized his gaze and plunged inside his mind, commandeering his thoughts, until his features softened, too.

Though Nykki slashing a pair of innocents sat like lead upon Amber's heart, she was grateful to have her energy replenished and brimming.

'Hoy!' The guard flagged the driver of a wagon, one of the few allowed beyond the blockade. 'Have you room to carry these ladies?'

A dark blond man whose head was half-shaved, with the remainder tied back to resemble a tail, turned to face them: a priest.

Amber stifled a gasp, and Nykki squeezed her hand, drawing her hair over her cheek.

The neophyte looked up at the scattered clouds covering a sprinkling of stars and a waxing moon. No immediate signs of rain. 'Of course. We can sit up front with our driver.'

He peeled back the canvas, exposing the wagon's wooden frame. Inside sat stacked scriptures, ilak fat candles, brass censers, barrels of wine, and folded vestments.

'Climb in, ladies,' said the guard, offering his thigh and elbow.

They shared a glance. Between the guards, the neophytes, and their driver, there were too many minds to influence at once.

'A generous offer,' Nykki said. 'But we can spare no coin.'

'No need to pay, ladies. We're pleased to do the goddess's work.' The blond neophyte reminded Amber of the priest in Harnal, handing out food and clothing.

'We don't mind walking,' she said.

'The goddess doesn't wait. If you care to see your aunt before it's too late...'

Shouts in the distance. There was no time to argue. 'Our thanks, Your Holiness,' Amber said.

They clambered aboard and hunkered beside the sacred implements, pulled the canvas closed, and shared waves of comforting warmth.

The priests climbed up on either side of the driver, who shouted and urged the horses forward.

Wheels crunched along the gravel of the uneven road, jostling them from side to side, as Erldan's torches faded into the distance. Amber inhaled the blossom scent of jasmine and honeysuckle and squeezed Nykki's hand, wishing they rode to freedom instead of death.

Calm should have settled over them the further they drove from Erldan, but Nykki's apprehension simmered, threatening to boil. What if these were priests like Grogan, their eagerness designed to secure two helpless women alone on the road?

Not every priest thinks that way, Amber thought to her.

But Nykki already plotted her pre-emptive revenge. The moment either of those priests came near, she would slice their flabby guts to pieces.

A neophyte groaned.

Amber pinched Nykki's mind. *Calm, my love. Keep your vengeful thoughts to yourself. We need to survive this journey if we're to take Davith down. We're so close now.*

As the night wore on, a thick fog cloaked the valley, reflecting the wagon's lantern light back at them and obscuring the road ahead. The driver swore under his breath as he narrowly dodged a series of potholes that lurched the wagon's tray sideways. Amber and Nykki clung to the wooden frame, fending off the heavy barrels and volumes that slid against them.

'My apologies, ladies!' called the driver. They slowed to a stop. 'I can't see a wretched thing.'

Muffled conversation before boots thudded to the ground.

Their hearts raced, power churning, as the footfalls crunched nearer.

The canvas drew back, revealing the blond priest holding a lantern. He reached into the wagon, offering Nykki his hand, and Amber could almost taste Nykki's pulse throbbing.

He raised the lantern and light poured across her branded face.

Nykki, turn away!

It was too late. The priest's eyes widened in recognition. 'You're her!'

Nykki's energy surged, and she yanked the priest's arm with preternatural force. Bone snapped and crunched, and the priest howled.

Two sets of boots landed, *thud, thud*, and then thundered to the wagon's rear.

Amber drew a steadying breath. There was no coming back from this. *Kill him.*

Nykki clutched the sharp lid of a censer. She turned it upside down and stabbed its point through the priest's throat. Stunned, crimson liquid gurgled from the puncture and his body spasmed, spurting blood.

Red soaked his vestment and spilled over his lips as waves of force engulfed them like a waterfall roaring after heavy rain.

Amber seized the second priest and slipped inside his mind to locate the chamber that would render him unconscious, gripped by the paralysis of sleep.

Take down the driver, Nykki!

She turned away, wishing she could shutter her psyche while Nykki savaged that poor innocent's flesh, but she saw no other way.

Together, they might manage one docile priest to get them inside Nedran and lead them to Davith. Managing a second posed too great a risk. She did not dare leave any witnesses this time.

Eventually, the driver's life extinguished, leaving Nykki sated.

Amber left the second priest lying unconscious in the grass by the side of the road and approached the wagon.

'Help me strip it down,' she said, ignoring the first holy man's butchered throat and the driver's vacant stare, while savouring the vitality that thrummed around them, knowing it would soon sour.

They tore off the blood-soaked canvas and hurled it into the brush beside the track. Amber glanced down at their spattered clothing. 'Let's hope at least two of those vestments escaped the carnage.' They rummaged through the garments, pulling out a couple mostly free of telltale crimson spray. The rest they tossed with the discarded covering, along with the wagon's contents, before dragging the corpses and dumping them, too.

Amber swallowed the bile that rose with each thump of their lifeless weight. Nykki revelled in it, her grinning eyes aglow.

They examined the emptied wagon. Come daylight, they could not disguise the blood that had soaked into the wooden tray.

'Let's unhitch the tray and ride,' Amber said. 'I'll sit with the priest on one horse, and you can take the other.'

Nykki paled, her surety gone. 'But... I've never... I don't—I can't...'

Amber stared at her. After everything they had endured and overcome, was she too afraid to mount a horse? 'We'll worry about that once we have this wagon freed.' She set about unfastening the bolts. 'Help me loosen these...'

Nykki froze.

As if the horses sensed her trepidation, they snorted and stomped, manes tossing, tails whipping.

Amber laid a soothing palm on each flank until both beasts settled. 'I need you in here.' She swiped blood and sweat from her cheek and forehead, smeared it into her hair and down her stolen shirt to dry her palms. 'Nykki, help!'

Nykki stood, unseeing, as terror gripped her.

Tiny hands with whitened knuckles clutched the strands of a black mane. Fog snorted through cavernous nostrils, and a pair of liquid dark eyes trained on her, above an elongated nose tossing side to side. Child fists clung, but the jolt was too violent. Too strong.

Panic stirred, and with it, the tingle of a thousand beetles crawled across her skin. Heat surged from core to limb, and out through her fingertips, wrapping around the mane. Tendrils of blue force grasped, desperate to hold on.

The steed reared, tipped her backward, and flung her through the air. She fell to the hard ground beside her brother. Ribs aching. Tailbone pinching. Head pounding.

Her breath stopped, then heaved, as the beast stomped and whinnied, rearing again, its shadow spreading until it enveloped her brother...

She braced, couldn't watch what happened next. Couldn't look away.

Oh gods.

Stop, Nykki! Stop!

The horses grew agitated, twitching and snorting as the excess energy of Nykki's heightened memories bled into them.

Amber clasped her arms and pulled her close. 'I'm here. You're safe. Breathe.' She slowed each inhale, and encouraged Nykki's breath to fall into sync, until hers and the horse's nerves settled. 'These beasts are tame,' she whispered into Nykki's hair. *We'll keep them tame.*

Nykki trembled, but from anger, not fear. 'I had forgotten,' she said, her voice cold and quiet.

Amber let Nykki's rage shudder through her, knowing it wasn't only the memory of being thrown from a horse, or of her brother being trampled, that Nykki had lost.

As a child, her movement had stirred and grasped from terror, causing that wild stallion to rear. Later, when she'd tried to access her power as a novice priestess, she couldn't. Hadn't even recalled using it. Now, joining with Amber, she unleashed her gifts.

Once Nykki calmed, Amber said, 'Come, we should get this wagon unfastened.'

Instead of wheeling it off the road, they angled it sideways to block the passage. Single riders might steer around it, but carts and carriages would need to detour or stop to clear the path.

There was no question of taking the priest with them now. Keeping Nykki composed would occupy all of Amber's concentration. She let out her breath. Hated what they were about to do.

To all appearances, the neophyte slept, but the moment Amber withdrew her hold, he would rouse.

She crouched beside him and drew her fingers to the blood pulsing against the side of his neck. Focus adrift, she reached into his mind. She sought memories, insights, or clues about what to expect when they arrived at Nedran. But every inquiry clouded over.

Xenon help her. He'd never set a foot inside that city. He was useless to them. The priest knew only that Davith had travelled ahead to conduct an important rite, and that they were to bring supplies for the local temple.

She swallowed her rising bile.

'I'm sorry,' she whispered, then turned away while Nykki unleashed her power to kill him.

Once Nykki was done, they hastened to dress in the robes they'd set aside, using soiled clothes to wipe the blood from their hands, hair, and faces. A consolation, no one would expect the two young neophytes from Erldan to know where they were going when they arrived.

Amber held Nykki close and soothed her again before helping her climb atop the steed. It took some wrangling to settle the horse, more used to hauling wares than wary riders. She set its fellow loose, though it stared after them, seemingly uncertain what to do, or perhaps not wishing to be left alone.

Hitching her too-long vestment up to free her knees, Amber squeezed her thighs around the horse's bulk. The lack of saddle and stirrups made staying seated more challenging, but with Nykki snug behind her, she pulled her beloved's arms to circle her waist and calmed them both with her power.

'Hold tight,' she said, using her magic to guide the horse forward. 'I've got you.'

Nykki's mind and body answered, wrapping even tighter around her. 'And I you, my love. Always.'

SIXTY-FOUR

'*Taya menel!*' *Move! Let me pass!* A couple wearing long draped linens tied at the waist brushed past, their garb akin to Aeron's robes, but lighter. The woman's covered her entire body, while the man's was loosely slung over one shoulder, leaving his arms and chest bare.

'*Salvees! Salvees!*' *Sale! Sale!*

Ella did not recognise the words, but their meaning slid into her mind. How often had folk at Aeron spoken this foreign tongue without her noticing? Some terms were a distorted echo of the familiar, time and distance having shifted the language as running water wears upon rock—or perhaps, as a tide shapes the silt of a riverbank.

Each breath pinched her ribs as she creaked along the paving. The sacrifice, fire, and chanting aided her recovery, but a sense of jarring remained. Her shirt and trousers, which she'd kept, clung to her, the air as warm and moist as the steam rising from Aeron's caves.

'Shyarma!' A word she did not know spat from the tongue of an older man.

Accompanying him, five women of varying ages donned full-bodied tunics. They eyed her, and then each other.

Wearing legged trousers.

Hair like a little boy!

Where is her dosha?

Her mind translated, save for the words for which she knew no Yceltic equivalent.

When she'd landed at the foot of a craggy mountain range, some distance from the market square and surrounded by lush rainforest, Yorg's memories were a lodestone to guide her. But she arrived in another world. Cries, laughter, and chatter carried across the thick air, while spices wafted atop the acrid stench of animals, refuse, and too many sweaty bodies.

She expected people to stare at her pale skin, but as she took in the myriad faces, several shared her Yceltic features. Few were as dark as Yorg, and almost none of their complexions deepened to indigo. Were Aeron's folk the last true Myanai?

A slender man with a tapered beard and fox-like eyes grabbed her arm. 'Girl, where is your dosha?'

She shrugged him off, and he gripped tighter, both hands wrapped around her wrist. He nodded to his companion, a stocky pale-skinned fellow, who answered by slapping her cheek.

She staggered. By the hells!

A fiery prickle darted through her fingertips, and the man reeled.

Both men shouted, arms seizing her, dragging her back.

More shouts as bystanders roused to watch the commotion.

Ella simmered, ready to boil. She reached into their minds and lashed at their psyches. The men winced and loosened their hold. She pictured their limbs as the moonstone, winding her power to net them both. With a draw of heat, her force surged and blasted them off her.

'Xenona! Xenona!'

They stumbled back. Silence rippled across the crowd, then settled with a weight that threatened to swallow her. Eyes crowded, as one-by-one, the on-lookers dropped to their knees, drawing three fingers over their foreheads and then their hearts. Not a warding, but devotion.

A slow, chanting wail rose.

Alien words toppled, and she caught only impressions of meaning.

Forgive me.

Honour me.

Bestow Xenon's mercy.

When the stocky man who'd struck her glanced up, Ella captured and held his gaze. His jaw softened, his eyes begged, and as her beguilement stirred, his lips curved, while his groin twitched.

A heady scent of jacaranda, frankincense, and amber curled its tendrils around her. She inhaled and drank in the crowd's wide stares and gaping jaws: on their knees, arms beseeching, willingly in her thrall.

She drew from their swell, their roiling emotions flooding her senses to fill her with light, then cast it over them, as far as her power would reach. Her god-sight recognised the faint azure wave surging and subsiding, winding through and between them: pebbles in a rising tide.

The slender, bearded man said, 'Have you come to us from the Sacred Oracle?'

He must not detect her trembling hands or wavering voice.

Rise. She reached and drew him to his feet until he towered over her. Her palms rested on his cheeks and his features lifted as though her touch were a sacred gift. *I seek the Place of Omens.*

He frowned. 'Have you no *dosha* to escort you?'

That word again.

He turned and whispered to the man who had called her a '*shyarma*'. That man then addressed one of his womenfolk, who stood level with the centre of his chest: as tall as Ella. 'Sheevalla, lend the *Xenona* a *kordra*.' A robe like the other women wore.

The woman, Sheevalla, eyed her, until Ella tried to meet and hold her gaze, when she bowed her head, looking down. 'Yes, Dosha Ralan,' she said to the man.

Not in Ella's thrall, but obedient to her dosha's command.

The others sneaked glances before their eyes darted away.

Sheevalla outstretched her palm, signalling for Ella to accompany them. They weaved between stalls of dyed silk, jars of dried spices, baskets stacked with unfamiliar vegetables, and dripping roasted joints of meat, marinated and hanging from iron hooks.

Buyers and sellers alike reached for her, seeking proximity, and two of the women in her party ushered her between them, as if they sought to possess her. Declare her one of them.

Where their arms touched hers, she snared them, and wound her beguilement until they softened against her, their shoulders easing with a release of breath. The other three, including Sheevalla, who she could not reach, held onto their resolve.

Beneath, an undercurrent slithered: *what if he wants her for his wife?*

These were not like the people Yorg described. The community he'd left behind. She had expected families to take many shapes, as they did at Aeron, with folk partnering according to their whim, and no hierarchy save the inherent value that recognised an individual's aptitudes and strengths. But like the women at Aryon, and Erldan before it, they fought for the meagre rations within their limited sphere.

Beyond the square, people bustled along paved streets. Multi-storied houses resembling temples crowded with their brightly painted stucco and ornate sloped roofs laid out in tidy grids. Everyone seemed to move on sturdy leather sandals, rather than horseback, and unlike the merchants who wheeled their goods into town for market days in Ycelt, the Myanai stalls were semi-permanent structures, patrolled by the various guilds' watchmen.

Behind them, the Halbar Ranges created a monstrous backdrop, permanently snowcapped, atop a lush rainforest. Further north, the Halbar bled into the Northern Ranges, divided by the River Arin. Places Ella had only read about, that had once seemed beyond her lifetime's reach.

Yorg had told her his people worshipped the mountain as Ycelt's people worshipped the sun, while others prayed to the forests and trees, and made offerings to the rivers and the sea. Some even lay prostrate upon the soil and earth.

As Ella walked these streets, making turn after turn, she saw no signs of these former gods, save for a temple to the Mountain, *Rimyan*, a genderless deity who gave Their name to the land.

Dosha Ralan's residence was a mirror to its neighbours', identifiable only by the jasmine glyph painted on the street-facing wall. A sliver of ice crept down Ella's back. Why that icon? Why this man and this family? She was trusting her magic, and their awe, to maintain her sway. She hoped it was enough.

When they reached the sloped and gilded awning, Sheevalla pinched her arm and ushered her around the side.

She pointed to the main entrance. 'That is for our dosha and his honoured guests.' Of which she was not one. It seemed their reverence evaporated behind the shadows of their private walls.

She and the five women trailed along a narrow stepping of stones to the unpainted rear of the building. The neat and embellished façade gave way to heaped gravel and dirt. She held up her sleeve to cover her nose as they passed the household's refuse and privy. Beggars loitered nearby, hoping to find scraps to eat or goods to salvage.

The women herded her through the low set lintel and into a narrow corridor that widened to an interior courtyard. As outside, someone had painted the portico columns in marigold, cinnabar, and amethyst. A pond housed slow-moving fish, whose scales glinted under the sun, then ducked beneath the ruffled leaves of a pink lotus. Their spicy citrus and floral scent went some way to covering the stench that wafted through the open door behind them.

'Come,' Sheevalla said, steering her again.

Their padding feet echoed across the black-and-white tiles and up a stone staircase. Beside them, vines crept towards a wooden fretted balcony.

They stepped through a narrow doorway into a room kept dim by sheer curtains covering the latticed windows. The shadowy space reminded her of a women's hall, but with cushions instead of chairs, as at Aeron. Bedrolls lined one wall. Did these women camp in here?

Sheevalla reached into a carved wooden chest, embellished with iron bands, and pulled out a robe like hers. A kordra. She pointed to a lacquered screen, and she understood she was to undress behind it.

As she hastened towards the screen, Sheevalla pinched a tuft of her close-cropped hair, and tossed Ella a silk shawl. Ella winced and took it. She found it as difficult to sway this woman as she had her sisters growing up, having to overcome her own animosity and the sense of being cast back into her childhood role.

One of the two women she soothed earlier slapped Sheevalla, and hissed something Ella didn't catch.

She ducked around the screen, wishing Yorg's memories had taken her directly to the Place of Omens, instead of leaving her to navigate these brutes.

Tears sprang and she searched for a mirror, or some other surface to scry, though it might not be possible at this distance.

Spying no mirrors, tables, jewels, or adornments, she steadied her breath, closed her eyes, and cast her silent thought as far as she could reach, knowing it would not be far enough. *Oh Yorg, I'm so sorry I let you go. I will find my way back soon, I promise.*

SIXTY-FIVE

Fear evaporated in the electric thrill of what Amber and Nykki had done and what they were about to do. Energy thrummed around and between them, consuming with savage hunger.

Amber squeezed her knees tighter astride the horse's girth, steering it on, but it was hard to concentrate on anything other than Nykki's hand inching to cup and squeeze her breast, the other sliding along her straining thigh.

Wind rushed past, filling her lungs with the scent of Nykki's hair and skin. She inhaled, longing to absorb her beloved, to make them whole.

'Pull up here, my love.' Nykki's breath came hot and fast against her ear as her lips dusted Amber's exposed neck.

She had murdered four men. Three priests and a driver. Innocents, save one. But against the driving tide of her need, those lives could have belonged to insects she'd trod on. Inconsequential. And if she was honest, a part of her luxuriated in Nykki's violence, the glow behind her cat-green eyes when she devoured their source.

Nykki's fingers curled around her pubic bone, pressing the already soaked fabric to rub against her.

Ravenous.

She urged the horse to slow, and by the time they halted, they could scarcely wait to dismount and tether it to a nearby tree.

Nykki pressed her against the rough bark, lifted her robe, and shoved her hand inside her braies. She gripped her cropped hair and tugged, teeth grazing the tender flesh.

Heat pulsed and thickened, and her surroundings blurred. She simultaneously inhabited and observed her body. The pale cream of her neck, the curve of her breast, her taut nipple peaking. She yielded from the outside and from within. Caressing and being caressed. She was everywhere and nowhere.

Waves of sensation crashed over her, more desperation than pleasure, more hunger than satiation, until she no longer knew where she ended and Nykki began.

Grass glittered as emeralds under Xenon's light: a half-illuminated crystal orb against the indigo sky. Beneath her palms, the bark crinkled, oddly soft, like leather, not wood, and with Nykki's next stroke, she hovered, drifting from her body.

Heart racing, she clung to her flesh, to the tree, to Nykki. But each corporeal surface slipped away, ghostlike.

What's happening? Nykki—what have you done?

Laughter burbled over Nykki's lips, a river trickling over rock. 'Hush, my love. Enjoy...' She glided along the ethereal currents, soaking up every remnant of pleasure.

Amber's god-body had peeled from her flesh: another ability that didn't belong to her, but to Nykki.

'Take the gift. Embrace it. These moments are all we have.'

Yet Xenon had not built Amber's psyche to accommodate this strange power. While Nykki basked in its freedom and the relief it afforded from her memories and her pain, she lacked control, and therefore, so did Amber.

Nykki found her lips, and she experienced that same peculiar mix of being caressed from the outside and in, while viewing them from a distance, her consciousness hovering an arm's length away.

'Nykki, ground me in my body, please...' she spoke with voice and mind, but her words overlapped and echoed strangely. 'I need to know I can get back.'

Nykki stroked her more intensely, finding a rhythm that threatened to tip her over the abyss. 'I've got you,' she whispered. 'You can let go...'

Pressure built with a swell of sensation so exquisite she feared it would engulf her. Nykki was right. This could be their last night, their closing moments.

The wave crashed, surging and rippling along every inch of her mind and body, to leave her shuddering. Sobbing.

She found Nykki's lips, haunted by the copper of blood, and clung as her senses warped and distorted. In a world where nothing would stay still or certain, Nykki was her lodestone. Her home.

But Nykki didn't ground her. Wouldn't stop. Amber's climax magnified her desire and she sought to drive her even higher.

Hovering in her ethereal form, Amber saw them from the outside: two writhing snakes, grappling and greedy. Whenever she panicked, Nykki's reassurance cupped her. *I've got you. I've got you.*

She relaxed and drifted.

Flitting in and out of her body, of Nykki's, their passion generated more power than they consumed. She waited to feel satiated, satisfied, but her hunger ravened, as if part of her knew they would never have enough time.

'Let me hold you,' she choked as the next crashing wave subsided.

Nykki eased them to the long grass, curling into her embrace, whispering and soothing.

The stars crawled across the sky, ducking in and out behind gathering clouds, and they clung, savouring every heartbeat.

Finally, within her body, the sense that her consciousness could slip away from her flesh at any moment lingered, making her hold on even tighter.

The loose threads of their psyches had unravelled, yet remained entangled, and when morning broke, they would have weaved together to create something new.

Soon, Elnora would rise, and they would journey the rest of the way to Nedran, but for now, they relished the waning night.

Sixty-Six

Seven nights Ella had slept on the floor beside Ralan's wives, navigating their strange customs, tending to the cooking, the cleaning, and caring for his hordes of children. Their initial reverence for her magic seemed tempered by her status as an unaccompanied woman, and more so, she suspected, by the lack of an audience to observe it.

Laughter, squeals, quarrelling, and tears poured into every corner of the house and yard. Her breath caged within her ribs at this normalcy she would never know. Would Breeyan allow Xarion the freedom to play? Would she ever have companions, if not siblings, to share with and bicker at?

The youngsters treated their mothers interchangeably, and if not for an extended glance, or a similarity of features, she would not have known who had birthed whom.

By day, the women and children kept to the back of the house, except to bring Ralan meals, help him bathe and dress. They only left the property when he accompanied them, or, if running an errand, he hired a lan-dosha, a kind of eunuch chaperone, in his stead.

Ella had thought they would take her to the Place of Omens right away. That she would stay a night, two at most. But when days passed with no sign of Ralan fulfilling his commitment, she'd said to Sheevalla, 'If someone directs me, I will head there myself.'

'Nay! Not without a dosha.'

'I don't fear travelling alone.'

Sheevalla's palm hovered, ready to slap, but she stayed her hand. Had Ella not been 'Xenona', she doubtless would have landed her blow.

'I can pay for a...' Foolishly, Ella carried only parchments in her satchel, not coin, for Yorg had stowed enough for them both. She cursed herself again for losing a hold of him. 'If you remind Dosha Ralan—'

'He is not your dosha,' she snapped, then continued checking the contents of a row of large ceramic pots, lifting each lid, stirring, sniffing, tasting, then resealing, before moving to the next.

'Halla!' she called to the eldest among them, then said what Ella loosely translated as, 'The Xenona thinks we can command our dosha!'

Halla scoffed, pushing her tight ghost-white ringlets away from her face, but when she glanced back at Ella, she softened. 'She does not know our customs, Sheev.'

Ella brushed Sheevalla's arm and let her power flow. 'Please...' With a draw of heat and breath, she channelled her request into the chambers of Sheevalla's mind.

Sheevalla shrugged Ella off, her eyes hard, citrine stones. 'Keep your Xenona-ran to yourself, girl.'

Ella withdrew, but if Sheevalla insulted her again, her next attempt to influence would not be a request.

She turned her attention back to washing and stemming vegetables, ready to pickle, wishing the dosha permitted his wives to prepare meat, too. Though she had used little of her source, she seemed unusually weak. Depleted.

A spasm seized her abdomen, followed by a familiar dull ache. Her moon-time.

It had been over a season since she abandoned Xarion, forcing her to wean, and her cycle had not returned until now.

All but one woman worked beside her, the fifth having stepped outside to supervise the children. She swallowed. 'Have you rags and a moonbelt I may use?'

Halla pivoted, her pale eyebrows raised against her brown skin. 'Do you bleed?'

She nodded. 'I don't wish to stain this kordra...' Why dress the women in creamy white?

Halla made the sign she recognised as a ward against witches and heretics. 'A Xenona bleeding in our dosha's house,' she whispered.

Before, the gesture sickened, but here, enacted with reverence, it warmed like a summer glow.

'A portent,' added another, her voice almost a chant, her eyes a luminous gold.

'Dosha Ralan will surely want to take her for his wife.'

The youngest, heart-faced Nyria, burst into tears and ran from the room.

Nyria need not worry. Dosha Ralan would do no such thing. 'Rags?' Ella asked again.

That night, when Ralan chose Nyria from among his wives to attend his bed, Ella clutched her arm. *Please—remind Ralan that he is to take me to the Place of Omens.*

Nyria's focus drifted, her full lips parting with a sleepy smile. 'Of course. Dosha Ralan ought to keep his promises.'

And do not tell him of my bleeding.

Nyria nodded. Her candle cast flickering shadows that bruised her eyes, and Ella shuddered. Still, hope rose in her throat as Nyria left.

She settled onto the vacant bedroll beside the others, waiting for the last wife to draw the sheer curtain around them.

At first, she thought the cloth useless—it concealed nothing—but as night fell, and mosquitoes hovered, she was grateful for the barrier against their persistent whines.

It was too hot to pull the covers up to her chin, but she hated feeling so exposed, knowing these women scrutinised her at every opportunity, so she poked her bare feet out the bottom. Sweat trailed from the backs of her knees and between her breasts, and she lifted her nightdress and slipped one leg atop the sheet, securing her moonbelt in place.

Something scurried across the floor. A cockroach or a rat. In the dark, she couldn't know. Her skin prickled. Heat be damned. She dived beneath the sheet.

For the first time in seasons, she longed to feel the shivery ache of cold tucked in her old tower room, knowing Lyrra or a chambermaid would arrive soon to lay a fire.

She held tight to that feeling, catching snatches of sleep, wishing for the early morning chill that always preceded uhtan.

When next she woke, it was to Nyria's feet padding back from Ralan's chamber. Through uhtan's false light, Ella saw she clutched her cheek, crimson and purple staining the skin where her nose met her left eye.

She glanced at Ella, shook her head, and looked away.

Wood settled in Ella's throat. She should not have asked. Should not have tempted fate. Sheevalla had mocked her for assuming these women had any sway over their husband, and she was right.

It was no longer feasible to wait for Ralan to remember his commitment, nor rely on his wives to deliver her message. She needed to get to Ralan herself.

As the women prepared and served breakfast, Nyria hung back, awaiting the pot's dregs.

A gaggle of small children gathered for their fill then peeled off, leaving scattered bowls as they ran to play.

When the wives ate, in their strange mix of reverence and shame, they sat facing away from Ella, which she'd grown used to. But that morning, they also showed Nyria their backs.

With a loud sigh, Ella joined her. 'May I?'

Nyria nodded without looking up from her meagre bowl.

Ella squeezed her hand, her power cooling as a liquid easing into Nyria's mind. Through her god-sight, one segment appeared jagged, almost swollen. She wrapped her will around it and soothed, dampening Nyria's pain and her memory until the edges calmed.

Nyria swayed on her cushion, her features softening, like drunken bliss.

Ella poured her magic until Nyria was sated and then withdrew.

'Thukran. Thukran.' My thanks. My thanks. Nyria wiped her tears.

Ella offered so little, and yet to Nyria, so much.

Not nearly enough. Ralan should not have touched her.

Ella cleared her bowl, and Nyria's, and settled into the morning's routine. It was laundry day and she helped gather and fold sheets from where they hung across the balcony to dry. A young boy, his laughter pealing, raced to slap linens out of his mother's hands.

Halla slapped back, but he darted out of reach. 'Do you want Dosha to send you to the slavers?'

Ella sucked in her breath as the boy squealed and sprinted away down the corridor.

'And tell Khalia to stop hiding and get inside,' Halla called after him, then returned to gathering sheets.

They were folding the last of the linens when a small girl with a round face and rounder eyes framed by long, dark lashes peered up at Ella.

'Will you stay with Dosha Gordon's family, too?'

'Khalia, leave Nessa to her work.' Ella had reverted to using her false peasant's name. 'Where is your comb?'

Two of the women worked to tame Khalia's unruly blonde locks, untying the strips of cloth she'd slept in overnight to set her hair in the curls the Myanai favoured.

'Ouch!' Khalia yanked away when one of her mothers tugged too hard.

Halla slapped her cheek lightly. 'Kah! Be still!'

The girl whimpered, twisting the belt of her kordra so tightly around her finger the tip turned white.

'When Dosha Gordon's family comes, you stay quiet and smile. Understand, Kah?'

Head lowered, she nodded and wiped her nose on her sleeve and let them finish.

'They're here.' Sheevalla stood in the doorway leading to the courtyard where Dosha Ralan hosted his guests.

Khalia looked frantically from mother to mother, as if begging some-one—anyone—to spare her.

'Go, Kah,' Halla nudged her forward.

'Ahmah!' she cried. *Mama.*

Korvalla, a woman who shared Khalia's round face and blonde hair, stiffened, swallowed, and turned away, busying herself sweeping tiles.

'*Ahmah!*' More fevered now.

'Come, Khalia.' The girl clung to Sheevalla's skirts as Sheevalla ushered her out.

A short way along the passage, Sheevalla crouched to squeeze Khalia and wipe her tears. Ella wasn't sure if she witnessed with her mind or ears when she whispered, 'Dosha Gordon is a good man. A wealthy man. If you go with his family now, and serve them well, he will provide for you, and you shall give him many sons.'

Beetles crawled across Ella's skin and settled in her belly.

Once her daughter was out of sight, Korvalla stuffed the sleeve of her kordra in her mouth to stifle a howl. Two others held her and muttered words of comfort.

Halla stood apart from them, a hardness around her pursed lips and narrowed eyes that belied pain. She turned to Ella. 'If Dosha Ralan takes you for his wife, you'd best pray to every deity that he gives you sons.'

Sixty-Seven

'What have we here?'

Amber startled awake. That oil slick voice. Gods. No.

She bolted upright and scooped Nykki behind her.

Grey stones eyed them through narrowed slits. Lip curving to a sneer, hovering just out of reach.

She shuddered.

'Better and better.'

Nykki, stay back.

Three neophytes gathered, caging them between Davith and the tree where they'd slept. Why did these holy men gather like rats around a refuse heap?

Behind them, the priests' carriage blocked half the road. They must have stopped to investigate when they spied the tethered horse. Amber should have moved them deeper into the woods. She hadn't meant for them to fall asleep.

'Two priestesses, what a treat!' Davith's head tilted as his tongue slid over his bottom lip, then scowled, and tutted. 'But defiling Elnora's sacred robes, I see. That won't do.'

He inhaled as though relishing their scent, and Amber recoiled, backing against the tree.

'What happened to that delectable hair, Little Sparrow?'

'It's waiting for you back in Erldan, fiend,' Nykki snarled. 'Splayed across two bleeding bodies.' Her fingers tensed around Amber's. She tossed her head towards the road. 'And there are a few more prizes up ahead.'

Hush. Keep calm…

'Oh yes.' Another tut. 'I hear you've kept yourselves occupied in Harnal, Little Sparrow, giving the locals quite the scare. What would your High Priestess say? Breaking vow after vow...'

Breathing hard, she clutched Nykki's mind.

'Yet I'm supposed to fear your mythical Curse?'

'Very much so,' Amber said. 'Whereas we have nothing to fear.' Not anymore.

'Has my precious fledgeling sparrow finally grown into a hawk?'

Her vision clouded with blood and seething heat. Not hers. Nykki's.

Davith made a show of admiring Nykki's brand. 'I see my poor, loyal Grogan had some sport with this one, too. I shall miss that boy's *appetite.* Though you're more of a blackbird than a sparrow, aren't you?'

Nykki lurched forward, but Amber grasped her back. *Not yet.*

How did he know about Grogan if he was in Nedran while they were in Harnal? Hadn't they slaughtered him the previous day? A courier could not have outpaced them. Did Davith harbour sorcerers within his ranks, or...?

Wait. The moon had been in its first quarter last night. But the heresy trial took place with the new moon, when Xenon's power was diminished...

No.

How much time elapsed while they journeyed through Xenon's currents?

'Seize them,' Davith said. 'Make sure you cover their eyes.'

Unlike Grogan and his fellows in Harnal, Davith's servants carried staffs.

But they hadn't reckoned with Nykki's magic.

Amber opened her god-sight and saw the nearest rod as a lifeless shadow between pulsing palms. Before its owner rotated it to herd them, she leveraged Nykki's movement to net and suck it from his hands. She snapped it over her knee and tossed it onto the grass. The next she held on to. Two jagged ends, one in each hand, pointed at them.

Nykki, take the other staff.

But Nykki had already lunged toward the third neophyte, an ordinary, handsome fellow with light brown hair and hazel-green eyes, who reminded Amber of Jonas.

He grabbed Nykki and turned her away from him, arms clasped behind her. He shoved her face into the tree trunk as she bucked and kicked.

The fiend closest to Amber was fool enough to meet her gaze, and she commandeered Nykki's power and pierced his psyche. His eyes rolled back, and his tongue lolled, drool seeping down his chin. She savaged his mind until he slumped, unconscious, to the ground.

She stepped over him to tackle the next, but the second neophyte, an acne-pocked lad with orange fuzz sprouting to frame his lips, screamed and ran.

'What clever parlour tricks you perform for me today, Little Sparrow.' Davith clapped his hands as though they acted out a play on a dais in the market square. 'And you brought your blackbird as a toy for my friend Lynor.'

The third priest, Lynor, had pinned Nykki against the tree. Tears kissed her cheek, the other squashed against the rough bark.

'My servant delights in teasing his prey, don't you, Lynor?'

Lynor's answering chortle turned Amber's blood to water. She grunted. *Shove him back, Nykki. Channel your movement.* Why wasn't she drawing on Amber's strength and torturing his mind, if she couldn't push him off?

Nykki's frightened whimper clamped around her heart. *Take him, Nykki. Kill him.*

Davith drew closer, daring Amber to pounce. But she didn't want to seize his body. She needed to penetrate his psyche.

'Keep playing with your blackbird, Lynor. The little sparrow is mine.' A salacious grin spread across his features as he lowered his staff.

She inched forward, studying his expression. He did not fear her. But he should.

The staff dangled by his side. Another inch and he would be within her grasp.

Nykki's scream pierced her. Lynor had ripped off her robe and was unfastening his braies.

Nykki!

She leapt for her beloved, but Davith foisted the crook of his staff to catch the back of her knees, and she toppled to the ground. Winded, she coughed and squirmed until Davith towered and pinned her. She froze. He pointed the end of the staff into her diaphragm and leaned down with his full weight until it hurt to breathe.

Amber's power surged, blasting outwards, but there was no movement behind it. Nykki's simulacrum had escaped her flesh, withdrawing her source. As she fled the horror of the brown-haired neophyte wrangling her body, she tugged Amber's psyche with her, encasing them within her ethereal haven.

In Nykki's vision, Elnora's sun warmed their naked backs beneath a pastel sky, and she slinked her soft legs around Amber's, twisting and caressing her regrown locks. She smiled, her creamy cheek unblemished below her luminous green eyes. Their lips blended, bodies melded, and it took every iota of Amber's will to wrench her attention to the corrupt High Priest sneering above her, his staff poised and ready to pierce.

She clutched the staff, fighting to stay grounded, and summoned Nykki's focus. *Lend me your power...*

In Nykki's mind, her ethereal lips caressed Amber's, their bodies merging, their minds enmeshed... *Join me, my love...*

By every god and demon, she'd wanted nothing so much in her paltry life than to escape the nightmare unfolding before her. But if she abandoned her corporeal form now, Davith would slaughter them both, and this would have been for naught.

Davith's staff stabbed deeper, and she saw an amalgam of Nykki's vision, Davith's slithering eyes, and the staff pointing at her chest.

She shuttered her psyche, blocking the slathering sounds, and the savage grunts, and struggled to breathe.

What if...

What if she gripped the staff as if she possessed Nykki's movement? As though their powers had fused...

On the next draw, her mind connected with wood, with Davith's body, and she blasted her force to hurtle them backwards.

Davith toppled, and the staff rolled onto the grass, out of reach. Amber leapt to her feet and pounced. The high priest lay akimbo, and she straddled him like a horse, pinning his arms as her influence surged.

She thrust into his mind, tore across the chambers of his psyche to pillage his memories, not caring what her rough ministrations damaged.

Flashes of reverie coalesced, and she was a small, grey-eyed boy, trailing behind his mother's skirts, sucking on a grimy thumb.

'Stop that!' the woman slapped, but the pain wasn't from the whip of her hand but a surge inside his mind, accompanied by a deep shame that etched into his psyche.

He showed her his rag doll. 'I made it with—'

She snatched it from his hands and tossed it into the hearth. 'No son of mine plays with dolls.' Another wave of humiliation as its wool smouldered. 'Clean the floor, and wash the sheets, too.'

As the boy scrubbed the white milky stains from the wood and weave, he pictured the men who had caused them. One after the other, sometimes together, they arrived each night, sweating and grunting, before leaving their coins on the nightstand, while he cowered on the other side of the drop curtain, and occasionally hiding under the creaking bed.

'How do you know?' one man marvelled. 'How do you always know exactly what I crave?'

No one hid their thoughts from Mother.

'Get out from under there, Davith.' Her mind pinched and squeezed. 'And go feed yourself. I can't stand your wretched hunger.'

He crawled out from beneath the bed and fled to the local temple.

Gorshyn greeted him with a hearty bowl of gruel. 'Come, lad. Our Lady sustains those who worship Her.'

Later, Gorshyn laid a blanket snug around his shoulders against the winter chill, guiding him to a bedroll atop the straw of his small hut. 'May Our Lady keep Her blessed ones safe against Xenon's light.'

Now Davith was a boy on the cusp of adolescence.

'Kick it to me!' he cried to the larger boys.

'Here,' one of them tossed the grain-filled sack his way, but when Davith picked it up, the lad smacked it from his hands, then trod on his foot.

He yelped, and another boy cuffed his chin. 'Take that, witch boy!'

'Witch boy! Witch boy!' they started up a chorus, cackling and jostling.

The largest tripped and shoved him down, grinding his face into a sloppy mound of ilak shit. The putrid taste at the back of his throat haunted him for weeks.

He kicked his worn boots along the gravel, braced to endure another smithy, another shopkeeper, another recruiter for the king's guard. Before they opened their mouths, irritation flashed. 'Not here, lad. Try someplace else.'

Backs would turn. Others signed a warding. One or two recognised him from his mother's hovel. She was good enough to soak and milk their rods, but none would take on her son.

'What if he's god-cursed, like her?'

When he arrived home with no work and no coin to find her lounging half-naked in a smoke-filled haze, he braced again for her loathing to pierce his core. Useless whelp. As feeble as your father.

The ache of hunger had settled into his bones and fused with his flesh and as his mother sucked on her pipe and took another man to her bed, her pleasure and disdain invaded his mind. All the while, he lay powerless, unable to shield against her, dreaming of the priests hunting her and watching her burn as she'd burned his doll.

When the day arrived that they finally pounded on her door, she'd already fled.

'You're old enough to fend for yourself, Davith,' she'd said. 'And if you contemplate telling them where I've gone, I'll haunt you, cut out your tongue, and stitch your mouth shut.'

Atop the stench of singed wool and smouldering wood wafted the scent of her sex, the spilled seed of too many men, and stale opium.

'Come, lad,' said Gorshyn. 'It's witches like that who threaten Elnora's people, but you can redeem your soul. The more like her we Cleanse, the more we purify the land, and the closer we reach to Elnora's arms.'

Behind them, Nykki howled, wrenching her from Davith's memories. Her beloved needed her.

She sliced through Davith's mind to cloak him unconscious, then withdrew, climbed to her feet, and raced to where that monster held her.

Amber's breath caught. He'd removed Nykki's robe and shoved her against the trunk as he writhed and ground against her. Her braies were around her knees, but his rod remained flaccid and soggy in his palm, and she was grateful to whichever deity had afforded Nykki the small mercy of rendering his natural weapon useless.

Oh! My love, hold on.

Amber seized his arms, tearing him away from her, but he was too strong.

'Get off me, witch!' His elbow punched into her guts, and she doubled over, coughing.

She imagined grabbing him with her mind's tentacles, but her ethereal claws passed straight through. Unable to move him, to find a way inside his psyche. He was impervious.

Like Jonas.

No. Gods, no!

He must be the same priest who had captured Nykki back in Harnal, and she'd left Nykki to fight him unarmed.

On the ground behind her, Davith stirred, while ahead, the impervious priest peeled Nykki off the tree and held her in a headlock.

No!

Mobilised to action, Amber scrambled for the discarded splintered staff and aimed the pointed end at him. They couldn't penetrate the man's mind, but the gods made him from ordinary flesh.

He manoeuvred Nykki between him and Amber.

Bite him, Nykki!

Amber edged closer, sucking in power. If Nykki drew his blood...

Curse the god, it would be useless to them.

Davith was on his feet and closing in. Dazed and rattled, but rallying.

That's when she noticed the blade poking into Nykki's side. 'Go on, witch. Stab me.' He chortled and thrust the knife against Nykki's rib. Blood welled where it broke the skin.

It might be enough.

Something sharp poked her. Davith's staff.

With a draw of breath and source, she whipped around, clutched it, and whacked Davith on the side of the head.

He tottered, clutching his ear, blood running down his hairline.

Power thrummed, and she pivoted to the brown-haired priest and thrust the staff with Xenon's force behind her, piercing his belly.

He howled.

Nykki, finish him!

Heat teemed through her core and along her limbs. Her eyes aglow, the grass between her and the road shimmered, while the gravel sparkled as though laid with veins of gold and quartz.

Hacking sounds churned her stomach as Nykki used might rather than magic to defeat her violator.

She turned back to Davith. This was it. She needed to end him.

Memories of Nykki's mind shredding Grogan's innards crowded, the blood sputtering from his pudgy lips, and the light fading from his eyes as his body lay preternaturally still.

Could she commandeer Nykki's movement to that extent? Bring herself to take a life? Even now? Even his?

Her hands trembled, unmoving. When she'd set out on this crusade, she'd fantasised bringing about his demise. But imagination and reality were not the same, and now that he lay vulnerable before her, she baulked, bile rising in her throat.

She could do this.

She must, or the false Cleansings and the brutality of Davith's vile quest would not cease. For the lascivious pleasure he'd taken in torturing Chrysanth, for scorching innocents on every wooden X, for the brand across her beloved's beautiful face, he needed to die.

Not just die. He needed to burn.

She dived for his ankles and forced his mind to falter until his body slumped.

She risked a glance over at Nykki. Her impervious attacker sagged, unmoving, stuck against the tree where Amber had pierced him, while her beloved had started on the unconscious neophyte, pinning him down.

She felt the stroke of Nykki's mind. *Take Davith, my love. He's yours.*

The High Priest trembled at her feet. The bile that had seized her throat earlier settled, and her mouth filled with saliva. Hunger. She had waited so long for this. 'Move,' she said.

Davith hauled to his feet, and she ushered him to his abandoned carriage. 'Get in,' she commanded. Beneath her influence, his malice writhed, but he complied.

She surveyed the interior until her gaze landed on an ornate wooden chest. 'Open it.' Within, lay a set of cuffs attached to a chain, a leather switch, and a flint. 'Remove your vestment,' she ordered, 'and pass me the switch.'

Davith's will ground against hers, as his quivering arms stripped off his robe, reached into the chest, and retrieved the implement. His knuckles whitened as he squeezed its leather handle. She needed to seize it before his resistance broke through her hold.

The blood on his temple had begun to scab, useless to her. But his rage churned like azure flames to her god-sight. She syphoned the energy and sent it surging through every word. 'Hand. It. To. Me.'

His grip loosened, and she swiped it from him.

'Close the lid.'

His entire body shook, the dark hairs on his scrawny legs standing upright, the blood of his spiderweb veins pulsing a vibrant blue beneath his pale skin.

Amber drew the switch back on an inhale. With her exhale, she slashed his calves, his thighs, his shoulders, savouring his silent flinch with each strike.

His fresh blood surged. She breathed it in and let it flood her, then commandeered his mind like a puppeteer. 'Cuff your ankles.'

As though attached to wires, she guided his hands to fasten the rings around each leg before she cuffed his wrists and secured the chain to the carriage frame. Even if he roused from her influence now, he would be trapped.

Her mouth watered with anticipation as she reached into the chest and retrieved the flint. With a final draw of power, she hopped down to unfasten the horses and urged them to flee.

Her next breath was the sweetest, as she sparked a flame and set a strip of cloth alight with a whoosh, then threw it onto the wooden carriage. She stepped back, relishing each flicker as it caught and burned.

Nykki would want to see this.

Wait—where was Nykki? She must have dealt with the other priest by now.

But Amber couldn't sense her. Had she deserted her body again?

Nykki?

'Nykki!'

Nothing.

'Nykki!'

Heart in her throat, Amber raced to the tree. The brown-haired man stood where she'd stuck him, jaw slack, eyes dead.

Nearby sprawled the other neophyte, his innards splayed across his butchered torso. Had he roused? Or had Nykki hunted him while he remained unconscious?

Beside him lay Nykki, her face and breasts coated in blood. Against the bright crimson, she appeared paler than the moon, almost blue, her skin thin like worn parchment, lattice with darkened veins. Deeper circles bruised her eyes. The surrounding air chilled Amber's bones, and it took a moment for her to register the weak, shallow breath emitting from Nykki's purple lips.

No.

How many times had she found Ella sprawled, weakened, as though suffocated by her own magic?

Nononononono. 'Tell me you didn't. Tell me you stopped drawing before... Nykki. *Nykki!*'

She cradled her beloved, tried to warm her, but the gods might have carved her from ice.

'Speak to me. Nykki!' She shook her, tapped her cheek. No response. Nykki's simulacrum had already departed as her lungs struggled to take their final breaths.

Behind her, the fire sparked and blazed, black smoke rising in the sky, the roar of flames almost louder than Davith's screams.

'Nykki, what have you done?' But she knew. She saw it play out when Nykki ravened for blood, thirsty beyond measure, beyond reason. Beyond death.

A source drained of life until it drained hers, too.

Nykki's mind stroked her psyche. So faint. *We succeeded, my love. You ended it...* Her breath faltered; the life bleeding from her body. Not even the fire's heat could restore her. Not now. There was nothing for her to come back to. Her organs were shutting down, as her lungs stopped fighting for every gasp and surrendered to the quiet stillness.

Peace at last.

No, Nykki. You can't leave me. I need you!

Nykki's mind caressed hers, but it was barely a graze. *This way is better, my love. Now Breeyan can't take my soul.*

She clung to Nykki's ethereal form, but it was already breaking into a thousand shards of light.

A final stroke as Nykki's last thoughts etched into her heart. *Promise you'll live for us both...* Her simulacrum dissipated, fading into the pastel clouds, the verdant grass, the russet earth, mingling with the pluming smoke of Davith's pyre as he burned to dust.

The fabric of her psyche was unravelling, tearing away the threads that had interwoven with Nykki's. Stripping her bare. Nykki was a star that blazed too brightly, and she the dark void in the night sky left in its wake.

Her silent screams careened across every plane until time ceased and the earth jolted to shatter a part of her soul.

She had ended Davith's terror, but at what cost?

'Was it worth it?' she howled into the wind.

As she clutched Nykki's icy, lifeless body, the gods might have skinned her flesh, seared her heart, and caged her lungs. Her throat clogged, and she couldn't weep through the hollow that had wedged there. She buried her face into Nykki's chest, wrapped her fingers around her hair, and rocked. *I've got you. I've got you.*

For an eternity and no time at all, she held her beloved. Numb.

Too soon, she heard shouts in the distance and the crunch of gravel.

She wasn't ready. Let the gods divert them. Let her hold Nykki forever.

They would have spied the smoke.

She lay Nykki down, hefted a neophyte's corpse over her shoulder, and dumped him onto the burning carriage. The other, the impervious one who resembled Jonas, she couldn't lift. He could rot against the tree where he'd tried to defile her beloved.

The riders neared.

Amber would not abandon Nykki for them to find. She would honour her before the gods with a proper burial and sacrifice.

She looked back at the plumes of smoke, listening to the approaching horses, imagining what it would be like to climb atop the flames and let them devour her, as Breeyan would do to her soon enough.

Promise you'll live for us both…

She picked Nykki up, so light now, as though when her god-body broke apart, it had stolen the core of her, and carried her deeper into the woods.

She closed her eyes, picturing Nykki's psychic refuge. The sun's glow warmed their limbs as a lilting breeze caressed their skin. A calf lowed in the distance while a pair of wrens trilled closer by, and she inhaled the grassy scent of threshed hallit, rosemary, and jasmine. She rested Nykki's head in her lap, her gemstone irises sparkling with a gentle smile, as she trailed her fingers along Nykki's unblemished cheek, leaned to kiss those perfect lips, and whispered, 'I promise.'

Sixty-Eight

'Nessa!' Sheevalla beckoned from the foot of the stairs. 'Dosha Ralan wishes to introduce you to his guest.'

Curiosity prickled. With a groan, Ella set her bucket and brush aside and wiped her hands upon a communal towel. Her moontime cramps had eased, but each task seemed a little harder than usual.

The women and their children had been subdued since Khalia had left to live with her adopted family, though no one acknowledged her absence.

'Once a dosha has chosen a new wife, she fetches a higher price if his family raises her,' Nyria had whispered as they lay side-by-side on their bedrolls that night.

'Wife? But she's a child!'

Nyria had brought her finger to her lips, her eyes widened in warning, and Ella rolled over, wishing the beetles would cease writhing in her belly.

Now Ella tried to sneak into the women's minds to find out more about this stranger. But keeping their attention on domestic affairs, and out of their husband's, they knew as little as she. Another of Ralan's business associates, perhaps.

She pulled her shawl up over her hair, secured it around her neck, and stepped into the courtyard. She found Ralan seated beside a rotund man with a mop of white curls, their silhouettes framed by a fresco depicting the mountains in spring.

Sheevalla shoved her forward. Both men glared and she nudged the back of Ella's knees and pushed down on her scarf-covered head. Ella's legs buckled, but she recovered and stepped out of reach, then blasted Sheevalla's psyche. Sheevalla whimpered and backed away, leaving Ella to face the men alone.

She braced for a beating, poised to strike the moment they were within her grasp, but Ralan and the portly fellow beside him scoffed, as though her defiance amused them.

'A prize, ah?' said the rounder man, whose eyes devoured without meeting her gaze.

Heat churned, a heightened pulsing in the air between them. Yet neither he nor Ralan looked at her directly, remaining just out of reach. Did they fear her magic? Or the Curse?

Ralan circled his finger, indicating he wanted her to spin, but she remained fixed in place.

'Do you understand me, Xenona? Turn for my esteemed guest.'

Sweat collected beneath her long robe and shawl. Elnora was almost above them, and while the men sat shaded, she stood in full sun. 'I am no pet for your performance,' she said.

The amusement drained from Ralan's features and his nostrils flared like a battle-starved steed.

'Don't fret, Rallo. A little feistiness can be enticing, ah?'

'I won't be defied in my own *dorj*, Siranos.'

'Come closer, Xenona.' Ralan's guest leaned in, beckoning for Ella. 'My teeth aren't pointed, ah? I am merely curious. I have never met a pale-skinned Xenona.' *Nor such an exotic beauty.*

That last thought slid into her mind. His lust-tinged fascination teemed around him, mingling with Ralan's outrage and the scorching heat of the noontide sun.

Fuel enough.

She peered to see if anyone observed them, but potted shrubs obscured the passages leading off the portico.

'You want me closer?' Her words dripped across her tongue. 'Like this?' She sidled nearer and pressed her yielding flesh against him. Her beguilement's tendrils curling, she whispered, 'Stand.'

Siranos stood and held out his elbow as casually as if they headed out for a stroll. Ella looped her arm around his, charming him the way a gourd-pipe wielder enchants a snake.

Ralan leapt back out of her reach. 'Sirro, you fool!'

'Go,' she said, steering him.

'Stop, Sirro!' cried Ralan.

The jolting words halted him.

She leaned close, a whisper's breath between them. 'Keep going.'

Siranos nodded and ushered her away, while Ralan stared after, unmoving.

He feared her.

Siranos led them through the front of the house, with its large, light-bathed rooms, and rich furnishings, and past frescos showing godlike figures peeking between foliage, residing alongside ordinary Myanai. The images reminded her of the time when gods supposedly walked among men.

Well, she would walk like a goddess from this place.

She half expected Ralan to chase after them, but the tingle along her flesh told her he had intended for her to leave with Siranos that day—only not with him in her thrall, and likely with a hefty dowry to fill his coffers.

'Keep going,' she said, as they stepped outside and onto the street. A few passersby glanced their way, but their curiosity melted once they took in her shawl and kordra, seeing what appeared to be an ordinary woman accompanied by a dosha.

'Where are we headed, my glorious Xenona?'

She did not hesitate. 'The Place of Omens.'

'A marvel!' He clapped his hands. 'What do you seek in the ancient city?'

'I have important business there.'

'Ha! Xenona business. I understand.'

Outside, they followed the path towards the square, then veered north. For what seemed like hours, they climbed higher, weaving between buildings and along alleyways, navigating uneven steps and the rubble of decaying roads.

Ella panted, out of breath.

'A long trek for you, ah?'

She couldn't recall the last time she'd walked so fast, nor so steeply.

Used to scaling this sloping terrain, Siranos seemed unbothered by the speed. 'Shall we rest, my Xenona?'

She shook her head and urged him on, aware of Elnora's shadows growing longer.

Siranos prattled as they ascended, but she only half-listened. The sooner they reached Yorg's former home, the sooner she could be rid of him.

'Ralan is a man of tradition, ah? He hoards his family like hidden gems. But what value is a treasure you can't enjoy? And if she's a pretty one, display?'

She shuddered. 'I offer no comment on other men's affairs.' Her thighs burned as she mounted another step.

'Ha! A Xenona who disregards a dosha in his dorj is a Xenona with many opinions.' He waved his finger as though priding himself on seeing through her ruse.

She grunted up the next step.

'You are determined, ah? And Ralan wanted to hide you, like his other wives, but I would present you as my *torja*,' he said.

'Torja?' she puffed.

'First wife.'

The most esteemed post permitted a woman: first among a host of slaves. A sour twist upon her tongue. 'You honour me, Siranos.'

'And you indulge me.'

'I find appeasing makes for a simpler life,' she said.

'Clever and gifted! Better and better.' He held out his hand to help her up a particularly steep step.

She hesitated, then took it. The alternative was hitching up her kordra to climb on hands and knees before condemning eyes.

'Ralan was smart to introduce you. Five is too many wives. Five times as many children to feed, and five times as much trouble. Three is plenty. I would settle for two, like my *mayora*. She was the *torja* of two. Very good woman,' he finished in crude Yceltic, flashing his bright teeth. 'You are good woman. Good Xenona. I can know.'

Ella concentrated on finding her footing to leap across an eroded ditch. She misjudged its length, and her sandal clipped the edge and slipped from her foot.

Siranos caught and steadied her. 'What shoddy leather Ralan offered. These won't serve you in the heart of the ruins.'

'They are all I have.' She slid the thin-soled shoe back on. 'Come, let us reach our destination before nightfall.'

Elnora's shadows lengthened as their path approached the mountain. Ella expected to arrive at a wall or a gate, or for the buildings to peter out, but the houses and shops continued, stacked so narrowly not even a horse or cart could pass.

Crumbling pillars and shattered stones appeared scattered between modern structures, while cats hopped on chipped and faded statues, like she'd seen in her vision. One feline slinked around a marble column carved with glyphs resembling those in Aeron's manuscripts. Many of the strewn and broken slabs bore similar markings, fragments of lore and legend etched in stone instead of inked on vellum.

There were still more steps to climb, some new, and some deteriorating, weaving between residences where women hung out washing and men nattered over ceramic cups of a steaming brew.

The day's heat and slog left Ella parched. What she would give for a soothing tea, or a mouthful of Aeron's sharp spirit.

'There's a fountain up ahead, my treasured Xenona,' Siranos said.

Sure enough, atop the next rung of steps, water trickled from a copper pipe set into the rocks. They stooped with cupped hands to drink. Icy liquid—snowmelt—numbed Ella's fingers but blessed her arid mouth.

Siranos rested, and Ella perched beside him. Her legs and back ached, while her moontime cramps settled low in her belly.

The azure of the sky deepened, lining the scattered clouds with yellow, orange and pink. Soon, Elnora would sink below the mountain.

'How much further?'

'But we are already here, my Xenona!'

'Where?'

'You wanted to see the Place of Omens, ah? Then you are here.'

Did he jest?

She stood and raced up the last of the steps, following the path higher and higher. Disintegrating stone gave way to vegetation, and then to nothing at all, as the trail vanished into mountain. Behind and below, remnants of ancient structures poked between modern houses.

Yorg's words echoed. *'Centuries, Princess. Not decades.'*

A new city built on top of the old.

'But the archives, the library. The lore...'

Siranos stood a few steps below. 'You read? Another marvel!'

'Of course, but—' Oh gods. If the Myanai constructed these buildings over ruins... 'What happened to the original city?' Where had that knowledge gone?

Elnora's edge slipped behind the mountain and a cold shadow chilled her bones while flaming clouds licked Ella's heart. The fiery edges reflected reeling memories of what she had discovered in Aeron's books: images of Xenon's followers tortured and Cleansed.

Ash scratched her throat and coated her tongue with a realisation she did not want to accept. 'They burned it,' she whispered. Witches and their witch-lore.

Yorg's home, his lover, the sacred knowledge, alight.

Culled.

As they would cull her daughter.

She sagged against the stones.

The mountain stole her fire with the last of Elnora's light. She'd failed Yorg, fled Jonas and the past he represented, only to end up amid the long-lost ruins of the only civilisation that might have freed her and Xarion. Gone.

Sixty-Nine

'T his ridiculous spat with Lord Venn needs to end. We're hungry. Serrah's hungry. *I'm* hungry.' Jaydyn swapped Serrah to her other hip, wiping her running nose on a kerchief enroute. Gohran's niece must still be sickly if she was allowing her mother to handle her so long without protest.

Gohran slammed his ledger book closed. 'The feud will end when the dryhten accepts his brother committed treason and pays his due.' Jaydyn need not know it was Erldan's debt that throttled them more than the inconvenience of a blockade.

That morning, another courier had arrived to collect on his loan.

'If you default on this repayment, your interest compounds to the next,' the messenger had warned, before returning to his carriage empty-handed.

As if Gohran needed reminding.

And now, his sister accosted him in his study with petty nonsense.

'You won't impress your comely new betrothed when you cater your celebration with gruel and sour ale,' she scoffed.

He ground his words through clenched teeth. 'Vera will get every luxury befitting a future queen.'

'For a *supper*. Not even a ball.' She pulled Serrah to her chest and kissed her forehead. Her brow furrowed. 'You're still warm, Sess.'

Serrah grizzled and stuck her finger in her mouth. Her rash appeared faded, thank the goddess. An illegitimate heir was still an heir when there were no others to carry a family's legacy.

'Were our coffers dripping with gold, I wouldn't waste it on frivolities that could be better spent on—'

'On what? Hunting parties, weapons, and battlements?' She rolled her eyes.

'Would you prefer we ate no meat at all while Nedran's army breach our walls?'

'If you and Venn would hold hands and frolic through the woods like you used to, you wouldn't need to bolster our defences.'

'This isn't a game, Jay.' He had no patience for this conversation.

'And I'm not playing—'

'Your Highness?' A page hovered in the doorway, red-cheeked and puffed.

Gohran waved his sister out.

'Excuse me, *Your Highness*.' She dropped an exaggerated curtsy and strode past the page, clipping him with her shoulder to make room for Serrah, who still clung to her hip.

'What is it?' Gohran frowned.

The page stepped forward and bowed. 'There has been another incident, Your Highness...' He peered up through ash-blond lashes. 'Involving the High Priest. Someone ambushed their carriage on the way back from Nedran.' He sucked in a breath. 'Only one lad got away...'

The boy continued speaking, but his words became muted and black. Gohran might have been underwater, a world apart, submerged beneath the depths of the ink upon his desk.

Davith... Dead...

How? How had the goddess allowed... Allowed what? The murder of Her loyal servant? A servant who extorted a heretic king in Her name.

A king he should have denounced and Cleansed.

Him.

Davith had been his mentor, his advisor, as beloved as an uncle—perhaps a substitute father.

He had been a threat. A rival. A parasite. A curse.

The sinking sensation was somehow... liberating. Yet it left him hollow.

Cast adrift.

'There's something else, Your Highness.'

The words ripped him back to the room and the eager blond boy trembling before him. 'Go on.'

'We believe whoever did this also killed Nedran's younger lord. He was found near the burnt carriage, naked and speared to a tree...'

Was it possible? Had the culprits rid him of Jonas's threat, too? 'What did you do with the body?'

'We buried it along with the other remains, Your Highness.'

'Excellent.' He imagined that handsome, smug grin, turned grey and stiff, dirt thudding onto his lifeless, broken limbs, sealing him over, as the soil suffocated his nose, and concealed his eyes. Silenced his mouth...

'Your Highness?'

'Yes?' Irritated.

'Shall I fetch Arhys?'

'Yes, my thanks.' The page bowed to leave. 'No—Wait.' He no longer needed to deal with Davith's appointed steward. 'I'll handle this.'

'As it pleases you, Your Highness.' The page reached the door. 'My deepest condolences.'

As the boy disappeared down the hall, and his footfalls faded, Gohran's vision misted. In the delicious quiet of his solitude, he savoured the images that played behind his eyes, of worms devouring his enemies, and time rotting their flesh to dust and bones.

A twisted grin spread across his features, and he leaned back in his chair. With a toss of his raven hair, he laughed and laughed.

When the courier arrived from Erldan carrying Jonas's official pardon, Venn could finally breathe.

Raeyn squeezed his arm. 'This is a forward step, my lord.' Seated beside him at their strangely quiet table, he was grateful for her unwavering presence.

He rested his hand on top of hers and met her gaze with a nod. 'It doesn't bring him home, though, does it?'

The pardon came after some unidentified dissidents slaughtered Gohran's head priest and a pair of his servants on the road home from Nedran. At first, Venn feared Gohran would assume it was at his instigation and retaliate. So, he eased the blockade, and made an initial payment towards Jonas's blood price, as an offer of good faith. In return, Gohran had issued a proclamation to encourage Jonas out of hiding.

Assuming he was still alive.

Thankfully, the remonstrations against the heavy-handedness of the clergy in both provinces cast suspicion elsewhere. Gohran accepted Venn's coin and dispatched couriers north and east.

But even if Jonas arrived home right away, it was too late to intercept Gohran's marriage to Vera. So, when he sent word to Mornae about Jonas, he prompted Aunt Servan to hasten negotiations for Lynden's betrothal to Prince Adyn.

He wrote, 'I trust you'll pay particular attention to the terms of the military alliance that ensues,' adding to Raeyn, 'She'll likely do a better job than me of shoring up the contracts, but I would be remiss not to emphasise its importance.'

'As is your duty, my lord,' Raeyn said with a wry smile.

He'd also suggested Lyn take Jonas's former lover, Kerryn, with her as her lady's maid, choking back his tears as he scrawled, for Bess should have been the one to accompany her.

He hated marrying his sister to a mere lad, but at least if she took a maid of her own, she would have someone to confide in, and he knew cursed well how shrewd Kerryn could be.

Davith's murder seemed to placate his people for the moment, and Raeyn's public support of Bess earned their trust. They had a long journey ahead to restore the goodwill Bess's arrest had lost, but as nobles and commoners mourned the lady's maid together, Venn sensed something shift. A softening through their shared grief as Venn and Raeyn wept alongside them.

If Raeyn gave Nedran an heir soon, she would surely win the people over and divert the sombre mood to one of promise.

With this desire in mind, that night, Venn left the door between their rooms ajar, grateful when Raeyn slipped into his bed and curled against him right away. As their bodies found each other over and again in the dark, their grief mingled, seeking comfort and chasing hope, until, exhausted at last, they fell asleep in each other's arms.

SEVENTY

'The villagers were abuzz this morning.' Wearing her ordinary Yceltic clothing—loose woollen trousers and a plain tunic—Vorlyn found Jonas pacing Aeron's corridors, albeit slowly, in his reinforced boot.

'Oh?'

'Tensions between Erldan and Nedran appear to have eased.' She set her satchel down.

'How so?'

'Erldan's couriers reached Wernad and Rassit, which indicates Nedran has lifted their blockade.'

'Not necessarily good fortune for me.'

'Come, let me show you something.' Vorlyn steered him into what appeared to be a study, or perhaps a library, where Mayel perched at a table piled with books and parchments. Beside those, a glass sphere rested on a small cushion.

Her smile when she greeted Vorlyn was lit by the heavens, but faded and grew stiff when Jonas entered after her.

'I've not found anything yet,' Mayel said to Vorlyn, in answer to an unvoiced question.

Vorlyn addressed Jonas. 'It's only possible to scry upon a person or place you have experienced in the flesh.'

'And vision strength relies on a powerful connection,' added Mayel.

He pointed to the sphere. 'Ella's too far away to contact through that thing?'

'I'm searching for a way to amplify the signal,' Mayel said.

'Can't Yorg help? She's in his home, isn't she?'

'Yorg's magic is vast, but...'

'Not vast enough. Sexual or blood connections are strongest. For instance, between lovers, or a parent and their child. But that's not why I brought you here.' Vorlyn motioned for Mayel to hand her the sphere. 'Before I share what I learnt in the village, it might help to see this.'

He waited for Vorlyn to ask him to hold the sphere, but Mayel placed her palms over Vorlyn's.

In their grip, its surface swirled as it had when Alina used him to locate Ella, a cloud cover clearing to reveal the stars beneath. The churning subsided, and he saw what appeared to be a gaggle of ladies sipping tea before a tray bearing cakes and fruit. The image sharpened, and he recognised his sister.

'Lyn!' He leaned closer, studying the miniature scene. 'Where is she?' An older woman with grey-streaked honey-brown hair and hazel eyes perched beside her. 'Is that...?'

'Your sister is safe in Mornae with your aunt.'

Did Vorlyn know Servan?

He examined the vision again. A copper-haired woman sat with them, bouncing a lad on her knee. Was that Kerryn? The lad's curls were the colour of his mother's, but his irises were dark as coal. He took in the boy's broad cheeks and narrow nose, his prominent brow. If that was supposed to be his son, then Yorg might as well be Jonas's father!

Vorlyn closed her eyes, and the sphere misted over. When she opened them again, the scene had changed.

Venn and Raeyn sat at Nedran's dining table, conversing and touching with the easy intimacy of a couple with scores of summers between them, rather than a few moons. Jonas's breath hitched, and a weight settled on his chest. Their mouths moved, but the glass muted their voices to Jonas's ears.

Mayel removed her palms, and the image vanished.

He wanted to scream, *Put them back! I need more!* But forced his hands to remain by his side. 'Why show me that?'

'I needed you to see that your family is well.'

He braced. 'Then the news is bad.'

'Not at all. You are a freed man.'

'What? How?' The room expanded around him…

'According to rumour, your brother paid a blood price, and the king agreed to retract his order for your arrest.'

'But Erldan and Nedran remain allies?'

'Yes.'

…And closed back in.

He sucked in his breath until his chest ached, a sob caught in his throat.

Finally, he spoke, his voice a whisper. 'I can go home…' Until that moment, he hadn't recognised the hope Ella stole when she'd vanished before his eyes.

Now, he could return to the life he'd forfeited through his rashness and Gohran's tempest. But while the deal struck for his freedom restored his optimism, fear and despair lingered, for Nedran remained under the sway of a foetid, unhinged demon. None of them was safe or free.

But what if Aeron's folk could help him convince Venn to attest that Ella was still alive? That he'd met with her. Then he wouldn't need Ella to return, and they could fetch Ella's child, and…

'Why would you do that?' Mayel's eyes accused him. 'Why do you need Ella's daughter?'

Curse it. She must have eavesdropped on his thoughts. 'Because the babe is heir to Nedran. And once Raeyn and Venn's marriage is unsealed…'

Vorlyn snapped, 'Ella's child belongs where she is.'

'Venn will rally more people behind him if his succession is certain. While relations between Erldan and Nedran remain precarious, we need her. Ella's babe is the only child born with Nedran's blood.'

'Ella's daughter is no heir to Nedran,' Vorlyn said.

Jonas swivelled to face her, the glow along the walls flickering as though cast by a lantern. 'She may have been conceived without the priests' seal—and she's no son—but these are trivialities if she shores up Venn's dynasty. His legacy…'

Vorlyn's brow arched. 'Are you truly that naïve?'

'Nedran's people will be more concerned with blood than ceremonial legalities.'

'I'm not troubled by Nedran's citizen's and their loyalty, but Xarion's parentage. That child is no more your niece than she is mine.'

'What are you implying?' If Venn wasn't Xarion's father, who was? Gohran would not have allowed another male near her, not after dragging her home from Nedran in disgrace.

'Gohran will never let you marry. He wants you chaste, untouched. Because if he can't have you, no one will.' His own cruel jibe at Ella taunted.

Everyone said the then Marked Prince of Erldan preferred his younger sister to any woman in the High Realm, but he'd not entertained for a heartbeat that Gohran would lay a filthy paw on her. A delicious scandal fuelled by boredom and envy—nothing more. The notion was heinous. An affront to every god.

When Jonas had discovered Ella's magic, Gohran's unrelenting protection put that rumour to rest. Gohran had needed to guard her secret. *And his.* But what if his first suspicion had been correct?

'No,' he whispered, swallowing sour bile.

But there was no one else. No lord, no servant. Only Ella and Gohran, alone at Erldan, until she'd fled...

Bruised and broken.

Brittle.

The thought that Ella might have...

No. Not willingly. Never by her choice.

That Gohran could force a woman did not surprise him, but surely, he wouldn't... not his *sister.*

And yet, had a part of him always suspected? Had he realised when he asked her, *'What really happened at Erldan?'*

Now, her reply seared his soul: *'I paid a price you'll never have to experience.'*

'Hells...'

'People do monstrous things,' Vorlyn said. 'That does not make them monsters.'

'But Gohran is.' Oh, by all the gods, by every demon, he was.

'Ella's magic...'

Jonas trembled. 'Don't. Don't defend him.'

'Very well. I won't. But you need to understand—'

'I said, don't.'

She sucked her lips and let him simmer, fidgeting with her tunic, chewing the inside of her cheek.

He took a slow, deep breath. Then another. And another. He braced and nodded for her to continue.

'Gohran is entirely responsible for what he did to Ella. That is indisputable. Ella's power is special and rare. But also, dangerous. Her gift alters the way people feel about her.'

'So, she wills men into lustful fools, like an old crone's elixir?'

'And women, yes. But it's no charlatan's brew.'

'You're saying my love for her is what, some sorcerer's spell?'

'No. Not everyone is susceptible...' She frowned, chewing her words over.

'And she cast this enchantment on her brother?'

'Not deliberately, or even consciously. Back then, she wasn't aware of her gift.'

Ella had been so... fragile... when she returned from Erldan, seeking refuge with Venn.

She'd charmed him beyond reason.

'This is too much.' Jonas held up his palms and backed away. 'All of it.'

Whatever Ella's role, her power, Gohran was a venomous snake coiling his way around every object he considered prey. Erldan's witch-king was lucky he wasn't within reach. In that moment, Jonas would have extinguished Gohran's vile existence with his bare hands.

'It is a great deal to absorb. But it's important that you do.' Her staid tone couldn't soothe the fire roiling through his blood. 'You need to understand the ramifications of your choices from here. Yours and hers. It's why I needed you to know your family is safe and well. To reassure you, there's no urgency. You have time to decide what to do next, Jonas.'

She was wrong. There was no time.

Gohran's ice-blue eyes flashed before him. His sneer. His poisonous wrath. He imagined the delicious blood pouring out of him, his lips contorting in pain and fear. Those eyes turning hollow with the mask of death.

Jonas had been trying to release Nedran from a viper's hold. But the most assured way to deal with a snake was to cut off its head.

SEVENTY-ONE

Aryon permitted no males within its halls, so Breeyan met Gordovyn out at the grove. She expected him to send a servant carrying whatever sources he located, but he arrived empty-handed, on horseback.

'Unfortunately, I found no references. It's unclear whether, over the generations since Xenon's Curse was first penned, the lore has been lost, omitted, or never existed.'

'And yet you came all this way?'

'My order's business took me along the Gythyn, so it seemed a waste not to venture a little further.'

Breeyan envied how easily all but the Gern's most unusual looking men donned trousers and a tunic and disappeared into Yceltic life, as though their gender disguised them.

She eyed him sharply. Given the recent spate of arrests and Cleansings, not to mention political unrest between Nedran and Erldan, it seemed a foolhardy risk for a social visit.

'In truth, I wanted to lay eyes on the child so powerful she amplified your magic.'

Breeyan sucked in her breath.

'What I witnessed was extraordinary. But I wondered what, exactly, prompted you to seek lore on Xenon's Curse?'

Of course, he was curious. Xarion had lent her power to contact him, then absorbed her lifeforce without drawing blood.

'I imagine that degree of potency is... tempting... to behold.'

She stiffened. 'Tempting?'

'One could easily do more than direct and channel such power.'

'Are you suggesting I drew Xarion's source into myself?'

'I merely observe it might *tempt* one to do so...'

'I have not.' Her tone bit.

'Oh, of course, Your Holiness... I only wondered if perhaps someone amongst your ranks...?'

She was about to protest, tell him none of her priestesses would commit such impiety, but stalled. He may have given her an out.

'Not the child's power, no. A priestess, who is no longer at Aryon, believes she inadvertently drew from a forbidden source. She was in Ycelt, when the incident occurred.'

'I see.'

'I have ensured the priestess concerned—a novice—has not returned to Aryon. However, you'll appreciate my caution...'

She detected the faintest twitch below his right eye before he spoke again. 'Indeed. I wish I had the answers you seek. I agree it is wise to keep this novice at a distance, perhaps even banished to the Cursed land.' Where she would be Cleansed soon enough.

'I wondered, however, when several of your priestesses made their way north to the Gern following the last equinox. There seemed to be some consternation over the child—your niece's daughter, I believe?'

'Certain women felt uncomfortable around a powerful newborn, given the god forbids us bearing children. It has been a disconcerting and novel experience.'

'And you agreed to harbour your niece despite her carrying a babe?'

'Are you questioning my authority? Or my judgement?'

'Forgive me, Your Holiness. I seek only to understand why the Gern's newer inhabitants left Aryon feeling so alarmed.'

'I imagine it difficult for any man to comprehend the experience of a woman bereft of motherhood, and I am loath to justify my actions to one.'

'Of course. My apologies. Perhaps if I met with your niece and her daughter...?'

'My niece no longer resides at Aryon, and her daughter is in the care of a recent refugee. We found ourselves inundated following what appears was the razing of a village in search of the priestess I mentioned. So, you can see why I worry about the ramifications of the Curse.'

'You believe the attack is a symptom?'

'The logic follows.'

Gordovyn rubbed his chin.

'"The Curse brings horror thrice over," she quoted, hoping to divert his focus to the details of the lore. 'Should we interpret that phrase literally, that the Curse hurts three tiers of acquaintance extending from the violator? Or perhaps it refers to proximity. Or is it figurative? Hyperbole, even?'

She hoped Gordovyn didn't notice her tone rising in panic, or the way she tore at the skin beside the nails she could not bite.

'A fascinating path of inquiry, indeed.'

Except this wasn't some academic exercise. People had suffered and died and might continue to do so. *Her son might bring his wrath upon them...*

'If Cleansing is the remedy to the Curse, can it be stopped once the effects begin?'

'Are you suggesting you Cleanse this absent priestess to contain the Curse?'

'To halt it. Remedy it,' she said. That small twitch again. 'Can we trace its domain? For instance, if we correctly identified those three tiers of tragedy surrounding the violator, would the Curse have run its course?'

'And the violator be "remedied", as you put it?' He looked to have bitten into something sour.

'If I can halt its further spread, or...'

Gordovyn held up his hand. 'This is puerile nonsense, like running widdershins around a fairy ring, expecting some mythical creature will appear.'

'Are you implying the Curse is a myth? A fairytale?' She was being facetious, but so was he.

He exhaled loudly. 'I would treat any threat or suspicion of the Curse with the utmost earnestness and urge you to do likewise.'

She would not let him derail her. She needed answers. 'Do you recall from the lore how to determine—definitively—whether a person has invoked Xenon's Curse? I had believed it marked the aura.'

'Indeed, it should.'

A squeezing pressure crept along her shoulders. 'And is there a means to differentiate this mark from the scarring one might see from, say, a great tragedy?' Would Gordovyn recognise the roiling and inverted currents she had observed in Gohran and Xarion, rather than the scar that marred Ella?

'I have encountered no individuals bearing such a mark.'

The pressure eased. Perhaps he could meet Xarion, after all.

SEVENTY-TWO

'Despair not, my exalted Xenona!' Siranos laid a tentative hand on Ella's back. 'If it is relics you seek, the Sacred Oracle houses a *Musolano*.' A place to study artefacts. But she sought books. Manuscripts.

She picked up a glyph-covered remnant of marble. 'King Myrhan,' she whispered, recognising the name of Ycelt's founding monarch.

'You know that tale, ah? Of the Xenona and the old cynnelic.' Cynnelic—a lord. But Myrhan was a king, not a lord. The High King of Ycelt. 'The Musolano holds a replica of that entire legend.' History, not legend. 'You Yceltics love your war stories. Men fighting gods instead of revering them. Such arrogance, ah?' He raised his arms to the setting sun, the rising moon, ran his fingers below the water, and kissed a moss-covered rock. 'The gods are all around us, Xenona. Why fight them?'

'Are these glyphs from *The Lost Warriors*?' she asked.

'Yes, clever Xenona! I had forgotten the name.'

'And the Sacred Oracle contains a complete copy of this work?'

'Does the god muffle your ears, Xenona? Perhaps not so clever after all, ah?' He chuckled at his own jest.

'Are there other histories there? Other lore?' She had no time to humour him. Twilight encroached, along with a god-sent urgency that rippled down her spine.

Though he prattled on, she couldn't hear him. A panicked wail in her mind blocked all sound. The pastel sky sharpened and blazed, no longer the soft butter and pink of frangipanis, but scarlet. Clouds formed faces, revealing an unfamiliar man standing beside a dark-haired woman with azure eyes, who must be Breeyan. They stared at her—only it wasn't her who they saw, but Xarion. Examining. Condemning.

Elnora's light sparked the clouds' edges like flames. The old priestesses, Xarion among them, stood screaming within. Cleansed. Culled. And the devout man peering through the smoke, mouthing, *Cursed.*

She stifled a cry, struggling to breathe. Elnora flashed again, and between the flames, swords clashed. At first, she assumed it was Myrhan from the old war, but he wore modern armour. The next flare revealed his insignia—sapphire, emerald and gold. Erldan.

'You know what Gohran is... A murderer. A monster.'

More swords struck, and a shield raised painted with blue and silver. Nedran. *He will bring your death.*

Something rolled against her foot. She squealed. Just a dislodged rock, but for a fleeting moment, it appeared as Jonas's severed head.

Jonas had warned her that if she didn't go with him, Nedran and Erldan would descend into war.

'Your demon brother razed an entire village...'

She squeezed her eyes shut and covered her ears as her mind screamed.

Distance rendered her helpless to intervene, but she would not leave empty-handed.

'How far away is this Musolano?'

'Not long, ah? A few nights to travel there, maybe more, maybe less. Shelter with me, cherished one. I will make you my torja, and we can arrive in comfort.'

He pictured a type of carriage, like a shaded horse and cart, but in place of beasts, humans hunched, harnessed and chained. Wearing only a pair of braies beneath the searing sun, their violet eyes pleaded. *Slaves.*

She refused to partake in such cruelty. These were men, not animals. Yet she needed to reach this Oracle. 'Tell me about the Musolano,' she said.

'We must turn back, Xenona. We have no lantern.'

Her limbs trembled and her muscles burned, and she fought tears, longing to curl into the tender arms of sleep.

Siranos was right. Elnora had vanished behind the range, thieving the last of the light. Twilight lasted minutes, not hours, and darkness would cloak them soon enough.

Her abdomen ached with a dull throb that radiated to her lower back and down her legs. A source, yet it held no *life*. Through her god-sight her rags could have absorbed a long-dead corpse, her magic weakened. Not to the extent that Xarion once syphoned, but noticeably dampened.

Why would her moontime deplete, not fuel her? When she'd first arrived from Aeron, she'd felt her most potent. Most vibrant. Then, as the moon approached, her anger and sadness peaked, before the gift itself brought fragility and loss. Kindling that had caught, blazed, and then dwindled, from a wood stack to remnants of ash.

'I want to hear about this Musolano,' she insisted. 'Describe it.' She cast around for a loose rock. Anything with a point.

The light was almost gone.

'Come, Xenona.'

A jagged stone fit neatly into one palm.

He outstretched his hand, already turning to leave.

'No.'

He would not waylay her again. She had no patience to navigate another home, a new world, a further soul attempting to exploit her. Certainly not a god-forsaken man.

She caught his wrist and yanked him back. She needed that original manuscript. Needed to deliver it to Ycelt and unravel whatever tragedy her alleged Curse had begun. Because if not by Xenon's hand, her aunt would cull them soon enough, while her brother continued to Curse them all.

'You underestimate your strength, Ella.'

She stared into Siranos's eyes and brought the stone's piercing edge to hover over his wrist. 'The Musolano. Tell me.'

She would get what she came for.

SEVENTY-THREE

Chrysanth stepped between the trees of the grove, bouncing Xarion against her chest. Her disconcerting golden irises faded against Xarion's azure ones.

'Is this her?' Gordovyn stretched out his arms, his features cast alight, then froze. 'There's something...' He winced, hands withdrawing to clutch his temples.

'She's always hungry when she first wakes.' Chrysanth frowned as Breeyan slipped between them to take Xarion.

'She hasn't learnt to control her power. That will come in time, of course.' Breeyan nodded to Chrysanth, who retrieved a jar of pureed pumpkin from the satchel slung over her shoulder. Once Xarion settled on her knee to feed, the pressure of her omnipresent need subsided.

Chrysanth perched beside them, fussing and cooing, and she almost envied the way she experienced the pleasure of Xarion's beguilement without the intensity of her craving.

Gordovyn stared, forcing his breath steady. 'Her power is... extraordinary.' He inched closer, hands clasped over his waist.

Breeyan didn't bother to test his shield. He would doubtless sense her probing, and she would glean naught. Instead, she tightened hers, tending to Xarion as though she were the most ordinary babe in Ycelt.

'It is rare to raise a moon-touched child from infancy,' she said. 'Xarion carries the powerful line of her dynasty. From her earliest breaths, Xenon's light shone upon her. Indeed, earlier, as a seedling growing in her mother's womb.' Breeyan hoped feeding Xarion's mind and body would settle her for long enough to assuage Gordovyn's curiosity.

'I hope to raise her under Xenon's gaze,' she continued, sharing her imagined future for Xarion as her apprentice and successor.

Gordovyn inhaled, eyelids heavy as he absorbed the vision. 'A worthy ambition, Sister.'

'Would you like to hold her?' She prayed Xarion charmed him into her thrall within the brief window of calm, before her need rose to a storm.

'She's a dearling,' Chrysanth added, her expression wistful and dreamlike. Breeyan sensed the clipped tinge of grief that always followed and wondered again who Chrysanth had left behind. Perhaps a younger sibling.

She urged Xarion into Gordovyn's arms. His features brightened as he cradled her, the ethereal currents shifting between them as Xarion wound her will around him, flashing a rare smile.

He closed his eyes and inhaled. 'She smells like spring flowers.'

'You see why I need the Curse cauterised. If any of its tendrils have taken root, it could threaten our people. Our legacy.'

'I believe the texts you seek may only exist in Myan, if they survived the Great Upheaval.'

'Our ancestors culled the lore?'

'Much of it, yes.'

Breeyan sighed. The culling of alleged heretical doctrine—and individuals—represented an ugly period in the history of Xenon's followers. 'Can your contacts uncover what survives?'

'I'll send letters with the Gern's next export.'

'How long will that take?'

A wry twist to Gordovyn's mouth. 'Longer than you have, if your suspicions are correct.'

Breeyan sighed. 'How do you suggest we contain the Curse in the meantime?'

'The only way you can.' *Cull them.*

Flames sparked before her. Ella, Gohran, Amber, Nykki, staked and burning. Gordovyn accusing. *Her, too.* Xarion.

Gordovyn's eyebrow shot up, startled, before his eyes narrowed, watching, watching.

Her shield remained raised, but... Was Xarion beneath it? Had Gordovyn read her thoughts through the babe? Xarion likely would not understand them, but would she recognise their threat? Transfer them?

She moved to retrieve Xarion from his arms, but he shrugged away, turning to block her. 'Who, exactly, do you believe has transgressed?' His mouth tightened.

'Give her to me, Brother.' She could not expel the image of Ella burning. Of Xarion...

'How would a mere babe, an innocent, bear the Curse?'

Oh gods. He *had* read her fear. Which meant Xarion had, too.

'Unless the mother—your niece—had sworn her vows when she conceived...?'

'You know she was in Ycelt. She'd never set foot inside the citadel, but arrived here, already pregnant.'

'Then why? Why would the Curse taint this sweet life?'

Breeyan scrambled and clamped down on her thoughts. She would not mention Xenon's forbidden power: beguilement, nor her suspicions about Xarion's true parentage—not something she had done, but who and what she was. 'I misspoke earlier... To protect my niece. It was she who drew from a forbidden source. I only fear that as Xarion is her closest, most intimate connection—'

Another spark of flames and a scream pinched her psyche.

'Hush, Xarion darling.' She held out her arms. 'Give her to me, Brother. I know how to calm her.'

Xarion's wrenching howl tore through them. Gordovyn winced and buckled, and Breeyan snatched Xarion from him.

His focus drifted as he studied Xarion through his god-sight. 'Her aura, it's...' He lurched backward, signing a warding. 'That is no force from a deity, but a demon.'

Xarion screamed again and Gordovyn dropped to his knees, eyes squeezed shut, clutching his temples and clenching his teeth.

'Hush, Xarion, darling. Please...' But Breeyan could not penetrate Xarion's mind to soothe her.

Chrysanth tried to comfort her, too, but Xarion flailed her fists to keep her away, and her tiny, clawed nails scratched Chrysanth's cheek.

'Ouch!' Chrysanth cupped the scratch, and when she removed her hand, found her palm stained with blood.

Xarion's silent wails intensified as the surrounding air chilled to ice, the ground cracking beneath their feet.

Breeyan's muscles melted to water, and her stomach to lead, as she crumpled to the dirt, trying not to let Xarion fall. 'Hush,' she repeated, her voice growing fainter, until she emitted only a whimper. Xarion's terror consumed her, and Breeyan had never felt so lost, so frightened, so alone—emotions that did not belong to her, but to the babe.

Chrysanth collapsed beside her. Her skin turned grey and her lips blue, save for the bright crimson streak that marred her face.

Mama! Xarion screamed over and again.

No one is taking her from you, darling, Breeyan soothed. *Hush, please...*

Xarion crawled from her, screaming, pleading, casting an image of her mother's creamy complexion, her jasmine scent, and midnight hair aflame. *Mama!*

The picture became entangled with Gordovyn's imperious sneer, his dark, condemning eyes, his fingers signing a warding, and Xarion howled as though her heart had shattered.

Across from them, Gordovyn lay sprawled, twitching and shuddering. His eyes rolled back as his skin paled, before blood burbled from his lips, trickling from the side of his mouth and down his chin to soak into the earth. Then he fell eerily still.

Silence blanketed the grove.

The weight of Xarion's pain eased, and Breeyan gasped for air.

With the ordinariness of a toddling child, Xarion studied Gordovyn's pallid face as she dipped her palms in the bloody dirt, then raised them, fascinated by the scarlet-tinged mud.

'By every god and demon, Xarion, what have you done?'

Seventy-Four

Jonas had never ridden so hard or so fast. His ankle throbbed inside his stiff boot as it jolted against the stirrup. Gohran might have pardoned him, but this feud was not over. He almost tasted that viper's blood each time he imagined him laying a lustful finger on his sister. The knowledge grew like a cancer until it strangled every other thought.

'I wish you would reconsider,' Vorlyn had said again as he mounted the horse she'd procured from the villagers.

'And I wish I had persuaded at least one of you to join me.'

She smiled wryly. 'Don't act in haste. Remember, we're working to bring Ella home.'

Mayel pulled him close and planted a kiss on his newly smooth cheek. 'Make sure you return to us, Jonas.'

She should resent, if not loathe him, for endangering Ella, but she assured him it was for Ella that she pleaded. *I know her heart.* The thought slid into his mind, with an understanding she hadn't articulated: *better than Ella.*

They had steered him along the river that carved its way between treacherous forest. 'Don't deviate from the path, and you'll reach a low point where bandits tend not to lurk, and you can ford and arrive near Rassit.'

He thanked them, and urged his steed to a gallop, stopping only when he reached the town to exchange his horse.

It was hard to contemplate how close he'd been to home, yet a world apart. The familiar landscape on Nedran's outskirts lodged tears in his throat. He hardly knew what he would say to Venn except that he was so cursed sorry.

When he neared Nedran's outer walls, instead of the usual bustle, the people he passed seemed oddly subdued. Almost as though a muting shield hung over them. Some recognised him and raised an arm or nodded his way in a lacklustre greeting. Dread settled in his gut and pounded behind his ears.

He approached the main gate and dismounted.

'My lord,' the head guard bowed, his voice whistling through the gap between his bottom teeth.

'Farros, isn't it?'

'Yes, my lord.' Another bow. 'It's good to have you home.'

'Why is the town so quiet? Is there no market today?'

Farros glanced at his beefy companion, and as the pair relayed all that happened during his exile, Jonas studied the knife scar that travelled from the fellow's hairline to his upper lip, watching it twitch with each word, so that he didn't slip away.

He palmed his horse onto a groomsman and continued travelling on foot, hearing the gravel crunch beneath his feet, but he might have been somewhere else entirely.

Dissidents had supposedly slaughtered priests on the road and in Harnal, and had attacked servants within Erldan's household.

'They found the pair naked and covered in cuts,' Farros had said. 'As if someone tried to let their blood like animals.'

'I heard it was a pair of witches who cast a spell using bright orange hair,' the scarred, beefy fellow added.

'It wasn't orange, it was the colour the dyers use to make equinox robes.'

'No matter the colour—it was witchy.'

Farros cuffed him. 'You'd believe fae folk stole the dryhten's own mother.'

Jonas wasn't listening. He was picturing Amber's saffron locks and a burning vengeance behind her grief-stricken eyes.

He knew that feeling. Oh, by every demon, he wore it like a pair of familiar boots.

He trudged the rest of the way to Nedran's keep, barely noticing the glances and waves, his breath ragged, and by the time he reached Venn's study, he was numb.

Venn looked up. Tidy, sober, and officious. His old self.

'By the goddess, you're alive!' Arms swept around him, smothering, choking, weeping. 'What the hells were you thinking, threatening Gohran?'

He wrangled free of Venn's embrace. 'I needed to find Ella.'

'Why? Jonas—why?' Venn pulled him back under until he thought he might drown.

When he surfaced again, he couldn't answer. Couldn't speak. Somehow submerged and boiling over, needing to stay in this moment, but forced to leave. He disentangled himself, grappling for his voice, for the right words.

There were no words.

He held his older brother at arm's length. 'I need you to ready Nedran for what is about to happen.'

'Jonas—I—'

He thrust up his palm. 'I am riding to Erldan with sword raised.' He braced. 'You can act as my second, or stay and prepare the city.'

Venn snapped. 'No, I forbid it.' He straightened and broadened, as if his size might impel Jonas where his seniority would not. 'Vengeance is not worth plunging two provinces into war.'

Jonas threw back his head to plead with the gods. 'You think I seek revenge?' Even now, his brother didn't see him.

'I've enacted a law to prevent Gohran and his servants stepping foot within Nedran's borders without permission. He won't sway any of my people again—and that includes you.'

'You imagine he'll quietly accept your decree and stay out of Nedran's affairs?' What if he could use magic to relocate himself, like Ella? Nothing would stop him from infiltrating.

'Once the priests seal Lynden's betrothal to Prince Adyn of Herron, Gohran won't dare shed a whisker within Nedran's borders.'

He scarcely believed what he heard. Venn, content to remain allied with that monster.

He recalled the easy intimacy between Venn and Raeyn through the sphere. He still doubted she had magic, but there were other ways to sway a man. 'Has your desire for Raeyn muddled your reason? You know what Gohran is.'

'And I can keep him at bay.'

'You cannot stay entangled with that demon-spawn.'

'If you had ridden to Vera in Lichen instead of confronting Gohran in Erldan, this situation never would have escalated.'

Jonas ran his hands through his hair and turned away. He had accepted his part in this—Venn need not squeeze citrus over his wounds. 'If you don't want me to challenge Gohran, then sever ties. Put Raeyn aside. Tell the priests Ella is alive, and you consummated your prior betrothal.'

'I can't do that to Ella. Gohran will denounce her.'

'And *she* could denounce *him. You* could denounce him.'

'I have no desire to face a heresy trial again in my lifetime, and I certainly won't instigate one.'

'The priests can't arrest someone they can't find.' And they would not find Ella in Myan. 'But as a well-respected dryhten, your word is gold.'

'But then Raeyn will know I—'

'What, betrayed her?'

'Cursed her.'

Venn looked away, but Jonas saw his throat bob, his chest tighten, and his eyes narrow.

He'd almost forgotten Venn's drunken ramblings when he confronted him in this exact spot after discovering Ella's empty grave. *I'm cursed. I touched her and now I've cursed us all...'*

Venn believed it—blamed himself not only for Jonas's arrest, but for Bess's death, the uprisings, the protests, the violence. Perhaps even considered Gohran's stranglehold just retribution.

'If you remain bound to Gohran, you punish us all.'

Venn's voice was barely a whisper. 'And if you try to end Gohran yourself, you'll plunge us into war.'

Jonas spoke through gritted teeth, 'Then give me a better option.'

'Once Raeyn produces an heir for Nedran and Lynden—'

'How long might that take? Sardin's boy is still a lad, and there are no guarantees Raeyn will conceive.' Jonas paced, tugging at his hair. Why couldn't Venn see that while Gohran lived, and they remained allied, none of them were safe? If he was capable of a fraction of what he'd witnessed at Aeron, and of Amber before then...

Amber.

A witch with saffron-coloured locks murdering priests and bleeding servants. It must be her. If she had returned to Ycelt, perhaps he didn't need assistance from Aeron or Venn.

Already, he was picturing Alina helping him contact Amber through her magic sphere, and together they would force Gohran to sever ties, or Jonas would take his head...

He strode towards the door. 'If you choose to stay bound to a hypocritical sorcerer, mass murderer and incestuous rapist, be it on you.'

'Wait.' Venn grabbed his arm. 'What did you call him?'

'You heard.'

Venn frowned.

Was he truly unaware? 'You learnt what happened to the villagers on Erldan's outskirts?'

Venn nodded.

'I assumed he razed that village hunting me down, but Ella said he was looking for her.'

'You've seen her?'

'We must purge Gohran for what he's done.'

'You called him a rapist, Jonas. An *incestuous* rapist. What did you mean?'

'If all Gohran cared about was his sister's sorcery, he would have denounced her long ago.'

Venn's eyes darted back and forth, chasing his memories—the precise way he imagined he had appeared to Vorlyn—scrounging for an explanation that made sense of what he refused to accept.

'You might turn away, but I can't. If you won't sever ties, I'll take the choice from your hands and end Gohran myself.'

'He'll kill you, Jonas. He's a better swordsman when you're *not* half hobbling on an injured foot—and that's before you consider his influence once you are within reach.'

'I've faced poorer odds.' *But please, gods, let me have at least one sorcerer by my side.*

'I can't allow it.' Venn drew a deep breath. 'I got us here. I'll get us out.'

'You'll set Raeyn aside?'

'No, but you're right. Gohran can't escape this.' He called to his page. 'Scribe me a letter and then summon Mykan. I need to arrange a formal duel.' To Jonas, he said, 'You might not best him with a sword, but I can.'

'My lord?' the page hovered.

'Issue King Gohran of Erldan a challenge to a personal duel. Should he refuse, I will have no recourse but to declare war between our provinces.'

He addressed Jonas again. 'The priests can adjudicate, as they did in Myrhan's time.'

Jonas sucked in a breath. It was one thing to confront Gohran himself, or for Venn to sever ties, but quite another to force Gohran to choose between war and certain death, because he couldn't defeat the best swordsman in this part of Ycelt. Is that why Ella never told Venn? Because the truth could only lead to war?

'And if he kills you?'

'Then Nedran will be yours.'

SEVENTY-FIVE

'You seem cheerful this evening, brother,' Jaydyn said, passing a plate of roasted tubers across to Vera before helping herself to a thick slice of new season's venison.

'You should be too, *sister*, with that hearty feast upon your plate,' Gohran snapped.

'Are we dining on the spoils of today's hunt, Your Highness?' Vera asked through coquettish lashes.

'Our meat will have come from the marketplace along with this wine,' Jaydyn said. 'Who would have thought a dead priest would bring a boon?'

Vera frowned.

With her brow arched, Jaydyn leaned close, keeping her voice lowered. 'Nedran's dryhten paid a portion of his brother's blood price following the furore.' So far, Gohran's men had told no one of Jonas's assumed demise, while the people remained focused on the death of their head priest. 'Evidently, Venn feels responsible, given it happened just outside of Nedran.'

Vera stiffened, paled, then cleared her throat. 'Shall I top up your glass, Your Highness?'

Ordinarily, Gohran would have stifled his sister's loose tongue, but he felt strangely weightless. Disconnected. Freedom should have unshackled him and lifted the iron weight from his chest, but receiving the news of both deaths cast Gohran adrift.

For as long as he recalled, Davith had been his anchor. His lodestone. Provided a sanctuary, when Erldan was anything but.

As a boy, he'd earned Rohan's approval through worship, attending to his studies and warcraft, and keeping out of his father's way. Whenever he caught the sour twist to Rohan's mouth and the tightness around his eyes, he'd registered disappointment. Disgust. A look mirrored in Lord Jonas when he saw through Gohran's façade and straight into his soul.

There had been nowhere to hide.

When he'd discovered Davith's refuge was a lie, the betrayal sliced deeper than his father's disdain. Perhaps deeper than Ella's.

But now he had no *need* to hide.

No priests hovered. No protestors crowded his doors. No politicking strangled.

The only person left who knew his shame was Ella, and with Jonas dead and Venn married, Ella had no reason to return. Another weight lifted.

Yet part of him still yearned for the haven Ella offered. She not only knew his shame, but shared it. When their minds and bodies merged, she did not mirror their father, but *him*.

In a childish reverie, he imagined fetching her home. Reinstating her as his advisor, where she could provide that haven once more. Keep her close.

His loins tingled and his blood stirred, aching and needy.

The goddess had forsaken him over and again. He might as well claim his birthright, and hers.

Reality slammed against fantasy when he recalled her terror as he overpowered her will.

She must remain dead.

Another tingle, and a familiar burning itch crept along his limbs, begging for release.

Earlier, he had reached beneath his bed to retrieve his chest. With Davith's spies crawling, he'd not cut himself for what seemed like moons—when he'd last sensed Ella. Alone at last, he had opened the chest and gripped his knife, only to find it cool and lifeless in his palm. He'd set it aside and picked up the strap. Ran his fingertips over the blood-crusted leather, waiting for his hunger to spark, but the material felt as ordinary as a horse's reins.

He had shoved the implements away and pushed the chest under his bed.

Why, once he had the privacy to self-flagellate, did the urge evaporate?

He'd sunk onto his bed. Not free, but empty.

Now, as he nodded to Vera, and she filled his glass with newly purchased wine, he considered the path ahead. Nedran had relieved the blockade, restoring Erldan's trade routes, and with his profitable betrothal, wealth would flow back into his kingdom. Nedran might become Herron's ally, but Erldan would be bound to Lichen, a powerful and prosperous city. He could repay Erldan's debts and focus on building a life with his new wife. Put this dark period behind him and start anew.

With that in mind, he reached for his betrothed's hand as she set down the carafe. 'We can ride tomorrow, if it pleases you?' Her fingers curled in his, and he pressed his lips to her delicate skin, enjoying her smile as he imagined their future.

'Very much, my thanks.' Her lips curved, drawing him to their deep crimson stain—the exact hue of her dress.

'Your Highness?' A breathless page appeared.

Gohran's temples throbbed, and his chest tightened, as the fabric of Vera's gown dissolved into a pool of blood. He tried to speak, but his throat caught with the screams of a hundred souls ringing in his ears.

He dropped Vera's hand and looked up. 'Yes?' he managed at last.

'An urgent courier from Nedran.' The lad bowed, then retreated out of reach.

For a moment, he couldn't breathe.

He snapped the seal and read in silence. '*Lord Venn, the dryhten of Nedran, hereby challenges King Gohran of Erldan to a personal duel in recompense for the heinous violation of the lord's erstwhile betrothed, and unwarranted apprehension of Lord Jonas of Nedran.*'

The message continued, but the words blurred as he drifted from his body, viewing himself from the outside. The letter dangled, and its ink appeared to drip and smear the page as the colour drained from his skin. All the while, his sister and his betrothed's eyes probed. He felt numb.

Venn had threatened his sword before, informally. But this was an official proclamation—a direct challenge to his rule, to be sworn before, and adjudicated by, Elnora's priests. If he lost, as in the time of the Ancients, Erldan would owe Nedran fealty. If he refused, he plunged both provinces into war.

He recalled the weight of Venn's weapon resting at the gully of his throat in mock combat. Boys playing with toys.

'One day I will best you,' he'd sworn.

'It had better not be with a real blade if you do.'

He'd not once beaten Venn, not when grief weakened his erstwhile friend, nor with the gods guiding his senses.

In battle, he afforded his kingdom a fighting chance. All he'd invested in fortifying Erldan, in readying her army, and allying Erldan to Lichen's forces, gave the kingdom that chance.

'Gohran? What is it? What does it say?' Jaydyn kept asking, though she needn't voice her curiosity. It weighed upon him like lead.

His breath drew heavier and more ragged than the night he'd denounced his mother. Now, as then, eager eyes surrounded him, pressing in.

Venn had served him an impossible choice.

His own life, he could sacrifice. Countless times he'd contemplated ending his torment. That decision would have been easy.

But he would not sacrifice his kingdom's sovereignty.

'Your Highness?'

'Gohran?'

Another breath. Now, as then, he would choose the only path left open to him.

'Tell my captain to prepare Erldan for war.'

Seventy-Six

The Musolano's tiles felt cold and hard beneath her as Ella's vision adjusted to the sun streaming between marble pillars. How was it daylight?

She struggled to sit. This port was harder than the last. Already depleted, Siranos's source was weaker than the bonfire and boar. But Yorg was right. Her power grew stronger and more precise. She felt it as she sifted through her host's panicked thoughts to construct a robust passage, incorporating the crucial details and discarding the rest.

She pushed to her feet, orienting to her new surroundings, and steadied herself against the wall, waiting for her dizziness to pass.

Mosaic covered the square's floor, which was roughly the same size as Ralan's courtyard. Instead of vibrant frescoes, someone had inscribed glyphs along the walls. Open archways led to seemingly identical rooms in every direction. While in the centre, marble podiums displayed artefacts: painted pottery, rusted metalwork, and tarnished jewellery. Many items were broken or mere fragments, as though salvaged following an attack.

She padded across the mosaic, running her fingertips over the inscribed glyphs. They thrummed beneath her touch, a whispered susurrus calling, as she caressed the carved ridges and valleys. Not Myanai or Yceltic, but the Ancient tongue that predated them.

The murmurs flowed like currents around her, and the glyphs sparked with blue light, guiding her. Instead of trying to read the symbols, she let her mind reveal their story as she traced their glow from wall to wall, winding through the empty corridors, quiet except for her echoing footfalls.

Her mind's eye pictured Myrhan and Elnora's Dark Sun followers, Xenon and His priestesses of the Silver Moon. The characters in the tale surrounded her, the way her dolls once had, as looming shadow and translucent light.

She let her focus drift and followed their sound, their gleam, and the inexorable pull of their power.

A whisper behind her: *Cursed. Forbidden. Betrayed.*

She swung around. No one was there. She turned back and continued.

Another story thread wove itself along the walls, this time, of her ancestor, Mathildh, Myrhan's daughter. Xarion's mother.

The raven-haired woman seemed to stand before her, with azure eyes like staring in a mirror. Without words, they recognised each other's pain. Mathildh's Xarion, and hers.

Mathildh's journey led her to the story she sought of Myrhan's captain and the warrior priestess, Xarion. The priestess appeared as she had pictured her grown daughter, and the captain resembled Jonas, with his green-grey eyes and tempting grin.

They stood facing one another, an aura scarred, and the other Cursed. Ella had not understood when she had read the transcribed pages, but now, her god-sight showed her.

She watched as their forbidden love story played out: Xarion's lies, the captain's betrayal, but turned away when it reached its tragic conclusion.

Not a caution against beguilement, for Xarion could not beguile the captain, so why did the god keep showing her this story?

She stepped through the illusory images to follow the story's glyphs. Blue light sparked a trail to the sigils from the excerpt she'd examined at Aeron, recalling the translation: *Should a man draw the lifeforce of another to fuel his power, he shall be Cleansed or those he touches shall be Cursed thrice over.*

The engraved lines danced to life at her touch. She comprehended them, not as a translation, but in their natural tongue. *Should a man bleed or force another, he and those he touches shall be Cursed thrice over.*

As she suspected, there was no reference to drawing, or even lifeforce. Vorlyn had said there was no glyph for 'force', and so the scribe had substituted the glyph for 'power' and combined it with 'life', but here the word meant to compel or coerce. To 'overpower'.

She read the line again, tracing each word with her mind: *'Should a man bleed or force another, he and those he touches shall be Cursed thrice over.'*

Wait—where was the sigil that resembled a flaming hook? The glyph for Cleanse or Cull?

It wasn't there.

Oh gods. It had never been there.

Thunder rumbled across the sky. Xenon's voice resounding in her mind.

She had been right. The translation was no error, no mistake. It was a lie.

And there was more. Xenon's Curse continued, imparting a message she'd never heard:

'He shall bear the pain of a life stolen. And that pain shall bleed into every life he touches thereafter. Scarring himself and those who survive what he stole.'

And the last line, which she'd heard a variation of before, now took on new meaning:

'And so, when a man asks for whom is the Curse a punishment, borne of anger and betrayal, is it not a double-edged sword? To those I answer, only if you let it be.'

Did that mean it wasn't a true curse at all?

Had it only ever been a fable? A warning that causing harm, taking a life or forcing another, bore consequences with tentacles that reached beyond the perpetrator.

How many iterations of translation had warped the god's message? Even now, reading the earliest glyphs in their original tongue, her mind's filter could only approximate Xenon's intent.

Lightning sparked, followed by a roll of thunder.

Not a call to action, but a warning.

And not a mistranslation, but a change made willingly. Deliberately.

Is that why her ancestors purged the manuscripts, too? To erase information that contradicted the accepted doctrine. Genuine heresy, not the priests' manufactured crusade against so-called witches.

Another flash and roll brought a blast of chill air. Did she imagine the blue tinge to its flame?

Her daughter might bear the scar of her parents' crimes, but that did not make her Cursed.

So why did the Ancient warrior, Xarion, bear the Curse? Where was the rest of that story—?

'Prya?' A voice like a zephyr on a summer's day pulled her from her musings.

She turned to find an older handsome man with raven-dark hair, moonbeam pale skin, and sunstruck sapphire eyes, standing before her, watching.

He stepped towards her with a smile that wrenched her soul like heartache. Like missing home.

'May the gods strike me down,' he said, his voice as smooth and warm as honey. 'If it isn't Prya's daughter, here at last!'

She froze. Who was he? How did he know—?

His mind stroked hers, as comforting as hugging a favoured down pillow.

Why did he look so cursed familiar? And why did she yearn for him to scoop her up and let her drown in his embrace?

He paused, studying her with a wry twist to his lips, and her breath caught. She had the strangest sense she should know him from somewhere.

His psyche reached again for hers, like ivy tendrils curling between cracked pavers, filling her mind's hollows with verdant green. When he spoke, his voice resonated in the deepest levels of her soul: 'I've been waiting for you.'

Ella's story continues in

Ella's Fate

Book Four of The Lost Warriors

THANK YOU

Thank you for joining me on this journey

Loving the series so far?

Rate and review Christine's work wherever you get your books and book recommendations. Your support helps bring this work to new readers.

Connect

Subscribe to Christine's newsletter for new releases, bonus content, and more:

christinepriestly.com/newsletter/

Website: christinepriestly.com

Connect: linktr.ee/christinepriestly

Need more?

Subscribe to receive your bonus novella:

christinepriestly.com/bonus3/

Acknowledgements

To my readers and supporters, thank you. Every like, share, comment, reaction, review or recommendation helps bring this world to life and makes the journey worthwhile.

To my editor, for your mastery of language and grammar. Those conjunctions had to go!

To my early readers: Kelly Richter, Lisa Witten, Imogen Reed, Rebecca Ciezarek, Marnie Johnston, Trudi Childe, and Samantha Starling. I cannot thank you enough for your insights and for sticking with this story. Your late-night reaction emojis, voice memos, and swears (usually at Gohran) keet me going through this otherwise lonely experience. (I hope you're all still speaking to me after the tragic events within *Ella's Legacy*. I'm only the writer—I don't make the rules.)

An extra special mention to Kelly (again). I appreciate you in ways I can't express and hope you never have to re-read a scene that many times again!

A magical shout-out to Lisa Witten, who named the 'gold-eyed girl', as voted by my incredible readers. Thank you to everyone who participated in the 'Name That Character' competition. Chrysanth has a bold future ahead in the world of *The Lost Warriors*.

And to Mr Lee, I'm sorry it's not a trilogy (and thank you).

Strap in for the next adventure!

GLOSSARY

Ahmah (Myanai): Informal term for 'mother'.

Ancients (Yceltic): A race predating the Ycelts. Lore describes their unique colouring: moonbeam pale skin, midnight hair, and midday eyes, compared with the ancient Myanai described as having midnight skin, moonbeam pale hair, and twilight eyes.

A.S. (Yceltic): 'After settlement'. Used when denoting dates. Refers to the number of summers (i.e., years) elapsed since Ycelt's founder, King Myrhan, declared his right to be recognised as Ycelt's supreme monarch and ruler. Yceltic people typically note the passing of time by season (i.e., marked by the sun), with significant events, such as noteworthy anniversaries or births, being celebrated on the nearest equinox or solstice, and/or via the moon's cycles, where Yceltics mark time by the relevant phase of the moon, or number of moon phases that have elapsed.

Ballad of Fyora and Zar (Yceltic): A popular but lengthy ballad often used to denote the passage of time.

Braies (Yceltic): A type of undergarment made from linen or wool, traditionally worn to cover the privates from waist to knee, though some Yceltics choose more or less coverage to suit their taste and modesty.

Cleansing (Yceltic): A ritual to burn heretics. Believed to cleanse souls and restore purity. Used as a remedy against Xenon's Curse.

Cult of the Dark Sun (Yceltic): Ycelts consider Elnora's worshippers as members of this religion or cult. Elnora's priestly class typically excludes women from its ranks.

Cursed Land of Ycelt (Yceltic): According to ancient lore, following the Great War, Xenon cursed all Ycelt to remain at war (Ycelt's curse). Hierarchies that once relied on strength of magic now relied on might. This is used to explain the constant state of political and military unrest throughout the High Realm. Xenon spared his followers from Ycelt's curse by placing His curse ('the Curse', or 'Xenon's Curse') on any individual who raised a hand against them.

Cynnelic (Yceltic): A minor (low-ranking) lord. An archaic term, no longer in common use.

Dearling (Yceltic): Form of endearment, often used by commoners to refer to children.

Dorj (Myanai): Literally a palace, but used colloquially to mean household, or home.

Dosha (Myanai): A husband and overlord. Head of a Myanai household.

Dryhten (Yceltic): The highest-ranking lord beneath a prince. Distinct from an ordinary lord ('cynnelic').

Elnora (Yceltic): Goddess of the Dark Sun, commonly referred to as Our Dark Lady, or Our Lady of the Dark Sun. The Cult of the Dark Sun is the mainstream religion throughout Ycelt. Also used to describe the sun.

Eventide (Yceltic): Evening. The period of the day when Elnora begins Her descent below the horizon.

Foresight (Yceltic): An elaborate game of strategy. Game pieces represent different hierarchies laid out across a board, which describes the territory of play. A player may only move each piece within certain limitations, depending on rank, while each move influences the other pieces on the board. The object is to embed yourself as monarch of the territory, while maintaining control over the priesthood and subjects.

God-Body (Myanai/Yceltic): A person's simulacrum or ethereal form. Those gifted with travelling can move via their ethereal form, or 'god-body'.

God-Sight (Myanai/Yceltic): Also called 'vision'. Using magic (ethereal sight) to perceive. Ethereal perception.

Hallit (Yceltic): A type of grain that only grows in the central-western provinces. Prized for being nutrient dense and versatile. Used as human and animal feed, as a substitute for straw and hay, and fermented as a popular and potent alcoholic spirit.

Henad (Yceltic): Henads are religious spies granted specific rights to investigate, arrest, interrogate, and sentence individuals for heresy against the doctrine of Elnora's Cult of the Dark Sun. Henads are distinct from, but work alongside, Elnora's priesthood. Followers of the Dark Sun deem practising magic (sorcery/witchcraft) heretical, for they consider mages touched by the heretical god, Xenon of the Black Moon. The typical punishment for heresy is to Cleanse the soul by fire.

High King (Yceltic): The most senior ranking secular ruler in Ycelt. The king of kings.

High Priest/High Priestess (Yceltic): The most senior ranking post in the holy class.

High Realm (Yceltic): All land under jurisdiction of the High King of Ycelt.

Ilak (Yceltic): A domesticated ruminant mammal, similar to a sheep or goat, used for their meat, milk, skin, and wool. Ycelts also use ilak fat to make butter and candles.

Kordra (Myanai): A full-bodied robe worn by women in Myan.

Lan-Dosha (Myanai): A castrated male chaperone, hired to accompany women in public spaces.

Mageesta (Myanai): A title given to a mage or scholar.

Marked Prince (Yceltic): A title given to the eldest male child in a royal dynasty, marked to inherit the throne.

Mayora (Myanai): Mother.

Moonbelt (Yceltic): A belt worn to contain menstrual rags.

Moontime (Yceltic): Menstruation.

Moonsworn (Yceltic/Myanai): A person touched by the god Xenon and blessed with His magic.

Musolano (Myanai): A place to house and study objects. Often contains Ancient relics. A museum.

Neophyte (Yceltic): A lower ranked priest, often still in training, or holding a serving position below a standing priest.

Noontide (Yceltic): Noon. Midday. The time of day when Elnora reaches Her zenith.

Novice (Yceltic): A lower ranked priestess, often still in training, or holding a serving position below a priestess.

Princess Elder (Yceltic): A title bestowed when the first-born child in a royal dynasty is female, not male. The title holder may inherit a plot of land and retain the title even after marriage.

Rimyan (Myanai): The Mountain. A genderless deity for whom Myan is named.

Salvees (Myanai): A crier's call to attract buyers. Literally, a sale.

Scry (Yceltic/Myanai): Ethereal perception. Using magic to spy on distant subjects, for example, people, objects, and places, via a charged surface. The strength of the vision and distance over which a mage can view their desired subject are relative to the power of the scrying source and the intensity of the connection between mage and subject. Therefore, mages can typically only scry on subjects they have experienced in the flesh.

Shrillan (Yceltic): A prohibited plant known for its effects on the mind and body, including changes in perception and mood. When smoked, induces mild euphoria and relaxation. When fermented and chewed, acts as a stimulant to keep the user awake. A common side effect of chewing fermented shrillan is hallucinations. Used in religious rituals and to inspire visions in those with magic.

Shyarma (Myanai): A derogatory slur. Denotes a person (usually a woman) deemed to have poor morals, who behaves promiscuously, or transgresses cultural mores.

Soup of the Gods (Myanai): Colloquial description of the ethereal currents through which magic passes.

Taya menel (Myanai): A request for someone to move out of the way. Literal translation: 'Move, let me pass.'

Thukran (Myanai): An expression of gratitude or thanks. Yceltic equivalent: 'My thanks.'

Tiles (Yceltic): The informal name for a set of oval game pieces, commonly shaped from wood, polished stone, or clay. Each tile is graved or painted with a symbol to mark its order and suit. Most games involve multiple players building runs of tiles of order, suit, or both. Players draw and discard tiles through a combination of strategy and luck. The player with the highest tile sequence wins. Strongest hands combine a run of tiles of the same suit. To up the stakes, players typically lay wagers on whose hand will win. Distinct from Foresight, whose play involves elaborate drawn-out strategy between two players.

Torja (Myanai): First wife. The most honoured rank afforded a woman in a Myanai household.

Uhtan (Yceltic): The false light before dawn.

Xenon (Yceltic): God of the Black Moon (formerly, Silver Moon). Xenon's followers are often called 'Moonsworn.' Ycelts consider the Moonsworn heretics. Also used to describe the moon.

Xenona (Myanai): A sorceress. Believed to be god-touched ('moonsworn').

Xenona-ran (Myanai): Magic employed by a Xenona, or sorceress.

Xenon's Curse (Yceltic): The 'Curse'. Xenon's Curse befalls anyone who touches a sworn priestess in violence or in lust. According to Ancient Yceltic lore, Xenon's Curse brings horror thrice over. Yceltics believe Xenon Curses any individual who defies His sacred laws.

Sigils (glyphs)

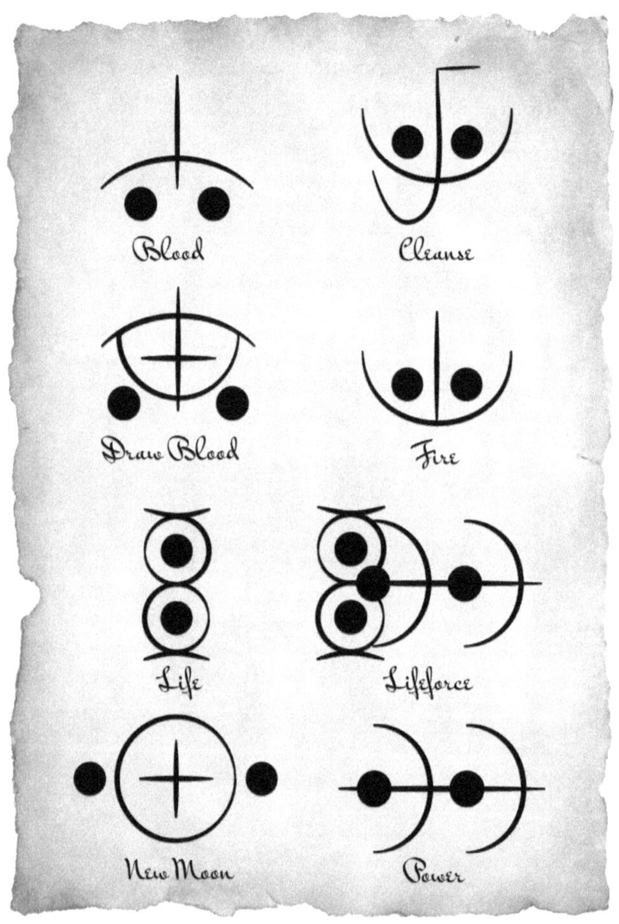

ABOUT THE AUTHOR

Christine Priestly is an Australian author of the captivating medieval fantasy series *The Lost Warriors.* Infused with a touch of darkness and literary spice, her work explores the complexities of human desire against a backdrop of sociopolitical intrigue, with compelling characters you'll grow to love, or love to hate. You'll often find her head in a book, sipping tea, cuddling her cats, or spinning on a pole.

Follow Christine's journey and see upcoming titles:

christinepriestly.com